Call Me Ishmaelle

ALSO BY XIAOLU GUO

Village of Stone
A Concise Chinese–English Dictionary for Lovers
20 Fragments of a Ravenous Youth
UFO in Her Eyes
Lovers in the Age of Indifference
I Am China
Once Upon a Time in the East
A Lover's Discourse
Radical
My Battle of Hastings

CALL ME ISHMAELLE

XIAOLU GUO

1 3 5 7 9 10 8 6 4 2

Chatto & Windus, an imprint of Vintage, is part of the
Penguin Random House group of companies

Vintage, Penguin Random House UK,
One Embassy Gardens, 8 Viaduct Gardens, London SW11 7BW

penguin.co.uk/vintage
global.penguinrandomhouse.com

Penguin
Random House
UK

First published by Chatto & Windus in 2025

Text design by Stephen Hickson

Map by Bill Donohoe

Set in 12.4/16 pt Imprint MT Pro
Typeset by Jouve (UK), Milton Keynes

Printed and bound in Great Britain by Clays Ltd, Elcograf S.p.A.

The authorised representative in the EEA is Penguin Random House Ireland,
Morrison Chambers, 32 Nassau Street, Dublin D02 YH68

A CIP catalogue record for this book is available from the British Library

HB ISBN 9781784745608

TPB ISBN 9781784745615

Penguin Random House is committed to a sustainable future
for our business, our readers and our planet. This book is made from
Forest Stewardship Council® certified paper.

Heaven and earth are indifferent;
They view all creatures as straw dogs.
The sage is likewise indifferent;
He too views common people as straw dogs.
Between heaven and earth, the space is like a great windy chamber:
empty yet inexhaustible.
Its turbulent air brings forth unceasing energy.

Tao Te Ching, Laozi

Contents

Whale in Different Tongues

WALVIS	Afrikana	HVAL	Icelandic
توح	Arabic	PAUS	Indonesian
鯨	Chinese	MÍOL MÓR	Irish
KIT	Croatian	BALENA	Italian
VELRYBA	Czech	鯨	Japanese
HVALT	Danish	고래	Korean
WAL	Dutch	TOHORA	Māori
WHALE	English	HVAL	Norwegian
ALYENA	Filipino	WIELORYB	Polish
VALAS	Finnish	BALEIA	Portuguese
BALEINE	French	ਵ੍ਹੇਲ	Punjabi
WAL	German	Кит	Russian
Φάλαινα	Greek	MUC-MHARA	Scots Gaelic
MUKTUK	Greenlandic	BALLENA	Spanish
KOHOLA	Hawaiian	VAL	Swedish
ותיווֹל	Hebrew	BALINA	Turkish
वृहेल	Hindi	MORFIL	Welsh
BALNA	Hungarian		

Characters

ISHMAELLE

JOSEPH   Ishmaelle's brother

SENECA   captain of the *Nimrod*

DRAKE   first mate

FREEDMAN   second mate

JACQUES (MAILLOT)   third mate

POUND BROTHERS   owners of the *Nimrod*

KAURI   first harpooner

TASHE   second harpooner

TYRONE   third harpooner

MR HAWTHORNE   surgeon

MOSES   cook

WOODY   carpenter

SIMON   cooper

ANTONIO   sailor

WASHINGTON   sailor

JACK   sailor

LOICK   sailor

MUZI   sailmaker and Taoist

FLAHERTY   steward

ROBERTS   steward

DILLY   cabin boy

TAIJI   Japanese translator

SHINYA   Japanese whaler

BROWN   captain of the *Royal Anne*

FITZROY   captain of the *Sirena*

MACKAY   captain of the *Thunder*

GLADYS   the cat

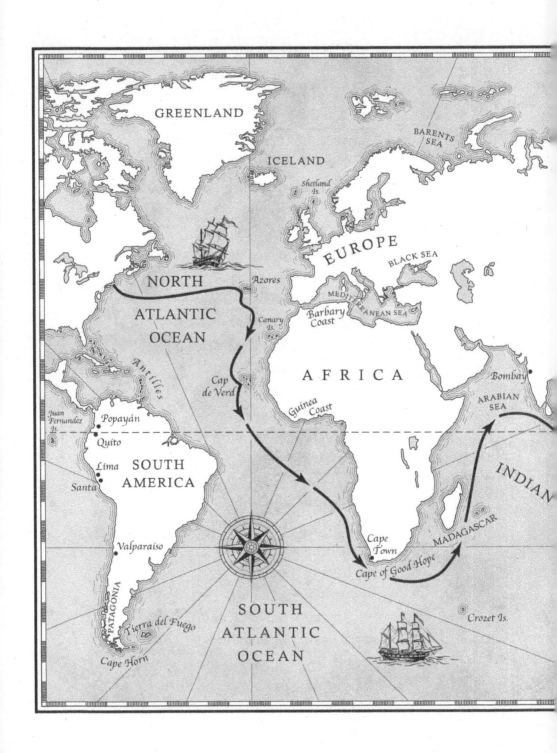

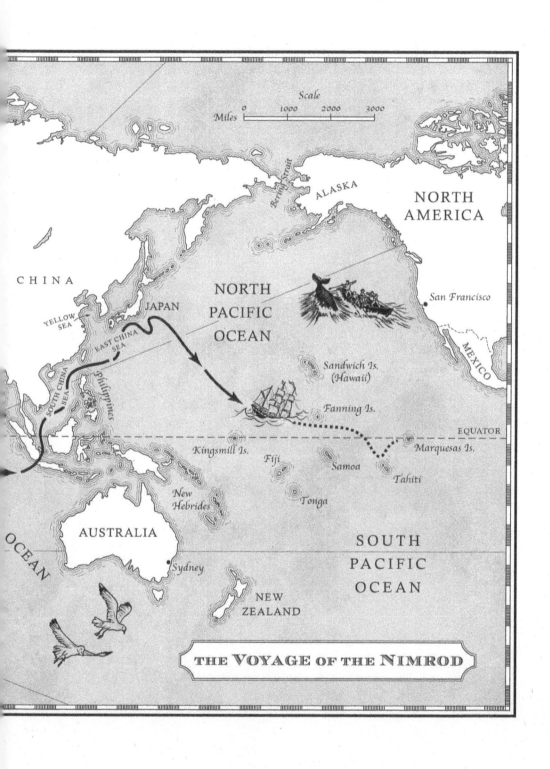

THE **VOYAGE** OF THE **NIMROD**

CHAPTER ONE

Saxonham

I

CALL ME ISHMAELLE. But know that I have not always gone by this name. Names carry much power and in my own case that power has defined my story. It is a saga that begins and ends with the sea, and in the middle concerns a fantastical creature. I will need to tell it to you gradually. Some memories are as clear as day, others cloudy, and I must pause to recover them. I hope I will be true, both to what happened and to what I am. But first, the sea.

I was born in a windswept cottage on the coast of Kent in the year of 1843. It was the month of May, when the geraniums of our village graveyard burst into mauve and white blooms. That was an auspicious sign for a birth. But the night I was born there was a storm, and according to my mother, a great flock of seagulls hovered above our roof. They squawked and squealed, just as I did, a slimy wrinkled creature in my mother's arms.

I grew up strong. I learned to walk like all children, but I also learned to swim. One summer, I remember the passing fin of a dolphin as I swam with my brother through the bay. That winter I watched grey seals and their pups, and I knew they came ashore to give birth on our beaches. During my early childhood, my brother and I lived in innocence, away from the great world, absorbed by sand, waves and marvels of the ocean.

In that great world, Queen Victoria sat on the throne of England. I knew nothing about kings and queens. But I remember when I was seven years old, my father told me that Queen Victoria was almost assassinated by an army officer! Miraculously, the queen survived and she managed to attend the Great Exhibition at the Crystal Palace the following year. I was very impressed by the idea of this woman king, who had already borne several children. I, who had never ventured beyond the coast of Kent, imagined within the plain stone walls of our house that I was Queen Victoria. I imagined the way she might walk and eat and talk. But, Ishmaelle, I told myself, you are too lowly to imagine a grand queen's life. And it was true. The only rich person I knew was the foul-tempered butcher near our house who kept pigs, rabbits and chickens in his backyard.

We lived by the sea near Saxonham, on the salty fields of Denge Marsh. Saxonham was a village – not much more than a hamlet in truth – a few miles from Dungeness. Our cottage was surrounded by hard shingles and bitter eelgrass. God seemed to have forgotten us from the very beginning. The two front windows overlooked the beach. At the back of the house, in open fields, were three large windmills. They had been there for as long as I could remember. My father said one of the three was built by my grandfather with the help of the villagers. There were windmills all along the marshes stretching as far as the port town of Lydd, where goods and horses were sold at market. Those windmills stood on mud and marshes amid samphire and pink thrift flowers, the only warm glow around our house. They looked ghostly, especially at night, but they were full

4

of life forms. Sea thrift loved to grow around their base in the spring. Then there were the robins and field puffins, they too liked to nest about the windmills.

When I was a young girl, I loved picking the white sea campions that grew on the coastal rocks. We called these flowers dead man's bells, though they had another grisly name: witches' thimbles. They grew on the edges of cliffs, and that was bad luck. Nothing should live on the edges of sea cliffs unless it is a sad barnacle or a fearful clam, my mother said. She told me that we should not pick white sea campions, otherwise some terrible disaster would befall us. But I did, in spring and summer. I picked them and made gallants and hung them around my neck. I hung them on our doorknobs too. I loved those little white creamy petals. Dead man's bells, I heard the children sing. Dead man's bells ring. One day, on the dock where my father worked as a carpenter, he vomited blood. A week later he was dead. He left behind my mother, my brother Joseph and my three-month-old sister who howled all day and all night. My poor mother had to work as a maid in the village. Every day, she left the crying baby with me and walked across the marsh to the village. I became a little witch. I stole potatoes and pig intestines from the butcher. I strolled to Saxonham and entered farmers' houses to steal clothing while they were out milking cows. But a witch with witches' thimbles was no good. I was a curse. I had toyed with fate, and disaster came.

II

FIVE MONTHS AFTER MY FATHER DIED, my mother became very sick. She was unable to get up to feed my baby sister for two whole days. On the third night she passed away. I was fifteen and Joseph was seventeen. Joseph had already left home to work in the shipyard near Lydd. He made a living on the dock, loading and unloading barrels and crates for the merchant ships. They called him a stevedore. I found employment in a rope factory in Saxonham, having no choice but to take the eight-month-old baby with me. After a few days of the work my hands became coarse and sore like the grass we used for binding. One morning as I carried the baby on my back to the factory, she began to howl. She wouldn't stop. I fed her some goat's milk, but I didn't manage to feed her again at noon as I was unable to stop my work. In the afternoon her eyes were glazed and, when I picked her up, her head was floppy. Before the work day ended she was dead. The women in the factory did not say much, since every woman had seen the death of an infant. In the evening light, I carried my dead sister back to the house. I laid the little bundle on the bed. That night, I didn't eat anything. Nor the next day. There were potatoes in the house. I was given a loaf by a woman in the factory too. But

I needed to punish myself. I had killed my little sister. Now I had to starve myself to know what dying felt like.

On the second evening, I took the spade from the shed. I could only dig a very small hole in the garden, as I had no strength left. I prayed to God after I shovelled the last spade of soil on the tiny grave. I asked Him to forgive me, but I was unsure if He could. I returned to the house, opened a drawer where we kept knitting cotton, and took out a small wooden idol. The head of the idol was that of a seahorse, with a curved neck with fine spines protruding from it, while the body was that of a woman, with small, rounded breasts. It was about the size of a cooking spoon. The seahorse lady was a heathen idol my great-aunt Gladys had prayed to when she was alive. It was brown-black and smoothed as if it had been used by many witches in the past. I lay the figure on the windowsill and prayed to her too. I used to see Aunt Gladys speaking to other fearsome-looking figurines, especially when someone in the village was sick or dying. Gladys died when I was eight or nine. My parents did not approve of Gladys's figurines and succeeded in throwing most of them away. But this seahorse lady was overlooked. Now I felt that this idol was somehow closer to me than God. She might actually forgive me. When I finished praying, I placed her at my bedside. Without taking off any of my clothes, I blew out the single candle, put my head on the damp pillow and stared into the darkness.

Lying on the bed where my mother had died and the tiny corpse of my sister had lain, I thought about fate. What was my fate? If I stayed here in Saxonham where I had passed fifteen years of such a bitter life, I too would soon be buried, perhaps by some unknown hands, next to my sister in the garden.

The following morning, I woke with a fire inside me. Leaping from my bed, I grabbed the stale bread and bit into it with all my strength. With a bowl of cold water, I ate half of it. As I was about to leave the house, my brother Joseph arrived. He had heard about the death of our baby sister. But that wasn't the only reason for his return home. He came back to pack some clothes and tools. He told me he had found work as a sailor, and that he would make more money than a stevedore. Come with me to see the ships, he said. I nodded. I wanted to, but what about my rope-making job? My brother said nothing, but he understood. Then, as he was leaving, he turned and said:

'You know, Ishmaelle, if you were a boy, I would take you with me on the ship. But you are a girl. Take care of yourself, my sister. May God bless you.'

I felt a stone stuck in my throat. I could not breathe, or utter a word. He left, and did not turn back. He knew I was watching him from the door of our house. He walked quickly over the shingle, a dirty canvas bag slung over his shoulder. Perhaps he was crying. Tears rolled down my cheeks. I could see the salty drops fall onto the shingle, and on the green thistles struggling to grow in between the rocks. I stared at the thistles for as long as I could, as if transfixed by the tiny hairy thorns around the pods, until I was certain my brother had disappeared. I turned and entered the kitchen. I found a pair of rusty scissors. One hand gathering a thick bundle of hair into a ponytail, the other gripping tightly the scissors, I cut, cut and cut! The chestnut-coloured curly fur fell silently onto the cold dirt floor. I looked down. The tufts moved, turning softly and unwillingly, as if they wanted to attach themselves back to my head. As if they were animals. Yes, the animals of my past. I didn't even bother to look for a mirror. Chop chop

chop, I cut more and more, until I felt I looked like a man, a man like my brother. Finally I placed the scissors on the stove, and surveyed the soft brown mass around my feet. I knelt down and gathered up a bundle of the still warm and living animals. I let them caress my face for the last time before I put them in the box where my mother used to keep her sewing kit. Let them be buried, along with those needles and string. Let them be gone from my body, forever.

III

CAPTAIN MACKAY HAD HUGE HANDS. That was the first thing I noticed when he entered the shipyard. Then I saw that he had sad grey-blue eyes that contrasted with his warm easy smile. I thought he was the most handsome man I had ever seen. I was sixteen and a half then. Along with my work in the rope factory, I was trying to find employment in the shipyard where my father used to work. Since my brother left, I had started wearing his old clothes. I had never been comfortable moving about in a skirt. On the dock, people came and went, and I was seen as a boy. The day when Mackay appeared with his sailors, I was cleaning up sawdust by the workbench. I heard his men call him 'Captain Mackay' in an accent quite different from the locals. Captain Mackay, who must have been in his early thirties, said he had come to the shipyard looking for my father, who had done some good work for him in the past. Whoever told him about my father's death must have told him that he would find Joseph working on the docks. But my brother had gone to the sea and Captain Mackay at first mistook me for him. Everyone used to remark that we took after our father. It was not that unusual for someone to mistake me for my brother. I was wearing Joseph's scruffy blue trousers with a frayed white top and my hair was short.

'You look like a young sailor back in my home town of New Bedford!' Captain Mackay said, smiling at me.

I asked him where New Bedford was. He told me it was in America, a country far away on the other side of the Atlantic Ocean. He had been sailing back and forth on a whaling ship for over a decade.

'On a whaling ship?' I asked curiously.

'Yes, a whaling ship! Every man in New Bedford works on a whaling ship.' He laughed. Then he said: 'I have to sail back in a few days.'

'Across the Atlantic?' I asked in awe.

'Across the Atlantic!'

'Gracious! How many days will it take?'

'It depends on the ship, it depends on the winds, and most of all it depends on who is captain!' Mackay answered. Then he gave me a lesson, just as my father used to give me a lesson on how to bevel a plank of wood.

'In Columbus's day, his first voyage across the Atlantic took more than two months. Good Lord, imagine that, for months on end, nothing to drink but rainwater, nothing to eat but dry biscuits!'

That was the first time I had heard of Columbus; no one had mentioned his name before.

'Then,' Captain Mackay continued, 'a hundred years ago, it took six weeks, if they didn't die while making the crossing.'

'What about you, with the *Thunder*, I mean?'

I was impressed by the name of his ship.

'On the *Thunder*? If the sails stay in good shape, I'll get to New York in fifteen days!'

Fifteen days. That seemed a long time to me, but it appeared to be nothing in Captain Mackay's mind. I had the thought that a fly could live for only fifteen days. And me? How much longer would I live? Might I cross this vast ocean in the lifespan of a fly?

Suddenly, I thought I heard the Lord answer. I knew what I had to do with my life to fight against fate – the fate that claimed my sister, mother and father.

Captain Mackay did not seem to notice that I was lost in my thoughts.

'In truth I can't wait to be back home,' he said. His eyes scanned the hills along the coast, as if he had seen the heavy clouds gathering above Dungeness.

'What is America like?' I asked.

For a moment he was silent. Then, reaching into the chest pocket of his coat, he took out a folded piece of paper. It was wrinkled and torn at the edges. But when he opened it out, I could see a drawing of a red house. In front of the house stood a man and a woman.

'That's my father,' he said, placing his index finger on the man in the sketch. 'He wants me back to help in the family business.'

I asked him how he would get to his house once the ship arrived in New York. I was surprised by my own blunt question. But Captain Mackay did not seem to mind at all. He explained to me that first the ship would dock at Southwest Battery on the southern tip of Manhattan, a few miles from his father's house in Five Points by Broadway.

'Southern Manhattan, Five Points, Broadway . . .' I repeated the words, as if to imprint the names and the places into my mind. 'Is Southern Manhattan different from here?'

He laughed and patted my shoulder.

'Very different! Our bread tastes better, and our beer less bitter!' Then, as though guessing the intention behind my questions, he added in a gentle tone: 'I wish you could be on the ship. But you know no women are allowed, Ishmaelle, even if you could sail. I'm sorry.'

I felt despondent. No women are allowed. Was that why along this coast there were so many lonely women and children, because the men all went to the sea? Some never returned. What a curse to be a woman, to be a girl. I hated my fast-growing hair, my soft cheeks and my small feet. But before Captain Mackay left the yard, he said: 'Ishmaelle, I can at least show you the *Thunder*, if you want to see what it's like.'

Next day, I went to look for him. It was then he showed me his ship, the deck and the sleeping quarters below. He was attentive and warm, reminding me of my father. But the captain seemed more content, because my father was often weary when he returned home from work. It was only on occasional Sundays that he spent time with us, showing us how to read and write. He used to teach us words from the Bible, and we would spell out 'heaven' or 'devil'. I remember once my father got cross with me as I could not spell 'damnation' – the m and n confused me. Occasionally he would lay his carpenter's plane on the workbench and show us how to make a bow and arrows from sticks. But my father was never as cheerful as Captain Mackay. I struggled to put into words the feelings I had developed for Mackay. This strong sensation in my stomach spread right down to my fingertips. My face had been flushed and hot as Captain Mackay pulled my arm to show me how to turn the windlass. Oh, I so longed to see America, and already I longed to see him again. Such feelings were enough to make me dizzy while I tramped through the wet salty marsh land alone.

IV

THE LAST TIME I SAW CAPTAIN MACKAY was the day before his ship left the Kent coast. He had mentioned the date the *Thunder* would sail, and I had been feeling very apprehensive as the day approached. It was as though I sensed I might never meet him again. That morning I went to the shipyard and watched as his men stocked the ship with supplies under his command. At first he did not notice me as he was very occupied. I decided to tarry there as long as I could. Finally, as the last barrels of fresh water were rolled onto the deck, he caught sight of me. With his large hand, he waved at me through the windy air from behind a pile of irons. Tortured by a yearning mixed with despair, I haltingly walked towards him.

'Ishmaelle, it's time to say goodbye!' was his greeting. He smiled from under his tangled blond hair and added: 'May God bless you, and may God bless the *Thunder*. I shall be happy to return one day to find you a fine grown woman!'

With a solid thump he patted me on my back as if I was one of his crew members. I looked into his eyes, and suddenly was overwhelmed by an impulse to weep. My throat hurt, and I could not speak. I suppressed a sob, and tried to eke out a smile, which must have looked to the captain like a pained grimace. I doubted Mackay even noticed my sadness, though. The sailors were calling him. He lifted his hand from where it rested on my shoulder, and turned to answer their queries. I wanted to stay to see the ship leaving, but I was so distraught that I thought the mere sight of his departure might kill me. With tears rolling down my cheeks, I staggered along the dock. I was a phantom. I could no longer think, I could no longer feel. How could I see him again? Could I cross the ocean to find him? Would anyone allow me on board when I was just a girl? I was a slave to my life, a prisoner of my world, a world I hated inhabiting. After Captain Mackay and his crew left for America, I felt completely numb. It was as though I had died. I was a ghost in our dead house. In every corner of this dim, drab little cottage I saw shadows of death. My mother's sewing reels and her dirty brown cotton threads, my father's worn sandals with broken straps, my baby sister's tiny hat which my mother had knitted and which she barely wore at all. There were rusty tools my father used for cutting the stubborn earth or for carpentry: saw, spade, hammer, nails and chisel. At night, all these heavy objects seemed to rise up and float about. They seemed to scream at me: Use us! Where is your old man? Use us! I had to move all of them out to the backyard. But the next night when I went to bed, even with my tightly closed eyes, I could sense that they all stood up like chickens at dawn, hovering over me in a dance of death.

V

ONE MORNING I AWOKE after dreaming about Captain Mackay. What did we do in my dream? The events were vague and confused. All I could remember was that we were together on his ship, and I was his spouse. We were in his cabin looking out of the window onto the open seas. He was standing behind me, and gently tucked a lock of hair round my ear. I turned to look at him; his grey-blue eyes were the same colour as the sea. But in my dream I could not touch him, as he was all of a sudden high above me on the deck of his ship, and I was transported to the dock, and all I could do was watch his ship pull away from the coast. My heart and the core of my body ached with loneliness, and my hands felt naked without anything to touch! In the morning gloom of the cottage I realised how abandoned I was, how desperately I wanted to be with him. I sat up from my bed, and looked around this house, which no longer held any warmth, love or kindness. I was living in a coffin, a coffin for my entire family.

I made up my mind to live in one of the abandoned windmills, the one my grandfather built. I knew every stair and every brick of that mill house. I dragged all the useful things with me from the coffin house and made a new home for myself there. Alone, I lived in my musty and damp windmill, alone as the moon in the sky, alone as a lizard in a crevice. My only company was a barn owl nesting in a crack in the walls and I watched it flying above my head during the night.

In the dark windmill I often thought, what if I had been born a boy? My parents had longed for a second son, after Joseph. When my mother became pregnant for the second time, my father named the unborn Ishmael, after the son of Abraham from the old Bible. But when a girl child appeared, myself, my father adjusted the name to Ishmaelle, strange as it was. From my early years, as a girl, I was attached like a shadow to my mother's life, a soundless maid, a slave to those of higher standing than us. My mother was a perfect drudge, whose days were filled with menial tasks for others. She had no time for her own needs. She even deprived herself for her children's sake. She never ate before we had eaten. She never knew how to read or write. She had no idea what her life might have been if she had not lived for us children or her husband. But perhaps the men were no better off, especially the poorer ones. My father too was a slave. He worked in the shipyard like a mule and died without a sound. My brother was a slave, though he might have had a better contract with his master than some others did. As for me, I did not fully understand what my life meant yet, all I knew was that I wanted to escape it. Yes, I must seek a new life, more adventurous than that of my fellows on this desolate salt marsh. I must find freedom on the seas.

It was in the windmill that I drew a map, a strange sort of map, which I could not show to anyone but myself. It was a map tracing a route, starting out from Saxonham, leading to the port of Southampton, then out across the Atlantic all the way to New York. Beneath the map, I reproduced the sketch Captain Mackay had shown me of a red house in Manhattan, complete with his parents standing in front. I added Captain Mackay beside them. I also remembered to write down the places he mentioned to me: Southwest Battery, Southern Manhattan, Five Points, Broadway.

VI

OR THE NEXT FEW MONTHS, between my nights
in the windmill and my days at the rope factory, I
learned how to be a forager. I collected wild
mushrooms, I gathered curative herbs, I cooked nettles and
garlic leaves for supper. I also discovered that the white
petals of sea campion cured my stomach aches, if I mixed
them with the roots of marshmallow in a mortar. I was able
to look after myself. I was ready to leave. On my seventeenth
birthday, I sat on a piece of driftwood, facing the ocean,
eating a cold eel pie. There was a storm heading for the
shore, but I stayed on the shingle, unmoving. I must make
a decision before the storm arrives, I thought. According
to Kent legend, when storms strike the Dungeness coast,
witches sail to sea in eggshells. I pictured my white-haired
great-aunt Gladys on one of the shells paddling away, her
skinny body wrapped in a black robe against the white. I
stared into the mist. The rain drenched me and gusts of
wind swept the spray. I saw no witches. I retreated from
the shingle beach and went home.

After that day, I never returned to the factory. I cropped
my hair even shorter. I wore only my brother's old clothes.
I walked all the way to Lydd. I was already older than most
cabin boys, who were as young as twelve. I told everyone I

was fifteen. I showed how I could heave heavy barrels and handle tools. I was a perfect young lad. After a few days in the harbour, I was given a cabin boy's job by the captain of a merchant ship. My pay was low, much less than the sailors, but my Lord, it was heaven compared to the pennies I received working in the factory. In my next life, I vowed I would be a real man and would grow a beard. Then I would go to sea as a sailor and become a captain! Now I was a man, no longer a fearful tame woman. Ships would be my home and oceans would be my fields. I did not tell anyone about Captain Mackay. All I cared about was crossing this ocean and arriving in America where Mackay resided. Then I could remove my boy's clothes once more and reveal myself to the world.

So here I was, a cabin boy on a merchant ship! I carried my father's penknife in my trousers along with Aunt Gladys's tiny seahorse lady. I thought leaving my homeland, and leaving my womanly guise, if not my womanly heart, must be a significant day in my life. After some enquiries, I found out the date was 3 December 1860. I must not forget that date, I told myself. Indeed, I should always keep in touch with calendars and clocks, since a seafaring person should keep note of the day and the hour, because when we are afloat on the wide sea with only the endless waves about us, we no longer have the streets and farms with their familiar marks to give us a sense of ourselves. Time, that strange thread running through my fingers, holds the secret of my present and my future, and my past. I was leaving the woman I thought I was behind, just as I was leaving the land upon which my feet had always trod. I told myself again, this is only a disguise for a journey to reach the object of my heart's concern. Still, something else murmured in me that this was not mere disguise, but that a truer me was somehow being born. I reflected on my seventeen years, and wondered about the transmutation of the worm that becomes the butterfly. Strange is that change beyond imagining. But my thoughts were interrupted – the ship was leaving.

After several hours sailing away from the rugged shoreline, at last we were on the open sea. My heart thrilled with both fear and expectation. The wind was as chilly as a witch's breath, but no icier, I reminded myself, than sitting in our grim cottage or my windmill, wracked by the violent air that always harried the villages of Kent. No more windmills and no more dwelling upon the memories of my dead sister flopping in my arms. Gone was the village of Saxonham and my drab past! Now the ocean was my brother, my father and my mother. The gales were my furious tempers, and the churning waves were my swirling thoughts. I knew that with each minute I was closer to where my love lived, but still I suffered. Oh, if only the Lord could make this ocean smaller! All this water, all this boundless white mist! But the fates have decided that I should endure my life on this water, this creation of boundless liquid mass.

CHAPTER TWO

New York and Beyond

I

DAYS PASSED ON THE ROLLING OCEAN. Occasionally, when I had a moment to myself, I thought that perhaps I wasn't living in *this* world, on this earthly plane. But which world was I living in? It was surely a much finer world than the hell of Saxonham, but it was not quite heaven either. Above me were dazzling blue skies dotted only with screeching seagulls or distant scudding clouds. Once a large white winged bird – an albatross – rushed down towards us, then glided away with grace and speed. I was told by sailors that albatrosses were mostly seen in the southern oceans and I should always inform them if I spotted one. They thought seeing an albatross in these waters was a curse. I had yet to learn what all this fuss was about concerning the albatross.

The first few days after our departure the weather was rainy and then misty. Sometimes, especially at night, when I stood frozen on the deck, I felt lost. No one on the upper deck explained to me where exactly we were. All I knew was that we were on the Atlantic Circuit, but I had no map to study the ship's path, because I was not allowed into the officers' or captain's rooms where the maps were kept.

A cabin boy is constantly busy, and the work is harsh. Fortunately I had become accustomed to hard work since my parents died. I helped with the cooking in the galley, and I would carry meals to the seamen and sometimes even to the officers in their cabins. In the beginning, I would run up and down so quickly with the heavy dishes and buckets that I would trip and fall. But I would pick myself up, and make sure there was no mess left on the deck. If there was a quarrel among the seamen, I would always stay out of it. In between meals, I carried messages back and forth between the officers and the mates, who occupied different parts of the ship.

I did not mind the work and never complained. Only one task, I have to confess, I did not appreciate. I was the lowest boy on the ship, and one of my daily duties was to empty the barrels of excrement every morning. I had to climb the narrow stairs on each deck and heave the awful liquid mass into the sea with all my might. The number of barrels I had to empty varied, depending upon how much the sailors' bowels had produced during the night. Yes I had done that sort of thing since I was a child in Saxonham – we had to pour out our chamber pots onto the beach – but I had never had to work on such a scale and with such intense labour. It was worst when there were strong winds or storms. I was told that in warm weather the sailors were told to shit directly into the sea, but now we were nowhere near the spring. Winter had only just started.

But the crew were not unkind to me. They called out 'Ishmael' loudly whenever they needed me to clean the deck or to help with pulling the sails. Occasionally the captain would summon me to run errands for him. Captain Chambers was a tall man with a tanned complexion. He was from Norfolk and had been a tea merchant. That was all I knew about him. He was calm, focused without being rigid in any way. When he was not writing in the ship's log, he liked to spend his time poring over large maps. Since my father had taught me how to read and write, I was curious about what was written in his logbook. If I knew what had been noted down, I could perhaps one day do my own logging, on my own ship. I let my daydreams run wild. Once when I cleared the teacups from the desk I managed to steal a glimpse of the logbook. His writing was very neat and it was easy for me for read:

Wind South, strong gales, bore away from the North channel; carried away the fore topsail; hove the log several times and the ship going through the water at the rate of 18 knots; rigging slack.

I noted those words, and when I went back above deck I quietly inspected the sails and the rigging, trying to understand what the captain meant by 'rigging slack'. I thought about 'Wind South'. By now it had turned: Wind North.

But it was not my place to tell him about the changing of the wind. I had enough to worry about. For example, how many layers of clothing I should wear to sleep, or remembering never ever to take off my jacket even if I stank and was itching like a dog, and never ever to piss or shit at the same time as anyone else. Whenever I needed to relieve myself, I had to double-check there was nobody around. I tried to go an hour before or an hour after everyone else's toilet time. Thankfully, every sailor slept with their clothes on as the cabins were as cold as iceboxes in December. Some never took off their shoes. I followed their habit and wore my shoes to sleep too. My greatest worry was my periods. I prayed that the mighty ship and the salty spray and the burning sun had the power to stop a woman's menstruation altogether, so that I could walk around in my sailor's suit, proud and free. All I needed was to endure this two-week voyage, or however long it would take, and arrive safely on the other side of the world. Yes, Ishmaelle, your brand-new world! You are a swift, a martin, a swallow! You are determined to leave behind your rotten Saxonham and make a new person of yourself! No more Ishmaelle. I am Ishmael! I am a sailor heading to the new world of my love, my captain, my new life.

II

I T WAS THE SECOND WEEK of our voyage. Most
days my legs ached and my arms were sore from the
deck work, but I always found a moment to stare out
across the ocean, while the sailors joked and told stories.
Though they were merchant sailors, the talk almost always
turned to whaling. I got the impression that most of them
longed to go on a whaling voyage. A few of them had been
on a whaling ship in their younger days. One explained
how a whale blows; another described a whale's tail so large
that the merest strike could capsize a boat. Our old cook,
Mr O'Malley, spoke of an Irish buddy – a harpooner – who
lost his life in pursuit of a grey whale. Apparently, the poor
man's head and torso were chewed up by the creature as if
it were eating a small squid. I wondered if that was why Mr
O'Malley preferred to work on a merchant ship. 'Indeed,'
he said, 'though you might make more money on a whaler
as whale oil will always be needed.' And he was patient
enough to explain to me that if I was willing to go whaling
I should get myself to Nantucket via New Bedford. He said
that New Bedford was where the whalemen were to be
found.

Well, I had heard of New Bedford, from my American
'friend' Captain Mackay, my secret soul, my spirit.

All this talk made me wonder if I would one day become a whaleman. But I told myself, whether I was Ishmaelle or Ishmael, the fates had given me this sea life, and what lay ahead, be it a whale or a man or a grand house on the southern tip of Manhattan Island, only the fates would know. They would guide me in some unaccountable way – and I endeavoured never to question them. All I needed to do was see what lay in front of me once my soles touched the soil of America.

III

M R O'MALLEY ONCE REMARKED that I looked
like a girl, because I could not seem to grow a
beard and my features were too soft. I was too
comely for a lad, he insisted. I shrugged that off. Mr Porter,
the third mate, called me to clean the deck at all times of
the day. He was a thin man from Essex and bothered me a
great deal, thinking me a poor excuse for manhood. He
took pleasure in shouting at me whenever I did not carry
out a task fast enough or to his liking. I did not utter a word
of complaint. How could I? I was lucky enough to leave
England.

We had a few nights of fierce storms. My first storm at
sea was a terrifying experience. The wind was so loud,
wailing through the rigging like a banshee, and the deck
ceased to be something one could stand on. The ship
heaved and listed, waves rushed over the gunwale, and I
feared a watery grave was close at hand. I was warned I
would get seasick, but surprisingly my stomach held firm.
Then relief came. The wind abated and we had calm days
after that. I had to help repair the sails after the damage
from the storm, and spent long hours on deck under the
relentless sun. My skin was burnt, which I hoped might
give me a more manly demeanour. Still, these harsh

working conditions did not bother me at all. But I did feel hungry all the time, and the food was terrible. We lowly seamen ate a diet of dry bread and occasionally salt meat. Only very rarely did we have a real meal with potatoes or fish. I also suffered from lack of sleep. I could never really sleep deeply because I was so worried someone might discover my true identity.

We were approaching the end of our voyage. The wind picked up and the mates said we were sailing fast. On the seventeenth day aboard the ship, I saw a sliver of land on the horizon. The distant and barely visible strip of white loomed larger and larger as our ship cut through the waves towards it. Every man on the deck shouted: America! America! Until they were told to mind the riggings as the winds suddenly changed.

IV

UPON ARRIVING AT BATTERY HARBOUR, I contemplated asking Captain Chambers or our first mate about Captain Mackay. They might know Mackay since they all ploughed the same sea route from England to New York. But I did not want them asking why. So I thanked them and left the ship. I stopped by the harbour and bought a cup of hot pea coffee, while asking for directions. Everyone seemed to know the neighbourhood I mentioned. They told me to walk north and look out for a pond near Lower Broadway.

When I saw the pond, I knew I had arrived at Five Points. A row of houses resembled the sketch Captain Mackay had shown me. Methodically, I knocked on all those doors, looking for Mackay's family home. My enquiries were not always met with kindness, but I would not give up. Eventually, someone pointed out Mackay's house.

It was the father who opened the door to me. I instantly recognised him because of the resemblance between father and son. When I enquired after the captain, he answered as a man might talk to a stray cat: 'Young fellow, my son has died on the sea.' Seeing my shock, he added: 'They could not lower his fever, and he died just before arriving at the harbour.' A bolt out of the blue, I said nothing and turned away, walking down to a street that led me back to the pond.

I sat by the pond that afternoon. I sat till the evening came. I sat there into the night. I saw the stars. Gemini was bright. I heard crows. There seemed to be hundreds of them. They squawked, cawed and screeched, as if applauding or laughing at my misadventures. They cried the mayhem of my night. I was a crow too, in my invisible black cloak. I screamed and moaned, bitterly lost in this new world that had now become a vast wasteland. I heard faint singing from a church somewhere nearby. It was a few days before Christmas. What was I going to do, alone, marooned, washed up in this unknown land, far from anything I knew or loved? Ishmaelle, what a fool you are! A hopeless case! I thought then I might as well die. Was the year 1860 a good year to cease existing? I would join Captain Mackay in oblivion or in God's heavenly kingdom.

The night further closed in on me, and the stars seemed to fade into a pitch-blackness. I could only curl into a ball on a bench in the freezing air and wish that sleep, or death, would release me from these desperate hours.

V

I WOKE UP THE FOLLOWING MORNING chilled to the bone. Still, warm sunlight bathed my face. I managed to get to my feet and staggered down the road. An old street baker delivering bread saw my sorry state, and held out a warm loaf: 'Son, you look like you could do with some victuals.' I thanked him and kept walking back to the harbour.

A young boy was hawking newspapers. 'Threat to Union' was written in large black letters, while lower on the page was a drawing of a solemn-looking bearded man. I noticed the name Abraham Lincoln. Everyone seemed to be captivated by the news. Is there a war going on in this country? I wondered. But I was in no mood to read the newspaper nor to stay in lonely New York.

Once I found out where the ships heading to New Bedford were docked, I went off with the intention of embarking on one. In no time at all, I was on a boat leaving the harbour. All I could think of now was to get on a whaling ship as soon as possible. My heart was still heavy with the shock of Captain Mackay's death. But I was no longer a woman; I had quit my woman's body. I would never know love for another man. If only I could grow a beard or have hair on my legs! But I hid my legs and my arms in my sailor's outfit. I carried a pair of scissors in my pocket all the time. I was tall and among the sailors I did not stand out. Most sailors were my age, some even younger. In my scruffy outfit I felt very much a real seaman. My low voice helped too. My mother's voice, hoarse and dry, perhaps the only useful thing she left to me.

On the ship to New Bedford, I overheard my fellow passengers conversing. Most of them were seamen, either returning home or going to Nantucket to join the whaling ships. Leaning against the railing on deck, I let myself daydream. I imagined I was working on a great whaling ship and making my money. All I wished for was to spend my life on the ocean and have no one bother me. I would become a useful Ishmael, a great sailor Ishmael from England.

It was growing dark as we docked in New Bedford; all I could see was a grey mass of houses extending out from the wharfs. Feeling alienated and utterly lonely, I wanted to move on to Nantucket so that I could find employment on a whaler. But it was Saturday; the little packet for Nantucket had sailed, and no other means of transport was available until Monday, so I had to find a place to stay for the night.

Mr O'Malley had told me, when we were still on the Atlantic, that New Bedford had monopolised the business of whaling, but that Nantucket was the great original whaling town. He also said that Nantucket was where the first dead American whale was stranded.

Now having two nights before leaving for the island of Nantucket, I needed to kill the cold and cheerless hours. Wherever you go, Ishmael, said I to myself, be careful. Be sure to enquire about the price, and watch out for the men, and sleep with your clothes on.

With faltering steps, I paced the darkened streets. I passed by the Seaman's Inn. It looked expensive, and besides, too many men there. There would always be men, but the fewer men the safer I would be, I thought. I must always be cautious. So I walked on, and followed the streets that took me waterward, for there lay the cheapest if not the cheeriest inns.

At length I saw a smoky light from within a squat building, the door of which stood open. The sign over the door read: The Two Hawks Inn. As the light looked so dim, and the place looked little frequented, I thought this dilapidated wooden house might not be too expensive for me.

The Two Hawks Inn was filthy. The windowpanes were opaque with layers of dirty grey frost, and the dark hues of the threadbare carpets seemed to dim the place even more. But no more of this complaining, I said to myself. I needed to go in and discover if I could pass the night there safely.

VI

U PON ENTERING THE INN, the first thing I noticed was a large map on the wall, showing the whaling routes from America. One of the routes from Nantucket went all the way to South Africa and then eastward to the Indian Ocean. The light was so dim that I had to squint to read the names of the stopping points in the China Sea and Japanese Ocean. I stood before the map, transfixed by the inky names of faraway countries. If only I could have this map in my hand!

In the public room, a number of young seamen were gathered, chatting loudly. I sought out the landlord, a hirsute man, and told him I needed a room. He told me his house was full.

'But can't you squeeze me into some corner even just for a few hours before dawn?' I begged.

The landlord thought for a moment, and asked if I would object to sharing a harpooner's blanket? I froze for a bit. I could not share a blanket with anyone.

Seeing me hesitate, the landlord said: 'If you're going whaling, you'd better get used to it.'

He was right. But still, I said that if I were to accept his proposition, I would need to know who the harpooner might be.

'The harpooner? A good chap! He wouldn't object to sharing a bed with you.'

I thought of the bleak coldness outside and nodded. I would just keep my clothes on as I had done on my seventeen-day Atlantic crossing. Then the landlord enquired if I wanted supper, before going off about his business.

A few minutes later several of us were summoned to our meal in an adjoining room. It was as cold as in Saxonham – no fire at all, the landlord said he couldn't afford it, nothing but two dismal candles. We buttoned up our jackets, and with frozen fingers held to our lips the cups of scalding tea. But the payment for food and bed was reasonable, and by the time we saw the dish – not only beef cubes and potatoes, but dumplings! – well, it was more than just reasonable! I did not expect warm dumplings for supper! I had imagined the innkeeper would feed us a few cold potatoes. As I was spooning the food in my mouth, I noticed a fellow in a seaman's uniform, using his knife loudly and violently, cutting into the delicate dumplings with almost a degree of hatred. He stabbed and chopped the food as he would stab a whale in the sea! What an awful manner. I hoped he was not the harpooner I would share the bed with later!

When the landlord came back with more tea, I asked him discreetly if that was the harpooner with whom I had to share a blanket.

'No,' he answered, laughing. 'The harpooner is a dark-complexioned chap. He never eats dumplings. He only eats meat.'

'Where is he?'

'He should be back soon.'

I began to feel anxious about this dark-complexioned

harpooner. I would sleep with one eye open to prevent any unforeseeable disaster.

After supper, we went back to the bar room. Some new sailors had arrived, wild mariners enveloped in shaggy coats and woollen hats, ragged and beaten-looking.

With the liquor in their throats, they began to sing. They were American sailors and they sang American songs, which I had never heard before. One of them reminded me of Captain Mackay, with his smile and the way he spoke. But I would not allow my thoughts to drift in that direction. No. My heart became inert. I asked the landlord to show me to the bedroom as soon as he had finished cleaning up the kitchen.

VII

WHILE WAITING FOR THE LANDLORD, I paced up and down in the hall and glanced at a bundle of newspapers. The top one was the *Massachusetts Chronicle*, its headline: 'Slave Act: South Carolina to secede from the United States!' I read a few lines and vaguely made out that some men in the south of the United States wanted to keep their slaves, who were forced labourers, black people held against their will by white slavers. But just as I tried to find out more, a sailor grabbed the paper.

Finding a corner to seat myself, fatigued and lonesome, I could not help but ponder my predicament later that evening. I was going to share a bed with a man! The only man I had shared a bed with was my own brother. My brother Joseph! I missed him terribly. Only the Lord knew which ship he had boarded, or which sea he was sailing. I could not tell him about the wild journey I had embarked on. But I wished I could tell him that I had become a man in this new continent, and that this very night I would have to sleep with a harpooner! Oh, my brother! I wish you all the best and you should wish me the same!

The more I wondered about this harpooner, the more I became fearful at the idea of sleeping beside him. It was fair to presume that, being a harpooner, his linen would not be clean. There might be lice. I began to quiver and twitch all over. It was getting late, too; a decent man ought to be home. So, when the landlord returned with a bunch of keys, I asked him:

'Does this harpooner always keep such late hours?'

The landlord chuckled again. It seemed whenever I asked a question, he always found it rather amusing.

'No,' he answered, 'generally he's an early bird. But tonight he went out peddling – maybe he can't sell his head.'

'Can't sell his head?' I could not believe my ears, as I had heard stories on the ship of those tribal people selling human heads. 'Is this harpooner actually engaged in peddling his head around this town?'

The landlord nodded. 'I told him he would never sell it here, the market's overstocked.'

'You mean with heads?'

'With heads.' He looked squarely at me, this time without laughing. 'I don't know where you come from, but don't you think there are too many heads in the world?'

Confusion rendered me speechless. I came from England, I had never seen someone selling a human head, and my great-aunt Gladys had never mentioned anything like that.

'I was even given a head last Christmas by a savage,' he added. 'It was painted, but I told him to give it to someone else. I won't hang it in my inn, I would lose business.'

I felt the blood pumping in my veins and my ears were suddenly hot and itchy.

'Landlord,' said I, as calmly as I could, 'I come to your house and want a bed; you tell me you can only give me half, so I am to share with a certain harpooner. And now you're telling me the most exasperating stories. Really, please! Tell me who and what this harpooner is, and whether I shall be safe to spend the night with him. Or I leave right now and won't pay for the dumplings!'

'Be easy,' said the landlord, peeling off dried candle wax from his fingers. 'This harpooner has just arrived from the South Seas. He is Māori or some other sort, from an island in Polynesia. I gather that's where he bought up his heads. He managed to sell them all but one, and that one he's trying to sell tonight, because tomorrow's Sunday, and it would not be proper to sell heads when folks are going to churches.'

If all this was true, how could I know that this Polynesian was not a dangerous man? Would I find my own head still attached to my neck the next morning?

'Don't worry, young chap. He seemed to be a noble man – whatever that means on his island. Besides, there's plenty of room for two to kick about in that bed. Come, I will show you the room.'

Mutely, I followed him upstairs, resigned to my fate. I was ushered into a small room, with simple furnishings. There was indeed a large bed, almost big enough for three harpooners to sleep together.

The landlord placed the candle on the centre table and told me to make myself comfortable.

VIII

GLANCED AROUND THE ROOM. There was a painting representing a harpooner striking a whale. The whale was twice as big as the boat! I was filled with wonder at the image, and felt that I had arrived in a land of whaling, having left behind a land of bogs and sheep. I noticed an old hammock lying on the floor in one corner, and a seaman's bag stuffed with clothes on a chair. But what startled me in the room was a long harpoon resting against the head of the bed. I went to touch it. It was heavy, the tip was sharp and it felt icy cold. It shone in the dimly lit room.

I sat down on the bed, waiting for and thinking about the head-peddling harpooner. I took off my shoes, but nothing else. I covered myself with the bedspread, beginning to feel very cold. I prayed that the harpooner wouldn't return, or better had met with an accident in the streets. Then I blew out the light and closed my eyes. Just when I was beginning to doze, I heard a heavy footfall in the passage. I raised myself from the bed, and saw a glimmer of light under the door.

Lord save me! That must be the harpooner, the head-peddler from the South Seas! I tried to lie still, and not to make a sound. The stranger entered the room, holding a candle. Good heavens! Such a face! It was a dark purplish colour, marked here and there with patterns. Lord, were they face painting or tattoos?

I continued to watch him from the bed, not moving at all. With a particular rhythm, steady and slow, he opened a big bag and pulled out something that looked to me like a tomahawk, which he placed on an old chest. I was unnerved upon seeing the tomahawk. Then he took off his hat and there was not a single hair on his head. I felt more and more afraid.

Meanwhile, the harpooner continued to undress himself. His arms, his back, all over were the same inky-black tattoos. What a mad whaleman from the South Seas! But then perhaps Māori would think the same of me if they saw me landing on their shores. Still, he was stranger, and a peddler of heads too, perhaps the heads of his own villagers for all I knew. He might take a fancy to mine!

I watched him as if I were at a village fair. He fumbled in his pocket, and produced a little object, like a wooden idol. He knelt before the fireplace and lit a small fire. I shifted my position to see what he was doing. First he brought out a handful of sawdust from his bag, adding it to the fire. With the wooden object in his palms, he began praying in a sing-song voice. As the fire smouldered, he placed the idol on the ground by the ashes. Then, without any warning, he jumped into the bed!

I could not help but scream. I rolled away from him and onto the floor. With trembling hands I lit the lamp again. I hated myself for such a cowardly reaction. A real man would not have reacted to him in this terrible way!

He sat up, looked at me coolly, and uttered: 'Kauri share bed? Kauri not fear. Kauri sleep good.'

I felt relieved upon hearing his last sentence. Despite his

45

imposing physical presence, he seemed calm, and even gentle. I moved back towards the bed and said: 'So the landlord explained to you, I hope?'

He did not seem in the least interested in what I said. He simply rolled over on his side and murmured: 'Kauri sleep now.'

I went to the other side of the bed and pulled the blanket up to my face. I kept my eyes open as long as I could. But the rhythmic breathing and light snoring of my bedmate soon sent me to sleep too.

IX

UPON WAKING THE NEXT MORNING, I found
Kauri's arm thrown over me in an affectionate
manner. Immediately, I touched my clothing.
My shirt and trousers were snug, all buttons were in place.
I knew then that he had not been unmannered. And
instinctively, I trusted him. Kauri was not an ordinary
man. I moved very slightly, turning my head to look at him.
I was not sure what I should do with his arm. It felt natural,
as if I had been his mate, or even his wife. But I was no
man's wife. Discreetly, I pulled his arm away from my
body, and placed it back gently on his chest.

My sensations were unfathomable. Since my parents
died and my brother went away, I had never had close
physical contact with anyone. I was a lonely girl in shabby
boy's clothing. Even with Captain Mackay, we had never
been physically close. But with this tribal man from a
faraway land, even though I hardly knew him, I felt we had
shared a certain intimacy. Perhaps this was the feeling men
describe as brotherhood. Yes, brotherhood would be a new
concept for me.

I felt my bedfellow shift. He was waking up. I sat up and
left the bed. I put my shoes on.

Kauri opened his eyes, then sat up straight like a dog on

alert. He looked at me as if he did not remember how I came to be there. I smiled. He nodded, still no words. As if this was the most ordinary thing – two strangers in the same bedroom sharing a bed. He began to dress. I was fully clothed already, so all I needed to do was lace my boots.

Since he showed no inclination to speak, I started.

'What does your name Kauri mean?'

'Kauri, big tree,' he mumbled, putting on his jacket. 'Kauri the old trees on our island. Father king not old. Turtle king not old. Kauri old.'

I guessed he meant the Kauri tree is older than his father or the turtles.

But that was not the end of the story about his name.

'Kauri, deer too,' he added.

'Tree *and* deer?' I asked.

'Deer eat tree, Kauri eat deer.'

There was something magnificent about the way he put words together. I had never heard anyone speak in such a calm and dignified manner. I pictured a broad-leafed tree under the burning sun on a white sandy beach, beneath it a deer munching on outstretched leaves. Kauri. Kauri, big tree. Kauri, deer. All this felt so different from the head-peddling man of last night!

Half an hour later we were walking side by side, like brothers, Kauri with his long harpoon, and I with my canvas bag. The innkeeper was surprised to see us leave together.

X

O N SUNDAY, we passed along a cobbled street lined with shops. Though they were closed, there were many attractive items displayed behind the windows. Kauri and I stopped and looked at these products through the glass. One shop sold the things a seaman or a fisherman would need for work: boots, gloves, fishing nets, rods, bait hooks, oars and drinking flasks. Through the bow window of another shop, I saw bottles filled with whale oil, with the label indicating the uses to which the oil could be put: for hair and skin, for candles, for soap, for perfume, for the lubrication of machines. One label on a glass jar caught my eye: 'The Best and Purest Spermaceti Oil for Your Lamp! Smokeless!' I also noticed a corset made from whalebones.

Pointing at the whalebone corset, Kauri remarked: 'See there, the humpback brother baleen live now as sister.'

I thought he must mean that the humpback's baleen had been reborn as a woman's intimate apparel. The corset struck me as beautifully made. My mother never owned such a fine object as this, though we saw one once in the house of a lady where my mother worked as laundress. I had never worn one. As I stared at the corset, Kauri, leaning his forehead against the shop window, took pleasure in looking at different-sized baleens, lined up together like soldiers.

We returned to our inn. Kauri lit up a little fire and set his feet close to the hearth. He brought out his little idol and once again performed his ritual. This time I took a good look at his black god he called 'Yojo'. It was a small tree-like man with many legs spreading out like roots. I put my blackened seahorse lady on the table, but I did not talk to her. The lady should see all and know all.

Kauri finished his prayer as I was mending my sweater. He looked at my seahorse figurine, without making any comment. He sat and smoked his pipe. When he finished his pipe, he announced: 'Ah, seahorse woman good for boat.'

I was relieved that Kauri seemed to approve of my idol. He then reached to the table and picked up the books the inn kept for the guests. One was a Bible, the other a Quaker book titled *Some Fruits of Solitude* which I had not had a chance to take a proper look at. Kauri placed the Bible on his lap, and began counting the pages. He counted up to fifty, then started again at one. His large black eyes occasionally stared at the words on the page as if he read the meaning through his counting. It was a curious thing to see. Why such interest in counting pages? Could he not read? Might he want to learn?

As I was watching him, I was struck by his peacefulness once again. He seemed very self-contained, in need of no other person or thing. It occurred to me that Kauri did not mingle with the other seamen at the inn. He appeared to have no desire to enlarge the circle of his acquaintances. It was as though his soul was intact. Ha, unlike mine! My soul was in pieces like the scales of a seahorse. Perhaps only the seahorse lady could pull my pieces back into one place. Or perhaps I needed to find my soul on the foamy ocean.

Here was a man some twenty thousand miles from his home, by way of the southern and northern seas. He knew the world, much better than I did. Perhaps he did not need or want to learn to read English, but I felt an impulse, something like an obligation which the pastor of my village church had taught me when I was young. I drew my bench near him, and explained that I could teach him how to read and write. I found a pencil and a piece of paper. I drew the word 'I', and pointed to myself. He nodded. I then gave him the pencil. He used his left hand, and made a thin line in quite a childish way. I then pointed to him and wrote 'you'. He copied the word, but this time his writing was queer. All the letters were warped and bent, as if he wrote them while being tossed about at sea. But he was earnest and tried out the word again – *you*. And then again – *I*.

I thought of teaching him our names too. I wrote my name: Ishmaelle. For heaven's sake! No, not *Ishmaelle*! Never! I crossed out my name violently, and rewrote it: *Ishmael*. He took this in quite naturally, but had a difficult time copying it, especially the letter s, the shape of which he inverted. He did the same with the h, so it faced the wrong way. I did not correct him. Finally, I wrote his name: Kauri. But as I was spelling it out, I asked myself, how do I know that this is the way his name should be? Would it be written differently on his island? *Was* there a written language on his island? But instead of taking the pencil from my hand to try out his own name, he asked me whether we were again to be bedfellows this night. I told him yes. He looked pleased and took my pencil. He clasped the pencil with his long fingers and wrote 'Kauri'. The K looked shaky, and had one more stroke as if he had drawn a tree branch. Well, Kauri is a tree. I nodded in satisfaction. Then he lit up his pipe as though to signal that our work was done. I coughed, which caused his eyes to gleam with mirth.

He offered me a puff every now and then. I had smoked before on the ship, so I was not shy. It also made me feel more like a man. We sat wordlessly, passing the pipe regularly between us. When we finished, he suddenly pressed his forehead against mine, clasped me round the waist, and proclaimed that henceforth we were bound. He said:

'In my country, my island, we are friends; like married.'

I asked him what that meant.

'It means Kauri die for Ishmael. Kauri strong friend.'

I corrected the way he pronounced my name. Ish-mae-lle. No, I revised myself: Ish-mael. He made no attempt, but said again: 'Kauri strong friend.'

And I took his words to heart. Kauri was a tree deer, or a deer tree. Kauri could be supernatural. The more time I spent with this Polynesian, the more I enjoyed his company. Although he said so little, and I did not understand all he said, I felt that Kauri could be a protector. I was half-woman half-man. We were both strays, far away from each of our queer countries.

XI

I T WAS OUR LAST NIGHT in New Bedford. Both
Kauri and I were looking forward to leaving on the
first boat to Nantucket. When night came, we
resumed the same ritual. Though this time I removed my
heavy jacket. I waited for Kauri to finish praying to his
little idol, hoping he would tell me about his island and
his past life. He did so, gladly. But sometimes I lost the
details and he seemed to speak in digressions.

Even though Kauri twice mentioned the name of his
Māori island in Polynesia, I was unable to fix it in my mind.
I would need to find a map, so that he could point it out to
me, if he knew how to read a map. He was the son of an
island chief and his family owned land. Some years ago, his
people were at war with a tribe on a neighbouring island.
During their tribal warfare, he had been to the tip of
Aotearoa, the land of the long white cloud, and he liked
what he saw. But what was important for him, he told me,
was that he had encountered there some white sailors from
a whaling ship. The white sailors then landed on his island.
He had watched their customs when his chief-father invited
them for a feast where presents were exchanged. In Kauri's
eyes that event was significant. A desire grew in him to see
more of Christendom. One day, a ship from America visited

his father's bay, and Kauri sought a passage to western lands. But the ship, having her full complement of seamen, did not want to take him. Still, Kauri was determined to leave. Alone in his canoe, he paddled to a distant strait, which he knew the ship must pass through. On one side was a coral reef; on the other a low tongue of land, covered with mangroves. Hiding in his canoe in the midst of the mangroves, Kauri waited. When the ship was gliding by, he clambered from his canoe and climbed up the chains to the deck. When the sailors discovered him, everyone was stunned. The first mate threatened to throw him overboard. But Kauri was the son of a chief, and struck by his perseverance, and his genuine desire to visit the western world, the captain relented. They put him with the sailors, and made a whaleman of him. That was how he got to New Bedford, far from his tropical island. In time he managed to speak the English language, without knowing how to read or write it.

'Will you not go back one day, since your father will grow old and you will become the new chief and rule over the island?' I asked.

'Kauri no return. Kauri sail in four oceans,' he said, finally lying down. His voice was sleepy: 'Kauri harpooner. Kauri with Ishmael.'

His speech was clear and as always when he spoke of us, his meaning was straightforward. There was never the slightest confusion around it. I wondered if he would ever use the two words I had taught him: 'you' and 'I'. He knew how to write them now, but it seemed that he did not wish to use them. Maybe he did not think it useful to say 'you' and 'I'.

He pressed his forehead against mine, then blew out the light. We rolled away from each other, and very soon were sleeping.

CHAPTER THREE

Nantucket

I

WHEN THE PALE DAWN LIGHT loomed on Monday morning, Kauri and I were already on the first ship to Nantucket. A gale was brewing, and the sea churned angrily. It looked ominous. Were these changes in the weather signs from heaven that I should not make this trip? I looked at Kauri, and followed his line of sight – his dark eyes were following two seagulls gliding above the grey waves. Suddenly, one of the gulls dived into the water and emerged with a small fish in its beak. Instantly, the second gull dived in and flew out with a larger fish vigorously flapping its tail. I saw Kauri smile. That immediately settled me, and I started to feel like I was fighting fit, as a man might describe himself. An hour later the sun broke through the clouds. My energy was restored, and I looked forward to our arrival on the island, where my real adventure would begin.

The passengers around us were my age, some younger. I noticed two boys, Indians, who could not have been more than twelve years old, accompanied by brothers or relatives, and a group of very lean black boys. Listening to their conversations, I gathered that most of them had worked as seamen before, but all of them were intent on becoming whalers. One sailor said in a fluted voice to his friend:

'You know how Mr Williams bought his 120-acre farm, and his twenty-room house? Do you know where the money came from? He bought it the very day he returned from his fourth whaling trip! He shipped back one thousand barrels of oil. And two hundred of spermaceti!'

His interlocutor responded with enthusiasm: 'I delivered five turkeys to that house last Christmas and I saw the purest candles burning brightly in their hall, white and smokeless! Just that light, it made me want to be a whaler from that very day!'

I listened to them with great interest. Then a man with charcoal-black skin said: 'For my people, money is not the thing! To be a slave, or to be a free whaler. That's the way of it in the world.'

His mate laughed raucously: 'Yes, there is no white or black on a whaler, there is only able harpooner or no-good greenhands. And we Wampanoag are the best!'

To be a slave or to be a free whaler? Even though I was not black, I would have felt like a slave if I had stayed in Denge Marsh. Something in his remark, or even more in the tone of his voice, resonated in a deep place within me. Perhaps we were all seeking our individual freedom on the seas.

I must have appeared as normal as any young sailor on board, since nobody seemed to mark my presence in any way. Kauri blended in with the blacks and Indians on the packet, though a few of the crew looked curiously at him and his long harpoon. One Indian, calling himself Tashe, seemed particularly interested in the harpoon. As the sunlight warmed us and the boat got closer to the island, our spirits were lifted, everyone chatted and laughter broke out. Kauri remained cool and serene. Now and then he brought his harpoon out of its sheath and inspected it. He seemed to possess a particular affection for his harpoon, which must have been well tested in mortal battles. The sharp end, Kauri claimed, 'it know the hearts of whales'.

Kauri's way of thinking always momentarily stopped me in my tracks, as I wondered about his strange mind. Could steel know the hearts of living beings? Did the steel of the harpoon's barbed head also have a spirit that would guide it through the flesh of the whale to the whale's beating centre? I remembered once when helping with my father's carpentry stepping on a nail sharply jutting from an upturned plank, the nail went into my foot, and I cried out as the cruel fire dug its way into my flesh. Kauri's art made the pain in a whale but a hundred times more. I looked at the harpoon's spiked head once again, and shivered.

II

AS THE FERRY WAS APPROACHING Nantucket, the minds of us passengers turned to the matter of sperm whales. Everyone had something to say about these mysterious creatures: the incredible size, the pure white oil, the powerful spout. I listened to all their pronouncements, and took everything in with the greatest interest. I had never seen a live sperm whale before, but I had seen a dead one. When I was about fifteen, a group of children from Saxonham told me about a stranded whale on the beach near Dungeness. Everyone wanted to witness this prodigy of nature. So along with other villagers, I set off to see things for myself. When we were in sight of the town, we saw from quite a distance its immense body, as though a huge chunk of cliff had been broken off by a storm and fallen onto the shingle. As we moved closer, we saw the monstrous dead whale – a sperm whale, they said – so huge, it did not look like anything I had seen on land! It had a giant square-shaped head with clusters of barnacles growing on it, its body was dark and leathery, and its skin looked old and creased, like black marble. I went to touch the skin. It was cold, strangely soft and taut, like I was touching a large piece of kelp. The stench from the carcass was repulsive.

By this time I was already alone, my parents and my baby sister had died and my brother had gone away for work. I was still living in our coffin house. I did not care about anything, so I stayed by the dead whale for a good while. At first I found it quite ugly – well, ugly is not quite the right word. But it had such a hideous aspect, made more hideous by its size. And so its misery, too, was enlarged, a hundred times more than the misery of some small dead fish. As I got used to its appearance, I found its shape truly incredible. What seemed most ghastly was the way the stomach of the whale was cut open. Blood oozed from it, mixed with small fish parts. Seagulls were whirling around us, and wouldn't leave the decomposing flesh. I wondered who or which animal had torn its stomach. Could it be a man? I was told that sometimes a school of sharks would attack a whale, and that even a huge whale was not safe when confronting hungry sharks. As dusk descended, I walked back to the village. All the way on the path to my house, I thought of nothing but death. The whale, my parents, my baby sister. No one was going to bury that whale the way my hands buried my sister in the earth. But it did not seem right to me that it should be abandoned on the beach. If the whale had to die, it should have died in the sea. The sea coffin was a better place to be.

That night images of the dead whale seeped into my dreams – its barnacled head, its leathery skin, its blood. The images would not go away. As though haunted by his spirit, I went back to the beach the following day to see the creature. Some villagers were trying to cut off the meat with kitchen knives and garden tools. Two men were hacking away at the head, hoping to locate the oil in there. Suddenly white oil like thick wax gushed forth, so quickly that the startled men were unable to capture it in their wooden buckets as it rolled down the whale's body and was absorbed by the shingle. I stood at a distance, watching the scene with horror and disgust. The dead whale was deformed beyond recognition. It had become a pile of ghastly body parts and organs, dripping white oil and blackened blood. I felt my stomach begin to heave. To prevent myself from vomiting, I ran as fast as I could back to my house. I did not want the ghostly image of the giant creature following me, but all the way home I felt haunted by its weeping spirit. The shade of that spirit now clouded over my mind as I looked down at the wake of the packet, as we ploughed through the waters, not far from the island of Nantucket. I imagined all those whales out there, waiting for the iron spears of men to rob them of their lives.

III

NANTUCKET! FINALLY we disembarked at a port that was busy, full of small and large crafts. It was so different from the beach in Saxonham. Instead of shingle, there were banks of fine golden sand. The sky was a vibrant blue, with not a single cloud in sight. The only trees were pines, their distorted trunks bent in the wind. The tall houses along the banks were handsome, all built with porches and colourful painted windows. Some houses had wells out the front, where women could be seen washing clothes. I imagined the locals had grown wealthy from the business of seafaring.

We were to station here until we managed to find work on a whaling ship. And even if we were lucky enough to get hired, we might still have to wait some time for the ship to depart the island. So we had first to find a cheap place to stay. After many enquiries in the streets, taking up a good number of hours, Kauri and I were directed to what looked like a hotel, with the strange name of Chez Requin. It sat on a hill overlooking the harbour.

It was colder and windier than in New Bedford, so we were glad to enter the hotel, but we found no one in the tiny lobby to ask for a room. Though we could see, in the kitchen adjoining the dining room, two large steaming pots on a stone stove. I was instantly hungry, but Kauri looked unimpressed. Then a large woman in a brown-coloured gown appeared. As she wiped her wet hands on her dirty gown, I said:

'I and my friend Kauri would like to have a room and supper. I am Ishmael.'

'Call me Madame Requin, you can put down your tings and les valises ici.'

Her small eyes above her chubby cheeks fixed on Kauri and his long harpoon, but she made no comment, beyond whispering 'oh là là'. She turned and shouted something towards the kitchen, then seated us at a table littered with the remains of a recent meal. Madame Requin removed the dirty dishes and asked:

'Would you laike la tourte au poisson or zee chaudrée?'

We hesitated. I could not understand whatever language she was speaking.

'Feesh or chaudrée?' she repeated, this time more simply.

'Chaudrée?' I asked, feeling almost embarrassed.

Then someone in the kitchen stuck out his head, and shouted to her:

'Sacré bleu! Je m'en fous. J'en ai assez de la cuisine, je m'en vais!'

The plump woman shouted back: 'Bon, fous le camp! Imbécile!'

Suddenly we saw a man with a grubby apron and red face storming out. He untied the apron as he left, throwing it on the floor. Then Madame Requin burst into irritated action, and rushed back to the kitchen.

I looked at Kauri in confusion. My Polynesian did not respond, but he did not look annoyed either. He was lighting his pipe and puffing slowly.

Then the madame returned with two steaming bowls, and air of triumph!

'Voilà, soupe de chaudrée, messieurs!'

Whatever it was, I was delighted by the look of it. Both Kauri and I wasted no time, and set about spooning the thick liquid into our mouths. From the first spoonful, I felt immediately blessed. It was hot, savoury and creamy, better than anything I had eaten in the last few weeks on my sea trip. It was made of small juicy clams, mixed with potatoes, sweetcorn, fish bits, pork bits, in a buttery broth. Kauri said nothing but by his slurping and chewing and swallowing I knew he was enjoying the food as much as I was. That cook may have been a foul-tempered foreigner, but he knew how to make flavours come alive. We scooped more, with no thought of anything else. When we finished the delicious soup, easing back in our chairs, we communicated by eyes alone. Then Kauri reached again for his pipe.

I supposed the madame and the cook were French. I knew that we, the English, had been at war with them many times, or so my father taught me. But food and war are two different things. And didn't we beat them in some great battle? Still, they clearly knew how to cook. Maybe if they had spent more time cooking than fighting, everyone would have been better off. My mother, God rest her soul, used to cook us potato and herring soup. My brother and I never knew if it was good or bad, we were always hungry, wolfing down mouthfuls without even chewing. But now, with my stomach full of delicious chaudrée, I think it was probably bad, although to admit this felt disrespectful to my mother's memory.

After supper we promptly retired to bed. There were two small beds, one on each side of the room. Satisfied, I fell asleep while Kauri was still performing his ritual. I swore to myself that I should always like Nantucket very much. The happy soup! And my own bed. After a few hours of deep sleep, I woke up. All around me was stillness and darkness. Only the faint sound of Kauri's light breathing nearby reminded me where I was. I looked over to his bed. I could make out the shape of his harpoon leaning against the window. He had not drawn the curtains on his side of the room. I could see the moon against the black sky, a full moon. Was that the reason I woke up? I thought of Saxonham, the abandoned house on the shingle, the windmills, and the tiny grave in the back garden for my little sister. I thought of Joseph, my brother, the only living family I had left. I wanted to reach him, but how? I wanted to write a letter to him, to tell him about my journey and where I was now. But where would I send the letter? I could send it to the postmaster in Lydd, but how long would it take the postmaster to find Joseph? I thought of all the villagers I had known around Saxonham, all those half-remembered faces who might take my letter and pass it on to my brother if he ever returned. But in truth I could not think of any friendly ones. My heart grew heavier. I heard the church bell tolling. Like seaweed gradually soaking into the brine, I fell asleep again.

IV

NEXT MORNING, Kauri informed me that his little
black god Yojo told him that we must go together
among the whaling fleet in the harbour and select
our craft. Well, that was exactly what I wanted to do of
course. After much enquiry, we learned that there were
four ships readying for three-year voyages. Only two of
them still needed a few hands. One was small and weary-
looking, named *Marian*. The other, the *Nimrod*, was bigger
with an impressive pointed bow. We were welcomed on
board, and a sailor told us that Nimrod was a great hunter,
but his mate disagreed and said that Nimrod built the
Tower of Babel in the ancient land of Mesopotamia. Well,
for me, whether Nimrod was a hunter or a tower builder, I
already felt a stirring confidence that the ship would be
sturdy enough to secure our life on the sea.

I had not seen many whaling ships in my life, but
somehow the *Nimrod* felt noble to me, even if it was not
especially large, about 25 feet wide and 120 feet in length.
What really caught my eye, though, was the figurehead of
the bow. It was a massive head carved out of dark wood –
Nimrod, I presumed. His expression was fierce and angry,
his eyes fixed intently upon some distant point on the
horizon. The hull was slim and sharply tailored at its end,

perhaps to achieve the best possible speed. There were three whaleboats hanging from wooden davits on the sides of the vessel, and one upside-down spare boat sitting atop a wooden frame mounted on the deck. The deck floor was buckled, and was blackened in part with pitch, which gave off a faint smoky odour. I imagined it must have weathered a heavy past – storms, whales, and injured sailors too. But right now, we needed to find the officer so that we could propose ourselves as candidates.

I found an elderly man on a chair reading a book. He was brown and brawny. Like most seamen he wore blue pilot-cloth and a brimmed hat.

'Are you the captain of the *Nimrod*?' I asked.

'What do you want with the captain?' he said, glancing at me.

'I want to go whaling.'

'Ever been in a whaler?'

I shook my head.

'So you know nothing about whaling?'

I was about to answer, when Kauri stepped forward with his harpoon, and confirmed he had sailed many times and killed many whales.

'I've worked in the merchant service, crossing the Atlantic,' I added. 'That's why I want to see what whaling is, sir.'

'Want to see what whaling is, eh? Have you clapped eyes on Seneca?'

'Who is Seneca?'

'Captain of this ship. Captain Seneca to you.'

Kauri and I looked at each other. So we were not speaking to the right person?

'You are speaking to Captain Pound, young man. The ship belongs to me and my brother Daniel. We are here to see the *Nimrod* fitted out for the voyage, and supplied with all her needs, including crew. But before you decide to go whaling, I want you to think on it more.'

'Why?' I asked. 'We want nothing in our life but whaling, sir.'

'Well, you should first observe Captain Seneca, young man. You'll notice he has only one leg. I don't suppose you want to have lost a leg or an arm by the next time I see you?'

'What do you mean, sir? Was Captain Seneca's leg lost because of a whale?' I was taken aback by this unexpected revelation.

'Because of a whale! Aye, it was crunched by the most monstrous whale that ever chipped a boat!'

I was alarmed, and didn't know what to say.

'Let me tell you that most greenhands quit after their first whaling trip!' Captain Pound went on. 'They cannot take it! The work is hard, the weather is foul, food is scarce after months on the sea, and if you don't get attacked by pirates, you might get torn up by the big fish when you are on the chase!' He paused, and observed me. But I remained firm. Then he continued: 'So now, young man, I have given you some idea about what whaling is; do you still feel inclined for it?'

I nodded in earnest. 'I just want to be hired as a sailor first.'

'Very good. From where do you hail? I don't think you come from around here.'

I hesitated for a moment, then told him I came from England, a place near Canterbury Cathedral.

He looked me up and down. Somehow, he saw in a different light.

'One last thing you need to know before you sign the papers. Many ships that leave from this port never return.

I have lived by this salty spray long enough to see that! Fortunately the *Nimrod* is still intact with her bow and her forecastle! Now if that still doesn't change your mind, come with me, you may sign the papers right away.'

Kauri made a move to follow me, but Captain Pound stopped him and said he only dealt with one at a time. Leaving Kauri on the deck, he led me below.

V

I N THE CABIN, seated on the bench, was a sturdy man in his early sixties with wild grey hair. He introduced himself as Daniel, co-owner of the *Nimrod*. The brothers were talkative, especially Daniel. He began to tell me the history of his life and I was forced to listen before I could discuss my employment. I learned that like many other Nantucketeers, the brothers were Quakers. I did not know much about the Quakers, but at the inn where we were staying, I had learned that they were a group of Christian folk who opposed slavery, and believed that women could be equal to men. These folk seemed good to me. Anyway, this old Daniel told me that he and his brother had both retired from seafaring, and had invested their money in whaling vessels, hiring other men to do their whaling for them. True, they did seem too old to go out on the waves themselves.

'Ha, after fifty years on the sea I'm happy to stay dry and profit from my well-earned income.' His laughter was loud and his speech endless, leaving me nodding my head like a dogfish.

'Daniel,' said Captain Pound, 'the young man says he wants to be on the ship. He says he is from Canterbury, in old England!'

'Oh?' said the brother. Upon hearing this information, he finally stopped talking about his seafaring.

'And shall we have him?' said Pound.

'He'll do,' said his brother, eyeing me. 'He seems robust enough, if a little soft in the face, begging your pardon, young fella!'

I felt myself blushing. Pound then brought out several pieces of paper with elaborate neat writing and placed pen and ink before me. I was already aware that in the whaling business they paid no wages for sailors. Rather all, sailors on the ship received a share of the profits. They called these *lays*. Lays were proportioned to the degree of importance of the seaman. I was also aware that being what was called a 'greenhand' at whaling, my own lay would not be very large. But when they asked me of my experience, I argued:

'Sirs, I am used to the sea, and thanks to my late father and the dock work I have done, I can splice a rope, sew sails, and passably use hammer and chisel. So can I receive a better lay?'

Captain Pound exhaled a tobacco-drenched breath and said: 'Well, Ishmael, to be honest, whaling business is not as good now as in the old days. Profits are no longer as great as they once were, so I can give you a 250th lay.'

That seemed very small to me. But the brothers assured me this was standard enough for a sailor, so I agreed.

After I signed the papers I told the brothers I had a friend up on the deck who also wanted to join.

'Maybe not right now,' said Captain Pound. 'Bring him back this afternoon after lunch.'

Oh, what a joy! I had found myself a place on a whaler! Kauri's little god Yojo had worked his magic. All he had to do now was get Kauri on the same ship.

Back up on deck with Captain Pound, I asked boldly: 'Now that I have signed up, I should like to see Captain Seneca, if you please.'

'I don't think he is present today.'

'When can we meet him then?'

'Not sure. But I know that Captain Seneca keeps to his cabin. He's a queer man.'

'How so, a queer man?'

Captain Pound would say no more. But his brother took up the topic.

'Captain Seneca is a man of few words, young fellow; but when he does speak, then you would do well to listen.' He paused, looking at me, and said in a quieter tone: 'Listen, Ishmael, never say this on board. Never say it to anyone. Captain Seneca is an unusual man. I sailed with him years ago; I know what he is. He is a strong-minded man, but moody, you could say. But it's better to sail with a moody worthy captain than a laughing fool!'

Then both men walked away, leaving me there on deck, my heart full of excitement, but also some unsettled feelings. I felt a strange awe of a captain I had not yet met, though knowing that he had lost a leg to a whale, and now I had just joined this crusade against those gargantuan leviathans for three years on the ocean! Folly, Ishmaelle! Utter madness! The sea wind blew on my face and the fear within my heart gradually dispersed. One thing I did know: I was finally on the right track in life. I was becoming a man, even though that thought seemed too daring and trepidatious. Could I really do it? Could I really face down the men on this ship, and convince them of my manhood? Or would my womanliness be betrayed? And, in my heart, I said farewell, to Mackay, who had been my love when I was still a woman. But it was now time to press such thoughts

73

out of my head. And as I looked up at the rigging of the *Nimrod*, which would now be my watery home, I also murmured farewell to Ishmaelle! Here I, Ishmael, come, a traveller in a new world, blue, boundless, wide enough for my wildest dreams.

VI

AFTER LUNCH, Captain Pound and his brother
returned. We were waiting at the end of the wharf
near the ship, Kauri carrying his harpoon and his
bags. The brothers looked at Kauri and Pound remarked
that he had not suspected my friend was a cannibal.

'I met many cannibals on my sea trips, but we don't let
them on board, unless they produce their papers,' his
brother remarked.

'What papers?' said I, now jumping on the bulwarks.

'He must show that he's converted.' Turning to Kauri,
he asked: 'Are you at present in communion with any
Christian church?'

Before Kauri could make a sound, I interrupted with a
hasty explanation:

'He's a member of the first Congregational Church.' I
impressed myself with my daring since I was making this
up. Still, I had learned that many savages sailing in
Nantucket ships came to be converted and joined different
churches.

'How long has he been a member?' Captain Pound took
a good look at Kauri again. Then he said in a jocular tone:
'Has he been baptised? I guess on the day the minister did

not rinse him long enough in the river. There's still some of that blue writing of the devil in his face.'

Kauri looked away calmly. His purple-blue tattoos on his arms and face absorbed the sunlight, as if manifesting the fact that nothing could have had the power to wash those body markings away from his skin.

'Captain, all I know is that Kauri is the greatest harpooner I have ever met. He has killed more whales than any man in this world, I dare say. When he was only a child, he had already killed ten whales on his island!'

To my surprise, both men seemed to accept what I said, especially with regard to Kauri's prowess with a harpoon. Captain Pound then waved his hand dismissively.

'Never mind about the papers. Tell him to come on board. What's that you call him? Kwari? Kooli? What a harpoon he's got there! And he handles it about right.'

Noble and always dignified, Kauri came up to him with his harpoon.

'I say, Coolie, I know your friend spoke highly of you. But tell me yourself – did you really stand at the head of a whaleboat and strike a giant fish?'

Without saying a word, Kauri jumped upon the bulwarks, thence into the bow of one of the whaleboats hanging on the side. He poised his harpoon and darted the iron right over Captain Pound's shoulder, striking a darkened spot on the boat with his sharp spearhead!

Then Kauri announced: 'Him whale eye, dead whale dead.'

'I say, Danny, quick, get the ship's papers. We must have this man in one of our boats!' Captain Pound cried. 'Look, we'll give you the ninetieth lay, and that's more than ever was given a harpooner out of Nantucket.'

When Pound had got everything ready for signing, he turned to me and said:

'I guess your friend doesn't know how to write, does he? Can he sign his name or make his mark?'

At this, Kauri looked in no ways abashed. He stepped forward, taking the proffered pen. In the proper place, he drew an exact counterpart of the queer little tree that was tattooed upon his arm – something like this:

All of us looked at his signature. The Pound brothers seemed amused and closed the deal happily. I thought to myself, now I know why Kauri wasn't interested in learning how to write his own name. He knew how to write it, and better than I did.

VII

WE WERE TOLD THAT we had three days left before the *Nimrod* would sail. During these days of preparation, Kauri and I often visited the ship, and each time I asked about Captain Seneca, and when he was going to come on board. To these questions, the officers would answer that he was expected aboard soon. Meantime, Captain Pound and his brother had been attending to everything necessary to fit the vessel for the voyage.

There was great activity on board the *Nimrod*. Not only were the old sails being mended, but new sails were arriving, and bolts of canvas, coils of rigging as well as hundreds of logs of wood, and polished planks as carpentry reserve. Captain Pound sat in his chair casting a keen eye over the hands. His brother went into the town for the purchasing of materials at the local stores. The men employed on the rigging worked long hours till evening.

We were all aware that we would embark for three years at sea. But not everyone knew what that meant. I certainly could not comprehend it. We were reminded that a multitude of things – bottles, saucepans, cups, knives, forks, shovels, tongs, nutcrackers and whatnot – are indispensable to the business of housekeeping. Not to mention the preparation of dry food and fresh stock: flour, corn, beef, bread, cabbage, potato, salt, pepper, water . . . We would be far from grocers, doctors, bakers and bankers. Due to the great length of the whaling voyage, Captain Pound told me, spare boats, spars, lines and harpoons were crucial. Though there was no spare captain, I thought to myself. There was only one captain, Seneca, and our only ship was the *Nimrod*! The captain was the ship. I hoped I was not wrong.

Like a pregnant woman, the *Nimrod* grew heavier each day. And I grew more excited and anxious in equal measure. I ought to write a letter to my brother Joseph, so I could deposit it with the packet from Nantucket back to New Bedford, and from there, God willing, that letter would be shipped to England. Gracious Lord, I had to do it before the *Nimrod* abandoned this land.

VIII

The *Nimrod*, 28 January 1861

My dear brother Joseph,

I am sending this letter to the post office in Lydd, hoping they will forward it to your ship. Brother, I cannot know when you will see these words, but I must tell you briefly where I am now. I am on an island called Nantucket in Massachusetts, in America. You will not believe how I got here! I embarked on a merchant ship which took me from England to New York . . . But it's a long story and I will have to tell you about it another time. The important thing is, Nantucket is where American whalers launch to the seas. I am now on the *Nimrod,* a whaling vessel, and we are finally sailing tomorrow. Hence my rush to write this letter!

We have a stout healthy crew and to all appearances an uncommonly good one. When I have been with them longer I will tell you how they are. You might be worried about me upon receiving this letter, but so far all I can say is that I am safe and keeping myself well. I don't miss Saxonham a bit. It is a great and queer

world here. Rarely have I seen a woman at the
harbour, but I did encounter a respectable old lady.
She was one of the tireless ones who did the fetching
and carrying. Aunt Margaret, as everybody called her,
was the sister of Captain Pound, the ship's owner. She
reminds me of our great pagan Aunt Gladys who
taught me how to make medications from herbs. And
Aunt Margaret is such a kind woman. She would
come on board with a jar of pickles for the steward's
pantry, or another time with freshly baked fennel
potatoes for some of us before the cold evening sets
in. Once she gave me coffee to drink. Brother, you
must try the pea coffee if you have a chance! When
she learned that I can read and write, she gave me a
bundle of papers, and a little bound notebook as a
present. That's how I am writing to you now, on her
fine paper! You can imagine I felt close to her and I
felt that I could have talked to her, in private
moments. But in the end I did not talk to her. I want
very much to be part of the brotherhood of the
Nimrod, and to sail away from the land. Joseph, I
must finish this letter now, before the last ship today
taking mail back to New Bedford leaves.

I should like to know where and how you are, if your
health is good, your mind at ease – everything about
you. I have been feeling sorry about leaving our home
without telling you, but I did not know where you
were, and still I do not know your whereabouts. I hope
I can get letters from you once I send you the address
of the next port of the *Nimrod*. May God bless you.

Your beloved Ishmaelle

IX

I T WAS A CLEAR MORNING and we were all on board busying ourselves with the remaining preparations. I still had not met the elusive Captain Seneca, the man who would rule over our life at sea. Approaching noon, after the final dismissal of the ship's riggers, and with the *Nimrod* hauled out from the wharf, we were introduced to Drake, the first mate.

Drake was a tall, tanned man with blue eyes. He was in his forties, and there was about him a definite air of authority. Instead of wearing sailor's garb, he wore a long Quaker's frock and breeches, which gave him the look of a Pilgrim. He had a bushy beard with no moustache. I liked his plain look. He was speaking to a squat black man with a round face under a mass of thick curly hair, who then ordered everyone to be silent.

'My name is Freedman, Mr Freedman to all on board!' the black man said. 'I am second mate. I hail from Cape Cod, and I intend to return there a rich man at the end of this voyage.'

'Aye aye,' a chorus of excited voices shouted out. I joined in, and clapped my hands.

Freedman flashed a warm smile that revealed his

gleaming white teeth. I felt an instant trust in our second mate.

Drake set his hand on the shoulder of a lean young man in a fur jacket. He did not look up to greet us, but continued coiling a thick rope.

'This is Jacques, our third mate. He takes care of the whaling boats and the equipment.'

Jacques had a pasty complexion and long hair tied in a ponytail. Reluctantly, he turned his face slightly towards the gathered sailors, revealing a cauliflower ear. I shuddered at the sight of it and averted my eyes.

Then the Pound brothers, coming up from the cabin, asked the chief mate if everything was set, as Captain Seneca was ready.

'I shall call all hands then,' Drake said. 'Everyone on board! We leave the island this afternoon.'

With everyone gathered on the deck, there must have been about thirty-five of us. Half of them were black. One of the harpooners – Tashe – was the Indian we had met on the packet from New Bedford. The cabin boy was also from the packet – I heard the men call him Dilly. And I could see that I belonged to the lowest rank on the ship – the greenhands, or first-time whalers. Five of us were first-timers, and the others were younger than me, around fifteen or sixteen. But all us greenhands were white. It seemed to be that along this coast, the Indians and the blacks were much more experienced whalers than us white folk.

As Jacques went to the riggings to check the sails, Drake briefed us on how things would work on board:

'Eighteen of you are foremast hands. You will perform the daily duties of taking care of the vessel and taking turns on whale watch. During a hunt, some of you will row the whaleboats. You greenhands will have to learn all the skills quickly so that you can help with the watch and row the whaleboats when needed.'

I stood up straight, like a soldier about to go into battle. I eyed my friend Kauri. To my surprise, he was looking up at the clouds as though he saw a sign of a rainbow.

'And, greenhands, you should know the harpooners here are of higher rank and share privileges with us mates and the ship's craftsmen.'

I glanced again at Kauri, who was standing beside Tashe and a third harpooner. I thought: already we belong to different groups! But he did not seem to be affected by this situation. Indeed, Kauri did not seem to care where he belonged, or which group he stood with. He was Kauri, the self-contained Polynesian prince.

I thought Captain Seneca would come out on deck to meet us finally. But I was told the first mate and the pilot would steer the ship out to sea. Captain Seneca would remain below.

Now Drake called everyone who lingered at the mainmast to 'strike the tent', the last command prior to heaving up the anchor. Then the anchor was up, the sails were set, and off we glided. I felt as though it was my own heart gliding over the silky harbour waters on the path to unknown places. A tiny shudder below my stomach caused me to move around the deck, lest anyone should notice.

It was late afternoon. The winter days were short, and the horizon was already merging with the coming night. The last remaining light tinted the wintry ocean here and there. A curtain was being drawn on the stage of the land where we had played our roles. New roles awaited us.

The two ship owners were no longer needed. The

Pound brothers came onto the open deck and embarked into a small sailboat that had accompanied us. I felt a tenderness inside when I thought of how the two old brothers had recruited Kauri and me. Now they were leaving us. As their little boat headed back to harbour they shouted farewell, and their voices mingled:

'Good luck, Drake, good luck to all you boys! And goodbye . . . God bless you all!' said one voice. And the other: 'When you return after three years, we'll have a hot supper waiting for you in old Nantucket. Goodbye!'

They would soon be home, I thought, and they would sleep soundly in their warm beds after a dinner of beef stew cooked by their wives. And here we were, a group of young men, myself among them, on a freezing night sailing into the darkness. A young man! How that came off the tongue! Yet I was not. Showers of doubt came. I was deceiving people. I was a fraud and an impostor. My existence here was a performance. I just hoped that in time my performance would become nature. All I needed was the courage to keep going. I am a man, I said to myself. I am a man.

CHAPTER FOUR

The *Nimrod* Sails

I

THE *NIMROD* WAS OUT OF SIGHT of land. We were surrounded only by green-blue churning waves. That morning I saw a dusk dolphin, its streamlined silver body so handsome in the glistening froth. As I watched it dance in and out of the water I thought how much larger it was than the ones I had seen on the coast of Kent. I did not see if its pod was following behind her, as I was called by other sailors to work. While adjusting the rigging, the sailors lamented that the business of whaling should be regarded among landsmen as a disreputable pursuit. One long-haired sailor, Antonio, of Portuguese origin, was especially talkative. He remarked that whaling was not considered to be on a level with what are called the decent professions.

'A butcher has more respect than a whaling man!' Antonio claimed. 'But once you have dragged a whale on board to do cutting, is it any different than working in a slaughterhouse!'

'Nothing can be worse than that!' a black sailor named Washington said. 'I worked in a slaughterhouse in Providence, I cut open twelve pigs every day with a blunted knife. They squeal and kick and the blood is all over! I don't fancy doing that again!'

'It's not the best job you can have, I agree,' another said. 'But in my village, I could not find work at all. Even the stinking tanner would not take me on!'

'This is my last whaling trip, I swear,' Antonio said. 'I'll be a landsman once I return home. Then I shall go westwards, to San Francisco.'

'Why to that city?' asked Washington.

'Gold,' answered Antonio.

'That's a fool's journey, there ain't gold in all them rivers and hills, there's only dust and mud and horse dung,' said our second mate Freedman. 'Lunch!' he shouted, bringing the debate to an abrupt close.

I wondered how Antonio had ended up on board if he really wanted to mine for gold. I agreed with them about butchery though, I would never want to be a butcher. But I might want to look for gold. Though I knew nothing about gold. No one in England ever mentioned where gold came from.

Now everyone was back by his hammock chewing on the dry bread. Our quarters were the forecastle below the front deck, and there were more than twenty of us in this crowded space, a jumble of indistinct human forms in a dimly lit and undivided room. Around the edges men had placed their travelling chests. These wooden chests, along with their hammocks, were a sailor's territory at sea, upon which no other man would dare to encroach. I did not possess a sea chest, only the old canvas bag from my late father. The ceiling was very low and the ventilation was bad. It was a world of shouting men and it stank of them! The officers' quarters were towards the back of the ship, with more protection from the wind and they were more roomy. They had their own bunk beds. The mates, harpooners, the surgeon, the cooper and the cook shared that space. The captain stayed in the quarterdeck right next to the steerage, and slept in his private cabin. I was told that he was the only one who had a bed which was strung with solid ropes so that the rocking of the ship was counteracted. Below us were the storage holds, where food, oil and supplies were kept. It was pitch-black there, and smelly, worse than the pigsty in Saxonham.

So far there had been no trouble. I managed to look after myself. I wore my mother's knitted muffler around my neck and face to keep the cold away, and I had brought my own herbal medicaments from Saxonham — the dried campion, ginger and mint powder to ease my stomach upsets. Yes, I had a normal woman's body, but I was passing as a whaleman.

II

EVEN THOUGH THE LANGUAGE I learned at my mother's knee was English, I was not acquainted with the strange speech of these seamen long used to life on the waves. I didn't know there could be so many different ways of describing wind, like zephyr, breeze, trades, squall, blast, bise, mistral, gale, blow, gust. The mates would use these words to refer to the various invisible airflows around the sails and riggings above us or across the decks, carrying salt spray or not, harbingers of fair weather or foul. At first, I did not quite grasp some nautical terms our mates used on board. But it was not difficult for me to remember them, especially after a few days of working on deck.

Apparent wind: the airflow that comes from both the natural wind and the headwind caused by the boat's forward motion. (I was shouted at once by one of the mates to 'set the sails by the apparent wind, you young land-lubber!')

Leeward wind: when the ship is sailing with the wind cast upon its stern, so it is, as the old hands say, *running before the wind*. This is the calmest way to sail, stately and steady.

Windward: a ship is sailing into the wind, therefore

beating against the wind. And a rough and raw way it is to cut through the sea.

Neck wind: the mid-air wind that can damage the mast, like a naughty spirit, but otherwise does not stop the ship from making its course.

Zhong wind: medium wind against the bow. (This is a coolie word that the California whalers and Asian sailors would use, according to the cook, who quipped: 'I cannot make a good stew when it's blowing.')

Apart from these many wind words, each with its own flavour and qualities, there were other terms that were also alien to me at first.

Watch: a period on the mast, usually four hours, when a sailor must keep his eyes awake and peeled to spy any danger or sign of a whale.

Head: that place on the ship where a sailor goes to relieve himself, unless he chooses to give vent to his excretions over the side.

Stove boat: a boat that has been damaged by a whale.

Clean ship: a whaler without any whale oil.

Gamming: visits and socials between whaleships at sea. (Oh, how curious I was about such a thing, and looked forward much to its happening!)

Loose whale: a whale with harpoons embedded in it and lines trailing, without any boat attached to it; one that has broken away. (What a terrible fate for one of God's creatures! Though I had not witnessed such a scene yet.)

Ground: whaling grounds such as the North Atlantic waters, Cape Horn waters, South Seas and Pacific Northwest waters. (How marvellous it sounded to me, the moving ground of the ocean!)

All this reminded me that on my Kent coast in England we had so many words for mud. My parents would use different words to describe the soft masses of earthy moistness that we dealt with daily. My almost every day was squelching through the marsh that lay near our humble house. Our boots were never clean; my fingernails always had a ring of crusted dirt. My father had a talent for description. A different word or phrase for the dirt we found in our marsh each season: sludge, cob, adobe, clay, muck, gravel, sand, ooze, slime, silt. Lord, praise this brown sludge, my dear father would say. And then he would lift his muddy boots and bury the heel again in the oozing ground with a look of both satisfaction and great resignation on his lined face. Off he would go with his carpenter's tools in his shoulder bag, whistling a tune, heading towards the old harbour.

III

LIKE MANY OF THE MEN ON BOARD, our first mate Drake was from Massachusetts. Since he was the man in charge, I listened to his instructions intently. Coincidentally, he was born in the same year as my late father, and that may have explained why I had taken a fast liking to him. Looking into his grey-blue eyes, you seemed to see there were images of a thousand perils he had calmly confronted through life. It was said that he had a large family in New Bedford, and he had seven daughters, but no son. He owned an eight-room house and a farm too. I listened to all this, and looked at the man. But I could not read much on his sun-baked face.

'I will only have whale-fearing men on my boat,' said Drake. 'Bravery is not the first quality for this business.'

By this, he seemed to mean that a fearless man is less likely to stay alive on the sea than a clever man who is advisedly afraid.

Then Freedman, the second mate, would chime in, in his simple but forceful way of speaking.

'Drake, see all these boys, fine lads, full-grown and true. They are as careful as any men you'll find anywhere, I say, across these waters or on land.'

I thought of how careful a whale hunter must have to be

95

when facing a perilous battle. I had to admit that I could not imagine actually killing a whale with my own hands. Could I do it if one day it should come to that? The biggest fish I had ever killed was a huge silver hake that got caught in a net my brother had cast; it was almost half as long as my body at the time. That was back in England, though, and I was a very young girl. Now I was a different person. Me, Ishmaelle, I was not a harpooner, but time would tell. One day I might become a woman Nimrod, a great hunter. For now I was hired as a sailor. I would only deal with a whale once the harpooners had ended its life.

'Take care of the staples, and not a piece to be mindlessly wasted!' Drake told us. 'Keep your spirits up for the work. I have no fancy for lowering boats for whales after sundown, nor for persisting in fighting a creature that is desperately fighting us back. Boys, we are in this lonely ocean to kill whales for our living, not to be killed by them!'

Off he went, down to the cabin, perhaps to see Captain Seneca, the mysterious man with one leg. What would he say to Seneca? What did men talk about in private, especially men of such gravity and elevation? I had some inkling, from my days at sea. Still, a veil remained between my knowledge and the reality of men.

IV

THE EARLY-EVENING HOURS were reposeful because we were not pressed for the whale sighting and had a stretch of time to relax after dinner. For me, the early evening was devoted to the songs that second mate Freedman played on his fiddle. Most evenings for an hour or so he played his instrument while some sailors hummed along. How I loved the way he handled that battered soundbox! I had seen musicians back in Kent, at the Christmas market, but they played their violins in such a solemn manner. Freedman played very differently. Sitting by the windlass, his legs crossed, he took the fiddle in his left hand and placed one end against his chest, while with his right hand he scraped the bow back and forth with vigour. The tunes he played were mostly Negro songs, often melancholic, and I loved the melodies. As the darkness descended on deck, the labours of the day seemed to be soothed by the music.

I was very much impressed by the earthy and jolly Freedman. He was a native of Cape Cod. Antonio said Freedman's father was a slave child but was freed by his master, who was a shipbuilder, and Freedman became an apprentice in the trade at the age of thirteen. That was how he became a great seaman and whaler. 'I know them nails,

planks, hulks as well I know the four strings of my fiddle,'
Mr Freedman liked to say, to anyone who would listen.

As well as playing folk songs on his fiddle in the evening,
Freedman was also a man of the hammer. He carried a very
small one around in his pocket, one you might use to crush
a walnut or to crack the shell of a lobster, or more likely to
flatten a nail head on the hull. He used his little hammer
almost every day, during his meals or to repair a battered
hatch on the deck. He claimed he had crushed a whale's
head with it too, despite its small size. 'When it comes to
death, it all goes down without making a fuss,' he said, as
if speaking a riddle. What he thought of death itself, there
was no telling. One evening, Freedman confessed that he
had not been a swimmer, even after some years of whaling,
and he had almost drowned during a few whale chases, and
I wondered if those experiences reflected his riddle.

'Is anyone here not a swimmer?' Freedman asked.

There were several of us with him at that moment. One
red-haired sailor named Loick nodded, half nervous and
half embarrassed. A year younger than me, Loick was thin
as a pencil.

'Ay, Loick, it's normal at your age!'

Freedman dipped the dry biscuit into the soup to soften
it as we all did with our awful food. The biscuits were
called 'duff', a mixture of flour and pig fat but as hard
as rock.

'In one of the chases I was thrown from the boat as the
damn whale tail capsized our vessel. I struggled in the
water, death came to me as I sank, until I was awake and
found myself on a deck with two men on me pumping out
water from my belly. When we landed at home, the first
thing I did was teach myself to swim. That summer I did
nothing but swim like a seal every day. I dived and spread

myself like an octopus in the water until my next voyage began.' He swallowed his softened biscuit, eyeing us up. 'So, don't sink, boys! We are as good and as bad as whales!'

Loick nodded in earnest. Then Antonio chimed in, telling us that a sperm whale could be underwater hunting for two hours without coming up to breathe. Antonio seemed to know a great deal about everything. But I sensed Freedman was not very fond of the long-haired Portuguese boy, for reasons I did not yet know.

Our third mate Jacques, with the cauliflower ear, was in his mid-twenties. He was the son of a Frenchman who had come from Brittany to Quebec to trap animals. Or that is what he told us. Jacques had a broad frame, and was cordial enough, but occasionally he was bad-tempered at night if he had taken some rum. Sailors claimed that Jacques had once saved Drake's life on the sea. After that, Drake recruited him as a shipmate whenever he went whaling. Half in jest, Jacques said that the whales were his brothers, but between brothers there was always war, they would have to fight and kill each other. And therefore he felt both honour and sorrow at killing his brothers.

'I was a whitey among the Indians in Quebec,' Jacques told us. 'I wore no clothes but for animal skins. My old man worked with the native trappers. Most of them led godforsaken lives. It was more than harsh, it was brutal. I saw plenty of them drink themselves to death. And all the kids fought each other and I had plenty of beatings. When I was thirteen, my father moved the family to Massachusetts. Thank the Lord, no more carving up the muskrats and the raccoons! Whaling has saved me from that way of life,' Jacques said, though he spoke with a visible sense of discontent, even some bitterness.

I once witnessed a dispute between Jacques and

99

Washington. By custom, our third mate was addressed by his first name; no disrespect was meant by this. But Jacques sometimes seemed disgruntled with the practice, and on one occasion exchanged harsh words on the matter with Washington, whom he instructed to address him only as Mr Maillot. I thought perhaps the reason he picked on Washington was because he was black, but Jacques didn't pick on the other black sailors, and our second mate was black, which seemed proof that we could be equal. In any case, the dispute was not my concern.

On the third day of the voyage, the first mate Drake was briefing us greenhands about how things would go about when a whale was sighted.

'Once the order from the captain is made, the three mates – Freedman, Jacques and I – will each lower a whale-boat into the water with the harpooners and the steerers. Jacques will make sure each boat has spears, lances and harpoons. The chase can go on for half a day or the whole day. But I have to warn you, the clever devil will often get away.'

'Will the captain remain on the *Nimrod* while you are out on the chase?' I dared to pluck up my courage and ask at the end of Drake's speech.

'Seneca?' Drake glanced at the quarterdeck where the captain was. 'He used to go on most of the chases when he still stood on two legs. But he is no longer the man I knew.'

We were all dismissed after that. I was told to group with other first-time sailors so that the mates could show us how to handle the ropes and sails. Those ropes, how they reminded me of my dismal factory life in Kent! But the ropes on the deck felt different, they smelled of hemp, and they felt purposeful in my hands.

V

LIFE ON THE SHIP was very hierarchical; each man and boy had his place on the pyramid, with the captain at the peak. But occasionally there would be movement on the pyramid and a sailor would be allowed in the cabin to talk or eat with the officers.

Being of higher rank than the rest of us, the harpooners were allowed to eat in the cabin once the captain had finished his dinner. Drake, the chief mate, had selected Kauri as his harpooner for the first whaleboat. Tashe, the Red Indian with few words and a lean body, belonged to the second mate Freedman. Tyrone, a giant native Nantucketeer, served the third mate Jacques in the third whaleboat. Tyrone had high cheekbones and round oriental eyes. He wore thick silver jewellery around his neck and arms, and had piercings in his ears. One of his ankles was ringed by silver hoops. They made music whenever he moved about.

The poor cabin boy Dilly – I never knew his real name – rushed about on and below the deck carrying this and that. I heard that he was a nephew or cousin of Freedman. Apparently Dilly was an orphan and the second mate had taken pity on the boy. To me, he resembled Freedman very much. They had the same curly black hair and black eyes.

He was a dreamy little lad, and I did feel for him sometimes. Once I saw him climbing a ladder by a mast. He did not climb high as he was not allowed, but it looked like he was practising how to be a lookout. After a while, though, the boy was still there up in the air, lost in his tangled thoughts. Oh poor Dilly, what was in his head? Then I heard a shouting from one of our men: 'Dilly-Dally, are you dreaming again? Come down instantly!'

Over the first few days after leaving Nantucket, I got to know everyone on board. I felt part of the group. I passed as a young man, as Ishmael. I always made sure that my breasts were bound tightly with the old cloth I brought with me from Saxonham, even though my chest was flat. My hair was cropped short, and I cut it every few days. I learned to walk and sit like the men around me. But my double life disturbed me at times. I could not laugh in the way they laughed, or curse the way they did. Occasionally they looked at me queerly. I tried to imagine how it might be if we were a crew of women, all chasing whales together. But that was impossible, even in my imagination. Women did not go on sea adventures. They stayed at home.

I tried to keep my focus on daily routines. I still had seen no sign of Captain Seneca. The three mates regularly relieved one another of duties, and Drake seemed to be the true commander of the ship. Every time I came to the deck, I would look around to see if a new face had appeared. But it was the most bizarre thing: Captain Seneca did not show himself.

One grey and gloomy morning, a favourable wind carried us through the waters with good speed. We were sailing south-east towards the equator, leaving the frozen northern winter behind as fast as we could. As I came up for my watch, I saw a stranger in a long robe standing motionless upon the quarterdeck, his eyes fixed on the misty waves.

Was this towering black figure Captain Seneca?

I stared at him from across the deck. There seemed to be no sign of infirmity in him. His tall, broad frame seemed solid and strong. He stood straight, even stiffly. A scar was visible under his left ear, a curved incision of pinkish skin against his black complexion. His grey hair and dark robe billowed wildly in the wind but his body remained firm. I looked down at his legs. Around the ankle of one, under the hem of his trousers, I glimpsed a strange white bit of stump.

This grim sight affected me deeply. According to Antonio and the others, what the captain stood on was the polished bone of a whale. I could not help but wonder how the captain could walk on such a leg.

Upon the side of the *Nimrod*'s quarterdeck was an auger hole, bored about half an inch into the plank. Seneca steadied himself by inserting the tip of his forged leg into that hollow. There was an infinity of determination and wilfulness in his pose and in his gaze too. It was almost like he had been crucified here on the quarterdeck under the black clouds.

Abruptly, he moved. His flowing robe prevented me from observing his gait. But I could hear that his false leg made a sharp and resounding tap with each step he made. Pounding on the deck mournfully, like some apparition by the River Styx, he disappeared into his cabin.

VI

Midnight. Quarterdeck.
Seneca stares at the moon.

A FATHOM SIX FEET the height of a sailor I shall throw all them into the water yes I shall let them all row towards the great fish cutting through these pale waters teasing my dusky cheeks a man can be teased but cannot deny he belongs to this deep six the depth of his soul can only be fathomed in the sea

Even in these warm waves the great fish is watching me from underneath and from the yonder I can smell the iron from his veins the sea monster of my grave he will also need this blue above the deck where I breathe in my rage and out into this unruly night my breath like a squall

The golden sun only knows the walk of my broken bones but knows not the rage hanging on the mainmast at night and knows not the deep sorrow of a failed seaman who has come from endless hills and cold valleys the past of a man this encumbered black spirit yet not destroyed yet more powerful still

I wear this Iron Crown this crown of thorns a nail from this son of man a nail in my bones walking each night on this blasted quarterdeck and conversing with him yes I see the nail on my crown it is bright with many a gem and I am the wearer of the darkling power

Shoot this sun like an albatross I am tortured yet the sunset soothes me then I need no more brightness yet the cooling dusk blinds the sharp steel of my nail and my crown and I hear the great leviathan whispering in the distance and calling out a song to my nailed bones the song wings its way to me across cavernous depths

Come forth from behind your harpoons mates come forth from behind your tombstones I have need of your perverse lives if we can call them that I can use your bodies and your minds' focus and the calluses of your wind-tarnished skins but come and see if you can serve me on this path to my purpose this path is laid with iron rails whereon my soul is fired to run through these torrents of the night

Throw those men overboard into the deep six the fathomless dark expunge and purge the pettiness of men the smallness of men Drake Freedman Jacques and all the rest who clamour after gold and comfort I am madness maddened I am torture tortured I am punishing the punished I am drowning the drowned and all men with the wheel of time will dive into this deep six in the sunset of the world

The stench of Mammon is all over their clothes and oozes from their pores each and every one Drake Freedman

Jacques and the rest they are all krill shrunken heads scrabbling like crabs stinking of dreams of lucre the smell of Leviathan will cleanse these under men the only glitter will be in the fire that consumes them come brave but blind spirits the black sea roils and the white death awaits

CHAPTER FIVE

Captain Seneca

I

THE AIR BECAME WARMER and the sea bluer as we sailed towards the equator. The long days were warm and humid, as if we were living a perpetual spring. As the *Nimrod* headed towards South America, the night-breeze turned softer. I appreciated the hours on the deck and the time under the starry nights in this tropical sea. But below the deck in our sailors' sleeping quarter, it was hell. Each of us stretched our tired limbs on a hammock to sleep. The stench, a mixture of sweat, urine, rotting food scraps and rodent droppings, was close to unbearable. The nights were full of noises, as the men, awake or dreaming, hummed, whistled, mumbled, rambled, raved, sometimes screamed at ghostly persecutors. Insects buzzed and sometimes crawled into our hammocks, and unseen critters scurried across the wooden planks beneath. Somehow I became used to this cacophony. It even seemed to bear me, on some nights at least, into a deeper slumber than I had known in the cottage back on land.

But over several nights, I heard above me the distinctive sound of Captain Seneca moving about again. As he paced the deck back and forth, his whale-leg tapped and scraped against the wood. The other night, I got up and crept to the head. As I went back to my hammock, I heard a man's voice. It came from the deck, and I thought it must be Seneca, talking to himself, as I heard no second person speaking, but I could not make out what was being said. Climbing into my hammock, I closed my eyes, but my mind would not shut. What ailed the captain? Was his wound, his deformed body, the cause of his sleeplessness? It felt like the old man was wrapped in a black robe of anguish, a misery none of us could truly understand.

The following night, during the small hours, I heard the same sounds above my head. Thud, thud, thud. The heavy leg pounding the deck. Thud, thud, thud.

Then I heard Jacques, the third mate, say with his lilting speech:

'If walking these planks at night would please you, my captain, then no one will stop you. But, dare I say, might there be some way of muffling the noise? A piece of cloth, or something you could wrap around the tip?'

'Am I as loud as a pickaxe?' Captain Seneca's enraged voice, bloated and choked, answered. 'Go back to your kennel, you dog!'

'Sir, I am not used to being called a dog,' Jacques said in suppressed anger.

'No? Then how about being called a mouse, or a cockroach?! They used to call me cockroach, before I proved myself. By the age of twelve I could steer a fifteen-foot rig. What do you prefer to be called, eh?'

Something seemed awfully wrong. There was no response from Jacques.

There were no further sounds from the deck, only the creaking timbers. A moment later the pounding resumed, but further away. Then I heard the staccato steps of Jacques, as he clambered down to his quarters.

11

I GOT LITTLE SLEEP with such a fracas unfolding on deck. How did a black boy they called cockroach become captain of a whaling ship? How did he turn into Captain Seneca? Truly a puzzle. This *Nimrod* was the vessel of many untold stories, and so many great souls I had yet to learn about. They were as mysterious as the colossal whales out there.

I lay awake in the darkness, among the sounds of snoring and snorting. I heard bodies tossing and turning in their hammocks. Perhaps they also, even in slumber, had been disturbed by the strife between Jacques and Captain Seneca. Then in the blackness, I saw a dim shape come to the hammock on my right side. I was suddenly alert, clutching the blanket tight around me. I knew things happened at night on a ship, but was he coming to me tonight? Panicking, I rolled myself into a ball in the blanket like a cockle shell.

But the man was not coming to me. Antonio always slept on my right side, and on my left was Loick. So the man was coming to Antonio. There were whisperings between the two men, then a rustling and a fumbling about. The breathing grew heavier, and the rustling sound turbulent. I remained rigid in my hammock, scared to move even an inch. Perhaps the noise had woken Loick too, for I saw his shape turning over. He swore in a breathy whisper, then turned back and continued to sleep. I heard more sounds, and swearing. Disturbed in all sorts of ways, my senses troubled, I could feel myself becoming distressed, with a palpable fear shooting through my spine. Would he come to me afterwards? Would this happen tomorrow night? Kauri could not protect me, since Kauri slept in a cabin with the other harpooners. But even if Kauri had been right next to me, what could he have done? He was a man after all. A man is a man, and the way of a man can be without constraint, remorse or mercy. Without shame. I lay frozen, confined to the narrow strip of my hammock. In my imagination I saw vivid pictures of everything that was happening beside me, even though I tried to shut them out. My heart shrank from a sense of repellent intimacy, I felt disgust. I wanted to flee from my canvas prison, but dared not move. I was the mute witness, compelled to hear, and to see darkly. I dreaded the idea of a hand reaching out to my body, and finding some lack there. My void, my secret. I tried with all my might to think of something else. And my mind summoned up Seneca's grey features, the troubled face, worn out by the wave-wrinkled sea. Seneca was watching me and all that was happening. The dreaded judge. But still I could not block out the low cries and the groans. The two next to me had become one with their pressing and pulsing and their jagged pumping, right by my hammock. Would the Lord strike them down, and me too, just as He wasted Sodom and Gomorrah, and would I too be turned to salt, a pillar in a coffin?

I heard a cry from one man, then the other. The deed

was done. The quickened breathing subsided. Now that they had finished that business, I called out, but silently, *please, Lord, release me from this purgatory*. Let me fly from these tortured souls and bodies, which, after all, are but the souls and bodies of ordinary men. Let the night take me to oblivion and the peace of sleep.

III

THE NEXT MORNING our third mate Jacques came to the deck with a frown on his face. He did not look like he had slept at all. Wrapped in his old fur jacket, he smoked his pipe alone by the windlass while we ate our breakfast. The eight o'clock watch had begun. Some went up the mast to do the lookout, others were working on the riggings. I watched Jacques approach Drake.

'Did you hear me last night?' Jacques said.

'You mean your talk with Captain Seneca?'

Jacques nodded grumpily.

'I would not bother asking him to walk quietly,' suggested Drake. 'He is a poor soul, after all. He is really not the same Seneca I knew from the past.'

Jacques seemed to regret what had happened in the night. 'No doubt you are right. But it has made a wiser man of me.'

They both glanced in the direction of the quarterdeck and Captain Seneca who, surprisingly, was out by the steerage. His spyglass raised, he was looking over the stern.

'Made you a wiser man? How so?' Drake asked quietly.

'Well, I now know that I shall just leave the old man alone; never speak to him, never take to heart what he says.'

Drake gazed at Captain Seneca for a while, as if trying to decipher a hidden meaning from the dark figure against the white mist. He then turned back to Jacques.

'It was surprising that Seneca suddenly decided to return to sea after being settled,' he remarked. 'When he lost his leg, he swore that he would never return to a whaler. So there must be something going on in his own thinking, of which I do not yet have a full grasp.'

Jacques nodded. 'Yes, it is strange that he came back to a whaler.'

'Well, whatever force is pushing him back to the seas must be very great – powerful enough for him to leave behind his wife.'

'Ah yes. The child . . .'

They said no more. Drake returned his gaze to Captain Seneca for a moment, then without a further word walked to the mast to tell a sailor to adjust the rigging. Suddenly, all of us heard a shout from Captain Seneca, his unique low and hoarse voice cutting through the air:

'Masthead, there! Look sharp! There are whales hereabouts!'

Everyone looked in his direction. A patch of white waves churned in the grey-blue water, not far from the stern of the ship. But the whales must have vanished back under the water.

'If you see a white one, roar out!'

Everyone was alert. Tashe, Tyrone and Kauri scanned the sea's surface with intense interest. The air was quiet and we could even hear Seneca's breathing. The captain's nostrils flared, and the rhythm of his breath was getting faster. Minutes passed. There was no sign of any whale.

'Captain Seneca,' said Tashe after a while, 'would that white whale be the same that some call Moby Dick?'

'Moby Dick?' said Seneca. 'Do you know the white whale then, Tashe?'

'I'm sure I saw it once on my last ship. A monster of a sperm whale, as big as this here *Nimrod*. Strange-looking beast. Not like other whales. His jaw jutted forward and his spout shot out white lava!'

'Did he have any irons clapped on his flanks? Harpoons lodged in his sides?!' cried Seneca.

'Yes he did. A number of harpoons with ropes attached!' Tashe confirmed excitedly.

'There you go! Then you know our quarry! If you see that cursed white beast, no matter how far, no matter at what hour, lower the boats at once and take me with you!' The anger and passion in Seneca's voice affected everyone around him.

That afternoon, I wondered about the white whale Captain Seneca seemed to be so intent upon finding. I had never seen a white whale. It seemed a marvellous thing, like a whale made of ivory alone. My childhood memories of whales came back to me again, and I tried to recall more vividly the minke whale I had seen on the Kent coast. My father was alive then. One afternoon, my brother and I were collecting cockles; most days we did a bit of scavenging at low tide. Then we saw a sleek grey body, like a long slab of rock, moving swiftly on the distant sea. It was so far away that I cannot say I really saw it. But I did see the blow, like a fountain squirting water during the Christmas funfair we once visited in the town of Lydd. It blew in a curious way. I heard my father cry out: 'Look, a whale!' I dropped the basket of cockles, running towards the water with Joseph. Before I could properly see the creature, it disappeared. Later on, my father told me it might be a minke whale, and that minke whales have two blowholes.

Then I remembered the great carcass I had seen ten years later – a sperm whale, like a dread shadow on the sand, a ghost of a seafaring dragon. I had come so close to it, touching its still smooth flank like black marble. But it was so unreal. Its spirit had left the world. And now here I was, an accidental whaler, who knew nothing of whales, except the festive spout in the distance and the unreal immensity of a sperm whale's corpse on a windy shore. How was I going to become a real whaler? And if the chance arose, if a monstrous whale came towards me and the ship, would I throw a harpoon to spear the beast? Could I? It would be me versus whale, but why would I have more right to live than the creature?

IV

IN THE AFTERNOON, the wind changed direction and a squall appeared. The horizon was blackened under the dark clouds. The sea was moody and the waves churned furiously. Even though I had been on the ocean for several weeks, I was still not used to the listing of the ship in stormy weather and sometimes had to steady myself by gripping the rail. But Loick and a couple of other greenhands suffered from seasickness, so badly that at times I had to perform their tasks. As I was helping to tighten the rigging, Freedman came to me. He said the surgeon was sick, and I should deliver fresh water to his cabin and check if he had other needs.

Having a good opinion of our surgeon Mr Hawthorne, I was glad to obey the order. He had a different air from the other men on board, and he dressed more finely. Other than the captain, he alone was spared hard physical work on the deck, nor was he required to chase whales, or climb the mast if we were short of hands. I went down to the hold and fetched some fresh water. The surgeon's cabin was close to the captain's at the back of the ship. I stood before his door and knocked on it. There was no answer. I hesitated and then opened the door. Mr Hawthorne was sleeping on his bunk. Well, I was not sure if he was asleep.

I moved closer and looked at him. His eyes were closed and his face pale, his lips dry and crusted. I did not wish to disturb his rest. Quietly, I put the water jar on the desk next to him. I dared not sit, I simply stood there and thought I should wait for a few moments to see if he woke up. Glancing around, I noticed many books on his desk, on topics ranging from medicine to nature, geography to history. Two books in the pile made me particularly curious. One was *A History of Medicines*, the other *Collected Plays of Shakespeare*. Back in my Kent home, we only had a King James Bible on our mantelpiece, and we also had *Dr Johnson's English Dictionary*, a battered book with pages missing, which my father inherited from his own father. I then noticed a journal opened on the desk, with a page written in small, neat handwriting. I could not help but glance at it.

. . . This morning I saw large flocks of birds coming from the west. I always pay attention to birds, their variety and their movements. They are both our friends and signs of nature's purpose. I hope to see flamingos when we approach Cap de Verd. On his voyage of discovery to the new world, Christopher Columbus, when he was just a few days out from reaching land, noticed an immense flock of birds flying from the west. The next day he decided to change his course, towards where the birds had flown from. He then spotted land, a thin strip of white and green, in the distance. What a sight it must have been. San Salvador – Holy Saviour – was indeed named by Columbus. The captain is keen to sail straight down south, but my interests are the natural and human wonders we shall encounter along the way. I shall write to Henrietta, a kind of log of my journey and my reflections on nature . . .

I was very intrigued by the name 'Columbus'. I had learned of him from Captain Mackay in Saxonham. I would always remember the excitement in Mackay's voice as he described to me the thrill of seeing a new land after months at sea. Now as I was reading the surgeon's diary, I could tell that Mr Hawthorne was inspired by a similar passion for finding the new and the strange, even among the exotic birds that flew above our craft. I wanted to read more, but my curiosity remained unsatisfied, since Mr Hawthorne, lying on his bunk, shifted his body, and coughed. I immediately turned my attention to him. He opened his eyes. It took him a few moments to notice I was beside him.

'The mate asked me to check if you were better. Do you want some water, Mr Hawthorne?' I asked, stammering a little.

He nodded, and raised himself up, betraying a lassitude and weariness.

I poured some water into a cup and handed it to him. He drank slowly. Then he said:

'Ishmael, will you open the chest there for me, and find a box?'

I noticed the chest by the desk and opened it. It looked like a medicine cabinet, with an odd assortment of objects neatly stored and labelled. I could read the labels on the bottles: laudanum, coca, morphine. There were also small glass jars labelled alcohol along with cotton patches, scissors and pincers.

'Can you pour a little bit of laudanum into a glass?' he said.

I did what he bade me and handed him the liquid. I watched him swallow it, and asked what he was drinking.

'Opium dissolved in alcohol. This will relieve, I hope,

my aches and pains,' he said with a faint smile. 'But one does not want to resort to it too often. It's highly addictive.'

I nodded. And asked him if he needed anything else.

'I could do with an assistant when there is an urgent situation, or if I fall gravely ill then someone able to help,' he said. He seemed to be in better spirits now.

'Mr Hawthorne, if you like, I can offer you one of my herbal remedies. It's a powder made from dried campion, mallow roots and mint. It has helped me in the past when I have suffered from muscle pains and aches.'

The surgeon gazed at me.

'My great-aunt back home was a great herbalist and curer in our area. She taught me many things about how to help the body with herbs and medicaments. I have never offered my powders to anyone else, but they are good. Would you like to try?'

He nodded, and seemed to be intrigued.

'Well, as a man of science, Ishmael, I am always willing to experiment, especially on myself.'

So I ran back to my quarters, fetched my herb powders and returned to the surgeon's cabin. Mr Hawthorne took a little ball of my medicine, hesitated for a moment, then swallowed it, drinking some more water.

'You're a dark horse, Ishmael.' He eyed me with a sympathetic but curious gaze. 'If this helps, I suggest some of your powders should be kept in the medicine cabinet.'

'Of course, Mr Hawthorne, though I have almost none left.'

'Whatever you are able to spare,' he said gently. 'Drake is unwell too — can you take some of the laudanum to him and check his condition for me?'

I did as he asked, went to see the first mate and then returned with an empty glass. Mr Hawthorne was looking slightly better. He was already up, sitting by his desk, and writing something.

'How was Drake?' he said.

'He does not look too bad to me, sir.'

The surgeon then remarked: 'Your miraculous powders seem to have brought about an improvement already. I thank you, Ishmael, and your great-aunt, if I may.'

Before I left, I stalled for a while. I wanted to ask if I could look at some of the books in his library, but I was too shy. And it seemed as if he wanted to return to his journal writing. So I exited his cabin.

V

THE STEWARD MR ROBERTS announced dinner, which meant that the first service, for the highest rank of men, was about to begin. I was surprised when he called me to the forecastle and informed me that by order of the first mate I should dine in the cabin today, as a reward. 'A reward?' I asked. 'Yes, a reward for easing his intestinal troubles. That's what Mr Drake told me,' the steward said. I was mortified, since I did not do much for Drake, nor for the surgeon either. I was embarrassed to be elevated above my peers even though I felt proud at the same time. Well, in truth, not so very elevated. I would still sleep in my hammock alongside the other seamen, and I was still one of the lowliest hands. Perhaps the other mates were also unwell, I thought, and needed my help. Or maybe even the captain himself.

There were two windows built into the rear wall of the captain's cabin. I was surprised not to find any pictures of whales or ships or tempests, as I had imagined there would be in a captain's private quarters. Instead I saw a lone engraving hanging slightly askew on the wall opposite the dining table. I took a closer look. Two figures, one bright in the sky, the other dark and in the depths of a sea, seemed engaged in combat. The bright figure had a long beard and a stern countenance, his right hand was raised and his index finger pointed upwards, while from his left hand blazed downward a terrifying bolt of lightning. The figure at the bottom of the picture was a coiled serpent of a man, looking up, his face contorted as the lightning bolt was about to pierce him. The Lord God smiting the devil, and conquering evil, I thought to myself. Then I looked around discreetly. On the desk below the image there was a Bible on top of some sea charts. I noticed there were two books stacked one upon the other just behind the Bible. One was called *Some Fruits of Solitude*, by William Penn. I vaguely knew the title. It was a Quaker book that I had encountered at the inn in New Bedford. I tilted my head to read the spine of the second book. It was *A Journey of a Long Travail from Babylon to Bethel*. Next to the desk was a small bed that seemed to be shorter than the captain. A brown-and-blue-patterned quilt lay neatly folded at the foot of it. That was all. The captain was already seated at the far end of the table. His eyes registered my presence. Then he looked beyond my shoulder, out towards the waves.

When the three mates were settled, Moses the cook began to serve the meal. I was given a place next to the third mate Jacques. No one paid any attention to me, apart from Drake, who acknowledged me with a nod as I sat down. I noticed Drake had exchanged his Quaker's frock for a quilted waistcoat. The atmosphere was icy and stilted, with Seneca presiding like a mute sea lion surrounded by his cubs. I thought the cook would serve everyone, but Seneca, as though impatient with Moses, quickly took over the role of serving. This seemed to be a torture for each officer. As Seneca strained to cut the beef, everyone's eyes fastened upon the old man's knife. The first mate received his meat as though receiving charity. I noticed that Jacques was especially restless; his pale white face had turned pink, and his cauliflower ear seemed to be more red and swollen than usual. I realised how lucky we lower-rank people were, to eat among ourselves, and not to have to suffer such an ordeal.

When it was my turn, Seneca did not serve me. Moses intervened, and cut the slice of beef for me. I was relieved. No one talked during the meal. I was surprised that no one wanted to enquire about my herbal medicaments. Perhaps they felt that sufficient gratitude was expressed by allowing my mere presence, and that no words were needed. I ardently wished to be released as quickly as possible. But I understood, without being told, that I had to wait until the captain had finished his meal. I kept my head down, chewing as quietly as I could, studying the grain on the table with care. There was butter, though I did not dare help myself. I watched Drake and Freedman cut butter for their bread, but since Jacques took none, I thought it best to remain humble and modest. Butter was a premium item on the ship; we lower-ranking sailors would rarely receive any of that fat and sweet substance.

After the first round of service with the three mates and the captain, everyone went on deck to smoke their pipes. And the next group came into the cabin. It was now the turn of the three harpooners, plus the carpenter and the cooper. Usually, the surgeon would eat with this group too, but I heard he had decided to eat alone, wary of spreading (or succumbing to) some new malady. The three harpooners were served first, and I was told to stay to help with the dishes.

Now without the presence of the mates and the captain, I was glad to be there. In contrast to the domineering ambience at the captain's table, the carefree ease and banter of the harpooners was a delight. I took pleasure in watching Kauri eat his beef. He still did not like to eat meat with a fork and knife, preferring his powerful hands. The other harpooners, Tashe and Tyrone, chewed their food with such relish that I wished I could join them for a second plate, since I had eaten little to nothing at the captain's table. Woody the carpenter and Simon the cooper helped themselves more liberally to the butter than the mates. Woody's speech was muffled because his mouth was stuffed with bread. Somehow Dilly had managed to sneak into the cabin. Normally Dilly would eat with us sailors, but perhaps he sensed that the situation today was unusual, and profited from it to get himself an extra piece of bread. Like a cat with a fishbone, the cabin boy quickly retreated to a corner to enjoy his prize.

VI

I T WAS MY TURN TO MAN the masthead. I was lucky that the weather was fine.

The masthead of the *Nimrod* had to be manned from sunrise to sunset. We sailors took regular turns, and relieved each other every few hours. In the serene weather of the tropics, it was pleasant to be on the masthead. There you stood, a hundred feet above the quiet decks, while beneath you the ship swam and below the ship the sea monsters slithered through the water. You could become lost in the infinity of this blueness as the winds blew and the sails billowed. No one would bother you, except there was one nagging purpose – the sighting of whales.

But that afternoon, though the weather was fair, my body was not. I discovered that I had my monthly bleed. My menstruation had been perturbed since leaving Nantucket, and had become irregular. When I was clambering up the ladder, I already felt the telltale pains in my stomach, and my legs felt weak. A gush of warm liquid came out of me. I always wore two layers of underwear and at that moment I knew exactly what had happened. Grasping the rope tightly in my hand, I blanked out in the air momentarily. Slowly I came back down onto the deck, and told the greenhand Joshua to replace me. I kept some coarse paper and a cloth belt I'd fashioned under my hammock, and I needed them right away. There were few people in the quarters at this hour, as everyone was on duty, so I grabbed my paper and the cloth and concealed them in my pockets. Then I went down below – to the bottom layer of the ship where we kept the oil and supplies. I had to be very quick because the chef frequently came there for provisions. I stuffed the paper and my cloth into my undergarments. It rubbed against the hairs around my crotch, stinging and prickly. I stood up awkwardly and went up on deck. I climbed back to the top of the mast. Cramps wracked my stomach, pains shot through my lower back, and my head was light for some time, but I just needed to bear it for a few more hours. Then I could rest, and sort out my blood when a moment of opportunity came.

The woman's curse was my curse. My blood was the mark that would betray the hiding Ishmaelle. I knew that three or four days of blood awaited me, the second day being the worst. Who on this ship would guess the truth about this bleeding sailor? Indeed, who could possibly believe, in seeing a bloodstain on a trouser leg, that the rough but sensitive Ishmael was something utterly other than he appeared?!

VII

NEXT MORNING, ON THE DECK, while I was
chewing a home-made medicine of mint powder
to ease my stomach pain, I watched a school of
tuna swimming by and grasped the edge of the gunwales.
Mr Hawthorne caught sight of me. Perhaps the surgeon
noticed that I was looking unwell, as he asked:

'Are you all right, Ishmael?'

I nodded. 'Yes, I am all right. Maybe just a cold, or
some ailment of the stomach.'

He looked at me, and said: 'We don't have much
medicine on board. If the pain worsens, you can try a little
opium. But I hope you won't need it.'

I thanked him, and noticed that he was carrying a big
book. He went to the side of the after house where a chair
was placed. He settled himself, and began to read. From
what I had observed, Mr Hawthorne was the only man
who spent his days on board the *Nimrod* devouring books.
Occasionally we would see Captain Seneca in his room
reading, but not as much as Hawthorne.

Now as Mr Hawthorne was absorbed in his reading, I
moved closer to him and caught sight of the title: *Systema
Naturae* by Carl Linnaeus. Careful not to alert Hawthorne
to my presence, I positioned myself behind him so I could

take a peek inside. The tome looked intriguing, its leaves covered in beautiful drawings of plants and animals. But I realised it was written in Latin, which I could not read. As I stood dumbly, the surgeon turned his head and smiled.

'Are you interested in books about nature?'

'Is that what this one is about?'

'Yes, it's about all the species in our world. This author named each species, from apes to jellyfish, from lions to insects!'

I knew the word 'species'. But I could not say I knew exactly what it meant, so I asked: 'You mean we humans are one species and whales are another species?'

The surgeon nodded. 'If you read this Swedish botanist, you would discover that he believed we humans and apes belong to the same genus, although many people feel offended by that idea.'

What a thing to say, I thought, humans and apes belong to the same group!

'You mean when God made Adam and Eve, He also made an Adam ape and an Eve ape?'

'Not quite, but that's an interesting question.'

'What about the whales and dolphins? They carry their babies in their stomachs like us.'

'Yes, whales and dolphins are mammals, just like us! Isn't it strange that we mammals live so differently? Whales live in the ocean and we can only live on land. Without this ship, we would all die horribly in the sea. But for the whales, the sea is their garden. If a whale is stranded on land, it dies.'

'And the baby whales suckle milk from the mother whale, like the child does her mother, or the calf the cow?'

'That's right.'

'But how did mammals get to the sea? If they are not

like fish, does that mean they are more like cows? They don't have gills but breathe the air like we do?'

'Ah!' Mr Hawthorne responded, as if relishing the thought. 'Yes, indeed. That may be one of nature's great mysteries. Perhaps once, the great-great-grandparents, the ancestors of the whales, roamed the earth, and decided that the sea might be better for them. They changed their form, their feet became fins, and their noses became holes on the top of their heads! The species can change.'

'Could we humans change? Or did God create us to be the way we were?' I thought for a moment, then hesitantly I asked: 'Would it be sinful for us to become something different?'

'We might change if God decides to change us. But some people think we humans are perfect already, as God created us in His own image. We are different from the animals.'

'So we are not animals?' I paused, and pondered what the surgeon had said. 'But aren't we still animal-like? Aren't the animals not so different from us? In my village there were many cows and sheep. Some of them were my friends when I was young. I named a few and I played with them every day. One old cow, Jemima, used to eat apples from my hand. One day I found her dead, covered in flies and maggots. I was very sad. Now, on this voyage, I have not yet learned much about whales, but if I could swim among them and could see them every day, would I feel the same way about them?'

'That's an interesting perspective, Ishmael. But we cannot get too sentimental about these creatures.'

He turned back to his reading.

What did he mean, sentimental? I dared not ask. If God created all these creatures, were they not all equal in His eyes? In the Bible it says man was given dominion over the animals. Does that mean man could pursue them till death, and take their flesh? Does that mean man can scour the sea and litter it with the skeletons of all the creatures he destroys? I thought more about men and women. Man was also given dominion over woman. Male over female. If God is a man, where is the God that is a woman? I remembered a half-woman half-man figurine in my great-aunt Gladys's house. That idol had a pair of breasts and also a giant penis. And Gladys said we are all half-woman half-man. As a small child I actually believed that, though I had not found the extra part on my lower body. But now I wondered if there might be in some other world a woman god with a penis? I wondered if Mr Hawthorne could explain this to me. But he was lost in his book again, so I hoped perhaps another time, when he was not so occupied.

CHAPTER SIX

Lower the Boats

I

By the carpenter's bench, under the mainmast,
Seneca stands and stares into the starry sky.

I THOUGHT THE WOUND was closed last spring when
I clutched my unmanly stump and saw Ruth knitting
under the sycamore tree heavy with child and I asked
for her forgiveness of my temper by her swollen belly I
thought all would pass and I would be a man of home and
the farm would be my final ship but the wound opened
again when the child was born I saw his blue eyes and the
skin pale as a baby goat's the sparse hair like golden spun
silk not my child a white man's child a white man who had
known Ruth and this child the fruit of that sin her doing
the midwife grimaced and looked away not letting her eyes
meet mine then covered the child hiding this white stain
and my dead mother's face appeared

Many nights I think of the small body of the child who did
not resemble me nor my own father I would not forget the
blueness a man looks into a child's face and wants to see his
own oh I could not bear that blueness his small cold hands
and pale cheeks no longer pink as he lay still all breath gone
he was so little that I felt I was holding a feather he had no
weight but sorrow and remorse weighed on me as I walked

with him to the final place like a dead man and now my days are without Ruth and without child but the white devil is out there and is waiting for me so he can destroy whatever remains of me

I am a lone man the stranger on the *Nimrod* I cannot be of good cheer or laugh with my white sailors nor the black men who toil on the decks if I am not given my vengeance against the white devil if the gods don't deliver him unto me then I fear the grave will open up and eat me alive that white ghost that stalks me that haunts the depths he knows me and I him his great animal whiteness against my black grim visage set on death either my harpoon will puncture his heart or I shall be cut down and pulled by this devil to the watery bottom

Yet my remorse is pricked by my wife's eyes that look at me from across the sea their coldness and their accusation their green lustre that like a pond I had once wanted to drown in when she saw me leaving in December's frost with the gales and gloom and I on my pegged leg half a man and half a corpse heading towards the harbour where the *Nimrod* awaited like a hearse I knew then that was the end of my earthly life only the life of great devils the whale and me and the devouring sea was left but no woman least of all her could understand the weight that draws me under and lets me tangle with the evil that once known can only be embraced

II

The whale's mating call.

CCcchhhiiiiiiikkkkkeeeee
Coooooommmmmmmmiinngg
Kkkkkkkkkkkkkuuurrrggghh
Coooooommmmmmmmmiinng
Kkkkkkkkkkkkkkuuurrrggghh
yyyyyeeeeeeeeeeeeeeeeeeeee
CCcchhhiiiiiiikkkkkkkkk
Kkkkkkkkkkkkkkuuurrrggghh
Yyyyyeeeeeeeeeeeeeeeeeeeee

I thought I had heard whale songs during the night. Perhaps they were mating calls, with two alternating streams of pulsations and whistling. The sounds were soft but sometimes powerful, like animals crying in a dense forest. They mixed with the creaking noises of the ship. The more I listened to them in the dark, the more I believed that the calls were from two whales, for I could tell the pulsations came from different directions. Then all was quiet for a while. Our chef Moses once mentioned that when whales mate, the male and female chase each other around and rake their teeth on each other gently. The female whale then lies on her side so that the male can get close to her. As I listened from my hammock, swinging gently back and forth and felt lulled into a kind of dream and strange peace, images of my old English village came to me. The early spring in Saxonham, my brother and I would be playing or lying on the shingles near our house, hearing the call of the rock pigeon, the returning migrant birds, and the scurrying squirrels leaping in the nearby bushes. Our two barren pear trees, now green with leaf, would as usual be without blossoms. Like witches they never gave birth; they stood in that way of mysterious seers casting spells but remaining wrapped up in their secrets. The colour would be rising in everything and everywhere – the pink sea thrift in the fields and samphire in the salty marsh, the green canopies of old oaks – and the longer days coming, bringing the world of summer light. But all that was far from me as I lay in my hammock. Now about me, beyond the thin wooden walls of the ship's hull, was the cold sunless ocean, alive with these clicks and chatterings, in the middle world between the surface and the seabed. That seabed far below where skeletons and wrecks lay. That's what we trekked over, steady on our course, to where? And what date was it? I had forgotten again the time. I did a mental calculation and I came to the conclusion, it must be the 4th or 5th of April, 1861. Did the clicking whales beneath know this date? What did that date really mean out here? Out here, far from kith and kin, as they say, far from hearth and home. My home? I had none, except for one wandering brother, whose whereabouts I knew not. But sleep came without dreams.

III

IN THE SMALL HOURS I woke, and went to the head to relieve myself in privacy. Then I went up on deck. It was pitch-black. I thought I saw distant lights. Was it a lighthouse? It could not be. It had to be some passing ship, with its navigation lights on. But still, the thought of a lighthouse calmed me.

When my father was still alive, he told us that my grandfather and many locals had built a lighthouse in Dungeness. My father said that over the years the sea had thrown up more and more shingle on the beach, so the old lighthouse was replaced later. The tower stood at the end of a pier. I had never seen it up close, but on a clear day it was visible from our village. It was the tallest building I could even imagine. My father said it was as great as the Eddystone Lighthouse off the coast of Cornwall, though I had no idea where Cornwall was. Our old man and some other locals were called upon to build lodgings for the keepers. All I remember is that when Joseph turned fourteen, my father was going to take him to help with his work for the lighthouse. That day, when everything was ready, and my mother had baked a huge loaf of bread for them to take along, my brother was so excited that he clambered up one of the windmills at the back of the house, just to tease me and to show off. He climbed onto one of the sails of the windmill and shouted:

'Ishmaelle, while you are here milking cows I will stand at the top of the lighthouse and see the whole world!'

My father and I were down on the nettle-filled path, looking up at him.

'I will find out what's on the other side of the sea!' he cried.

'Do you think you will see those strange creatures,' I said, filled with envy, 'the ones without a head but with eyes on their chest like the images we saw in Aunt Gladys's house?'

Both my brother and I were fascinated by the images we had seen at our great-aunt's house. She pasted them to the kitchen wall, next to a string of dried garlic and a long-handled broom.

'Aye! Surely I will see all those creatures, Ishmaelle! Farewell!' he shouted down again, his left hand stretched behind him, as he tried to grasp hold of the rotor of the windmill.

My father cursed him.

'Get down, you fool! The other side of the world is no different! It's just Frenchmen eating the same cod and banging the same nails into chairs and tables and coffins!'

My father had never left England. The furthest he went, according to my mother, was somewhere to the north of London.

Joseph leaned forward, then suddenly there was a tearing sound as his jacket caught the edge of a sail, followed by a dull thud as he tumbled from the windmill. He fell in a dense patch of nettles a few yards away from where I stood.

The day was ruined. My father left for Dungeness by himself, taking the haversack my mother had prepared for two people, and the loaf. My poor Joseph was in bed for two weeks. He limped for months after, and swore that he would never get close to that cursed windmill again. A few months later, my father returned from Dungeness. The first thing Joseph asked him was:

'Were you up there on top of the lighthouse? What did you see, Father?'

'What did I see?' My father sat down on a chair below one of our pear trees. 'I saw the same waves! The same wet godless water! Even though I managed to climb up on top of the world! Listen, son, Saxonham is as good as anywhere!'

Then he got up and stormed off to the kitchen. He sat at the head of the table, where my mother had cooked for him a homecoming meal: a leg of mutton with potatoes, drenched in thick gravy.

So that was the memory about my poor brother Joseph injuring his leg before his first big adventure. A few years later, he did pass by that lighthouse, but he never said what he felt about it. Nor did he say if he ever climbed up there to look at the other side of the world. Between Joseph and me there were no doubt too many things unsaid, but we did not always need words. Perhaps we were mirrors of each other. Perhaps that was why whenever I felt unsure, I thought of my brother, and what he would say, if he were here. But the ships he had found work on were merchant vessels sailing along the English coast, and I did not think he had ever been beyond Liverpool. He did not need to climb the rope ladders like me to sight whales in gales and rains, hoping that I would not fall from the top of the mast. Yes, not fall and be tossed into the sea. All the adventures of life would then amount to nothing.

IV

WE BROKE FOR LUNCH. All the sailors were on deck. Around me was a cacophony of shouting, horse play, relentless outbursts of male energy. I moved towards the bow, and sat down on a knot of ropes, desperate for a moment to myself. Who would have guessed that I would be crammed in with thirty men on this small floating castle? An absurdity! But one I had brought on myself in a quest to find freedom. I had started this strange journey to become *myself*. And here I was, not myself. The loneliness I felt on the *Nimrod* was different from what I had felt when I lived in Kent. I had escaped England to escape the limitations of being a woman. And I *did* find freedom here, of a sort. But I was seeing the limitations it came with. If only I could talk to someone. Don't we all need to tell someone about ourselves, so as to bear the weight of living? Only if one can let out a bit of one's own truth into the ear of another, and feel the warmth of an understanding gaze, can one breathe. But that was barred to me now. Concealing myself in the midst of this fraternity, I had lost all community. Would this always be so? Could I live like this, as Ishmael, for the rest of my life?

Would I forget my womanliness one day, and become so comfortable in this role that it would be second nature to me? Maybe then my body would change. Maybe the blood would stop coming every month, and my breasts, small as they were, might sink further into my chest. Maybe a beard would begin to sprout. Mr Hawthorne told me that creatures can evolve and change in form. The caterpillar becomes a butterfly, the tadpole a frog. Nature is not always fixed in its design. Maybe it boils down to the will inside the breast. I breathed in deeply and stood up.

It was Thursday, a day for meat, which was rationed on board. Every hand received a slab of pork, which had soaked all night in water. But it was still so terribly salty that I could barely taste the meat at all. Regardless of his cooking, which according to the sailors was no better or worse than that of another, our chef Moses was one of the most important men on the *Nimrod*. He could spoon a few extra potatoes for any man who had found his way into the chef's good graces, just as he could short-shrift another who displayed a lack of respect. For my part, I chewed the rubbery flesh without complaint. At least we found no cockroaches in our meat this time. There had been plenty of these in our meals over the last few days. As Moses liked to say: 'Boys, the cockroaches can eat our meat, but if it comes to it, we can eat the cockroaches!' After the meal everyone was thirsty, and we had to drink deep draughts of water to cleanse our palates of the cloying tangy aftertaste.

Then work resumed, as the sun beat down hard. Antonio climbed up on the mast for the watch, singing a pirate song. I had heard it before, so I hummed along:

They call me hanging Charlie,
Away, boys, away!
They say I hang for money!

So hang, boys, hang down!
They say I hanged my mother,
Away, boys, away!

Suddenly Antonio stopped singing, and cried: 'There she blows! there! there!'

Drake and Freedman immediately ran out from the after house and scanned the horizon in the direction he pointed.

'Where?'

'There! About a mile and a half off! A school of them!'

Instantly there was commotion. The harpooners and sailors all gathered on deck, and even Captain Seneca appeared among us. He looked intently through his long spyglass, one eyebrow cocked, the other squeezed tight into a ball of concentration, his dark skin glistening under the sun.

Moments later, we could see a whale blow in the distance, then another just beyond it.

'Lower the boats!' Drake ordered.

The harpooners and steerers rushed to unfasten the whaleboats. We brought out the wooden tubs with their freshly coiled ropes, as well as extra lances and spears. The three boats were lowered. Drake and Kauri went in the first one with their men, Freedman and Tashe the second, with Jacques and Tyrone in the third. I remained on the *Nimrod* with others to mind the rigging.

While all this was going on, Captain Seneca stood motionless, observing through his spyglass the course of the school of whales. But he was frowning.

'A pod of females and cubs . . .' he grumbled, lowering his spyglass. 'The white whale travels alone!'

Still, the *Nimrod* followed the three whaleboats

southward. The whales travelled fast, and we chased them for two hours or so. Then, as the boats came close upon the target, a squall arose, bringing mist, and soon one boat was out of view. Shortly after, we lost sight of another. We could see only Jacques's boat now, thanks to the bright yellow paint on its side. As we tried to maintain our course, great waves broke and crashed on the bow of the *Nimrod*. Two men went to the front deck to bail out the water. By now all three boats were lost, as spray and mist obscured our view. Captain Seneca stood by the engineer on the quarterdeck, observing the scene. He seemed to be losing interest, and presently returned to his cabin.

By sunset two boats, Freedman's and Jacques's, had returned. Freedman's crew had made no kill, though his harpooner Tashe said they almost hooked one whale, but the boat got tangled in the line. To save his men he had to cut the ropes and let it go. Jacques caught a humpback, but lost some lances and ropes. We waited for the third boat to return. A while later, in the darkness, Drake and Kauri's boat got back with a grey sperm whale, more than half the size of our *Nimrod*. The huge creature was roped and fastened onto the side of the ship. Drake was pleased, despite the fact that Captain Seneca did not even come out from his cabin to greet the return of his chief mate.

V

EXT MORNING, upon finishing our porridge, Kauri and Tashe stole a moment for their pipe smoke.

'In my tribe, we say smoking a pipe together means we will never fight one another, or steal the other's wife,' I heard Tashe say to my Polynesian friend.

Kauri nodded stoically, without responding. I thought he must be remembering what he had said to me at the inn in New Bedford after sharing the bed and then a pipe. 'We are married,' he had said. 'It mean Kauri die for Ishmael. Kauri strong friend.' I trusted Kauri, though we now hardly had a quiet moment to spend together. But sometimes our eyes met, and I felt there was an understanding that we shared a certain secret.

Drake had changed his Quaker's frock for a rough overcoat and oily trousers, and chivvied us on.

'No time to waste! All hands are needed. Let's get to the head!'

All was commotion, with sailors rushing back and forth, barely avoiding collisions. After capturing the whale, the first task was to cut off the head part, which contained the best oil, and haul it on deck, leaving the carcass attached to the ship's side. We would cut a hole in the head and bail out the oil with a bucket. Some of us went down to the hull to bring up the barrels, others prepared the brick furnace on the deck in which the blubber would be boiled, the rest carried stacks of firewood. Apart from the captain, everyone was needed for such laborious work. There was barely anywhere to stand since great blankets of whale flesh, barrels and buckets had taken over every inch of the deck.

While Drake and Freedman were directing the cutting work, Captain Seneca swung onto the deck with a steward following close behind. The steward, Mr Flaherty, carried a tray with cups and a silver flagon full of alcohol, rum by the smell of it.

Standing by the enormous whale head, Seneca clenched his fist and spoke furiously:

'Stop all this useless work! Stop! It serves no purpose to our great quest!'

'Captain Seneca,' said Drake in a sombre tone, 'may we fill our barrels with oil first? We cannot sail homeward until we have enough oil.'

'Call the harpooners!' Captain Seneca shouted, ignoring Drake.

Jacques summoned the harpooners. All three were already busying themselves with the cutting, their hands and their clothes dripped with blood. They lined up in front of Seneca along with the three mates.

Not knowing what this was about, the six men eyed the captain, waiting for whatever madness he was preparing to unleash. When the old man's wild, bloodshot eyes met theirs, they saw a tortured and wounded man.

'Drink and pass!' the captain cried. Taking the flagon

from Mr Flaherty and pouring the dark liquid into a cup, he held it out to the nearest man. 'Swallow!'

Kauri gulped the drink down in one draught. The cup was instantly refilled by the steward. Tashe drank from it, then passed it on to the next, and the next.

'Well done, almost drained. Steward, refill!'

Mr Flaherty filled the cup a last time, and handed it to the captain. Seneca raised it to his chin, set it to his lower lip, and tossed the contents down his gullet.

'Now you have drunk my wine, all of you listen: if you don't find the white whale, you can skew me with your lances and harpoons, run me through with the iron barbs of your trade, and crucify me on this great mast. Ready your souls now for the undertaking, the dread task!'

Everyone was stunned upon hearing such a strange speech. Even Drake, outwardly always so composed, seemed disturbed.

'If you find no white whale, and fail to kill that evil spirit,' Seneca went on, repeating the message, 'then stab me to death, tear out my gizzards, and stop my beating heart! Death or the white whale. Nothing else!'

Then Seneca turned to each harpooner and reiterated his speech with particular stress.

'Kauri! Listen like you have never listened before, and know in your dusky breast that all the flames of your hate must burn only towards that end. Death or the white whale! And Tashe! Tyrone! From now on leap forward once there is a sign of the white evil. Death or the white whale! And all you others: stand firm, strong, resolute, without wavering, and not even a breath of hesitation!'

While the three dark-complexioned harpooners stood alert and animated, the three mates seemed uneasy before this scene. Freedman and Jacques glanced sideways towards Drake, but the eyes of the first mate were downcast.

Now the six men were dismissed as Seneca abruptly moved off, staggering towards the quarterdeck. They all watched the captain's black robe flap in the wind as he pulled himself further away.

VI

ON THE DECK, the long pikes and saws made a steady stream of cutting sounds. The spell cast by Captain Seneca's powerful presence still held sway. The six men were momentarily dumb, and then, as if waking from a dream, the three harpooners turned on their heels and went back to their cutting work, whereas the three mates remained in place, looking at each other with ponderous expressions. I went to fetch a barrel, walking past them.

Drake looked pale. Freedman and Jacques seemed unsure about how to react. They waited for some words from the first mate. Hearing none, Freedman started.

'The old man doesn't care much about getting blubber oil!'

'No oil, no pay,' Jacques added plainly. 'That's the God-awful truth!' He spat on the deck.

'He wants to sail the southern seas as soon as possible to hunt his godforsaken white whale,' Freedman said.

'The white whale!' hissed Jacques. 'He's been chasing that mirage since his leg got chewed off! A fool indeed, who is playing us all for fools!'

Freedman sighed, his bushy eyebrows crumpled together like two caterpillars.

'I have known Seneca for many years, and he was always a strong, reliable man of sound mind. He was liked by every seaman from the first trips we made together! It's unfortunate that he lost his leg, but maybe his bad luck began with his marriage.'

'Ah, les femmes! There's always a bitch to drag a man down!'

'You're a bitter one, Jacques.'

'Why shouldn't I be? I've been used by whores and strumpets, and I've had my bellyful. Why should he be any different?'

'His wife was no whore,' Freedman cut in. 'When Seneca met Ruth, he was already an old man and she a young girl. She wanted everything a wife should have deserved. And why shouldn't she? He managed to buy that farm for her and everything appeared rosy. Then something happened. The birth of a child! Something went wrong but I could never discover the detail of the matter. I know only that since then the captain has been a changed man.'

Drake nodded knowingly, and added in a hushed voice: 'Everyone could see that. Something was a blow to Seneca, poor soul.'

The three men went quiet, and eyed the captain's cabin. I continued pushing the barrel past them, my mind spiked with curiosity by their communications.

Then Jacques hissed: 'He should have killed that white man! Instead, he turns on the white whale! I reckon there's no damned white whale out there. Only in his cockeyed cranium!'

Freedman shook his head. 'Seneca is not in his right mind, but he knows whales. The white whale is out there. They can live as long as two hundred years. You know that, Jacques?' Freedman turned to the first mate. 'Drake here caught a humpback once and found an ancient harpoon stuck in its back!'

'True enough – I've got the head in my study at home. Carved flint, that harpoon, with a razor edge, but very old. Could have been lodged in that humpback by some Eskimo who knows when. At least a hundred years or more!' Drake lowered his head, mumbling, 'Whales outlive us. And they have long memories.'

'That white whale has escaped death from all the whalemen's harpoons that have ever been hurled at him so far. He may be immortal after all. We should stop chasing after him, and let him be, I say. Otherwise, we tempt fate!' Freedman intoned.

I had tarried long enough, and the conversation seemed to have petered out. I had to get back to the cutting work. All men on the ship had to take part, and I must be seen to do my share. The furnace had been lit and now the blubber was to be put into the large cooking pot and the empty barrels had to be readied to receive the oil. This processing and diabolic cookery was the work of many hands, mixed with sweat and cursing. And here I was, a phantom woman playing my role as a young burly man as best I could. A heavy cloud formed above the ship and the wind furrowed the sails. The ruffled sheets seemed like the complicated folds of my own thoughts.

VII

THE WIND HAD CEASED and the Atlantic was once again calm. We were close to the equator, and the sight of green islands on the horizon lifted everyone's spirits. Land, finally! Our bodies gained strength and our minds gained levity. Boredom and hardship had worn us out, even though we knew we were still at the beginning of our voyage. It would be a relief for everyone to set foot on solid ground even for just a day or two. Yesterday we were told that we would anchor off the island of Santiago, one of the more populated islands of Cap de Verd, where we would get new supplies and water. We also heard from Freedman that Captain Seneca would pick up some new crew members and in particular a special sailmaker. The fact that Captain Seneca knew a special sailmaker on one of the islands of Cap de Verd was an enticing detail. Perhaps the old man had always anchored at Cap de Verd on his whaling routes, and perhaps this special sailmaker was one of the very few who might manage to lift his wounded heart.

Once we anchored, everyone was given a task. Only the three mates could have free movement on the island, the rest of the seamen had to stay in a designated place or on the ship to carry out their duties. Particular assignments were made for the cook, the carpenter and the cooper as they needed to find their supplies. Joshua, Antonio and I were assigned the task of fetching fresh water with three harpooners. Others took the opportunity to wash our sails as the seawater had formed a salt crust on the canvas, and as a result the sails had become hard and would break easily in the wind. Then if we managed to finish our jobs we would have a bit of time for personal items such as doing our own laundry, cleaning as much of the lice and fleas off our bodies and clothing. I longed for a bath. There would be nothing more crucial than washing myself somewhere privately, without any man nearby, without a soul watching.

CHAPTER SEVEN

Cap de Verd

I

THE ISLAND OF SANTIAGO was brown and dry, the air clear and the horizon marked by ragged mountains that seemed to cut into the sky. The barrenness of the shore was matched by the sharp, powdery taste of the gentle wind that wended its way from the harbour and lodged in my mouth. A desert surrounded by a sea. A place to dry up in and become a shell. As far from the moist spongy world of my Kent coast as one could imagine. The first vegetation I saw was coconut trees. I had seen a picture of them back in Dungeness in a pub where my father once took me. Sheer happiness possessed me when I looked up at the crown of leaves and the young green coconuts hanging down. Mr Hawthorne told us this was a volcanic land. As an English girl, I knew about chalk and limestone along the Kent coast, so this was a very foreign landscape to me.

During the time we stopped in Cap de Verd, we were in good spirits. Just to sit on a patch of grass or on a rock, to feel sheltered from the violent shaking of the sea, was a pure blessing. Despite the wondrous sights on the land, we were to stop here for only three days. No time could be wasted. The official exchange for food supplies would be carried out between the mates and the natives because every transaction had to be recorded in the logging with precise notation of the sums spent and goods received. And we could only hope that Drake or Freedman would get as much fresh meat and fruit as we desired.

The water house was built by the natives on the bank, not far from the anchoring point. It was the place for all the stopover ships to get fresh supplies. But even with such a short distance, we were soon exhausted scrambling over the rugged rocks to fetch the water. I was on the point of falling to the ground, and had to catch my breath on the bank. Then Kauri appeared, holding in one hand a bowl of some sort of stew, in the other a stick.

'Sugar cane? Cachupa?' he said.

I did not know what a cachupa was, nor what a sugar cane looked like. But I knew that Kauri had been to Cap de Verd twice on previous whaling trips, so he knew this place better than most of us. Perhaps he felt at home here, since he came from a small island with a warm climate. I took the sugar cane from him, broke it into two bits, and handed back one half. Using my teeth, I peeled the hard skin of the cane and bit into the wooden fruit. Lord, this was the sweetest juicy thing I had ever eaten! I chewed the fresh cane and swallowed the juice to quench my thirst. Kauri did the same. So we sat there chewing our sugar cane as if this was the most pleasurable thing men could do with time off from a whaling ship. We both stared at the brown and barren mountains around us, thinking of ethereal things; all the places we had lived, all the people we knew, seemed so far away. The stories and faces in our memories felt like they belonged to a previous life, with no connection to this foreign landscape. This was the land of black rocks and dry thistles. Yet it was something we had right now, even for a brief moment.

The hierarchy of the ship made it impossible for Kauri and me to spend time together on the *Nimrod*, let alone share private moments such as this. And it was something I very much needed. After finishing the sugar cane, Kauri handed me the bowl of stew.

'Cachupa best, Kauri like.'

He still managed not to use the words I taught him: I, you. Nor did he use many verbs. Wordlessly, I spooned up some of the saucy stew. It was a delicious mix of pork, chicken, corn, beans and sweet potatoes. It was so tasty that I wondered why we could not bring a whole barrel of the cachupa back to the *Nimrod*. Moses ought to improve his cooking! I could not bear the thought that we would continue eating the mouldy bread and worm-filled beef for the next two years!

11

FREEDMAN AND MR HAWTHORNE were walking back from the post office. In a stopover like Cap de Verd there was a designated mailbox for seamen to receive their letters and newspapers. Both of them carried a bundle of paper and letters. I thought of Joseph.

'Sirs, I don't expect to receive any letters from England, but wondered if you saw any mail for me?'

Freedman shuffled through his, shaking his head.

'Nothing for you, Ishmael, I am afraid. A few letters for Drake and myself only.'

Mr Hawthorne too leafed through his collection of papers. It was larger and included journals and newspapers. I noticed some titles. One was the *Quaker's Voice*, another the *Great Liberator*, then another the *Massachusetts Spy*, with some illustrations on the front page.

Seeing me slightly disappointed, Hawthorne comforted me.

'Well, Ishmael, you can borrow one of these if you like – plenty to read here.' He handed me the *Quaker's Voice*, saying, 'I am quite keen to read the *Great Liberator* right away. There are reports of battles between the southern states and northern states. How strange that we are on the sea and not in the battles!'

I took the *Quaker's Voice* and saw a headline with a drawing of the new American president, Mr Abraham Lincoln.

'Yes, how extraordinary!' Freedman remarked. 'Lord, it might be a civil war! Frederick Douglass stirred this up after he returned from Britain as a free man.'

This was the first time I heard my officers mentioning Britain, and mentioning it in a nice way. I took this as a sign that it was safe for me to interject.

'Who is Frederick Douglass?'

'He is a freed slave, one of the bravest and most intelligent men on earth!' Freedman spoke in a solemn and respectful tone. 'Britain had already freed the slaves, and Douglass managed to jump on a ship sailing to England. He toured there and made public speeches about slavery. The English raised money and paid for his freedom from his master in New England. He returned to America and led the abolitionist movement.'

Both Hawthorne and I looked at Freedman. This was an impressive story, and it struck me that on the sea we rarely thought of slaves, but here on the land our black mate brought us back to reality.

'I am lucky to be on a whaler,' Freedman continued, 'and I am grateful to God that I have even been promoted to a mate because of my skills. On land I would not dare to look a white man in the eyes, but on the sea as an officer I can flog a white sailor for misbehaviour.'

We fell silent. Each of us sat on a rock, gazing at the *Nimrod* in the harbour and lost in our own thoughts. The sun was hot and the rocks warm. I was sweaty but I only dared to unfasten the top button of my jacket. Kauri was topless as he often was. I watched him as he walked away, perhaps to get more cachupa or fruit. Freedman took off his jacket and bit into the sugar cane that Kauri had offered. He began to read the newspaper with a certain urgency. I thought about our captain. I thought, isn't our ship a free place, since our captain is black?

As if reading my thoughts, Hawthorne spoke softly:

'No black man is free, if all black men are not free.' He paused, before adding: 'That goes especially for Captain Seneca.'

'How is Seneca not free?' I asked. 'He lost one of his legs, but he is fortunate compared with other black men.'

'Seneca is tortured by demons from his past,' Freedman remarked, raising his head from the newspaper. 'He might be the king of the *Nimrod*, but he would be the last man to feel free.'

Hawthorne nodded, but without making further comment. I pondered upon these remarks. I was not sure if I understood much about Seneca. But one thing seemed certain, from all the brief asides about him, our captain must have been hurt terribly in his life, and that made him above all human. A human who suffered. And did I not suffer too?

When Kauri returned with a cluster of bananas, both officers stood up and prepared to return to the ship. I was holding the *Quaker's Voice* in my hand.

'May I keep this for a day or two, sir?'

'Certainly,' Hawthorne said, while glancing at the front page of the paper again. 'Do give it back to me once you finish, as I would like to know what our president wants to do in Georgia and Virginia.'

We walked back to the ship, the two officers ahead, talking about Mr Lincoln and the war between the states. I had only the barest inkling of what it was about. All that seemed like it was from some other world, one that both

Kauri and I had no dealings with. A world of great ideas and events, of nations plundering each other. My father used to talk about history, and I knew of a few kings and queens, and of the Protestants always fighting with the Catholics. But my knowledge was enveloped in a great cloud of my ignorance. I watched the two men talking enthusiastically as they trod along the harbour path, while Kauri and I remained quiet behind.

III

NEXT DAY, EVERYONE was again assigned a particular task. The barrels of fresh water were on board the ship, and now we needed to carry back firewood and cloth which the mates had purchased the day before. Our surgeon Mr Hawthorne also needed to go to the apothecary to get replacement medications, and he asked me to go with him, which I was glad to do.

The path to the apothecary was carved into the cliffs that rose steeply from the ocean. We saw some white-bellied larks and sparrows, and my eye was caught by large spiky cacti. Gracious! Nature in Cap de Verd was very different from anywhere I had been. Hawthorne told me the names of some plants I had never seen before: sagebrush, lotus bellflower, Cape euphorbia. I had been thinking about our last conversation about plants and animals.

'Mr Hawthorne, the other day you told me about a book by that botanist who named all the species . . .'

'Oh, you mean Linnaeus. Carl Linnaeus, the Swedish botanist.'

'Yes. He said men and apes are in the same group. But what did he say about plants?'

'Plants? He said that flowers and plants have different sexes.'

Ah, the flowers and plants have different sexes! I had always known that plants had different sexes and some were male and female in one. Growing up in the marsh, I had discovered that some apple or pear trees were fertile and bore fruit every year, but some were barren – they did not bear flowers or grow fruits. Like the two barren pear trees in our garden in Saxonham. My brother and I would call them widow trees. The two trees seemed to be immortal, standing there in our overgrown garden for eternity.

'What did this botanist say about flowers . . . do they have different sexes?'

'He said the petals are the bed in which the bride and the bridegroom meet each other. Flowers are the place where insects have sexual relations.'

I imagined two wasps meeting on an apple blossom. The hairs on the wasps would pick up the pollen dust, and then they would climb on each other . . . that image sent some shuddery feelings through my body, so I stopped thinking about it.

'Linnaeus was very interested in the sexuality of plants,' Hawthorne continued. 'For example, he invented the classification of plants by organising them according to their number of *stamens* which are male parts, and *styles* which are female parts. He imagined that plants had vaginas and penises, and here he was going too far, I think. He was treating the plants too much like us, or the higher mammals.'

Hearing those terms, I was even more curious, but we had just arrived at the apothecary. As the surgeon ordered his medications at the store, he communicated with the storekeeper in a mix of languages. I was supposed to learn the names of the medicines but I was lost in our conversation about the sexes of plants. I thought more of what Mr Hawthorne said. Even though I knew it, when I stared at a butterfly or a bee crawling on a campion flower in my Saxonham, watching how the insect carried the pollen from the centre of the flower and then flew onto another plant, I would not know how to explain this activity. Was this the difference between a learned man and an unlearned man? I was not a man, but I was not unlearned – my father had taught my brother and me how to read and write. What slightly disturbed me, though in a quite stirring way, was that Mr Hawthorne felt able to talk to me about the female and male sex of plants. No one else on this ship would ever speak of these things except in a very coarse way. And I, Ishmaelle, a female wrapped in male clothes, was nervous about this idea of 'sex'. I never allowed myself to think about it, though it was at the back of my mind, even when I was climbing up high on the top mast, like the most fit and powerful seaman in this world. If that Swedish botanist was alive and witnessed my being on this ship, what would he name a person like me? Which group would I belong to? Do some female flowers ever disguise themselves as male? Do some male insects ever pretend to be female? Would they fool the Swedish botanist if he came across such creatures?

On the way back to the ship, I asked Mr Hawthorne:
'Why did God create two sexes?'
Mr Hawthorne grunted and chuckled a little.
'Some things are mysteries. God divided the heavens and the earth, the sky from the land, and day from night.

So, He also divided male from female. He did not create three, like the Holy Trinity. He made man and woman.'

I pondered on that. God did not create three sexes. I thought of the bearded lady I once saw in a carnival at the Lydd market. Was she not the third sex? I felt the light down on my own cheeks and chin, wondering if it might ever grow stronger. What if it became a beard? Suddenly I saw myself as that bearded woman in the fair, looking out at all the gawking passers-by, at the pointing children and the guffawing men. Why did they all find it so funny or shocking? Would God laugh too? I felt certain that the seahorse lady in my pocket would neither laugh nor complain. She heard all and saw all.

IV

IN THE MORNING we were told that everyone had to return to the *Nimrod* by lunch, and we would be leaving that evening, so all the supplies had to be on board. I was allowed a moment of freedom alone, after I reported to the surgeon and the chief mate that I had to collect some herbs since my home-made medicaments had been used up by the sick mates. Mr Hawthorne gladly allowed me an hour or two to hunt for the herbs. So I went up on the hills, where most of the vegetation seemed to be growing on the steppe. As I zigzagged between the rocky paths, I caught a glimpse of a small pond. With no one around, I ran towards it. Quickly I stripped off my clothes and submerged myself in the water. It was one of the most pleasurable and nerve-wracking moments in this voyage. Once I had washed the dirt and grease from my skin, I hurried back to my clothes and dressed my still wet body. My heart pounding, I raced back to the path, trying to tear the weeds from my hair.

As I climbed the hills looking out for the plants, I recognised, from the illustrations in one of Mr Hawthorne's albums, some date palms. But the dates were very green and small. I could not collect them yet. There were sweet-odoured dog roses, their flowers pink and their thorns sharp. I also saw many lizards, climbing in and out of the cracks of rocks beneath my feet. The flora here were quite different. I was unable to find sea campion, which I needed for my medicine, but I did see large bushes of mallows. So green and lush, they were not exactly the same as the ones I knew back in England, but the pink flowers and large leaves were almost identical.

I dug up the roots. They were a strong cluster, like the mallows on my salty marsh. I shook off the soil and peeled the skin off the roots so I could taste it. The inside was white, and tasted sweet. This was the useful mallow root I was looking for. It could ease cough and respiratory problems. So I pulled out a huge pile of roots and took them down to the ship.

By the afternoon, everyone was back on the *Nimrod*. We saw Drake had brought a few animals on board. Some were in cages, others were roped together. There were two pigs, a few chickens and geese. The chef and steward took the animals down into the hold, and Dilly, carrying two sacks of cut grass, followed the animals down below. There were also bags of rice, bananas and sugar canes. The last thing the mates brought on board was a basket of fireworks. I had never seen the actual fireworks before. They were all wrapped in red paper, in all sorts of sizes. I heard Drake speaking to Freedman: 'Now I shall be content on the Fourth of July, this was the last package the Chinese merchants were selling!' and Freedman said: 'Surely, without them we cannot have a proper celebration!'

As the dusk light descended, everything was in good order, and the sails had all been washed. We were informed that it was the time to receive the new crew. Just before our supper, they came on board. Captain Seneca was on the deck observing them. We saw four men, three of whom were Africans, and one who looked oriental. This particular man had light brown skin. He was small, compared to the other three. There was a special kind of aura around him. His black hair was neatly tied into a bun on top of his head. He wore a white silk shirt and black silk trousers. None of us wore silk on the rough whaling trip so he was a wonder for our eyes. As soon as the four men were introduced to the mates, Seneca walked with his stick straight to the Chinese man. The oriental man's body language was animated when he saw the captain, and it looked like they knew each other well. We could not hear what was said between them, but we saw Captain Seneca grasping one arm of the Chinese man, who bowed slightly to Seneca, folding his palms together and lowering his head.

'Is he the sailmaker that our captain wanted to have on board?' one of the sailors whispered.

'Indeed he is. I met him on one of my previous voyages!' the knowledgeable Antonio exclaimed. 'A monk, too, a Taoist or some similar sort! They call him Muzi, and he is also a mystic man!'

'A mystic man?' I asked.

'Yes, he can foretell the future!'

I was intrigued by such a revelation, and by this oriental man who could make sails and also foretell futures.

'How did a Chinese man end up in Cap de Verd?'

'Ha! How did we Portuguese end up in Asia three hundred years ago? People have always been moving around, even those Chinese – they turn up everywhere!'

I nodded, wondering about those oriental travellers from long ago.

'Cap de Verd is New Bedford in the middle of the Atlantic!' Antonio said. 'It is where ships transported slaves, exchanged goods and swapped oriental treasures.

Not only could you find a Chinese monk here, you could find all sorts of churches, and plenty of former pirates retired here too!'

I had heard rumours that Antonio used to be a pirate when he was young, but I was careful not to ask too many questions, lest someone became curious about me. During supper, the three men from Cap de Verd ate with us, but the Chinese sailmaker did not join us. He must have been dining with the officers in the cabin. The newcomers spoke Portuguese and only Antonio could understand them. From the way they grimaced while eating, I could see that they were not impressed with the way Moses prepared the chicken. But the rest of us were more than happy with our freshly boiled chicken and sweet potatoes. It felt like we had finally earned our special meal, and we hoped there would be at least another meal or two like this on the *Nimrod*.

After supper, everyone took up their pipes, while I opened the *Quaker's Voice*. Then I noticed our cook coming up, not in a great mood. 'What's the matter, Moses?' I asked. 'Well, they did not bother to find some cats on the island! And now we are leaving!' he cursed. Oh, the cats. Yes, the ship desperately needed a cat or two to catch the rats and mice. They were everywhere in the food hold, as well as crawling on our hammocks and across our noses during the night! But I doubted Captain Seneca would care to linger to find a cat.

The evening was warm and pleasant. The ship moved off in peaceful waters. The island receded, merging itself in the dark gloom of the sea. Kauri came on deck to smoke, and I joined him. We sat together carving whalebones with small knives. He was carving a ship, while I tried unsuccessfully to carve a windmill. Everyone was joking and gossiping on the deck. Freedman and Jacques had fed us a bit of news, saying that Muzi the sailmaker would be given a place to sleep right next to the captain's cabin. 'Captain had known this Chinese man for decades, before he lost his leg to the whale.' Then we were sent to our own hammocks.

V

THE *NIMROD* WAS PLOUGHING its way across the Atlantic. The three mates were anxious about collecting more whale oil as we had not gathered much in the last few months. Seneca was also shouting to his men at the mast whenever the lookout was happening, wanting us to pay extra attention to the 'white one'.

It was a blue and warm afternoon. The sailors were ordered to clean the deck. Kauri and I were employed making ropes along with a few others. All was quiet until a sudden roar rang from up in the air.

'There she blows! There!'

We all stopped our work and looked at the direction.

'There, another one! There she blows! A mile or so to the east!'

The mates were calling everyone to prepare the lowering of the whaleboats. Captain Seneca came out with his spyglass. He steadied himself, taking a good position and watching the distant actions through his glass.

The harpooners quickly fetched their weapons and other equipment they needed. When the groups went to lower the three whaleboats, the Chinese monk appeared on the deck. He was beside Seneca as the captain suddenly cried with excitement:

'I saw white waves, Muzi! I saw his evil hump!'

Then the most extraordinary thing happened. Seneca ordered the fourth boat to be lowered, the spare boat that was placed upside down on the deck, which was never used for the chase. It was reserved in case the other boats were damaged. But, on his order, the fourth boat was lowered. Now the Chinese monk equipped himself with a harpoon and jumped onto it with a few oarsmen as two stewards helped Seneca onto the boat. They used a specially made rattan chair with ropes on both sides, which he could grip on to.

Suddenly we seemed to be short of oarsmen. I was told to go down to Drake and Kauri's boat. I jumped in with the others and together we rowed with all our might.

With four whaling boats heading fast towards the east, the *Nimrod* was kept away from the wind, and she sailed on gently behind us. We kept close to Freedman and Tashe's boat, and heard Freedman report that the whale was heading leeward. We turned the bow and saw Seneca's boat behind us. The captain was seated in the middle, on a raised platform where he could sight the whale through his spyglass. Even though the waves were crashing loudly we could still hear his excited voice now and then, while Muzi stood upright on the bowhead with his harpoon raised. He looked as experienced as Kauri, and seemed ready at any moment to throw his sharp weapon at the whale.

VI

THE WAVES AND MIST obscured our sight as we rowed madly towards our target. Soon I grew exhausted, my arm began to hurt and the oar in my hand lost its movement. But then we came across a school of the whales and followed a large one. We had lost sight of Freedman's and Jacques's boats, but kept close to the captain's. More turbulence came, then suddenly our boat hit something hard. All of us jumped and I was nearly tossed into the water. In the maddening chaos, we realised water was leaking into the boat from a crack which we could not locate yet. I was instantly ordered by Drake to bail out the water while other men rowed on. Then in the midst of all this, we heard the distinct cry of Captain Seneca:

'Pull, pull! Pull hard! Now spike him again! Pull, and spit out your teeth if you must! That's it! Pull with the blade between your teeth!'

We turned towards the captain's boat. I could see the Chinese man standing on the bow. He had thrown aside his silk shirt, and displayed his naked upper body while wrenching at the lines from a whale, which was submerged in the water. Seneca sat on the raised platform, one arm managing his steering oar while his other waved in the air as he shouted orders. His oarsmen were rowing towards the whale with furious strokes.

I was bailing non-stop, but more and more water was pouring into the boat. Suddenly Drake spotted something and shouted:

'Every man, look out along his oars! Kauri, there!'

Kauri turned and raised his harpoon. The boat was tossing violently and he tried to steady himself on the bow – only to fall into the water. But he grabbed hold of the plank on the side and climbed back on board. Good Lord, he was still holding his harpoon! Kauri the island prince, Kauri the tree! Drake was also struggling to balance as his boat was tossed around in the foamy water. Perhaps the whale was beneath the boat. For the first time, I was afraid. Such a small whaling boat like the one we were on, we could be easily destroyed by the giant beast.

While Drake and Kauri tried to figure out what they should do in the midst of dread and confusion, we could see nothing but troubled water churning around us. Then, all of a sudden, a puff of white vapour hovered over the water, before disappearing. The creature had managed to sink into the depths of the sea again. The air vibrated and tingled. Was it playing games with us? Now I understood why a chase in a small whaling boat might take so many hours, sometimes a whole day, to even locate an intelligent whale, let alone to hunt one down!

Drake discovered the crack in our boat was on the side of the bow. He cut a piece of canvas and tried to nail it on the plank where the crack was. Meanwhile, a bowman stopped rowing and stretched across, trying to give us a hand. It was Joshua – he was a new seaman like me. As

Joshua resumed his steering, we heard Kauri cry out: 'There! The whale! Turn!'

We turned, in desperate pursuit of the spot he had indicated. It was at least half a mile off. Freedman's boat was on the right side of us, a quarter of a mile or so away. Captain Seneca's boat was visible, on the left side ahead of us. The three boats formed a triangle. It was perilous because the whale lines from each boat could be entangled and thus our movements would be trapped between the boats. The captain's boat had already thrown out two lines and they were now pulling the target desperately. But the whale swam much faster, and it dragged the boat forcefully along with it.

VII

THE THREE BOATS were driven apart as Drake gave chase to two whales we had seen to leeward. Our sail had been raised, and was catching the blustery wind as the boat cut through the surging waves. We were lifted up high, then crashed down with a thud into the swell. Hours passed, enveloped in a veil of mist. Neither boat nor whale was to be seen.

'A squall is coming,' observed Drake. 'We need to be quick now. There's white water again! Get close to it!'

Kauri, harpoon in hand, sprang to his feet. When a whale appeared on the surface of the water, Kauri launched the spear with full force, striking its vast back. The rest of us minded the ropes, which spun out from a wooden tub in neatly coiled lines. Now Kauri began to pull on the line, as we rushed towards the target so Kauri could throw out a second spear. The waves heaved around us and we were on the verge of being thrown out of the boat at any moment.

'That's his hump. See it, Kauri? Give it to him!' Drake directed.

There was a sharp whoosh, Kauri's harpoon shooting through the air. In the commotion, I felt a great invisible push from astern, while forward the boat seemed as though it had struck a ledge. The sail snapped and exploded into pieces; a gush of vapour shot up nearby. Something roiled like a coming earthquake beneath us. Before I could grasp the tub, I found myself jolted then thrust into the water. Blinded by the biting spray, I could see no boat or plank to fasten myself to. Was this the squall, or was it the angry whale whipping its tail? Or was it the tangled lines of harpoons that had upset the boat and plunged me in?

Was death upon us? I flailed in desperation like a fish trapped in a net. I was swallowing great gulps of water, choking and gasping for air. Finally I managed to raise my head above water. I swam until I caught sight of our boat, but none of the crew members were on it. Dread settled in my stomach, but I mustered all my strength to swim towards it. The storm had descended on the water, rain poured down, blinding the world before my eyes. But I managed to latch myself onto the side of the bow. Though half filled with water, the boat was mostly undamaged except for the shattered mast. I hauled my exhausted body over the side, and lay flat on my back, trying to recover my breath. Then I picked up the oars and tried to row towards a few dark spots in the distant water, but the visibility was still poor, and the wind was howling. The squall roared and crackled around me like a white fire, the clouds grew darker and there was no sign of any other boat. Surely we were very far from the *Nimrod*, otherwise we would have been rescued. The violent waves thwarted my attempts to keep the boat on a steady course. Still, I rowed with all my might towards a figure. Kauri grasped hold of an oarlock and hoisted himself into the boat. Together, we rowed towards the spots in the distance. We reached Drake, then the others, who had managed to remain close to one another.

But once we settled on our boat, we realised that one

crew member was missing. It was Joshua. Still recovering from the near drowning, we looked around the furiously roaring waters. We could see no sign of him.

'He was the one who could not swim,' said Drake, his voice grave.

We turned pale. I shivered from the cold, and could not think of anything but death.

'Search again,' Drake ordered.

So we rowed on, looking for any sign of movement in the water. We rowed for an hour or so, until we saw our ship *Nimrod* coming towards us. Beside her, along with the captain's boat, were the ship's two other boats. Did they see Joshua? Had they managed to pull him out of the water?

A while later, everyone was back on board the *Nimrod*. Muzi and the captain had caught a whale, a dark-coloured sperm whale, not the white one the captain so desired. But we did not feel better. We had not found Joshua. The *Nimrod* continued the search, even though the darkened sky shed no light. The mates lit many lanterns in case the man was still alive and struggling to get to the ship. Many of the men were exhausted from the chase, and went down to sleep, but others stayed on deck in the vain hope of finding the young sailor.

VIII

KAURI SAT ON THE DECK, looking out over the inky waters. He had lost two harpoons in the chase and had cut the ropes in an attempt to prevent the boat capsizing. He was almost in despair, but he said nothing, just smoked his pipe silently. From time to time, without turning his head, he handed the pipe to me. This was my first true battle in the sea against whales, but what had it proved? It was an insanity. Heavy doubts rose in me, along with the sad thoughts about Joshua drowning.

Dawn was slowly arriving. Neither Kauri nor I returned to our quarters. The air had turned cold. A mist still hovered above the sea, and the lanterns were still lit on all sides of the ship. But we knew that Joshua was no more. I imagined his body already shredded and torn up, his arms digested and his eyes plucked out by some fierce fish.

'Kauri, does this sort of thing often happen?' I asked.

He nodded.

Our eyes were fixed on the brightening horizon which the sun was already touching with its first faint rays.

'Then I shall make a will, and you will be my executor,' I said.

Kauri looked at me with his black eyes. 'If Kauri live!'

I nodded too. But I thought, even if I left a will, what would it be for? I, Ishmaelle, with no valuable possessions, had nothing to leave. The only family I had in this world was my brother Joseph. I could only leave him our memories together, but for that I needed no will. All I needed from Kauri was that he remembered my passing, and would recall me in his mind while he smoked his pipe.

Returning to my hammock in the dawn light, I fell asleep in exhaustion. I dreamt of Joshua. He was not dead. He was drifting on the sea, lying on a piece of wood, carried away towards a distant shore. I dreamt of him living on an island, feeding himself with berries and slaking his thirst from wild streams. A man now consigned to aloneness, but finally free from the horrors of whaling life. Oh, bless him. Don't we all need that, to be away from the violence either on land or on sea?

I didn't hear the whale call during the night, but I dreamt of a sleeping whale, a great whale, still and unmoving in the water. All was quiet around her. She was fixed in a vertical position with her head close to the surface, like a huge upright log in the sea. One of her eyes was open during her sleep. An extraordinary sleeping eye that was wise and alert. It did not blink. Was she keeping an eye on the danger around her? Sharks and men were her enemies, even though she was the biggest creature in the deep. Then she rose to the surface for a breath. Like us she needed the air above. Sinking down again and resuming her vertical position, she continued to sleep. And she dreamt. I dreamt her dream, of squid and echoing calls from great distances. And then suddenly an attack. Shadows skimming over the surface and the sound of oars ploughing the water. A whale's nightmare. She woke up, both eyes open wide, and dived down deep to escape the sharp spikes of the killers from above.

I woke up, both eyes open wide. I saw the dark shadows of my quarters. And my brother Joseph's face came to my mind. His eyes were closed, yet he spoke to me. Ishmaelle! Beware of the sea. Fear men, but not the fish of the sea. One day we shall know the truth, sister! And then he faded into the gloom.

IX

Cap de Verd whaling ground, 23 May 1861

Dear Joseph,

I dreamt of you this morning. In the dream you
spoke, strangely, of things I did not understand.
I miss you and your happy wise words. Oh, I
hope you are well. Months have passed since my
last letter to you. Did you receive it? Where are you?
In case you have received my letter I shall tell you
that our ship – the *Nimrod* – will be heading
towards the African coast, and we hope to arrive
there in July if wind allows. If the weather is
bad then we might not make it till a month later.
If you ever receive this letter and write back to
me, you should mail it to the whaling dock at
Cape of Good Hope, Cape Town, directing it
for the *Nimrod*. I believe that our mates will be
fetching the mail there. I have no idea how it
works but some of the crew members,
especially the senior ones, received letters at our
previous stop.

The last few months have been hard because the food has deteriorated. We had so many cockroaches in our meals and the bread was mouldy and you could see the worms crawling! The weather last month was awful, half of our sails were destroyed. We have a new harpooner who is apparently a great sailmaker – a Chinese man we picked up from Cap de Verd. He is the first Chinese man I have ever seen, and he is quite a mystic. But he only talks to our captain in his curious stunted English, mixed with gestures and handwriting signs. I watched him patch the ripped canvas and sew the sail the other day – and all I can say is that he is indeed a master sailmaker. He even brought on board rolls of cotton as our old sails were made of flax linen and they were heavy in the wind. So this Chinese man sewed the sails with cotton, and now our sails are lighter and should last longer if there are storms.

You probably know all these oddities about seafaring, but do you know this custom? We did not have enough rain last month, so the sailors were told to pee directly onto the sails which lay on the deck, so their piss could help to wash the salt off the canvas. Because sails drenched in salty water can break in the stormy wind after the canvas becomes dry and stiff! Fortunately, I was not one of the participants of this sort of jollity. Still, it is hard being on a whaler, harder than being a farmer in Saxonham, I now can say this, quite surely.

I must finish this letter now, as I am on the next round of watch today. And I will be climbing up

the mainmast and will have to stand in the air
for at least two hours. Imagine if the weather
goes wrong!

God bless you, my brother.
Your beloved Ishmaelle

CHAPTER EIGHT

The Whale is Both
Angel and Devil

I

*Captain Seneca, by the gunwale, gazing at
the great vaulted ceiling of the morning
sky heavy with clouds.*

GREAT FISH THE DAWN BREAKS do you sleep still
do you swim through your dreams time to rouse
yourself you dreamer and face the nightmare that
waits with hull and sail with its cargo of dreaming men
dreams of my childhood that land still haunts my sleep this
very night it came back to me the night when Papa Po died
I was out and about starving and stole corn in Master
Cutbush's backyard and roasted it in the fire by the
mulberry tree when I pulled the corn from the ashes I
burnt my fingers and the white man's dog came running
towards me and tore at my ankle and the master's son threw
stones at my head shouting go bite that negro cockroach I
cried out blind in the showers of stone and the savage dog
but kicked myself free and ran from my persecutors

My father dead that father was dead to the boy whom he
had filled up like an empty vessel with his tales of his woes
and his pains O how many times Papa Po told me about his
sea voyage from Africa and how he had come to the new
land with whipped bleeding back and starved like a dying

ostrich and sold from one farm to another until the Quakers bought him and freed him hear me whale this is the world of us men not the mindless life of fish breathing in water and riding the swells till the hook grab you or lance skew you

Fish what would you know of rage I sucked my father's hate like the milk from my mother's dugs mother told me she feared papa's fury but she wanted a man with solid hands on the farm so mama married Papa Po and a Wampanoag woman had better rights than a slave I would have an easier life she said and I would be a free man and I was born free I am no more Papa Po negro with a bleeding back and chained neck

So summer passed with my wounded ankle and Papa Po was no more and mother was never home I avoided Master Cutbush's dog as I walked along the dusty path watching my boots crushing acorns the townspeople said my father did not die of illness he was killed by a mob of white men but I believed Papa Po died of fever that's what mother said she also said my silly little Sam go to Mr and Mrs Eldredge's big white house north of the orchards if one day your mother is not back home Mrs Eldredge is fond of the children she will feed you roast turkey and boiled potato if you nice and obedient will you my little Sam my poor baby

Then Master Cutbush came one night I saw that white man in our house I knew he came to mother and I wanted to kill that man but mother feared him the fear of a Wampanoag woman scared for her meagre life for her squash her beans her corn her hut her well her chickens her firewood her child no husband there to protect her and keep safe fear swallowed her life and she ran away abandoned everything leaving me alone without her gods

Oh Lord I ought to say a prayer to Mrs Eldredge her kindness when she pressed the Bible in my hand and sat beside me to teach me the first words I learned to read in the big white house and I was no more little Sam no more negro cockroach I was Seneca and I was the child of the Eldredge house I was a fortunate soul of the Friends my life should have remained with the Quakers but anger and desolation possessed me I was not a good Quaker nor was I a good black man I was looking for another way another path another life

II

THE MORNING AIR was fresh. Usually, at this hour, Captain Seneca would be alone on deck, watching the waves. But as I climbed the mast, I saw Seneca and the Chinese monk sitting together at a table by the steerage, playing some kind of game. In truth I could not be sure if it was a game, or some form of fortune telling, with stacks of wooden sticks like the chopsticks Muzi used to eat with, but shorter. A well-worn book lay open to the side. I could not see its title. Muzi spread the sticks over the table, then Seneca set down an individual one. Muzi looked intently at the pattern made in this way, and said something to the captain. Seneca nodded, listening to the Chinese man's words as though he were an oracle. Was it some sort of divination, like the one my great-aunt once performed back in England, when I was a child? It was all mysterious to me, but what was most curious was that in the presence of the Chinese monk, Seneca comported himself with great modesty and a deference I had never seen before. For the two hours I spent up on the mast, they threw the sticks, noted the results on a piece of paper, then threw the sticks again. From beginning to end they were completely absorbed in this activity.

At noon, I came down for my break. The captain and

the Chinese monk had retired to their cabins. Drake told us we needed to change the position of the sails and tighten the rigging, as we were altering our course. The command confused us. For several days we had thought we were going down to Rio de la Plata, and now we were told that the *Nimrod* would head east towards the African coast. Why such a shift?

'Our captain has changed his plan' was the only explanation Drake gave. He did not look very pleased.

As Washington and I worked on the rigging, we got a bit more information, but not much.

'Seneca is in a hurry to get to the Cape of Good Hope and from there onward to the east,' Freedman informed us.

'To the east! Ha!' Washington remarked knowingly. 'Seneca is a Wampanoag – the People of the First Light! Of course he has to head to the east!'

'If only I knew what the Chinese monk told the old man!' Freedman whispered, as Washington secured the thick cords. 'Muzi is practising a sort of witchcraft or necromancy with our captain, telling him where the ship should go!'

'You know, my mother knew Seneca's mother,' Washington said. 'I remember Ma once said to me that only one Wampanoag family would never convert to the Christian God. That was Seneca's family.'

'And why was that?' I could not help but chime in.

'Why? Because Seneca's ma was a hard-headed woman. Among all them heathen gods, she only worshipped Neesuckquand – a goat god, a tricky mischievous spirit. She would be always consulting Neesuckquand about something, like when to sell her corn, when to buy her clothes, or when to kill a chicken. That god was her personal counsel. The rest of us turned to the white

Christian church, and had only the one God. I was baptised when I was only five days old. I reckon Seneca is just following the ways of his old heathen mother. Except his new god is the one that Chinese monk talks to.'

'So you are saying it's no surprise that Captain Seneca is consulting another non-Christian god, like a Chinese spirit?'

'Aye, Ishmael, it is true! Seneca is not made from the stuff we are made of! He is a queer one, he's part Christian, part pagan and part God knows what else! Maybe he is still worshipping that Neesuckquand, like his ma, or he has conjured up a new one. I am sure he thinks the world's full of demons, so he needs something to worship.'

'We know the real demon in our captain's mind. That's the white devil itself!' said Jacques, appearing from behind the ropes of the mainmast. He looked grumpy. 'I bet his Chinese friend told him that the white whale is not around here, and that's why we're changing course.'

Even as we altered the topsails and skysails, we were all eyeing our chief mate to see if there was any new instruction. But Drake did not say much. As always he held his opinion to himself. We knew that his first aim was to get enough whale oil so we wouldn't go home empty-handed. I wondered how Drake got along with Seneca, since their priorities for the voyage were so different. And for heaven's sake, we were at sea for months on end not because we wanted to murder a particular white whale, but for a more collective purpose – oil, and our share in the sale of it. I could perhaps claim that I wanted something other than oil and shares, something to do with adventure. But leaving that aside, to chase after one particular whale, a supposedly evil one, seemed indeed a strange fixation to me.

Thus far, no one other than Seneca had spoken with Muzi. Since he ate in the captain's cabin with the officers, and slept in a bunk in the stern, we did not learn anything of his habits or his past. But often, in the very early morning, just before the sunrise, or in the late evening when there was no rain, I noticed Muzi performing rituals on deck. One night, all was quiet. I was about to go to the head, when I heard a soft humming from above the deck. It was a man singing or chanting. I got up, and went to the head and quickly did my business. The humming was persistent. Curious, I climbed the stairs. Muzi sat alone on the deck with his hands folded over his knees. He was facing the north, looking out to sea in a meditative manner, though I could not see if his eyes were closed or open. He was not moving, just chanting softly. I tarried a while to watch him. Then, over the sound of the waves, a beautiful soft ringing echoed through the night air. By the light of the lamp set beside him, I could see he was holding a small cymbal-like instrument. Just as the sound was about to fade into silence, he tapped his instrument again with a little stick. Again the gong resonated softly but distinctly, melding into the ambience of the waves and the mechanical sounds and creaking of the *Nimrod*. It was profoundly peaceful to my ears.

So this was one of the rituals the Taoist would practise. It reminded me of the first time I saw Kauri pray to his little black god at the inn in New Bedford. Kauri still performed his ritual every night, but he had been instructed to do it without lighting a fire or drawing attention to it. Everything on a whaling ship was reduced to the most rudimentary form. And I certainly never showed my seahorse lady to anyone. The mere sight of her breasts would have disturbed every man on board.

I did not want Muzi to notice that I was watching him, so I silently slipped down to my quarters to sleep. But as I lay in my hammock I wondered how long he would be sitting on deck chanting, and when he would sleep, since we sailors rose with the dawning light.

III

I AWOKE AT DAWN to the sound of a fiddle, its rich
melody wafting down through the wood from the
deck above. It was a pleasing tune accompanied by a
jaunty voice, Freedman's voice, and Freedman's fiddle.
When I went up I asked him what the song was. He told
me it was an old Irish folk song called 'The Banks of Red
Roses'.

'About a young man who takes a girl to a cave and kills
her, burying her on the bank, from which roses then spring.
My father used to play it after dinner.'

I was surprised that such a dark story would be clothed
in a happy melody.

'Why does the man kill the girl?'

'Who knows why men might want to kill girls. That's a
mystery, Ishmael! Maybe he wanted to possess her. Men
can be greedy and brutish.'

'What sort of men?'

Freedman looked at me with a twinkle in his eye.

'Not your sort, Ishmael! You, I see, have a gentle
nature!'

Freedman put away his fiddle in its battered wooden
box, and got ready to start work.

'Men come in all shapes and sizes, like whales!'

I noticed that Captain Seneca was near us, having his morning tea by the bulwarks. He must have been listening to the music too. Perhaps he knew it as well. The song echoed in my mind. It disturbed me. Such a jolly tune about murder! The man in the song wanted to possess a woman. But why kill her! And why bury her along the bank? Are possessing and killing so closely tied in some men's minds? Men are strange, and dangerous.

As I pondered, I watched Freedman talking to the captain, both leaning against the gunwales. Then I heard the captain say:

'You will not play that song.'

'Oh, why, Captain?' Freedman asked, though he did not sound surprised.

'One should not let love spoil one's mind. Love is a sinful indulgence we men cannot drown ourselves in.'

Freedman paused. He seemed to understand what Seneca meant.

'I know, Captain,' he then said. 'That's why we are on this whaling vessel, having left our wives and children behind. Man has his duty.'

This remark somehow infuriated the captain.

'You know my past, Freedman, but you do not know my mind! My young wife was impressed by my power and my knowledge of the sea but she was not impressed by my body, so she betrayed me. What lack of spirit, and what dearth of intelligence! Women ought to be thrown into the sea and to see this devilish folly of the gods play out, and thereafter they would gain some knowledge and know the weight of things! But ahoy, away with the ignorance of women, away with the sordid land of comfort! We are here, at least and at last, free from them!'

Freedman listened, so did I, while chewing the cold

porridge mixed with molasses. I did not totally understand what the captain was saying to his mate. Nevertheless, I was drawn to Seneca's comments about his wife. How could this black man, towering in height and spirit, be so entangled in fury about this soft shadow of his wife?

Then Freedman responded, in an almost humble and placid tone:

'Sir, we both were brought up in the Quakers' way. I am sure you remember Crisp's words from *A Journey of a Long Travail from Babylon to Bethel.*'

'*For there were many who I perceived had been travelling in that narrow way,*' the captain recited mournfully, '*and had fallen into the mire; some on the right hand and some on the left, and they lay wallowing full of envy . . . So, keeping in my narrow way till I came to the end of the boggy valley, I then found firm ground under my feet.*'

'Exactly,' Freedman said. 'So, Captain, we all ought to walk down that narrow way, the Christian way, and forgive whoever is mean to you and to us, as the Lord would agree.'

'No, Freedman! We are not the same people! Even though we have the same black skin, and even though your father and mine came from those same slaves freed by the Quakers, I don't see myself going down the same narrow way! My way is there, in this wintry cosmos, in this murky sky and land to fight with a white devil, greater than the greatest iceberg errant in the sea! Leave me, Freedman, you do not know my mind and the fiery cold forms that dwell in it. Go tell the men to watch for the devil to appear!'

Freedman was stunned to hear this, and so was I. Quickly, I managed to disappear among the men on deck, and go to work. As Freedman called out to the crew to tighten the sails, the captain, with a heavy shambling gait, went back into the quarterdeck.

IV

THE MEN WERE ALL ON DECK and the day's labour began. The horizon was clear and we could see far out to sea. In no time, the man on the mast signalled a white mass in the distance. We looked to where he pointed, and after a few moments, a great white creature broke through the surface of the water.

Drake and Freedman had rushed to the bulwark to observe the creature, and now Drake gave orders for lowering. Three boats were lowered.

I joined as a steersman on Drake's boat, with Kauri at the front.

Tashe and some oarsmen boarded Freedman's boat. But this time, Freedman called upon Dilly, our cabin boy. Usually Dilly would never go down onto the water, as he was only twelve and could not swim, leaving aside his total lack of experience. But perhaps Freedman wanted the boy to have a taste of the chase, or to swallow some bitter water so he could get used to the sea. He ordered Dilly to climb down into the boat, and pushed an oar into the boy's hand. Dilly looked awkward and afraid.

Up on the bulwark of the *Nimrod*, we could see our steward looking down at the boy. Mr Flaherty was another one who never went out with the boats, though he could swim. He was older than most of us, in his early forties. Apparently his heart was weak and he stayed on board to serve the officers. Truthfully, I did not like this man very much for the queer way he looked at people. It was perhaps also to do with his missing teeth – whenever he opened his mouth a cavernous hole appeared ringed by grey-pink gums.

'Learn to tread water, boy!' Mr Flaherty shouted down to poor Dilly. 'Otherwise you are as useless as tits on a bull!' He watched the boy as we began to row out.

The three boats headed towards the white mass. But the creature was very quiet, and did not make the movements a whale would usually make. When finally it rose again above the water, Kauri hurled his harpoon. The creature struggled and thrashed, causing huge waves around us. Perhaps because Freedman got too close to it, or perhaps because the creature swam under Freedman's boat, Tashe lost his balance and fell into the water. We could see their boat was raised up by the white creature underneath, and saw Dilly follow Tashe into the sea. Neither Freedman nor any other man moved to rescue the boy. Perhaps he was thinking there were two boats in his wake, and one of them would come upon Dilly quickly, and pull him in. But it was a dangerous calculation, for Dilly was sinking. Thankfully, Tashe, already in the water, swam towards him and dragged him back to Freedman's boat.

The creature surfaced again and showed its great flank. Kauri threw another harpoon. When we finally got alongside it, we realised that the white creature had changed its colour to brown. We laughed, from both mirth and surprise. It was a giant squid! How could that be? Giant squids are creatures of the deep. They are like the krakens of myth. Why was one up here so close to the surface? Had it been chased by a whale?

The creature was smaller than a whale, but it was massive all the same. Behind its giant-eyed body floated eight thick arms and tentacles. We headed back to the *Nimrod*, dragging it along with us. I thought to myself: won't our captain be furious when seeing this creature? What were we doing, a bunch of headless men on this thoughtless ocean?

As we turned, Freedman's boat was behind us with Dilly lying in the boat in deep distress. Freedman was pressing Dilly's chest and we could see water coming out of the boy's mouth. After some moment of compression, he seemed to recover his senses, and gasped for breath. Now the attention turned back to the creature we had speared. Seagulls gathered above us like flying raindrops, and the smell had attracted sharks.

A few moments later the sharks were tearing apart the giant squid in the water. We had to quickly pull the whole damn creature up onto the deck so we could get out from the shark attack. Once we were safe, and the boats were pulled up too, we began to carve the creature. The cutting of a squid did not need special skills, and Dilly was again called to help with the work. The poor lad, barely recovered from near drowning, and still wet, had to bring out a large saw to deal with the slimy creature. Perhaps Freedman decided that the boy should learn some proper skills, rather than hiding in the kitchen with the chef.

Dilly had probably never used a saw in his life, but now had to kneel on a huge tangle of squid arms. And of course, he broke the ink sac as he pulled the blade across its head. Ink flew everywhere, causing a huge mess on the deck. The black liquid oozed and spread as we dismantled the body parts. Such was life, cutting up a giant squid just to feed our stomachs. In the midst of our chopping and scrubbing, the mastman spotted a real whale. As soon as the sound of 'There she blows!' was heard, Drake sent all of us back to the water. Dilly was spared this time, staying on board with the Chinese man and the cook and the craftsmen, who would have to deal with the remains of the mollusc.

V

THE CHASE WENT ON FOR HOURS. My stomach began to cramp terribly, and I instantly knew that the curse of my monthly blood was coming. But I showed no sign of pain, just kept rowing frenziedly. The weather was steady at least, and the wind did not rise as we rowed away from the *Nimrod*. At one point we lost sight of the whale, but Jacques's boat hunted down the creature. It was a sperm whale, judging by its head and long flukes. The tail lobes were triangular, thick and flexible. The creature was grey-coloured and plump, especially in the middle of its body, where it bulged out enormously. I suspected it was a female, and it may have been one carrying a little one inside her. But I was not sure, since I did not know whales well.

A red tide now poured from the grey whale. Her tormented body rolled in her own blood, which bubbled and seethed. The slanting sun playing upon this crimson pond in the sea sent back reflections into every face, so that we all looked like red-powdered clowns. I felt a doomed sense of our collective fate, us seamen and the whale, and this doomed sense of my own fate in this bleeding hell. Was all this part of men's survival instinct, men's bravery and men's power over the creatures out there roaming in the world? But my fearful and inert pondering did not get far. No time to think in that calamitous situation. The whale still fought violently and tried to escape, and we needed to throw more spears so that she would die sooner. And all the while, jet after jet of white smoke mixed with blood was agonisingly shot from the spiracle of the whale; her tail swung and flapped which made the sea around her a troubled typhonic pool. Then Tyrone flew out one more lance onto her body and Jacques straightened the line again and pulled the ropes with his bowman. All the faces were red, their eyes, their hands and the blood in the water around us.

Now their boat closed the distance with the caught whale. It ranged along her flank. Reaching out over the bow, Tyrone slowly plunged his long sharp harpoon into the whale's blowhole, and kept plunging in order to penetrate the whale's lungs, a sight so violent to watch – 'killing hell' were words that described the scene for me. One could look away but one could not stop imagining how a whale gradually surrendered to, agonised destruction. My own heartbeat and my woman's sympathy seemed about to burst out from me. 'Stop this! Stop this murder! Stop this bloody deed!' I wanted to shout. 'It's dying anyway! Don't make it suffer more!' But I remained silent, and just watched the blood, so much, from the whale's heart. And the great heart of a whale could weigh three hundred pounds or even four hundred. A great pouch of blood, to keep the great creature alive. I imagined the heavy mass beating slower and slower, then stopping altogether. Though the innermost life of the mammal ceased moving, its tail and head still moved, even its melon-sized eyeballs were turning blindly in its final oblivion. Now the creature wrapped herself in the red bleeding spray, she once more surged from side to side, spasmodically dilating and contracting her blowhole, then, at last, she fell back into the sea. Her body merely moved along the water passively, as the wind and waves carried her mournfully.

'It's dead, Jacques,' reported Tyrone.

All of us rose from our boats, gazing at the vast corpse Tyrone had made.

VI

WE TIED THE DEAD whale along the side of the *Nimrod*. We needed to flense her upper body in order to haul the sheets of blubber onto the deck, a task that had to be performed quickly, before the sharks turned up to get their share. As I suspected, the whale was pregnant. When the men cut open the whale's stomach, Jacques and Tyrone pulled out the foetus. It was pink and pale, already dead. 'Looks nigh on six months gone, or seven months,' Jacques remarked. I was astounded at the way the men simply let the dead foetus float off into the water to be devoured by sharks. The sight made me unable to continue with the work. The other men continued cutting indifferently.

While others were busying themselves with the cutting, Kauri and Tashe were assigned to kill as many sharks as they could in order to protect both the dead whale and the living men. Standing on one of the whaleboats, Kauri darted a lance into a shark; Tashe did the same from another boat. Sometimes, a killed shark was brought on the deck, because we wanted to harvest its skin. Otherwise, we had no interest in those tough-finned, sharp-teethed, cold-blooded, hungry creatures.

Kauri did not seem to like killing the sharks. He said: 'Kauri no care what god make shark, but to make shark is a damn thing for god to make.'

Everyone agreed. No one liked sharks, and we all liked whales, for different reasons. Though I could not say this applied to Captain Seneca. 'Like' was a light and meaningless word in any case. In truth, I could not say if I 'liked' whales or not. Each time I was thrilled to encounter one, but at the same time I was frightened by them. Yes, absolutely frightened. The killing was a torture for me to witness. Let alone the sight of a dead baby whale thrown into the water from its mother's opened belly. I felt I was at once both the mother whale and the foetus, a double death experience beyond words. But I repeated to myself, in a kind of incantation: I am a whaleman (well, a whalewoman), our job is to hunt the creature for its oil. The oil is our gold. This is precious to us, and we deserve to get it. We are good sailors and whalers.

But there were times when saying this would not work. I wondered if we could find similar kinds of oil in other materials, instead of cutting into a whale's head and body every day. We did use vegetable oil and animal fat to light our lamps, though they might not be as good as sperm oil. Did the great God never manage to invent some oil better than sperm oil? What did I know, Ishmaelle, an eighteen-year-old girl from a muddy village in England? I wondered if the whole venture was about something other than money. Was it something in the heart of men? Digging out rapeseed for its oil is not the stuff of heroes. Riding on ocean swells, armed with harpoons, plunging lances into the guts of beasts, taming the wild and testing one's strength – that was the stuff of heroes. Men have to throw themselves into the jaws of danger, taste blood, overcome the dark out there in the depths to overcome their own darkness. That's why I was bobbing up and down on this cork of a boat, in the wild sea. Not for money, but because men are restless, without peace, and because they have to hunt shadows to escape their own.

VII

THE MECHANICAL LABOUR of grisly doings continued. I had sought adventure on the high seas but here was a factory of death. For hours our hands were immersed in the fat as we massaged away the knots and bumps. Our fingers turned to eels and snakes. Sometimes we squeezed other people's fingers without even feeling them. We became part of the whale's body and its murdered life. Were we seeking a nauseating intimacy with the body of the slaughtered creature? It was like a holy communion, or rather an unholy one, with the body of the sacrificed one.

Muzi the Chinese monk joined us. He sat cross-legged, stretched out his long, slim fingers, and helped with the task of squeezing the globules of soft blubber. The work seemed never-ending, we had long since stopped speaking and had entered a state of half sleeping half working, only our hands moving. Muzi's eyes were closed as he pressed the lumpy oil. He did it as if he was meditating. What was in his head? Nothing or everything? I gazed at his dark brows above his closed eyes and his topknot tightened by a single chopstick. I liked this strange man, someone who kept quiet about himself and did not impose on others. But I feared him as well. At that moment he appeared like a mute witness, an angel of purgatory. It was unfathomable to me that Seneca trusted this man. I wondered if the power he seemed to have over the captain was also somehow exercised here over us. I looked across at him and, without opening his eyes, the faintest of smiles graced his lips. A mere shadow of knowing. Did he know something about me? My secret? Men are strange, I told myself, stranger than whales. And yet he seemed beyond male or female to me.

The next step in the process was to reduce the blubber to the gold of oil. This was called 'try work', a most peculiar phrase. On the *Nimrod* there was a brick kiln in the middle of the deck. Two huge 'try pots' sat atop the furnace. By midnight, the furnace was going full steam, and the ship was belching sooty fire. We needed to mind the wind so that the flames would not burn the rigging. From a distance, it must have looked like the fires of hell, on a ship, lost in the sea. A moving hell. And how far off would that description have been?

VIII

THE TRY WORKS LASTED TILL DAWN. We worked as if we were the demon slaves of an infernal master, who ruled over a hellish landscape of black soot and white oil. In the chaos, the greenhand Loick, exhausted, was caught in the flames by a sudden change of wind. His hair started to smoke and his shirt caught fire. We poured buckets of water over him and wrapped him in a heavy blanket, as he lay groaning, while someone went down to fetch the surgeon. Mr Hawthorne knelt down beside poor Loick and inspected the burns, then pronounced that he was seriously injured.

The surgeon sent me down to his cabin.

'Ishmael, you know where the medicine chest is. Fetch the aloe vera we brought from Cap de Verd.'

I nodded and immediately rushed below. The room was lit by a single candle on the desk, but I knew where he kept the medicine so I found the aloe quickly. I ran back to the main deck. Everyone had already resumed the work. I stood by, watching poor Loick writhe in agonising pain. Mr Hawthorne applied the unguent to Loick's arms and neck. He then instructed me to return the medicine to the chest, and to fetch some cotton and a pair of scissors. I did as he bade me.

Back in the surgeon's cabin, I looked around for the cotton and scissors. I knew they were located in a wooden box, but I could not find it. I fumbled about, opening one drawer after another. Finally in the middle drawer of Mr Hawthorne's desk I found a pair of scissors lying on top of a leaf of paper covered in small, neat handwriting. It was a letter.

Dearest Henrietta,

How I miss you. I miss your soft hands on my shoulders when we stand on our veranda and look out over the land below. It has not been too hard yet on this ship, thank God. I have been meaning to tell you that I saw beautiful flamingos when we stopped at Cap de Verd. You would be impressed by their pink feathers and elegant necks. Dearest Henrietta, can I tell you that I also miss your intelligent counsel, your sympathetic gaze when I labour with some difficulty in my undertakings . . .

I was taken aback by these private words from a man of whom I knew so little. But I also felt guilty about being so intrusive, so I closed the drawer and opened another. There I found some cotton strips. I went back on deck.

Mr Hawthorne attended Loick at length, until he was able to go down to rest, along with most of us sailors, leaving only one man for the night watch and another to take care of the furnace. I laid my tired body in my hammock and tried to sleep, but I kept thinking about 'Dearest Henrietta' and the way Mr Hawthorne wrote to her. How tender and affectionate he was. Soft and intimate. Could men be like this? I supposed Henrietta to be his wife. Was this an ideal marriage? I thought about Captain

Seneca and Ruth, but then shuddered, finding it inconceivable that Seneca could ever write such a letter, or feel anything that was expressed in the surgeon's note. Mr Hawthorne must have been longing for Henrietta, and probably wished she was on board with him now. It seemed a kind of madness that men had to isolate themselves from the opposite sex so as to do their gargantuan tasks. Or perhaps this separation from the women in their lives is the cause of the madness of their ambition. Perhaps these men were already alienated from women, and this was why they chased after whales. The whale was the woman they wanted, but transformed into a demon lover, or an avenging hag. Such a horrible fate for men, to be so far out at sea and so far gone in their own minds' fevered imaginings. Here I was, a woman, in the midst of these women-less men, in a ship dedicated to violence. How could I possibly survive?

CHAPTER NINE

Violation in the Dark

I

T HE SKY ABOVE US WAS PRESAGING CHANGE, a change for the worse. A tempest is coming, predicted Freedman, squinting into the grey curtain of melted sea and sky. There was still some cutting work to finish, and we knew we must hurry before rain came down to ruin everything. We barely rested. All of us were covered in grease. But the mates were pleased. 'Let the Lord be praised!' Drake finally remarked. 'At least we'll have a decent amount of oil when we reach the Cape of Good Hope.' Freedman added: 'In the meantime, keep up the hard work, boys!'

The furnace was still belching smoke, and would do so till the last of the blubber was cooked. The smoke blinded my eyes and everyone's face was black with soot.

'Now you all agree with me, whaling is not a decent profession. It's a working hell! Even being a pirate is better!' Antonio said, while pouring a bucket of blubber oil into the burning pot.

There had been gossip about Antonio being a former pirate for as long as we had been at sea. So when we had the lunch break, some of us wanted to hear a saucy story while smoking a pipe. The third mate Jacques was always straightforward in his way of speaking, so he asked Antonio:

'It is not my business, and I am sure you are one of the best seamen here, but, Antonio, were you really a pirate, in your former life?'

Antonio was taken aback by such a question. Perhaps he did not really want people to know about a shady past. But since he was talkative and had brought up the subject of piracy he answered it frankly.

'I was not a pirate to start with. I was working for a Portuguese merchant ship along the African coast. I was only sixteen then, but already a proper sailor!'

Antonio seemed to have a lot of bluster whenever he spoke about himself. I was always suspicious about his stories. But we urged him on.

'We were sailing from Gibraltar under our captain's command. But it was only a short two weeks before doom arrived! Have you heard of a pirate called Red Howell? They say he was originally from Wales. Maybe so, but he operated along the coast of West Africa. He had a long orange-coloured beard and wore a red robe. I heard that he had taken at least a hundred ships and collected a huge amount of treasure. In short, Red Howell captured our ship and killed most of our men as well as our captain. I will spare you how brutal he and his men were. But he kept some of us alive, and about ten of us became forced labour on his ship.'

'So you became a pirate, under Red Howell?' I asked before anyone else could ask him anything.

'Well, if you can call a forced labourer on a pirate ship a pirate, then yes, I suppose,' Antonio said. 'No one in my position could choose. I was more a slave than a pirate. I did not want to die. But I detested the way this brute controlled his people. He was very fond of torture. When I tell you how he liked to punish his people, you will understand how I desperately wanted to escape.'

Antonio's gold ear piercings shimmered under the sun. I had often wondered about his earrings. Some said pirates wear gold earrings so if they die the earrings can be melted down or taken as a payment for a burial and a decent funeral.

'If someone failed to carry out a duty, Red Howell would punish that fellow with "keelhauling"! He did it with two of us sailors because they became sick and could not serve the pirates.'

Antonio paused, as if trying to remember the terrible details of the torture, or hesitating to speak of these past events which had traumatised him. After a moment, he continued:

'Keelhauling was not the same as walking the plank. It involved throwing the man into the water underneath the ship, with a heavy weight on his legs to make sure he stayed underwater. Then the ship went on, pulling the body until the man died. That was a way to kill a man who could swim. Ever since I had been captured, I was looking for a way to escape. And I did, one day, when we landed in the Azores: I ran away and hid myself on the island until I found an American whaler to take me on as a sailor. I then stayed in America and learned my English by working in the port, and eventually I managed to join the *Nimrod*.'

Everyone was astounded and thrilled by such a story. Even Drake and Freedman were greatly entertained.

'I heard that some pirates practise a kind of marriage on the ship – a matelotage, is that the word?' Freedman asked.

Antonio nodded. 'Often an old pirate, no longer very fit, unable to swim any more, would get a young and healthy pirate to be his partner. So the younger man would be asked to join the older one in a matelotage and to live together, and they could share all their plunder, even inheriting it in the event of death.'

Some of us were laughing, others were intrigued. I could not help but ask:

'So were you persuaded to join this pirate marriage?'

Antonio did not give a clear answer. He just chuckled and joked:

'What do you think, Ishmael? Someone like me who could swim fast and steer well? Luckily I got away as early as I could!'

Laughter broke out, everyone satisfied to have a brief moment of entertainment. Now Captain Seneca arrived with a stern look, followed by Mr Flaherty. Today the steward also wore black, so he looked like a shadowy ghost of the captain, only smaller and shorter. Mr Flaherty had heard the story and he laughed too, revealing his pinkish gums in his half-empty mouth. Then he eyed me up and down in a strange way. I never liked this steward, and my intuition told me that something ungodly might befall me from this man one day.

Upon seeing Seneca, everyone returned to work. The burning of the blubber oil resumed, but I couldn't help wondering about a man's fate. If I was captured and taken to a pirate ship, would I manage to escape? Or much worse, what if I was forced to marry one of the sickly old pirates – would I even survive the first night? The mere thought of such a situation sent shivers all over my body. No! Stop! I poured the blubber oil into the steaming pot. Let it burn. No, I did not want to imagine the situation. I would kill myself with a knife rather than submit to such a dreadful fate!

II

ALL NIGHT, I was tortured by nightmares, one after another, about encountering a pirate ship. Antonio's harrowing stories replayed themselves in my head with my own variations. I was forced to labour on the pirate ship. I could not understand where the pirates were from, as they did not speak the language I knew. They shouted at me while I cleaned the deck. I saw knives and weapons clipped on their belts. Then came a forced marriage, between me and a one-eyed dirty pirate. He had a red beard and his appearance was in every way disgusting. What happened then, my Lord? I struggled and shouted as the loathsome pirate forced himself on me. But at some point, I realised something was going terribly wrong with my body.

What was going on? Suddenly I woke up from my dreams to feel the crushing weight of a body on my back! I realised with shock that my bottom was exposed. I was in acute pain because: my back passage was being penetrated. Deeply confused and horrified, my first thought was that I could not scream or make any noise which would wake up others. The hammock was swinging madly and he had pulled down my double-layered trousers from behind and managed to enter me. My upper body was still wrapped tight in my clothing and he did not seem to be touching other parts of my body, though I could not be certain in my shocked state. Everything happened so quickly that his violent thrusts were muffled by the noisy waves and wind outside, as well as the snoring noises filling our quarters. Paralysed in that position, I was in agonising pain. Very quickly he finished and the movement gradually slowed down. But my horror was deepened as his hand reached round to my front and searched for my supposed male part. Lord! I almost screamed as he reached my pubic area. Suddenly both of us were frozen, as his hand discovered there was no man's part there but instead an absence. He abruptly twisted my upper body towards him so that my face turned to his. Lord, even in such a blackness I could recognise that it was the steward Mr Flaherty. His eyes locked onto mine as if to say: 'What the hell, are you a woman?'

Instinctively, I pulled my hand out and covered his mouth while I shook my head. I shook it again, as if to say clearly: 'DO NOT TELL ANYONE.'

His hand froze on my body, around my vagina. But it did not move further. In that stillness, I felt the liquid product of his repellent lust slowly oozing down from my bottom. It would have been better if he had strangled me at that point, and I could have died with my shame. But he didn't. I could have knifed him, I felt the blade in my trousers, if I had had the guts to do so. But I didn't. Undoubtedly, he was in a state of shock. I kept staring at him in the dim light shed by the lamp hung from the ceiling. DO NOT TELL ANYONE. I thought he had got the message from my eyes. Coldly, he withdrew from me. He put his feet on the deck, pulled up his trousers, and disappeared into the dark. I knew where his hammock was.

It was on the aft end of our quarters. But I was in such pain that I was unable to move or think. Like being stabbed, I lay in my hammock, in my sweat and in this man's sperm.

I stared into the darkness. My thoughts were simple beyond my physical trauma. Would he tell the mates? Would he tell anyone? How would they punish me? Would they flog me as they did with anyone on a ship who committed a crime or who misbehaved? Would they dump me on some island, leaving me with some primitive people without shipping me back either to America or to England? Or worse, would they cast me into the sea? Murder me?!

After another hour of deep distress, I pulled myself up. I left the sleeping quarters and went up to the open deck. I did not know why I was up there. I simply told myself: *Ishmaelle, swallow this. Pretend nothing has happened. You are a woman and this kind of thing was bound to happen, sooner or later. Nothing special. Take it. Be it. You are done. You are still alive. You will have to see what God decides for you.*

As the salt-sea wind blew across my face, a sense of living returned to me. No, I did not come to the deck to throw myself into the sea. I would live on. I stared into the darkness. I felt the knife and my seahorse lady in my trousers. I slipped my hand into my pocket and took out the little idol. In the blackness my fingers felt the smooth breasts of the seahorse lady and her spiny head and tail. No tears came. I wanted to pray. But I did not know what to pray for and I did not know how. The vast black night and ink-coloured waves were all I had right now. I heard a slight rustling nearby, and turned. There, near the windlass, I saw a shadowy figure. Was this my assailant, about to pounce upon me, and cast me into the dark waters, or beat me down? I held my breath and froze, and scrutinised the shadow. The shadow was still, and then a soft chant arose from it. It was Muzi the Chinese monk. He was sitting in the same position as the last time I had seen him, with the same posture. The thin sliver of the moon emerged from behind the obscuring clouds, and now it shone above us. The Chinese monk noticed me. But he did not immediately stop what he was doing. Gradually, his chanting died out, and he turned to me. He spoke a strangely accented simple English.

'No sleep?'

I shook my head, unable to utter a word.

We were both silent for a while. He looked back into the sea.

'Sit, like me,' he said plainly, but in a gentle way.

With his hand on his knees, he sat cross-legged, his face towards the north, and began to hum. The humming sound involved no words, but arose from deep in his stomach, and into his throat, then out through his nose. It was a grounding and soothing vibration for my ears and my erratic heart, which still pounded in my chest.

I sat down, some yards away from him. I placed my hands as he did. I felt an inexplicable calmness coming from Muzi. But I did not hum. With my eyes closed, I listened to the sea, and to his humming. I did not know for sure how long I was sitting there, but when I opened my eyes, Muzi was no longer present. The moon was now to the west. I stood up and went down to my quarters. Lying on my hammock, I waited till the dawn light broke through the cracks of the ceiling wood, and thought of my brother Joseph.

III

NEXT DAY, at breakfast, I saw Mr Flaherty eyeing me while biting into his dry bread. He did not utter a word. We passed each other and went to busy ourselves with our own things. No exchange at all. Strangely I did not have any hatred towards him. All I wondered was when he would tell someone. When would judgement day befall me?

The day was passing in a state of despair. I did not know what I was doing even though I was told to do this and that. I saw Kauri on the deck at one point, but he was making a harpoon and his eyes were glued to his task, tying leather on a wooden lance, and did not notice me. I watched the foam on the waves. My heart was dead. The foam, churning and bubbling and falling apart and then forming again just to break apart again. Such a ceaseless effort. A woman's life.

I never had such a dreadful experience with my own body as the event last night with the pathetic steward Mr Flaherty. Was this God's punishment? Had I trespassed upon men's domain? Was there worse to come? I stared at the foam on the sea; the windswept language of the waves gave me no answer.

In the afternoon, there was no wind and the murmuring of the waves was hypnotic. The sea was holding a mighty power but no one knew what it would lead to us. In that stillness, we noticed an old ship coming towards us, heading in the opposite direction. As Drake watched it through his telescope, I could see he was frowning. And some of us thought, what? Are we encountering a pirate ship? Why this frowning?

We watched the ship as it drew closer. Soon I could make out the name on the hull: *Royal Anne*. But it did not raise a flag, which was unusual. We could see the sails were torn, the canvas hanging in pieces. An officer hailed us, his English accent immediately recognisable to my ear.

'He is English!' I said.

There followed more shouting and greetings from men on the deck, all in an accent which I could locate – from the southern part of England, not far from my county.

'So it is a British whaler,' Drake said, putting down his telescope. 'It probably got into some trouble on its way.'

Now Captain Seneca was out. Steadying himself with his stick against the bulwark, he leaned out and cried from the top of his lungs:

'Ship, ahoy! Hast seen the white whale?'

No one on the *Royal Anne* answered. An older man came on the deck, ordering his men to lower a boat. We watched him go down to the small boat with two sailors, who rowed towards us.

When they clambered onto our *Nimrod*, we saw that the elderly man had only one arm. We looked at his hollow sleeve, but did not say anything. He had a tanned skin, and when he smiled, the wrinkles around his eyes rippled like a little stone being thrown in a pond. He introduced himself as Captain Brown, and greeted everyone on deck.

He waved his one arm to me – well, I knew he was not waving to me alone but to a group of us, including me. But I was instantly affected by his manner – he had a fatherly kindness. Drake and Freedman were in good spirits, and they ordered Dilly to get some rum and dried meat. I was so curious about this *Royal Anne* that I wanted to ask where they had come from. But I resolved to wait, until a better moment presented itself.

'Your sails are in a jolly good shape, as neat as my wife's laundry!' The English captain was mellow with a sense of humour which I was familiar with. 'This makes me even more homesick for my wife's sheets and bloomers!'

I smiled to myself, and liked him straight away. He was the first English person I had met since last December.

'We got smashed these last few days in the storm, but luckily we are on our way home!' Captain Brown said. 'Even so, we have to repair our sails before we can go on.'

Without making any attempt at basic socialising, Seneca repeated his words coldly:

'Have you seen the white whale?'

The English captain was taken aback by such a blunt question. But he did not take it too seriously and answered:

'Yes, surely, a monster white one!'

'Did you?' Seneca was excited.

A gust of wind blew the empty sleeve of the Englishman's jacket. I imagined the short stub inside his sleeve, and wondered how he had lost his arm. Now Brown noticed Seneca's ivory leg.

'Aye, let us shake bones together! An arm and a leg!'

Dilly brought out the rum and sliced beef. Chairs were placed. Pointing to his missing arm, the English captain spoke with a wry smile:

'An arm that never can carry, do you see; and a leg that

227

never can run! But we are all still whaling! How many barrels have you got so far?'

Seneca did not answer.

'Not many, about thirty-five barrels,' Drake said, and went to pour some drinks for the English.

'Captain Brown, where did you see the white whale? How long ago?' chased Seneca.

'I saw him there, on the line, last season,' said the Englishman, looking towards the south.

'And he took that arm off, did he?'

'Aye, he was the cause of it. But I had a good surgeon on board – I got my life back at least.' Then he eyed Captain Seneca's ivory leg. 'And your leg, too?'

'The devil did!' Seneca spat out his words.

Drake handed a cup of rum to the Englishman and one to Seneca. Both gulped down the contents. Then they sat and looked in the direction of the south, as if they could see the trace of the white whale. Several of us were cleaning the floor of the stern, including myself. I was eager to know more about the English ship, and to ask some questions, so I moved my bucket and brush closer to them.

'I was ignorant of the white whale at that time. Well, one day we lowered for a pod of four or five whales, and my boat fastened to one of them; we were on the stern and on the outer gunwale to slice the whale. We did not pay attention to the water, until we realised an angry whale was following us. Suddenly he bounced from the bottom of the sea, and we saw a snow-white head and hump, with a damaged jaw and very wrinkly skin.'

'It was he!' cried Seneca, suddenly letting out his suspended breath.

'Our whaleboats were capsized, and we were all thrown

into the water. But our ship was only slightly damaged, thank God.'

'Did you see two harpoons stuck on his hump?'

'Yes, there were at least two harpoons on his back, before we all capsized,' Brown said, slightly sarcastically.

'Aye, they were mine – *my* irons!'

Drake and Freedman looked at each other. Drake walked away, shaking his head. We could all see that he was not pleased with Seneca's proclamation.

Captain Brown forked a piece of beef, chewed it slowly.

'Captain Seneca, you do not seem to be saddened by our misfortune,' said the one-armed commander. 'We were really in a bad state. Most of us were in the water, and the men on the ship had to quickly equip themselves to throw spears at the white whale. It was hell. In brief, the devil caught me and took my left arm . . . I floated, barely conscious. When I got my senses back, I was on the ship, and our surgeon was cutting the bits off from my arm . . .'

Brown paused. No one said anything. I stopped my brush on the deck, a few yards away from them. I stared at the soap bubbles seeping into the boards, thanking the Lord I still had my two arms and two legs.

'We lost three men,' Captain Brown continued.

After a few more drinks, his spirit was lifted again. 'But we have enough blubber oil to go home. An old man cannot complain too much. Now if I may, we would be grateful if you could lend us a spare sail and I would be glad to pay.'

'A spare sail?' Seneca was almost disappointed. 'But what became of the white whale?'

'Oh, dear God, we did not see him again, and hopefully we never will!'

'So he is still out there!'

'He is. But you should leave him alone, Captain Seneca. I am glad to go home and retire. You and your one leg should do the same. No more of this folly!'

'No, I will get him, Mr Brown. Which way is he heading?'

'Bless my soul, and curse the foul fish,' cried the Englishman. 'I say we would do better to keep the other limb. What's the point of getting that senseless creature when I have only got a few more years to live!'

The conversation finally died out, as Seneca was losing interest. When the beef and rum were all gone, Drake came up and told Brown that he could have a spare sail from us, though he would prefer to exchange for oil. Seneca retired to his cabin, and the talks between the officers continued. In the end, we were told that the *Nimrod* would receive three barrels of whale oil in exchange for the sail Captain Brown wanted.

During all this time, I was burning with the desire to speak to the Englishman, but there was no chance. Then again, I did not have anything specific to say. Should I ask about England? Perhaps I should ask if Captain Brown knew Denge Marsh by the Channel? Or even if he might be from there, somewhere near a village called Saxonham? How absurd, I thought to myself. Laughable too. Should I ask him about the Queen of England – Queen Victoria? I knew very little about our queen but she was someone I related to that piece of land, even though I was not sure if I would or could ever return to that old ground.

It was only a few months since I had sailed from England, but I felt I had left half a lifetime ago. I felt I had become an old mariner, as old as Captain Brown or Seneca.

I did not know until that day how terribly I missed that wet soggy land I had once detested. Was this ocean, this endless unsheltered life, to be my entire life, my only home? I could not know. Turning away and taking the soap-smeared brush, I resumed cleaning the deck.

IV

I LAY ON MY HAMMOCK, and the image of Mr Flaherty's face came to me. His mouth opened, his pinkish gum exposed and his lower teeth missing. He spoke filthy words. In the pitch-black, my body was stiff and I was anxious about what would become of me on this ship. Finally, at dawn, I fell asleep in exhaustion. I must have slept late. I was woken by the sound of an explosion on deck. In almost six months on the sea I had never heard such a violent noise. The ear-splitting explosions continued. Disturbed, I jumped to the floor, wondering if there was a war.

I followed a few sailors up to the deck. There were small American flags tied along the gunwale, and plumes of purple and yellow smoke lingering in the air. Surrounded by a group of seamen, the mates – Drake, Freedman, Jacques – stood by the windlass. Our captain stood in front of them, and he seemed to be in a good mood. Squeezing myself through a gap in the crowd, I saw that Muzi the Chinese man was the focus of attention. In his black silk trousers, he was the one orchestrating the fireworks. Jacques spoke in an excited tone:

'Go on, the chef won't serve the meat until you finish off these damn crackers!'

The other men laughed and agreed. Then Drake said to Seneca:

'Shall we, Captain?'

Supported by his wooden staff, the captain nodded. Dilly wriggled his way to the front of the crowd, holding a tray of cups and mugs, followed by Mr Flaherty with a big jug of rum. The sight of Flaherty made me step back. A sense of horror invaded me despite the cheerful atmosphere.

Pow! Pow! Pow! The fireworks exploded, and a cloud of blue and purple smoke rose above the deck. I jumped back and covered my ears. A Roman candle threw off sparks of every colour. Some sailors danced to avoid the exploding firecrackers.

So this was the Fourth of July, American Independence Day. Over the last few days I had heard the sailors talk about it during dinner, and our chef Moses had killed a few geese the day before, and had plucked the feathers from the birds. I vaguely knew that it was the day that America managed to become independent from the British, but since I was English, in fact the only English sailor on the ship, I did not dare to ask more, nor did I want to remind anyone that I was English on this proud day of the Americans.

We were spared work because of the celebration. The geese were boiled for the great feast, there were cuts of beef for everybody, and the rum flowed. Moses cursed when he burnt his hand at the fire, and Dilly had managed to spill a half-gallon of the best rum. Food was served to everyone on deck, including the officers, who ate with us and not in the captain's cabin. This was so far the biggest celebration we'd had on the ship, but I remained quiet. Being English and being a woman under Mr Flaherty's spiteful power made me cheerless and uneasy.

While Freedman played his fiddle, Mr Hawthorne took out his newspaper he'd got from Cap de Verd and pointed at the front page.

'It's not going to turn out well, I fear. The confederates are recruiting! But no black men will be allowed to join any side!'

Seneca glanced at the paper, and said in a cool tone: 'The armies won't use black men to fight. I am not surprised by this!'

'But what if the war becomes uncontrollable, what if the southern states start winning? We would have to get back and get all the white and black fellows in the north to join the army! Captain, do you agree?'

Seneca did not respond. Stabbing a piece of goose breast in a furious manner, he looked over at Freedman. He was playing a song I recognised, a piece I would hear at Christmas back in Kent. Putting aside his instrument, Freedman took a break and joined the conversation.

'If my father was still alive,' Seneca said, 'he would be first in line to join forces with the Union. But I was adopted by a Quaker family, so I have Quaker in me still. And war, weapons raised against our brethren, these are not the way!'

'Captain, what are you saying? How can you forget the sufferings of our fathers?' Freedman burst out. 'Both our fathers were child slaves before they were freed! They worked on Mason's farm, and Mason was the most savage monster. My father remembered that often he would be awakened at dawn by the most heart-rending shrieks. And Mason would whip the man's naked back till he was covered with blood. The louder he screamed, the harder Mason whipped. That monster brute even slashed a slave child's head because that child ate an extra piece of cornbread!

How can you say you are not interested in fighting this war? Yes, we are fortunately free men, but think of those ceaseless whips and cries and bloodstained bodies in the south on those plantations, Mr Seneca!'

'I hear you, Freedman.' Seneca frowned, then after a brief moment of silence, he said: 'My war is not with the confederate soldier in the field, it is not with any man, it is with a leviathan in this goddamn lost place. That monster waged war on me and wounded me so that I live as a cripple. I am fighting against evil! But evil manifests in different ways. The white whale is one of them! It's an abomination of nature! No real whale can be white. It's a sign of evil!'

'What about a white man, sir?' said Freedman. 'If a white whale is an abomination, what of a white man?'

'White men are not part of nature. No men are part of nature. Men are not like whales that come with a certain natural form. Whiteness in nature is a sign of death. Like the bones stripped of flesh on the sand shore. A white whale is an inversion. It wears its bones on the outside, like a perversion! That is evil. And so is that whale's implacable hate. That's not natural!'

The sailors who had been listening settled into silence. Seneca surveyed us all with his bright black eye, as if waiting for any sign of dissent or dispute. Then, in a calm voice, Mr Hawthorne, clearing his throat, made the remark:

'Captain Seneca, albinism is not uncommon in nature. It's a natural result of some defects of heredity. Nothing more!'

At this, Seneca turned on Hawthorne, with a volcanic and glowering look.

'Don't dare to educate me with your scientific cant! Go

back to your microscope and pinned butterflies, and stick to doctoring the sick!

Whereupon he threw his plate onto the deck, heaved himself up on his ivory leg, and stomped his way towards his cabin. On deck there was no more music, and no more laughter. It looked like the celebration was over.

V

AFTER THE FIRST NIGHTMARISH event with Mr Flaherty, he came to my hammock again, on the third night. He could not wait, could he? Now that I was his easy prey, he would not let me be. Maybe he spent the night before deciding if he should report me or if he should keep coming to my hammock to use me. What could he lose? Nothing. A spiteful revolting worm in my body and in my life now. This pitiful life. Since my sleep had been disrupted very frequently on board, I was awake when he climbed onto my hammock. But this time, he was not entering me from behind. Now that he knew that I was a woman, he made his way clear. He was breathing heavily, much more excited. Or was he nervous, since I was a woman in this senseless sea life? When he loaded himself on the hammock his large body crushed mine, and clumsily he reached, first, under my layers of shirts. As if testing something, he found my breasts. His hands were cold and rough, my nipples went sore and hurt terribly. I could not breathe. I tried to push him aside but there was no way I could escape from this. Mr Flaherty gripped me as if I was a floppy rabbit. He could strangle me or bite me at any moment if I fought back. Now one of his hands continued to squeeze my breast, while the other reached down my trousers and grabbed my loins. Oh, I thought that I would have to stab him. My knife was waiting, down in my trousers, but I was in a panic about whether I should take that extreme measure. If I killed him then would I not be killed by the seamen? I would be the accused one, the deceptive one, the liar, the abomination. Who would stand by me? No one, not even Kauri. I would be the one who would have to be punished. So in my quandary, my horror of indecision, I let Mr Flaherty's finger enter my woman's place. Lord spare me or strike me with a lightning bolt! Or burn me or cast me into hell flames! His finger then moved, and his body pressed against me, and his hand rubbed my maidenhead. He then took it away, and I felt something else pressing brutally in. I knew what it was. He had put in his cursed cock. My whole body hurt. I could not breathe and I could not move, while he took his lowly satisfaction. He thrusted, he groaned, he pinched. I bit my own lips until my mouth was salty. I choked and I must have been bleeding from the mouth. He then reached that point of goat-like release, with an awful shudder. He withdrew from me. Like a dog done with his bone, he was no longer interested in me. Then he left me there, a corpse on a violently swinging hammock.

I could not stay there, but had to drag my wracked limbs to the water store. I got a bucket of water and went down to the bilge. There I tried to clean out his cursed seed. I squatted with a rag in my hand and washed, again and again, hoping I would remain invisible and safe.

Later I went back to my hammock. I did not go up onto the deck, to see if the Chinese monk was there, doing his chant. I wish I had done that. But I was in utter misery. I could only lie in the abyss, among the creaking stench and the sailors, a den of men. The great question of what to do lay on me like a succubus. What was my life, what was my very being? The hours seemed to stretch to eternity. If Mr Flaherty were to visit me again, and surely he would, should I kill him? That would be to risk eternal damnation. Was Flaherty evil? Or was he just a man, doing what men do? In the eyes of God, what was Flaherty? What was I? Or should I end my life? To hell with damnation. I curse the God who let this happen anyway. I curse God who put men in control of the world, to rule us with their absurd desires and pointless ambitions, their strutting pride and their stupidity.

Or . . . was there some other way? Perhaps by escaping this sea coffin. We would have to make land soon. The next port was only days away. Yes, I would have to jump ship. I would escape as soon as I could, run for the hills. But what a thought. What would I be running to? A foreign country, a wild land, a place of cannibals and savages, and thieves, and men of low means? How would I ever make my way thence to home?

VI

The sound of a whale at the bottom of
the sea after being harpooned.

Sssssssssssssssssssssssssssiinkkk

Ssssssssssssssssssssssssssssiiiinkkk

Airairairairairaiaraiairairairairair

Menmenmenmenmenmenmenmenmen

mmeeeeeeeeeeeeeeennn

mmeeeeeeeeeeeeeeennn

mmeeeeeeeeeeeeeeennn

mmeeeeeeeeeeeeeeeaaa

CHAPTER TEN

Cape of Good Hope

I

W HAT KEPT ME ON BOARD THIS BARK? On this churning sea and in this sinful forecastle where men slept through the night, tossing and sleepwalking and dreaming and snoring while I was ravished and abused by a man in silence and poisonous hatred? What kept me here, on this ship of knaves and fools?

Night again. My black hours. The king of the night. Here it came, the mayhem of my night. My nightmarish night. My punishment. A hole for men, this man and that man, this dog and that dog. I could not blame all men, but I could blame most of them. Not little Dilly, not Kauri. They were innocent. And perhaps Captain Seneca too. He was innocent. He would never be interested in me, nor in gold or gain. His king of the night was the whale, that whitest of whales, his Holy Grail. He was tortured, he was insane, therefore beyond redemption. I was tortured but I was not insane.

I could not speak to Kauri. Or could I? Did he secretly know? Had his subtle native mind guessed? When we were in Nantucket, when we were still waiting to find a ship to recruit us, my Polynesian told me that he had sworn to celibacy. He would never touch a woman again in his life.

He was not made to live with a woman, he told me, in his simple English. He told me that when he was around fifteen he had killed his own brother because of a girl on his island. The girl, two days later, threw herself into the sea after discovering that her lover had been murdered. Kauri watched the girl's body being fished out by the villagers on a canoe. That body was pale and swollen and bloated. They buried the lovers together. Kauri helped to dig the grave for the two. His father, the chief, did not want to punish him, but he had to do something. Kauri could stay and be confined forever, or choose exile. The son could leave on the next western ship to depart the island. Perhaps in his exile, Kauri would grow into a wiser man, his father hoped. Kauri left. This was the real reason he left his island. And he vowed that he would never enter into a life with a woman. How could I ever forget, after our first night in New Bedford, after we shared a pipe together, how the wise Polynesian touched my forehead with his, and said we were bound together? How incredible that moment was! Words cannot describe the warmth of it. And now that moment returned to me. If I deserted the ship, I would have to say goodbye to Kauri, and to this borrowed life which removed me from the limitation of being a woman. But how could I stay, with the misery inflicted by Mr Flaherty?

I had grown to love this wooden sea chariot. When I would rise from my sleep in the night, and walk out from the confined wooden hold onto the decks, to find the Chinese monk sitting in his holy posture, chanting softly, I would discover beguiling illuminations: the lamps lit around the deck, under the mast, by the quarterdeck, and beside the windlass and bulwark. Lamplight, its glistering and its warmth, its affirmation of this wonderful and sinful life, all given by the great whales we hunted. For the blubber oil granted us this light and hope. We humans. Without lamplight, we would live in the dark. We would eat and dress in the dark, we would think and talk in the dark. And what was in the dark for me? The darkness for me meant brutal penetration from Mr Flaherty, the most hideous, the most repellent, the most grotesque, the most shameful, the most immoral act a man commits against a woman. What was I but a woman, a simple hole, a witch and liar in this floating life? I loathed the whole of humanity. I loathed and detested the sexual organs we women were given by You, Lord. A lack, a wound, a bleeding hole. An unhealable wound. A wound that ought to be eliminated from life. I wished to be no woman, no gender, no identity, no body. I wished to become one of the bubbles of sea foam out there. Cast me away. Annihilate me! Now.

There were times, though, when I said to myself, stupid Ishmaelle, life is a gift and you should be grateful to be on this wide-open sea with the company of Kauri, Hawthorne, Tashe, Tyrone, Jacques, Freedman, Drake, Owen, Loick, Moses, Washington, Antonio and even little Dilly-Dally; all the men with that sinful thing between their legs, they were my brothers for better and for worse! I never had a sisterhood which could protect me or challenge me or educate me or destroy me. Better to be challenged and even to be destroyed than to wither and rot in Saxonham on the salty and desolate Denge Marsh. Oh, was all this true? Did I miss England or not? Did I want to return to that land before a watery grave swallowed me or not?

I did not know. Lord. I did not know.

So should I desert this ship? Should I say to myself, I cannot endure this disgust this rape this spite this hatred this sadism, I cannot let Mr Flaherty's cock penetrate me on any night under this sinful sky? And when should I take out my knife, to kill, but kill him or myself?

I could not decide. Oh, Joseph, tell me! And help me! I love – yes, love – this ship on this sea despite the misery it has brought upon me. I could not think of being alone on the land, a weightless individual traipsing on foreign soil, without the feel of a wooden deck under my feet and without seeing the sails up on the mast billowing above my head.

I was condemned.

II

W E WERE HEADING for the Cape of Good Hope, and would soon be there. Three nights had passed and Flaherty had not come to my hammock. I had spent the nights clutching my blade. What had stopped him? Guilt, or some glimmer of pity?

Later I thought I was becoming a *Flying Dutchman*, sailing towards nowhere and living as a spirit. I did not know anything about the ghostly ship until our chef Moses told us about it one morning, just before we anchored.

'They say that the *Flying Dutchman* was caught in a hurricane in the South Atlantic, so it headed for the Cape to escape the bad weather. But every man on the warship was either diseased or dying. Most of them suffered from scurvy and infection. Listen! Eat the sour cabbage! It's good for you!'

Moses digressed in his storytelling, as some of us did not like to eat the cabbage that he kept in a large container in the hold. The pickled cabbage was not popular. It was worm-ridden and it stank like cat's piss. But it was one of the only ways we had to get the vitamins we needed to avoid the scurvy, according to Moses. I did not mind the sour cabbage and I preferred it to the mouldy bread. And so far I did not have any scurvy. Some did, and gums bled, and their skin bruised all over.

'So the sailors were weary and disoriented after weeks of awful weather, and when they got to the Cape they could not even find an anchoring spot. The captain, who was especially ill, led the ship back and forth around the rocky banks and eventually they lost their way!'

'Did they manage to anchor somewhere else?' Owen asked.

'Well, no one knows! No one has seen the ship since. A year later, the Dutch dispatched another ship to find it. That man-of-war weathered the gales, and finally arrived at the Cape, but they found no trace of the *Flying Dutchman*. Nor did they find any seamen from the ship. Having refitted, the captain decided to return to Europe. But as they were leaving the Cape of Good Hope, they were assailed by a violent tempest. During the night watch, a sailor saw a vessel standing immobile in the sea not far from them under a press of sail. The ship was very old and broken apart, but it had an orange glow around it. The sailor thought this was the ghost of the *Flying Dutchman*.'

'Did that ship survive?' I asked.

Moses shrugged. 'I don't know if any of this is true! If there was a real ship, perhaps it could not get into a harbour, or perhaps *would* not because it was loaded with great wealth, or some act of murder and piracy had been committed on board, so the man in charge was reluctant to anchor in a place where people would discover its secret.'

Everyone went quiet at this point. We only had some barrels of blubber oil on the *Nimrod* – was that a source for a possible battle? Though surely we had some gold which Captain Seneca was in charge of, for purchasing the supplies along the way, but that could not be much. Or maybe Seneca would be the source of the conflict!

As everyone was thinking of all the possible dire situations for the *Nimrod*, Moses drew his story to a close.

'All I can say is that I hope we don't all perish when we anchor later!'

We would anchor the next day. I was unhinged. I did not know what to do. And perhaps this would be my only chance if I had to desert. But, really, did I want to do this?

This night, I thought Mr Flaherty would spare me, take mercy on me, as the last three nights he did not come. But he did come. He resumed what he had done to me, a brute to a woman. He became more savage, more sadistic, grasping my breasts and tearing at my loins. Flaherty could not go down to the sea to chase a whale, so he had to annihilate a weaker member of the crew? What was this sick pleasure of annihilating others? When his body crushed mine, a painful urge of revenge rose and filled my heart and head – a whale must also take revenge on the men after him or her. I felt the knife in my trousers as Flaherty entered me. But I kept telling myself, tomorrow we would be on land. I would make up my mind once we moored the ship in the harbour.

III

E WERE TOLD THAT we would be anchored at the Cape of Good Hope for four days to get supplies. Upon docking, I thought miserably about what I should do. I decided that for the first two nights I would not do anything, so as to avoid suspicion.

A flock of ostriches greeted us upon arrival. Their necks and legs were long, their stomachs plump. I had never seen such a big bird in my life. As soon as we were allowed on land, I headed towards the flock on the rocky bank. But once I got close to them, they began to run. Lord, how fast they could run! Only lions or leopards could catch them, not us men!

Now I was on land, solid land. What should I do? Had I made up my mind? No, I could not. I wished that I were less confused. I wanted to live. That was the only thing I was clear about.

Beneath my feet were hard rocks. I should be like a rock, a stone, a pebble, a hard thing from Denge Marsh, from my Saxonham. I should bear no pain, have no feelings, know no remorse.

I was not alone on land, scrambling over these rocks. With four seamen, I was assigned to work on the harbour sorting out the ropes. We were not allowed to venture into the native land alone. This afternoon after lunch, some of us were sent to ferry water, while others repaired the sails. I needed to be alone, so I could clear my mind. I went to ask the surgeon and our first mate for permission to collect herbal roots. Since they had allowed me to do so in Cap de Verd, and since I proved that I could assist with the medical treatment of the sick on board, they agreed. I was relieved to be able to roam freely. Despite what had happened to me in the last few days, I, Ishmaelle, had proved myself to be useful on this ship. So now, when other men were down in the food hold with their lamps clearing out the rats and cockroaches, I was heading to the mountains to look for curable plants! Lord, you are watching me.

'If you happen to see a cat, catch it, Ishmael! Bring her on board!' Moses had shouted after me as I stepped from the deck. 'We cannot let the rats run the ship!'

The cook was going crazy with the infestations on the *Nimrod*. But my mind was not on catching a stray cat. And I knew how a cat behaves. A cat did not want to jump onto anyone's lap unless she was an overfed house cat that would never chase a mouse, never mind kill a rat. I was a stray cat, but I had been un-strayed for a while, I thought, thanks to the *Nimrod*. The sea had adopted me. But now what? Was I to be forced to be a stray animal again? I could not think what tonight might bring, and how I should react if Mr Flaherty climbed into my hammock.

Huge ferns and mountain cypresses grew on the hills of this majestic foreign land. The wind was strong, and seemed to come from every direction as I climbed. The sea below churned and beat against the jagged and dangerous cliffs. This was an alien landscape for me, not gentle and not tamed, but beautiful and powerful all the same. I saw some plants that I recognised: pink sugar bush, flowered lilies, a strange-looking fig tree with spiky fruit. I also saw blooming heath and milkwood. But I could not use them, neither their leaves nor their roots. I did not have enough knowledge about these plants. Besides, my mind was not on collecting the plants.

I met a few locals on the hills. Their dark skin shone under the scorching sun. One of them carried a large basket on her head. As they got closer to me, I saw a mother with three children. The mother wore a colourful robe and a gold-coloured headdress. The children were completely naked. When the woman saw me, she took down the basket from her head and showed me oranges, plums and some milkwood fruit. I guessed that they were going down to the harbour to sell the fruits, or to exchange them for other products. Neither of us understanding the other's language, I was not sure what to do with her. The mother picked up a small orange-like fruit and handed it to me. It was larger than a gooseberry, yellow-skinned and delicate. I bit into the fruit, and a sudden gush of sweet sour juice flooded my mouth. My tongue was shocked by the acidity and the intense flavour. What kind of citrus was this? After so many months on the sea, my taste buds had forgotten the sensation of sun-kissed fruit. What else had I been missing in this sea life?

Before we parted, the mother grasped a handful of the citrus fruits and handed them to me. She smiled warmly, her teeth a vibrant white against her dark skin. Off they went, the children turning back as they walked to look at me. They spoke and giggled. What made them laugh? They must have thought that today they met a dishevelled white seaman in scruffy dirty clothes and there was no joy on his face. As I continued my climb up the hill, sticky juice flowing over my hand, I opened my palm. The four fruits were tiny and fresh, each of them with intense wrinkled yellow skin. They belonged to Ishmaelle's herbarium, though it was not for any illness. It was for my soul. My soul had forgotten the spirit of the land and, perhaps, the spirit of a woman. What was a woman in me, apart from my hole? My missing part? When I saw that African mother with her children, I felt something so dear and so warm. Something melted in me, something spoke to my soul, something soothed my pain. I could not describe what it was. It was about her smile, her white teeth, her colourful robe, her golden headdress, the handful of small berries she gave to me, and finally, the absolute safety she emitted in front of me. Yes, the safety and peace between us two women, without any need for words or translations.

IV

ALONE AGAIN, wandering over the hilltop, I collected a few plants, even though I was not entirely sure of their usage. I thought I ought soon to return to the ship, before the mates began to inspect everyone's work. On the way to the harbour, to my surprise, I encountered a black cat, crouching in the middle of the road. A stray, lean and small. As if she had been waiting there for me all this time. The path was overgrown with bushes, but I could somehow smell her. On the stony path, she stared at me with her almost frightful white eyes, her black tail straightened up behind her. An imp-like creature. She did not move away as I walked carefully towards her. I did not have any food with me, and I was certain she would not let me pick her up, so I decided to pass her by. As soon as I got to the harbour, I went to look for dead fish. I picked some up and put them in my canvas bag. I returned to the path where the cat was. At first I did not see her, then perhaps the smell of the fish lured her back. Out of nowhere, the black creature appeared again from the bush. I threw a small fish to her, and watched her swallow it. Then I walked away and threw another fish to her behind me. I kept walking down to the harbour as she followed me and the bag of fish I had.

Half an hour later, the cat was aboard the *Nimrod*. When Moses saw her, he was very glad.

'Ishmael, you are more useful than most of the lads I know around the galley!'

I told Moses that I would call the cat Gladys, after my great-aunt.

'Ah, was Aunt Gladys a good woman?'

'Yes she was. She taught me about herbs and medicines,' I said, and let the cat roam on the deck.

But now I discovered that the mates had ordered everyone to bathe because we had got fresh water from the harbour. All of us had to wash before the ship left the harbour again. Some used a tub on the deck, others stood and poured the water over themselves from a small barrel. A few of them were completely naked. I saw Mr Flaherty among them. Our gazes met. I immediately found an excuse and went to Mr Hawthorne's cabin to show him the herbs I had collected.

Night came. And I waited.

V

SLEEPING IN A HAMMOCK in the harbour was very different from when we were on open seas. There were barely waves or wind. The snoring from the forecastle was louder than usual in this gentle soundscape. But I was in such a state that I felt almost feverish. I was waiting in agony for the intrusion of Mr Flaherty.

In the midst of my sleepless torment in the dark, the cursed man came. I knew the way he breathed, the way he searched my loins through my tight trousers, and the way he fumbled with his cock. But this time, I had the knife ready in my hand – I had held it for hours before he came to me. I was waiting in my hammock prison, my palms drenched with my sweat and the handle of the knife wet in my tight grip. I felt his heavy body crush me. As soon as Mr Flaherty's hand reached my loins, I brought out the knife, but at that moment the hammock swung violently and my hand and the knife became entangled in its ropes. I struggled to extricate my hand, but he pressed me so hard that I screamed out. Suddenly, the knife dropped onto the wooden boards. Lord! With all my might I pushed him away from me, the hammock tipped over and we both fell to the deck, me on top of him. In the confusion, I found the knife and grabbed it instantly.

Holding the knife towards Mr Flaherty's face I hissed, 'Do not touch me again. You will have this if you do!'

Flaherty froze. The struggle had woken some of the sailors. A man – Owen – rose up from his blanket and murmured, 'What the hell is going on?'

Then another man near us raised his head. It was Antonio.

Antonio and Owen were sitting up and staring at us in the darkness. I had no sense of what I should do next. Suddenly Mr Flaherty lunged at me and tried to take away my knife. We fought over it in the black of night, but before I knew it, many arms were pulling both of us away from one another. The knife fell to the deck again. By now almost half of the men were awake and observing the commotion we had caused. Some of them came over holding lamps.

'It is no fault of mine.' Mr Flaherty's face was red and his veins were bulging as he defended himself. 'She is no man! She is a woman!'

Everyone stared at me. My trousers were half down, and my jacket was open as the buttons had been ripped off by Mr Flaherty in the struggle. Owen released his grip on me so I could arrange my attire anew.

'This is a woman! Put your hand there and look for yourself!'

'What are you talking about?' Antonio cried.

The cursed brute repeated with a raised voice, 'She is a woman! She deceived us, all of us!'

Some were dumbfounded, others were outraged. Before any of them could reach me, I ran, as fast as I could, to escape the poison of their eyes. I fled to the deck above.

VI

AS THE DAWN BROKE, so did the lie and the truth. Everyone was on deck. My fate had come, the Lord had made the decision. Drake ordered Flaherty and me to report to the captain's cabin. All three mates were present. We were to make clear our involvement in the incident. There was nothing much to say on my part, once I confessed that I had been a woman all along. This led to further enquiries about who I was and where I originally came from. I told them my name was Ishmaelle – not so different from the one I'd adopted. And I told them I was from Saxonham in England, which they knew long ago.

Seneca sat at the rear of the cabin, with a sea chart spread out in front of him, listening to my confession. I told the officers what Mr Flaherty did to me, and how many nights he came. Drake, Freedman and Jacques were in disbelief the whole time, but Seneca remained impassive. Mr Flaherty did not deny anything, all he said was: 'What would you do if you found a lad at night with breasts and her lady Jane down there?'

As he said this, Seneca's eyes were looking through the porthole at the waves. There was a moment of icy silence. Everyone waited for Seneca's judgement. Finally, Seneca turned his eyes from the waves and stared with baleful intensity at Flaherty, emitting a barely audible hiss:

'Put him in irons!'

Mr Flaherty blanched and then began to tremble. Drake looked at Seneca with utter disbelief. Freedman gaped at Flaherty then at me. Then Seneca ordered Freedman and Jacques with a solemn tone to take Flaherty out right away and put him in the brig. He then turned to me, and bade me remain in the cabin.

Now I was alone with Seneca and Drake. Drake asked me if I realised that a woman disguising herself as a sailor would have to be sent back to the United States to be put on trial. I kept silent, my trembling hands thrust deep in the pockets of my trousers as if to conceal my fear. My fingers found my seahorse idol. In that suffocating silence, I realised that my seahorse lady had broken in two, no doubt from the fight below with the steward. I dared not move my hands. I dared not look at the captain and the mate. I did not see how I could argue against this fate. A terrible fate.

All of a sudden, Seneca said:

'Drake, and you, you will wait for my judgement!'

We were told to leave. In our stead, the Chinese monk Muzi was invited in. He came with his book and his sticks. I caught sight of the book cover. It was a drawing of a cosmos with lines and dots.

We waited outside the captain's cabin. We could not know what was happening inside but we could hear the sticks being thrown on the table. Then the sound of the sticks being placed, picked up and rearranged. The seamen on deck were quiet. Freedman and Jacques returned sombrely. I was unable to think or feel. I was unable to look at the mates for the deep shame I had suffered, but more

259

pressingly, the frightful consequences I would have to face once the verdict was rendered.

After what seemed like half a lifetime, we were called back into the cabin. There, the cosmic book was lying open on the table. The sticks were neatly stacked beside the book. Muzi and Seneca were sitting up straight, their eyes resting on the page where the strange lines and the Chinese characters were written.

'Would the captain tell us, please, what should be done?' Drake asked, standing like a harpoon.

'Nothing will change.' Seneca spoke in his low, heavy voice.

'Nothing?' Drake looked incredulously at the captain. 'Nothing, sir?!'

Seneca barely looked at him, and as if speaking from some oracular depth, spoke again, almost intoning a prayer.

'Nothing will change. We proceed as before!'

Seneca then looked at me, and then at the Chinese monk. I too could not understand what I was hearing. We all looked at the cosmic chart, the sticks, and again at Muzi, whose quiet countenance remained aloof and unperturbed.

'There is more here than mere human affairs,' the captain pronounced. 'We shall not deviate from our single purpose. The way of things is written into the course of the world. That course, that way, has been revealed. As I have said, we go on as before, nothing changes!'

'Sir, we are a Christian boat. We are men of the Christian faith. We are not to consort with dark spirits or the ways of heathens!' Drake ejaculated, almost in a fever.

At that moment the Chinese monk moved to the chart table, and folded the cosmic book. Now the back page revealed an ornate symbol of interlacing shades and colours.

The monk turned to Drake.

'The I Ching has made its judgement. It is not the work of dark spirits,' the Taoist said quietly. 'It is the way.'

'The I Ching?' Jacques repeated without comprehension, his brow about to break out in sweat, his eyes glittering. 'The I goddamn Ching, on this Christian boat?!'

'What do you know of God?' the captain said, with barely suppressed rage suffusing his now grim visage. 'What do you know of Christian faith, Jacques? Only the prating nonsense of the Sunday school, I'll wager, an addled preacher with wine-stained apparel, filling your empty head with the tired and useless phrases for children and imbeciles! You will not lecture me on Christian ships and Christian men. We are not only Christian men here. We are not sheep and timid cattle, to be led by the nose, with fairy tales of sin and redemption. We are beyond that. We are here for one thing only. And I will use any means to guide us to that purpose. If it is the I Ching, it's the I Ching!'

Jacques's face had turned pale. Silence reigned. The boards creaked and the wind softly moaned.

'Aye, mates! She can be kept on board,' Seneca resumed. 'There is no harm, and no importance. Nothing shall be changed, and we don't want to disturb the white devil!

Now get the men on the mast and watch out with eyes wide open! We are in the line of the white whale!'

I was in disbelief, and did not entirely comprehend what he meant. Then the Chinese monk folded his arms and, without looking at us, said:

'Heaven and earth should remain as it is. Women and men should remain on board till the China Sea. No penance should be done. Such is the way.'

Pondering these enigmatic words, we were abruptly dismissed from the cabin. Out on the deck, Drake told me that they would move my sleeping place to a different part of the ship. Instead of sleeping among the sailors in the forecastle, I would sleep between Muzi's bunk and the officers' cabin. Amid the turmoil of my heart, I felt buoyed up. All was not lost. But the future was not clear.

VII

Under the mainmast, Muzi's thoughts.

上起
Like bamboo shadows under the moonlight the shadow is
colder than the night and to tell the difference between the
shadow and light one shall look at the movement of things
as there is neither shadow nor light if there is no movement
明月

清风
To look at the lines of the white whale's face one should
look at the pattern of his tail as the tail is the forgotten
moonlight and the thrown-away time one should decide
the age of its tail the endurance of its tail and the strength
of the tail so that one decides if the whale should be the
fate of us or not
水火

时运
To feel and to touch the wrinkles on the head of the whale
is to speak merciful things to the creature the touch is the
gesture of a man though one cannot touch the leviathan but
if one can touch it and call the time to freeze to call the

motion to stop just for that finger to point and to touch
then we will make peace
开启

命冥

One should always look into the faces of horses birds pigs
serpents chickens lizards tigers foxes monkeys hyenas and
one should always make sounds like them when their faces
move and change as if to say I am one of you and one of
the beings there and here and we are all there
龙月

田野

To judge that men and women were worthy to live is to
compare them to whales the old mammal fish have lived for
aeons of time but we men and women have only lived a
life of a grain a dragonfly a newt a gust of wind lost in
the season the mammal fish have been spouting all over
the four oceans and nine continents and playing in the
gardens of the deep so why not worship them instead of
diminishing them
明冥

死命

To kill is to say we will all leave the place together and
return to the watery grave and we will be born again as
starfish as corals as seaweeds as kelps as worms as rainbows
we want to return by perishing our beings and becoming
one being
种草

上世下世
上世下世

上世下世
上世下世
上世下世
上世下世
上世下世
上世下世
上世下世
上世下世
上世下世
上世下世
上世下世
上世下世
上世下世
上世下世
上世下世
上世下世

CHAPTER ELEVEN

Indian Ocean

I

OW THAT I WAS EXPOSED as a woman, of course things changed, despite the captain's words. In one sense I found my lost freedom; in another, new obstacles beset me. A few men on board were resentful. But I had the respect of the captain and the mates, and I had a very different relationship to the ship. Nerve-wracking moments such as washing or using the head or hiding my period were no longer so problematic. I liked my new bunk, with its makeshift curtain fashioned from sailcloth. Being placed right next to Muzi's bunk made me feel much more comfortable than the slum of hammocks I had endured for all these months. I thought I had a secret protector on the *Nimrod* (though I was not sure if this protector was Kauri or Muzi). In any case, I had never thought I would survive being discovered. Another borrowed life. Lord, how many borrowed lives would I have?

Even though I was an able seaman by now, Drake assigned me lighter work. So I did not need to heave the heavy barrels of oil up and down, like the greenhands had to do. Instead I helped the officers. I was also able to spend time with the carpenter. All this because I had proved myself useful, shown myself to be necessary among men on this ship.

I could say I knew carpenters well, though in my entire life I knew only one carpenter, my late father. But knowing one was like knowing all. Being a carpenter was a noble job. The carpenter on the *Nimrod*, Woody, shared some similarities with my father. He was practical, patient, slow and deliberate in his movements. He would not let me call him Mr Entwistle. 'Call me Woody, like everyone else would call me, lad.' Well, Mr Entwistle still treated me as a lad, as I did not have any women's clothes to wear and I looked like a perfect young lad.

Woody was efficient and always in demand: making harpoons and barrels, repairing a whaleboat, refining the shape of oars, et cetera. But even when he was busy, he liked to tell stories or make jokes. His jokes were not always funny. One morning as I was helping him, he said:

'Ishmaelle, now we know you are a woman, you should have a wardrobe. If I have some spare time I'll make one for you.'

I thanked Woody, but said I did not think I would ever need a wardrobe. Nevertheless Woody launched into one of his stories while he was hammering a nail into a plank of wood.

'This one is about a carpenter and a wardrobe,' he began. 'One day, a woman asks a carpenter to fix the wardrobe in her house, because when the train is passing by the house, the wardrobe shakes and makes a noise. When the carpenter arrives, he tells the woman: "I'll go inside the wardrobe and close the door, and when the train passes by I'll check which part of the wardrobe is causing this problem." A few minutes later the woman's husband comes home and opens the wardrobe. He sees the carpenter and says: "What the hell are you doing here?" The carpenter says: "Will you believe me if I say I'm waiting for the train?"'

I burst into laughter. I told him it was funny, and that I did not think my father could have made such a joke. My father was always serious, concentrated on his work. I even felt jealous when my old man worked, because it felt that he loved his tools and wood more than us children.

Woody shook his head.

'How can a man love his tools more than his children? It's only a job to feed his children. I make things with my hands, so I earn respect as well as bread. Life is nothing but one task after another task, lad. Fixing a man's teeth is really no different from fixing a whalebone leg. Making a mast for sails is just like making a wardrobe for a wife. It is just a task. Everything is a task. Living is a task. There is only one thing that is not a task.'

'And what is that, Woody?'

'Death. Death is not a task.'

Well, I thought he was right. Death is not a task. But that was like saying a carpenter is a carpenter, a fish is a fish, a boat is a boat. There was no need to interpret these things. But to be a whaler was different. A whaler had a mission and a desire to conquer, to kill. Life for a whaler was not about one task after another task. Life for them was a huge heroic mission involving killing or being killed. I was never sure if I was a real whaler. I did not have this desire to conquer or to kill. I did not have this unstoppable urge to chase. But I did have the desire to know about the world, and to discover. So I was neither a carpenter nor a whaler. I was not sure what I was. For the last several months, I had been a man called Ishmael, now I was a woman called Ishmaelle. Though to myself I was both.

Yes I was both, and I wondered if Kauri saw me as both? We had been close friends since New Bedford, before we found the *Nimrod*. And Kauri never questioned my gender. For him I worshipped a seahorse lady idol like he worshipped his tree man Yojo. I also wondered if Muzi the Chinese monk saw me as both. Would his strange faith and understanding let me straddle both sides, both man and woman? Or even Captain Seneca? Did he now see me as a mix or cross-breed? At those times when I was comfortable and safe, I had little sense of having a woman's body, or being the outward shell of a man. I was simply a sailor doing all the tasks I was assigned. I would climb and watch and I rowed and I hunted and I ate and I rested among men, in common comradeship. But whenever I felt unsafe, I sensed the woman's body was speaking to me. I felt that I could be hurt because others did not see me as manly, ready for the rough and the hard. I could not become a brute even though I felt very much a brute when I carved the whales with a flensing pike, or gutted squid, or cut off the heads of turtles, not to mention all the fish I stabbed and killed and bashed on the deck. But who said being a brute was one of men's qualities, necessary to be a man? I felt perfectly manly when I behaved as a useful being, not tearing apart life, but simply climbing a mast. I felt in a place between both, floating between being a woman and being a man. Yes, the menstruation blood reminded me that I was a woman, but that womanly feeling was nothing when I saw the pool of a whale's blood whenever we toiled at killing and dismembering the giant mammal dying alongside our boat. Each time I saw a whale dying in its own sea of blood I felt that I was dying too. I wondered how the other seamen felt. No one talked about feelings in the midst of a slaughter or even after the killed creature was still. Feelings did not help the task, and therefore I could not be a good killer. I had chased the whales, plunging my oar into a surge, as we skimmed across the sea, but I had never thrown a spear or a harpoon onto any creature striving to escape its pursuers. I was not made of the right stuff to be a harpooner for sure, I knew I could not kill with that lightning strike of clear decision that the true killer must have. And did that mean that I, Ishmaelle or Ishmael, was not a man, a proper seaman, an able whaler? So was I just a woman, even though I could kill if I had to?

Often, when my mind wandered, I thought of the African woman I had met on the hills in the Cape of Good Hope. I thought of the way she smiled, the way she brought down her basket and showed me the golden-coloured citrus fruits inside, the way her small naked children stared at me and the way she gave me a handful of her produce. I still kept the fruit in my canvas bag, though they were all dried up like little stones, like shrunken infant heads. I did not show them to Mr Hawthorne, even though the surgeon might have been able to tell me the name of those citruses. They were like secrets of womanhood, of my unspoken bond between me and that woman. Another woman. That encounter had been safe and peaceful, on that hill, above the Cape. Like the way I had encountered the stray cat, Gladys. She decided that I was safe to her, so she followed me all the way to the harbour. She trusted me. Since then Gladys had lived on this ship, though I hardly saw her.

273

Occasionally I glimpsed a black tail disappearing below the deck, and we did see the half-eaten corpses of rats and mice here and there every few days. She was a good one, my Gladys. But she could only be good if she could feel safe, in her own place.

II

EVEN THOUGH THE CAPTAIN and his adviser Muzi allowed me to stay on board as a woman, and even though the mates were not unkind to me after discovering my identity, some men despised my presence. Under the influence of Mr Flaherty, a rigger named Jake had become hostile to me. Sometimes Jake made cruel jokes, and sniggered under his breath. 'Ishmaelle, I noticed my beef tasted a little strange. You haven't been handling it with your bloody fingers, by any chance? I know you are using your rags at the moment.' Or, 'Only a woman would eat that pickled cabbage because you are used to the smell of a woman's privates!' All I could do was swallow his talk. I could not complain. We had to cohabit on the *Nimrod*, which was hard even among the men themselves.

During one dinner, Antonio eyed me and remarked:

'Ishmaelle, make sure you don't climb the mast again, or we won't get any whales! That's why we have so little oil thus far!'

Some of the men laughed, others remained indifferent. I said nothing and chewed a piece of whale steak. Often after hunting a whale we had to eat whale meat every day.

'No one thinks a woman on board will bring good luck,' Jake said. 'So you better get off at the next place we anchor, Ishmaelle!'

Taking my plate, I climbed the stairs and went out onto the open deck. There, on the starboard, under the mainmast, I sat on the deck and ate alone. The whale steak had no taste, after eating so much salted beef the last few months.

As I tossed the hard meat into the sea, Mr Hawthorne came on deck. He carried a big book, and was heading towards the chair by the after house. When he saw me, he asked in a knowing voice:

'Were the men unkind to you? Is that why you came here, to eat alone?'

I nodded.

'Oh, those young thoughtless lads.' He sighed. 'If some of them were married, and had a child, they would speak differently. They would have some sympathy for you.'

I did not say anything. The surgeon had always been kind to me, but I did not think that was only because he was married and had children. I thought his kindness was from his cultured nature and knowledge of the world and his study of science.

'You know, Ishmaelle, from the very beginning of this voyage, I had thought you might be a woman. And after a few months, I was sure that you were a woman. So when you were discovered, I was not surprised at all.'

I stared at him. 'How did you know?'

'Well, I noticed you never washed with anybody. Maybe that's not such a big thing, but you never showed evidence of a beard at all – every man on board needs to shave but not you. I know you are young, but still. I also noticed that every month for a couple of days you seemed unwell. You looked pale and you ate mint powder, just like my wife Henrietta does.'

'So you already knew . . . yet you kept it to yourself,' I mumbled, feeling ashamed.

'Well, it is not for me to decide if you should be on board or not. For me, you are as fit and skilled as any sailor on the *Nimrod*, and that's the most important thing.' He smiled. 'Remember we talked about Linnaeus – the Swedish botanist, how he divided up the species?'

'Yes, of course.'

'Well, you are like a species in disguise! Even he would have a hard time defining you!'

We both laughed. But somehow my laugh felt sad, and sorrowful. I fell silent. Something was stuck in my throat, and I felt a prickling wetness in my eyes. I turned away to the sea.

'But it is a strange thing for a physician to say this: I noticed that you are a woman not so much because of any physical difference that marked you, rather it was the way that, occasionally, you would look at men, and at me. It is hard to describe that look, but it reminded me of how my wife looked at men.'

I turned back to him. I could not know how I looked at them – the men on this ship. All I knew was that I looked up to Mr Hawthorne. I admired him. If Kauri was my wordless spiritual friend, then Mr Hawthorne was my fatherly friend. I needed both. Without them, my life on this sea would have been unbearable.

At that moment, the mention of his wife reminded me of the letter I had read in the surgeon's cabin. The letter written to 'Dearest Henrietta'. That phrase was lodged in my mind. Even though I felt my question might be unwelcome, I asked:

'Mr Hawthorne, your wife, what is she like?'

'Oh, my wife . . . Henrietta.' He paused. Then he said quietly: 'She passed away some years ago.'

The silence that followed was punctuated only by the sound of my breathing as an image of 'Henrietta' formed suddenly in my imagination, alive with all the vivacity that I had given her. She could not be dead! How was that possible? I hesitated for a moment, then I had to confess to him:

'Forgive me, but the other day when you asked me to fetch medicine for Loick, I caught sight of your letter, and I saw it was addressed to Henrietta . . .'

Glancing at me, Mr Hawthorne looked surprised. He frowned a little. Was he angry, or was he perhaps relieved that I had seen his letter? I did not know.

'She died in childbirth. I may be a good surgeon, but I could not save my wife.'

Oh, poor Mr Hawthorne! That was pitiful. How I sympathised with him!

'I am sorry to hear it, Mr Hawthorne. Please forgive my prying.'

'No need to apologise to me, Ishmaelle. I don't cling to any privacy.'

'May I ask about your child, sir?'

'The child died with the mother. They share a grave in New England. Since their deaths I have learned what grief is, but somehow I have moved beyond it. Still, the memory of my wife remains dear to me. I know she is dead, but her presence continues by my side. When I visit her grave, I talk to her. I touch the tombstone, tend to the plants that now grow there.'

He fell silent. We stared at the white froth on the waves rushing against the starboard. It was misty. I wondered about his communications with the dead. I knew the letter he wrote to his wife was very recent, and the fact that he continued to write letters to her was beyond sorrow, and beyond my understanding. How could I comprehend this bond, this longing between men and women that survives death? I missed my brother Joseph, but I did not feel this immense yearning which entangled Mr Hawthorne and his dead wife. I missed Captain Mackay for a time, but no longer. He died before I could learn more about him and his life. I could not imagine writing a letter to the dead captain. But writing to the dead is not so different from speaking to them, perhaps. I occasionally thought of my father, and spoke to him. And sometimes I would dream of the dead, and the dead would speak to me.

As the dusk descended, I watched Mr Hawthorne leaving me, returning to his cabin. His footsteps were heavy and his clothes were no longer neat and fine as they used to be at the beginning of our voyage. Now he wore a loose-fitting sailor's shirt, stained with red-brown spots. The heels of his shoes were worn thin. I felt desolate. Hawthorne's story seemed again to prove that womanhood was a misadventure, a tragedy from beginning to end. Perhaps that's what I had tried to change, by disguising myself before coming on board. And now that I had returned to being a woman, I could no longer hide away from womanliness. But the last resort for me, perhaps, to avoid womanhood, was never to get pregnant. Never to give birth. I remember that Gladys had a knitted octopus made from red wool. She told me that a female octopus only mated once. When she began to produce eggs, that was the beginning of her death. The mother octopus would find a hiding place in the depths of the ocean and would lay her eggs, thousands of them. She would stay in that hiding place and mind her eggs, fighting any predators. During the hatching, she would stop eating; a few months later, she would die. When Gladys said this, she twisted her woollen octopus, distorting those arms into a tangled mess, as if to show me the last look of a dying mother octopus. I was very young, perhaps only six or seven. I had never thought a mother might die in the same way as an octopus. But now, many years later, this memory suddenly resurfaced upon hearing the story of Mr Hawthorne's wife, and it made me dread to think of being a mother. Never, Ishmaelle. I would rather die young, die unmarried, than be a wife, a mother, a devoted dying octopus.

III

I T WAS AUTUMN, but the weather in the Indian Ocean was very warm. The sky had been perpetually blue and calm for weeks, until a sudden rainstorm fell last night. In the morning, our chef Moses went down to the main hold to fetch a bag of flour, and almost slipped on some oil leaking on the wooden boards. So he sent little Dilly up to tell Drake. Drake went down to the hold with a few of us. We discovered a mess there, as the whale oil had leaked from the casks.

Drake instantly went to the quarterdeck. Seneca was by his window watching the weather.

'We have to stop the ship, Captain. All hands must go down to the hold, and bring up all the oil casks so we can check each of them and repair the cracked ones.'

'What a thought! Now that we are in the middle of the India Sea, we have to halt to tinker with some old hoops?'

'Either do that, sir, or waste in one day more oil than we may make good in a year. What we came a thousand miles to get is worth saving, sir.'

'So it is, if we get it!' Seneca seemed to have already moved on.

'I was speaking of the oil in the hold, sir.'

'And I was not thinking of that at all. Begone! Let it leak! What are you worrying about, Mr Drake? The *Nimrod* is not only full of leaky casks, but those leaky casks are in a leaky ship with a leaky captain, and that's a far worse plight!'

'But what will the owners in New Bedford say, sir?'

'Let the owners stand on Nantucket beach and curse the storms! Who cares about the owners? You are always prating to me, Drake, about those miserly owners, as if the owners were my conscience.'

Drake went quiet. This was a mad speech – even I knew it would be unacceptable to every crew member on board.

'But, Captain, all men here are slaves to the oil! It is the very reason, the *only* reason, they are on board the *Nimrod*. How can they return home without all the barrels filled?'

'What small thoughts! You speak to me of home, of money! You know what a home is for me, eh, Mr Drake? Home for me is a stagnant pool, a dead pond! After my father died and my mother left, I was given a bed and meals by Mrs Eldredge. Then I was sent to sea at the age of twelve. I caught my first whale when I was seventeen. I sailed all over the world without a thought of home! You know I have no home, I am an orphan! I thank the Lord I was homeless! Here is my home! This ceaseless sway and swing! This spirited water! I sailed for thirty years until the white devil took my leg! So, without my leg, I went back to the land and I made myself a home. A home! A home with a woman! Lord, that was the most spiritless thing for a seaman to bear! A home, with a stupid roof, a coffin wardrobe and a dusty rug. Without the scorching sun, without a crescent moon, without waves, without storms – all I had were the lit lamps and a woman's pregnant stomach! What does a home hold for me?

Nothing, Drake, nothing! Home is a slow-burning hell. And I had money, from years of seafaring! But what is money for? For trivialities, for a bread softer and less mouldy? Does a man have to eat softer bread? Does a man need a rug underneath his feet? I'd rather have no money, no home and be hanged under this mast! Be hanged along these sails! Be hanged by the bow! Be hanged by the yardarm under this scorching sun! Listen, I am not getting all the hands on board to fix the casks for money or for a home, Mr Drake!'

Freedman and Jacques stood stiffly by, their eyes fixed downwards. Neither of them dared to challenge their captain.

'I understand you, sir,' Drake said in a muffled voice, as though suppressing his anger. 'But shall we not understand each other better than hitherto, Captain Seneca?'

Abruptly, Seneca turned and seized a musket from the rack. He raised the musket and pointed it towards Drake.

'Understand better? What for? There is only one captain, one lord of the *Nimrod*!'

Everyone froze. I had never seen such rage from Seneca. For an instant, seeing a flash in the eyes of Drake, I thought he would snatch the musket and there would be a mutiny on board. But, controlling his emotion, Drake said in a restrained tone: 'Do not insult me, sir; I am not your enemy.'

At this moment, like an invisible gust of wind, the Chinese monk was suddenly among us. Saying nothing, Muzi approached the captain and quietly took the musket from his grasp. He returned the gun to the rack. Then he was quietly gone, back to his work repairing a sail.

Captain Seneca, his rage subsiding, turned gloomy.

'Drake, you are a good fellow,' he said. Then to the

mates: 'Bring up the casks in the main hold. Sail on.' With that, he disappeared into his cabin.

The mates looked at one another, saying nothing. I wondered if the captain's talk about home and his wife's pregnant stomach reminded Freedman of his own happy family. Drake too? We knew that Drake had seven daughters in New Bedford. He owned a great house surrounded by land, and he would never, ever speak about home and wife in such a dreadful way. But I felt pity for Seneca. How familiar those images were to me – a woman with a swollen stomach, a burning lamp under a dark roof, a dirty rug. How much this reminded me of my mother, my little sister, and my Saxonham. I felt I understood the captain, even though he was so devilish. But are we not all wounded and damaged, and either we were devils ourselves or fighting with the devil?

For Drake's part, he followed the captain's orders. All the oil casks were brought up on the deck for inspection. But we sailed on.

IV

THE DECK WAS FULL WITH OIL BARRELS. After searching, it was found that the casks last struck into the hold were perfectly sound, and that the leak must be deeper in. We again went down to the dark hold, heaving out the oldest casks from the bottom of the ship. That was a huge effort, and I was not spared for the labour. Our mates and the carpenter Woody carefully inspected a few mouldy casks, and discovered that at least four of the barrels were leaking. So now the carpenter and the cooper needed to repair them.

But all this time Kauri was seized with a fever. He lay in his bunk, but he was burning and Mr Hawthorne decided to bring him up on the deck. He said the fresh wind might lower his temperature. My poor friend, he did not look good. A week before, he hunted two whales with Drake, and during that day-long hunt he spent many hours in the water. Though everyone admitted Kauri was the best harpooner and one of the strongest on the *Nimrod*, he was exhausted.

We made a special den with cloth and canvas for Kauri to lie in the stern. But he was sweating even on the open deck and at the same time he was shivering. Our medicine cabinet did not have many resources. The surgeon gave

Kauri some opium; he took it and went quiet for a while, but it did not seem to bring his fever down. We used to keep willow-bark syrup for dealing with fever, but Dilly had drunk it all in the last few days as he too was ill. On my part, the herb medicine I kept was not useful for Kauri. All I could do was to wet Kauri's arms and forehead with cotton. His lips had turned white, with a cluster of salt at the corner of his mouth. His tattooed arms were burning dry, as if the skin would burst and peel off from his flesh. His eyes were glazing and he began to speak a language no one understood.

'Et t ni ya no ta no ti . . . ge he yop li hup ia . . .' Kauri murmured deliriously. 'Ni hy ni ta wo yk wy ka ka ti ri bi bi ye ja . . .'

The night was passing. No wind or rain. Kauri lay in the little den on the deck, and I managed to stay a few more hours with him. Muzi was on the deck too, and when Kauri began speaking and shouting in a manic manner, Muzi came to him. He sat beside my friend, folding his two palms together, and he prayed.

Dawn arrived. Both Muzi and I went to sleep. A nightwatchman was on the mast, keeping an eye on Kauri.

As the sun rose, Mr Hawthorne said we needed to take Kauri back below to the shade as he did not seem to be improving. Kauri was half conscious, very much thinner than even a day ago. His cheekbones grew sharper, and his eyes seemed to be widening. The black eyes looked out at us and tried to say something but he was unable to speak his words.

Later, Kauri managed to make himself clear, in simple English. He said he wanted to speak to our carpenter, so I went to fetch Woody.

Kauri's English was slightly confusing for Woody, but

with my help we understood that he wanted him to make a special canoe-coffin. He said in his tribe the prince and the nobles would be placed in a canoe. Then the canoe would be sealed with the body in it and it would drift in the sea.

Our mates learned the news, and Drake came down too since his whaling boat relied on Kauri and now it seemed to be a huge problem for the next whaling task. No one questioned that Kauri would die. The carpenter set straight to his work. I told Woody that I would be his assistant since he had witnessed that I was good at shaving planks and hammering.

Handing me a rope, Woody said to me: 'Ishmael, you must measure his exact length, so we can fit him in properly.'

I took the rope, measured my poor fellow from head to toe. I did not want to think much as I stretched the rope along Kauri's burning body; it was too grave to think that the wild life this Polynesian had lived would be sealed in a canoe-coffin.

It took Woody and me most of the night and the whole next day to make the coffin. Simon the cooper came to help too. We needed to make sure it would be tightly sealed and no water could get in. We did not take a break, and all day we just shared a loaf of bread. Indeed, as Woody said, life was about one task after another. We were on the mission of finishing a task, true. But in this case, the task was for death, or the dying. Did Woody still believe that death was not a task? It seemed to me that death was a grand task, or the greatest task of all.

The lid was placed aside, and I was told by Woody to nail all the sides firmly. When the last nail was driven in, and the lid duly planed and fitted, Woody lifted the coffin and lightly pushed it forward, as if to see how it would float in the water. The men on the deck all came closer, watching the ominous new object being handled, their mouths half open. Even I, the daughter of a carpenter, had never seen the whole process of making a coffin, let alone made one with my own hands for my friend to be placed in.

'Ishmael,' Woody said – he never seemed to remember that was not my real name – 'take the brush and oil it thoroughly.'

I obeyed, and brought out the Chinese tung oil which we got from Cap de Verd. We would have to oil the wood a few times before it would finally meet the sea.

Hearing the hammering work and the talk of the men on deck, Kauri, to everyone's surprise, called out. Apparently, he wanted the coffin to be instantly brought to him. Woody was certainly displeased, as, for him, the last task was not finished and the wood must be oiled properly. But Kauri insisted, so Woody gave in and said: 'Since the poor fellow will shortly stop troubling us, I will let him be indulged.'

We brought the coffin down to Kauri's bedside. The Polynesian then called for his harpoon, as well as one of the paddles of his boat. We brought these and placed them by the side of the coffin. He also wanted a piece of sailcloth to be rolled up for a pillow.

Kauri now asked to be placed in the coffin. Little Dilly was crying as he watched. Kauri closed his eyes for a moment as he lay inside the box. He then brought out his little god Yojo from his pocket, crossing his arms on his breast with Yojo at the centre. His breath became less troubled, and his face less hot-looking. He then called for the coffin lid to be placed over him. We eyed each other, no one dared to do so. Clearly this man was still very much alive and still speaking!

Then Woody said: 'Kauri, a carpenter is only a box maker. He is not a surgeon or a murderer. I have to report to Mr Hawthorne about this.'

Woody went to see Mr Hawthorne, and returned with him a few minutes later. Hawthorne looked at Kauri in the open coffin. He touched my poor friend's forehead and felt the pulse of his wrist, then he said: 'You won't need this for now, Kauri. I am afraid you might have to wait.'

Kauri murmured something, then the surgeon gave him some water and rum. Moments later, Kauri sat up. We watched him moving his arms. He put his little god back into his pocket. He grasped his harpoon and oar. Still sitting in his coffin, he said: 'Kauri no die. Kauri hunt more whales.'

'My friend, do you think death is a matter of your own will?' Mr Hawthorne asked.

Kauri looked at him with glazed eyes.

Then Woody said: 'Listen, lad, you have more tasks to do before you die and I have too. Better you get out so I can oil your coffin!'

Kauri slowly got himself out of the wooden box. And Woody resumed the oil work.

Later, after dinner, when we were gathering on the deck for a stroll, Antonio said that Kauri would not die as he had overheard that Muzi had done the I Ching with the sticks and believed that the coffin was not useful for Kauri.

'What does that mean? Who was the coffin made for then?'

'How would I know?' Antonio looked at me blankly. 'All I heard was Muzi saying to the captain: the coffin and the harpooner will not remain together in the watery depths.'

The coffin and the harpooner will not remain together in the watery depths. How should I think of this?

After a day's rest, Kauri regained strength. In the morning we saw him sitting on the windlass vigorously chewing a piece of salty beef. On the plate, there was a greenish lump of pickled cabbage which surprised us. It seemed that he even took the surgeon's advice to eat pickled cabbage. When he saw me on the deck, he leapt to his feet, and pointed at something in the water by the bulwark.

'Turtle soup for you, turtle steak for Kauri,' he said, beaming.

I looked down at the sea. Yes, a large turtle was swimming there in the clear and green water. It seemed ready to be sacrificed, for Kauri's regained life.

V

MR HAWTHORNE INFORMED ME that Captain Seneca had been ill for several days, and that he had taken little food in that time. He recommended that we take on board as much citrus fruit as possible at the next port. He was certain that fresh fruit would be as useful as his limited medicine when it came to dealing with various sicknesses on the voyage.

'Can you help me to take care of Seneca today?' Mr Hawthorne asked me after lunch. 'And perhaps remain by his side till he sleeps? I have had little opportunity to rest since he became ill.'

'What is the nature of the captain's illness?' I enquired.

'I wish I could be certain. I had thought it to be cholera because of the pain in his stomach, but no one else on board has any similar problem. From what I have observed, it might be some ulceration of his intestinal lining. He was feverish all last night, but I hope he will recover soon, with rest and what medicine we have to offer, and without need of intervention on my part.'

The surgeon told me to fetch fresh water and the last remaining lemon peels and bring them to the captain's cabin. We'd had a basket of fresh lemons from our anchoring at Cap de Verd, and the cook had preserved the peels to use for tea and for digestive ailments. The peels were dried up like scorched earthworms, black and mouldy in parts. I gathered them up in my hands along with a jar of water.

The captain was lying on his bed, motionless and with his eyes closed, covered with a blanket. Putting the water and lemon peels on the table, I stood beside the bed and looked at him. His grey eyebrows trembled slightly. His cheekbones were protuberant. His full thick lips were dry and cracked, and a blister was forming at the left corner of his mouth. Suddenly, he opened his eyes. Startled, I began to explain myself in a shaky voice:

'Captain, the surgeon sent me to see you. How are you feeling?'

He did not respond right away. He just stared at me, as if he did not recognise me, or was perplexed by my presence. I stared back at him. I was in his private space, and never had I been so close to him. I noticed that his eyes were no longer burning with their usual intensity, but looked dim and colourless.

As though he had not heard the words I had spoken, the captain said: 'Ishmaelle, you are a woman! Tell me, won't you tell me? I implore you . . .'

I was confused. What was going on with Captain Seneca?

'You are a woman, you must know this.'

He paused for what seemed like almost a minute. I said nothing.

'When Ruth met me, she was a simple girl, and she confessed that she had never felt such affection for a man. I had never needed a home, and I had just lost my leg. So I rejected her, out of shame. But Ruth would not be dissuaded. And for that I felt grateful, and I married her.'

The captain's eyes turned towards a book beside his pillow, *Some Fruits of Solitude*. He gazed at the book for a few moments, then continued in a low and sorrowful voice:

'Never marry but for love; but see that thou lovest what is lovely.'

I sensed the captain's breath grow heavy, as he went on, and I struggled to understand.

'The day I married Ruth, I stood on my peg leg and swore I would never return to sea, and that I would share my remaining years with her. We bought a farm and built a house. She seemed to be content. But two years later, something had changed, I knew this. She went for a long walk almost every afternoon. With this ivory stump, I could not follow her. I knew she was visiting a man. I knew him, a white man. Then came the final humiliation, when the child was born . . .'

I stared at the captain.

'The child?'

'Yes, the child. The first thing I saw in that child was his blue eyes. I saw the devil in them! What a fool I was! How could I know that such loveliness as was Ruth's could deceive? My black arms reached out and took the white baby from Ruth's breast. I grimaced, and said to her: now everyone on the land knows I, Seneca, have been deceived. I am a damned black even though I was born a free man . . . You, woman, have defeated me! If it be God's will, let that child die!'

I held my breath while listening to all this, as if the air would explode if I exhaled or moved an inch.

'The child was sickly, also Ruth. And within the month, the child was in the grave.'

The captain was no longer looking at me. He seemed now to be speaking to himself.

'She betrayed me, yes, but worse, I betrayed myself before God. I made a foolish act in quitting my celibacy. I let myself be humiliated. I have no more honour, no more pride, either in body or in spirit. I am just an ivory stick on this wretched deck. I should have thrown myself straight into the whale's jaw when the devil took my leg. I should never have returned to land!'

The captain's anguished black eyes were looking down, gazing at the obscure pattern of the wood planks. Some dust danced in the faint light. The dust was like his departing spirit, rising up slowly in the air in a ghostly way.

Unable to think of anything adequate to say to the captain, I uttered lamely: 'You have been sick, sir. The surgeon says you should drink water with lemon peel.'

I put the withered lemon peel into his cup, and poured water into it.

A moment of silence passed, as I tried to comprehend his words.

'Captain, I am moved by what you have told me,' I then said. 'But it is a sin to end one's life. To give your life up to the whale is no solution. You must resist such thoughts. You cannot know what purpose lies ahead for you.'

Suddenly, as if finding his old furious self again, the captain raised himself up on his arms. As he swung round brusquely from the bed, the blanket slipped to the floor. What was revealed before my eyes was distressing, no doubt simply because it was unprecedented. The captain, upon taking to his bed, had removed his fake leg. Now, even though he wore trousers, I saw the shape of the mutilated stump. But what struck me was the void below it. In the dim light of the stuffy cabin, it was as though the missing limb still dangled within the empty linen fabric. I averted my gaze, but felt a great and inexplicable sadness in me, a wave of deep sorrow that seemed to emanate from that hollowed part of his body to my body, and to which I was unable to respond.

VI

I T WAS THE END OF SEPTEMBER, when the monsoon
season would normally recede around the Indian
Ocean. But the rainstorms persisted. We had
encountered frightful thunderstorms in the last few days.
The torrential rainfalls were blown horizontally by the
westward winds, pushing our ship towards the east and the
shore. The deck was a perpetual whirlpool, and everything
below deck was drenched. Bolts of lightning zipped across
the marble-like dark sky, as if to say 'Go home, you fools!
Return to land, fear this liquid hell!' Between the flashes
of lightning and claps of thunder, I heard Kauri praying,
Muzi as well. Perhaps every man was praying, under his
breath to his own god. I prayed to the Lord, as well as to
my seahorse lady. I wondered if the seahorse lady would
laugh at me, in her queer way. The seahorse was a creature
of the sea, she was in her element there, and knew every
shade of the ocean's terrible temper. Still, if my seahorse
could cope with nature, I should too, if I was truly blessed
by her.

We had already reefed the sails before the worst weather
arrived; still we did not act quickly enough. The main
topsail, the fore-topsail and the mizzen topgallant sail were
all torn apart. When the storm subsided and the sun

emerged at last, we had to repair them before we headed further east. A group of us was assigned to sew the sails under Muzi's direction. Beneath the burning sun all the stewards joined us for the task, since most of the sailors were out hunting whales.

I had tried to maintain some distance between myself and Mr Flaherty ever since the incident. But today, he stood right beside me working on a pile of cloth. He was holding a pair of scissors to cut out pieces of the material from a fresh roll. I was measuring lengths of calico to be stitched together. I felt a soft touch sliding along my left arm and a gentle purring sound. Then I caught a glimpse of a black tail. It was my African cat Gladys, my stray cat. Well, no longer stray since she was now the cat of the *Nimrod*, the chief rat catcher of our ship. She was sunning herself behind me and licking her paws, her tail occasionally twitching. I let her move about, and continued my work. All of a sudden, Mr Flaherty got a grip of the cat as she passed him. With a firm grasp, he struck with his scissors and cut off the poor creature's tail! There was an unholy screech, and a geyser of blood splattering the white cotton with red flecks. I leapt to my feet in horror to witness the cat streaking away across the decking. The brutish features of Flaherty were twisted into a ghoulish grin, with an eye to me, gleaming. All the sailmakers had frozen in their tasks, and watched dumbfounded.

'What have you done?' I cried out.

'Ah, nothing, my scissors caught the sail and the cat's tail!' He laughed, the half-bloodied tail still grasped in his hand, which he now flung across the deck. 'Who would have thought it had so much blood in it? Spoiled our sails!'

'You are a cruel brute, Flaherty!' said the old steward, Roberts. 'I saw what you did!'

And that was that. Someone called out 'back to work', and we set to our labours again. Moments later, when everyone was busying away, Mr Flaherty moved closer to me.

'Watch out for your tail too, woman,' he murmured, his teeth clenched.

I moved away from him. I pretended I had not heard.

Later in the evening, the surgeon reported that we should leave the cat alone without doing anything. 'She will survive with only a tail stump, poor creature, though she might not have the same balance as she had before.'

Gladys had not shown herself again, and was still hiding. She was somewhere down in the dark lower decks. All I knew was she was in pain. I tried to find her but in vain.

Later, all the boats had returned. Each boat had caught one whale. This was our greatest success since we had caught three after leaving Cap de Verd. Drake said everyone would be given an extra ration of rum tonight. And the chef was told to add more meat for the officers and the harpooners as a reward.

VII

THE EVENING WENT ON infused with plenty of rum. Freedman played an old ballad with his fiddle. It was a song called 'Springfield Mountain', about a young man's death by snakebite in Massachusetts.

He took the serpent all in his hand,
and he quickly went to Molly Bland.
Oh, Molly, Molly, oh don't you see,
that wicked serpent bit me . . .

Jacques sang along to the slightly discordant tune. As usual, he drank too fast and too much. His cauliflower ear was reddening as his voice grew in volume. I drank some rum and ate the boiled potatoes, but I had no appetite. Across the deck, I watched Mr Flaherty drinking and talking loudly to the men. He did not feel any remorse. What would he do next? Watch out for your tail too, he had said. What was he going to do with me? Seek revenge for his three days in irons? He had not been punished severely, nor had he been ostracised by the other men. But his resentment must be brewing.

With a lit candle, I went down to the hold. I was worried about Gladys, but I could not see her or hear her. So I went up to the officers' sleeping quarters, thinking the cat might be hiding there. There was no one in the quarters apart from Kauri. He was doing his ritual alone by his canoe-coffin. The coffin was now his bed. He had arranged things as if he were living on a tiny island of his own. I watched him praying to his diminutive idol Yojo, but I did not want to disturb him. As I turned back with my candle, Kauri stopped praying, and said in his familiar compressed English:

'Cat Kauri saw. Cat hurt.'

I looked around, but I could not see her.

I came back to the deck, and most of the men were on the verge of total drunkenness. Almost everyone was there, even little Dilly, though as usual the Chinese monk and our captain were not among the group of carousers.

'Don't drink so much, Mr Flaherty,' said Drake, even though the first mate himself was holding a full beaker of grog.

'Why not? Why can't a man, a real one, get drunk when he wants?' Mr Flaherty gulped down more rum. 'We will either perish from chasing whales, or die from eating each other! Have you not heard of the wreck of the *Essex*?'

'Who could not know about the tragedy of that whaler?' Drake was visibly saddened, and his voice had become subdued.

'Well, then! It won't be the only whaler to suffer such a dire fate! On every Lord's day at least three ships are wrecked at sea! Ahoy, when will our day come, Drake? Maybe our captain knows, or his Chinese brain knows! Go and ask him, will you?'

'The men on the *Essex* died not because of shipwreck!' Freedman chimed in, also quite drunk, though he tried to hold himself straight. 'It was because they made the wrong decision when they got in the three small boats! They sailed to the wrong destination!'

'That was the quarrel between the captain and the first mate!' Mr Flaherty cried out. He turned so that he was face-to-face with our chief mate, as if challenging him. 'What do you think, Drake? If you had been on that damned ship, what would you have done, eh?'

Everyone fell silent. As seamen of the *Nimrod*, we all knew the disagreement between Drake and Captain Seneca about the purpose of this voyage, and what it might lead to if things got worse. As for the *Essex*, we were superstitious and avoided all mention of it on board. The infamous whaling ship left Nantucket in 1819, but her fate was doomed by a sperm whale a year later. The ship sank and the men had to save themselves in the three small whaling boats, in the midst of the ocean. The captain wanted to set out for the Marquesas Islands, 1,200 miles away, but the chief mate feared the islands might be inhabited by canni-bals. So he took two boats and headed towards the coastline of South America, but it was much further away. Slowly they began to starve on the ocean and eventually they had to eat each other. Avoiding the cannibalism they so feared, they had to commit it themselves.

'Devil got them,' Antonio mumbled. His eyes were wet, and he could hardly speak after so much rum.

'The chief mate survived,' Drake said. 'The chief mate returned home a year and a half later, and learned he had a fourteen-month-old daughter. Because of the trauma, sometimes he could not speak to anyone for days on end.'

Drake put down his cup, signalling that the day should draw to a close. I watched as he and Freedman went down to their quarters. The sky was dark. No moon at all. A storm was threatening.

301

Since Drake and Freedman had left, now the third mate Jacques raised his cup:

'Ahoy, let's finish this and go to sleep. Men cannot hang on to such sad tales!'

Most of the men drained their cups and silently left the deck. But Mr Flaherty remained, though he could hardly walk straight. Trying to steady himself, he took out his cursed member and attempted to piss into the water, not with great success. It was time for me to leave too. As I turned, I saw Kauri at the other end of the deck, a still and strange shadow. What was he doing? Since Kauri drank no rum, it was odd that he should be on the deck at this late hour, especially since I thought he had been praying. Perhaps he wanted to smoke his pipe before he went to sleep. I said nothing, and crept down to my bed.

The night was drenched by rains. Thunder roared and a fierce swell shook the boat. Next morning all was calm, though the deck was wet and slippery. The rum beakers lay strewn around along with a few scattered plates. We cleaned the deck of vomit, and other products of men's drunkenness. But when Captain Seneca called for Mr Flaherty to deliver his breakfast, no answer came. At that moment, no one took much notice of the fact that Mr Flaherty was nowhere visible on the ship. Only later, just before lunch, did we think something was awry. We began to search for the man.

What had happened in the night? The last time I had seen the brute was when he was trying to relieve himself, his bare member dangling across the gunwales. The only other presence on deck had been Kauri.

In the course of the day, everyone was speculating on the missing steward. Flaherty had been drunk and so he must have fallen overboard and drowned. The storm must have claimed him when a wave swept across the deck.

Kauri was smoking by the brick furnace. He made no pronouncement. I looked at him. He looked at me. As he held my gaze, he gave the subtlest of nods, which only I could have read. Then he looked away, and out over the sea.

VIII

TWO DAYS AFTER THE 'DISAPPEARANCE' of Mr Flaherty, during the evening break after supper, I caught a moment when Kauri was alone by the bow. He was in the midst of carving a turtle shell. I sat down next to him, observing his carving. There seemed to be a half-sculpted volcano on the shell.

'Smoke . . .' Kauri said.

I nodded, though I was not sure if he meant the volcano he carved would be smoking, or he wanted to have a smoke. Then he put down the turtle shell and knife, took out his pipe from his pocket and lit it.

We took turns puffing on his pipe, not talking much. It was like the old days. Why did I say 'the old days'? It was only nine months ago when we met in New Bedford, when we had shared the same bed at an inn, but it felt like such a long time ago, a half-century into the past. I was not the same Ishmaelle now as the one then. That one would not recognise the seasoned sailor who now sat on the deck. I wondered what Kauri thought of my transformation, if he noticed it at all.

'You . . . Mr Flaherty . . .?' I said, in a hushed tone, turning round quickly to check if anyone was near us.

Kauri stared at the setting sun on the distant waves.

'He no good. He dead an evil death.'

The tattoo on his brown skin shimmered in the dusk light – those shapes of tree branches had always been mysterious to me. Kauri the tall tree, Kauri the deer, Kauri the island prince. And Kauri the silent killer.

I thought that was all he wanted to say, but after a few more puffs of smoke, Kauri said in his typical way of self-made English:

'Kauri know Ishmaelle hard life. Life hard on water. On my island a bad man is punished. We take his head and cut him open and take the eyeballs and get chicken to eat eyeballs and we hang bad man under Kauri tree.'

I was startled to hear this, and was prepared to hear more gruesome details about how Kauri's people would punish a bad person. But Kauri said no more. He picked up his turtle shell and knife and began carving again. A melody drifted into our ears. By the after house, Freedman had begun his evening fiddle session, and this time I could make out the song. It was one he played every now and then – 'Follow the Drinking Gourd'. This time Moses and little Dilly sang along with him:

Follow the drinking gourd
for the old man is awaiting for
to carry you to freedom
if you follow the drinking gourd . . .

CHAPTER TWELVE

Java and South China Sea

I

Ishmaelle's dream.

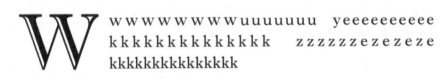

W wwwwwwwwuuuuuuu yeeeeeeeee
kkkkkkkkkkkkkk zzzzzzezezeze
kkkkkkkkkkkkkkk

First I hear the faint whistles then clicks far below me kkkkkkkkkkkkkkk ze ze ze ze ze ze ze ze kkkkkkkkkkkkkkkkkkkk the clicks become clearer and clearer the whistles fainter and fainter so I swim towards the clicking sound there must be a sperm whale there or a killer whale but I cannot see anything as I dive further and deeper all I see are slow-swaying kelps and tropical fish and corals red and green and orange those corals they are like mini mountains and cliffs overhanging the sea in my Saxonham

As I dive deeper I hear the click sounds more and more frequently with a kind of bursting pulse I feel that something is going on something is urgent and there is a calling from the whale and there is a communication between me and the whale so I swim towards the invisible whale who is calling out its song yes I am sure the whale is trying to speak to me then I hear the sound moving upwards this must be the whale going up to breathe yes it needs air it has lungs it is just like we humans and it has to go vertically up and up and up above the water to respire

Yeyeeeee kkkkkkkkkkkk zzzzzeeeeee kkkkkkkkkkkkkkk now the intervals between clicks from the whale become shorter and louder the whale sends the signal more and more rapidly and I sense that the creature must be near me and I should be careful as I also try to go up to the surface of the water perhaps the whale needs me otherwise why this urgent clicks louder and louder and as I swim further up I see a giant whale with a huge belly and humped back and it swims vertically yes it swims upwards

Then I realise it must be a mother whale delivering her baby Lord how did I know that and I think I have understood the clicks and the whistles those special sounds are definitely a mother whale trying to give birth

I have never been a mother but I saw my own mother giving birth to our baby sister and it is a wretched business it is beyond pain even though I was only watching the whole scene through our dirty windowpane but I could see my mother lying there in her blood what a torture perhaps the whale's birth is not much different from my mother's birth and from us humans we women have to have the baby in the right position in our womb and the baby has to be head out first into the world otherwise the delivery will be dangerous both for the mother and the baby I now understand that the rapid clicking sound means danger it asks for help but what can I do I am only a human I am neither a fish nor whale let alone a sea midwife

I see the giant mammal now giving birth to her child and I see the whale turning its enormous body perhaps she is in pain and suffering and I see blood around her and gradually I see a tail coming out from the mother more and more tail part being pushed out and more and more and more and more and more and more blood and I see the whole tail is out then I see the fins are out and more and more body parts are pushed out and I see the head and the head is huge even though it is a baby whale and slowly I see the baby is out and out and out

Oh that tail makes the first splash and the second splash in this watery world and the child whale is born the baby whale is there in the world have I done something or have I just been a witness for that birth or I did something without knowing what I have done

I then see the mother whale swimming around her baby and she squirts the milk into the mouth of the calf the white milk must be from her glands for nursing calves and the milk looks very thick like liquid silver it looks like the fat and the blubber oil we seamen have hunted all these months the rich oil the fat milk then the baby whale gulps down the fluid and then sucks more flowing milk from her mother through the blue water lord this is magical

Now the mother whale pushes the baby whale's fins and head towards the surface and she nudges the child to come above the water so that the calf can breathe but the calf is disorientated and she is not a good swimmer yet and I see the mother whale tries to lead her to the surface but the calf does not understand and she stays floating horizontally without getting her head out of the water so now I am worried so worried I know without breathing the baby whale will die so I swim towards the calf and push her fin towards the surface of the water and now the calf is above the water yes she is breathing and breathing yes

Me too now I must come up to breathe or I will die I must swim up and up and up and up and all the way vertical yes just like a seahorse will swim vertically so I leap above the water like the child whale I gasp for air yes yes yes I see the sun the sky the clouds and I open my lungs and yes I breathe and breathe and breathe

II

WHEN I WOKE UP I DID not know who I was or what I was. It was dark. The clicking sound still echoed in my ears, my body rocking slightly, left to right, right to left. Was I still in the water? I felt pain, a cramp, low down in my stomach. For one moment, I believed I was a whale, a female whale, the mother whale who had given birth. I *was* the whale. The whale *was* me. Just one body, one whale thinking.

Gradually the surroundings pulled me back to where I was. The bunk beneath me was hard, my back hurt. I looked around. No, I was not a whale. My body was still rocking from side to side. But it was the ship that was rocking on the water. The wind must be churning the waves on the ocean. I rose and looked my own body up and down. I did not have a tail. I had two legs. I was a human. A woman. A bleeding woman. I had woken up in my own blood.

Up on the deck, everyone was already on duty. Had I slept late? How long had I slept? I saw land not far away from the ship, clearly visible. I saw Muzi in the captain's cabin, both of them studying the sea chart. I saw Drake and Freedman ordering the men to gather the empty barrels for the new supplies. Indeed, we would be anchoring soon.

Another alien land. Another season. Though the *Nimrod* was seasonless. It was autumn now in my Saxonham, I reminded myself. I wondered what the Queen of England was doing, on this day, in this season. Queen Victoria, she resided on the land where I came from, while I, Ishmaelle, eighteen years old, floated on this ocean, chasing a white whale I had never encountered and that I did not aspire to kill. I wondered if I would ever return to England. And if I returned, would Saxonham still be the same village I had known?

III

TIME SEEMED ETERNAL ON THE OCEAN. We hunted whales, stored the oil, suffered typhoons and hunted whales again. We were on the line of the equator, heading south-east. Very soon, we would be in Sumatra, anchoring at Batavia.

As we headed for Java, our first mate showed us the sea chart and briefed us about the busy and disorientating whaling ground we would be entering. The names on the chart sounded very foreign. Sumatra – we had to learn how to pronounce it – then Nias, Mentawai, Enggano, Krakatoa. The names would not lodge in our ears, even though we repeated the words again and again.

For three consecutive nights Antonio dreamt that he was encountering a Sumatran tiger. 'I had to fight the beast with my bare hands! His teeth tore into one of my sleeves and pulled me towards him! I kicked and swung and boxed with all my might and eventually I ran for my life!'

'Why didn't you use your harpoon?' said Jacques. 'Surely he was not as fast as a whale! A well-aimed throw and he would be done!'

'But have you seen a tiger, Jacques? A tiger does not run in a straight line, unlike a whale! A whale swims straight and away, so your harpoon flies in a straight line!'

'Why didn't you just knife him since a tiger is so much smaller than a goddamn whale? Not that we have seen many whales on this cursed voyage!'

'And what would we poor labouring wretches earn, even if we were to murder all the whales in the South Pacific?' Antonio spat on the floor, and rubbed in the saliva with his shoe. 'Tiger hunters make more than a lowly whaleman.'

'I earn more than you, and I am still in debt!' Jacques grumbled. 'I should have gone to the west coast for the gold like everyone else! Only idiots like us would stay on a whaler . . .'

They went on, continuing to argue what was the best way to deal with a Sumatran tiger, forgetting that the tiger was only appearing in Antonio's dreams. Dreams had invaded their waking reality. I thought of Seneca. Was our captain chasing the biggest dream of all? And was he not leading these men into despair? Jacques seemed for a moment to take on the aspect of a wild beast. His eyes flared and glittered.

'Curse these tigers! But curse these worm-eaten planks, and these worm-infested biscuits that they pretend to feed us with! And curse all the whales that haven't tasted the steel of our harpoons!'

However, the talk soon turned to expressions of antici-pation about the island we would reach. Drake told us that Batavia had been the territory of Dutch East India before the French took over. After that the British ruled the place before the Dutch returned and caused wars around the region. All this sounded very complicated to me. Drake concluded: 'Those old Europeans want to take over the islands of the South Seas. We Americans are not part of it!' Though Freedman said: 'But if we have a chance, our marines will surely take over the land, as well as the tigers!'

The sails and shroud lines were pulled and adjusted so the bow could turn in the direction of Batavia. Presently, we encountered a British merchant ship – the *Highland Explorer*. Each time I saw a British ship, I prayed that our captain would be up for the gam. But since it was a merchant ship, Seneca had no interest, not even in sending greetings. Drake and Freedman thought we should have communicated with the *Highland Explorer*, because normally a British ship would be carrying cotton, coffee and opium. And we needed cotton, but more crucially we needed opium for our medical cabinet. But Seneca did not order us to stop. So we sailed on towards Batavia.

IV

AS WE APPROACHED THE HARBOUR, the fog became heavier. The wind died down, the sails were still, and the ship stood immobile in the water. We waited in the dense fog. It seemed a sign, somehow ominous.

Drake lowered a boat so he and Freedman could try to get to the shore to find a clear anchoring point. Jacques, standing by the starboard watching them leave, remarked:

'The water is so shallow at this hour, the ship will have to wait to get into the harbour, no matter what!'

I saw Antonio and the rigger Jack go up to Jacques. The men whispered among themselves. But I could not hear what they said.

As we waited, the surgeon informed us that the old steward Mr Roberts was bleeding and he needed some assistance down below. We knew that Mr Roberts had scurvy, and we had run out of medicine to treat him. If we could not get onto land soon, the steward might die. The situation distressed everyone. Captain Seneca was in a furious mood. Waiting for the fog to disperse, he paced back and forth on the deck, his ivory leg making its customary sound: thump, thump, thump. Then we heard

Mr Roberts's groans. No one said anything. The silence amplified the sound: thump, thump, thump.

Still stranded in the static water, some of us went below to Mr Hawthorne's cabin. Mr Roberts's skin was purple and scaly, as though bruised all over. He bled from his gums, and from an open wound on his right arm. It was a terrible sight. As we looked on, he tried to speak. His speech was garbled, but we understood some words.

'I detest the sea . . . bury me on the land.' That was the last clear sentence Mr Roberts said. We all heard it. He inhaled violently, more blood oozed from his mouth. He was gone.

Mr Hawthorne told me to tell the carpenter we needed a coffin as soon as he could make it. Even though we already had a coffin made for Kauri, we could not use that one. It would be an offence to him. So Woody and I went down to the hold to find some planks. While Woody was making a coffin with help from Simon the cooper, others struggled to carry the dead weight of Mr Roberts back up to the deck, so we could place him in the cloth and sew him up right away. Muzi would know how to sew it up securely.

The fog was still thick, though not as dense as before. I noticed something was amiss. It was eerily quiet on the deck. Where was everyone? I knew that in this heavy fog some men had gone down to their quarters to sleep, because there was no work to be done now on the rigging, and Captain Seneca had returned to his cabin. There was nobody on the deck apart from those who had helped the surgeon carry Mr Roberts's cadaver. Muzi appeared with some new sailcloth. I sensed obscurely that something strange was occurring with the shipmen, but I was preoccupied with sewing up the body with Muzi and Mr Hawthorne.

Gradually, the fog dissipated, the harbour was now clearly visible in the near distance, and we soon saw Drake and Freedman's boat coming back towards the *Nimrod*. Captain Seneca emerged from his cabin and began to pace on the deck impatiently. I walked to the starboard and looked over the side. Seneca joined me. Almost simultaneously, both of us realised that a second whaling boat was missing! Where had it gone?! My first thought was to look for Jacques. Did he take the second boat, to follow Drake? Jacques was nowhere to be seen.

'Ishmaelle, call all men on deck!' Captain Seneca cried.

I was petrified. I could not call the men on deck – I was only an ordinary seaman. And Drake was still in the water with Freedman, rowing towards us. So I rushed to the officers' quarters, calling for Jacques. When I got to the bunk where he slept, all I saw was my cat Gladys. With her stubby tail, she crouched on the empty bunk, staring back at me. I knew something terrible had happened.

Everyone was gathering on deck, standing before Seneca. Four men were missing: Jacques, Antonio, Jack and a greenhand called Samuel. They had disappeared with a whaleboat! They must have taken their chances in the heavy fog, while the two mates were away and the rest of us were below deck sleeping or helping the surgeon. Now Drake and Freedman arrived back with their oarsmen, and learned the bad news.

Drake was in disbelief that Jacques might have led an escape.

'I would have never guessed Jacques would commit a crime!' Drake said, his face darkening.

'Oh, that lad has not been happy for months! Did you not notice, Mr Drake? A few others too,' Freedman grumbled.

'And why was that, Mr Freedman?' Captain Seneca asked, suppressing his temper.

'Why? Food is bad, and we don't have enough whale oil. Anyone can see that.'

This remark enraged Captain Seneca. He raised his stick and, pointing to the two mates, shouted: 'Go back! Chase the damned deserting scum. That perfidious lying offal!'

Instantly, the two mates went to lower the boat again. The oarsmen followed. Meanwhile, Captain Seneca came at me, pushing something hard into my hand.

' 'Go along with them,' he said. 'Jump! Make sure you shoot the damn deserter if he does not turn back!'

I looked at the hard object in my palm. It was a pistol. A Colt revolver. I had never held a weapon before. Though the mates had shown us how to shoot it the other day. Stunned, I stared at the captain. But his eyes were those of a wolf, or a lion, fierce and wild. There was doubt in his piercing gaze. Before I could say anything, Drake called me to the rope ladder, and we descended in all haste onto the small boat.

V

THERE WERE FIVE OF US, Drake, Freedman and me, along with the two oarsmen, labouring towards the harbour, in pursuit of the deserters. If the deserters had gone on land, said Freedman, the boat would be anchored somewhere. But we saw no sign of it. The conclusion was that they had sailed to another island, but had they sailed north in the direction of South Sumatra, or, as Drake thought, had they headed south to East Java? In haste, we turned our boat to the south towards East Java, though we knew we had already wasted an hour or two on the sea.

We chased along the Java shore for another hour, steering the boat with all our strength, Drake and Freedman having to do so while tightly watching for any sign of a small boat along the shore. The noon sun beat down, and we were losing our energy. Because we had left the ship in such a hurry, none of us had brought water or food supplies. So we had to make a decision: to go on with the chase, risking our own lives for the men who had obviously managed to advance far ahead, or to return to the *Nimrod* to ensure there was no further disturbance on board.

We decided to turn our boat back. We could not afford to leave the *Nimrod* there without its mates.

But when we returned to the ship, before we even climbed up on deck, we saw Captain Seneca looking down upon us, furious at finding no sign of Jacques. 'Dogs! How could you let that coward trapper's son go?! Whoa! Is this some plot? Of all against me, eh? I shall flog the lot of you!'

'But we came back for you, Captain,' Freedman said. 'We feared some dreadful unrest aboard the *Nimrod*. We come back to stand with you.'

Seneca said nothing. Brusquely, he pivoted on his leg, and his reddened face disappeared from view.

After such a long and stressful day, we finally anchored in Batavia that evening. Captain Seneca sent abroad the message that, other than the mates, no one was allowed to be on land by himself. There would be severe punishment for anyone who disobeyed. Moreover, the mates were to monitor those of us assigned to fetch supplies. Though, by now, we no longer had a third mate. Counting the dead and the deserted ones, we had lost five men in one day!

Mr Hawthorne sent me to the captain's cabin for permission to leave, so we could transfer Mr Roberts's body for burial. This was a task that the surgeon and I had to accomplish, according to his will. As I stood on the quarterdeck, Seneca nodded, but did not say a word. I was on the point of leaving when Seneca suddenly spoke:

'Ishmael!' (He still called me by my male name sometimes.) 'Keep the pistol. And you will replace Jacques.'

I stared at him, but he was already turning from me, as he went to sit down to write in the logbook.

VI

THE CARPENTER WOODY CAME TO HELP us with the burial. Arriving on land, Mr Hawthorne, Woody and I carried the heavy body of Mr Roberts ashore. We moved towards a hillside, and tried to find a spot. All around us were tropical plants and dense bushes.

We dug a hole with the tools Woody had brought with him, and placed the coffin inside. Mr Hawthorne said a few terse prayers over the grave. Then the carpenter said: 'We need to mark the spot, in case Mr Roberts's wife and sons want to find him in the future.' Well, Woody had known Mr Roberts's family for decades as they were from the same town in New England. So we agreed, and began filling the plot with earth. As I shovelled the soil back into the hole, I thought about the last time I buried a body. It was my baby sister, and it was in our garden in Saxonham. How desolate that day was. The garden in my England was barren and frozen in frost, and I was a broken person there, alone and lonely. Yet here, with the surgeon and the carpenter as we buried Mr Roberts, I did not feel lonely or bleak in any way. I was sad for the steward, but this sadness was not persistent. The overwhelming smell of the tropical jungle, the humid sweet air of the region and the exotic birdsong brought me a sense of joy and freedom I had rarely felt in the past few months.

After we closed the hole, the carpenter went to look for something to mark the spot. He brought back some white rocks, and placed them at the head of the grave. We stood and looked at the spot for a while. Something was still missing. The rocks, like a mound of tiny white skulls, seemed forlorn. I looked around, and saw a young pine sapling. I dug it up and brought it to the grave. I used the spade to unearth enough ground to replant the young tree. The little pine sapling would grow on top of the grave, surrounded by the skull-like stones, its roots reaching into the grave, to draw out the sustenance it would need from the remains there interred. Perhaps Mr Roberts's family would find this spot one day. Perhaps!

On the way back to the harbour, Mr Hawthorne told me that the surrounding islands harboured many seamen who in the past had deserted their ships.

'Some of them lived among the natives, and never returned home.'

'Really? Because it is so beautiful here?'

'Yes, but also because the length of time on sea, when they arrived at this far-flung station, had become unbearable, to the point that some of them decided to quit the harshness of the sea life altogether.'

'Well,' the carpenter said, 'only those lads who have no wife or children waiting in Massachusetts would risk their life to hide here. I would not want to live among cannibals and mosquitoes!'

As Woody spoke, he swung his hand and killed a few flies on his arms and legs.

After we had returned to the ship, I was immediately sent back with a group of harpooners under Freedman's supervision. We were to transport the food provisions. Freedman exchanged a long musket for five chickens and some coconuts. We also got some green tea, soap, oranges, eggs and cotton cloth for the offer of a barrel of gunpowder. Like any whaling ship, the officers kept gunpowder for self-defence, in case we encountered pirates or violent natives. It seemed that by now all we had left to offer were our weapons!

VII

I STILL HAD THE PISTOL that Captain Seneca had given to me, and I thought I should return it to him. The deserters were gone and I could not see any use for it.

When I was allowed into the captain's cabin, Muzi was there, looking at his I Ching book, while Captain Seneca was placing the divination sticks on the desk. Neither of them raised their head, and Seneca simply said:

'Wait there.'

So I stood by and waited.

Muzi made a sign with his right hand, then Captain Seneca picked up a handful and threw them down.

'Bottom: yin line, broken. Up: yang line, unbroken,' the monk said enigmatically. 'Six, nine, six, six, nine and nine. Yang is strong.'

Muzi wrote in his brown notebook. I could see the script, but I could not read it. Perhaps it was in Chinese. Then he asked the captain to pick up the sticks and throw them down again.

The monk pronounced a few more perplexing words and numbers:

'The lower part, broken lines. Up part, unbroken. Middle part, nine, nine and six and nine.'

Again, Muzi noted something in his notebook, and again the captain gathered the sticks and threw them down, but by the fifth or sixth round, Seneca mumbled impatiently:

'Ahoy! Should we not look at what the Book says?'

Muzi shook his head, while he tidied up the sticks.

'Do not ask the Book more than one time the same question, Captain Seneca,' Muzi said in his idiosyncratic English, 'and do not ask petty questions. The Book does not tolerate vanity.'

I watched them continue the ritual. I understood nothing. But one thing I sensed was that it was a ceremonial procedure involving change each time. Yes, change. It seemed that not once were the directions or the numbers of the sticks the same when they fell on the desktop.

After a while I heard the monk say:

'Now, Captain, you have completed the eighteen changes. We can determine your hexagram shortly.'

He opened his book, the one with the cosmic drawing on the cover. With his finger pointing at a specific paragraph on the page, he started to read the text in silence. Suddenly, the captain realised I was watching and waiting.

'What is it?' he said.

'I thought I should return this, Captain,' I said, taking the pistol from my pocket.

My hand grasped the pistol and I tendered it to Captain Seneca, but he did not move from his chair. Instead, he was annoyed.

'You think this is a toy, Ishmael? You think you can play with it for a while then return to your nurse?'

I pulled my hand back; the pistol was slightly wet in my sweaty palm.

'Listen, you! First you were a man coming onto the

Nimrod! Then you revealed that a sharp witch is your true identity, and I was glad! You know how to cure the men and how to deal with diseases. And now we have come all this long way to the South Seas and you were one of the good lads I can depend upon. You are here to help me! I am no Christian man, even though I grew up among them. They tried to mould me into their ways! But I am Seneca! I know a witch when I see one! And Ishmael is a witch, a hunter! You are going to help me find that white whale!'

Frozen, my mouth went dry, and I struggled to swallow.

'The Book tells me the change of the universe,' he went on. 'You are part of this change, Ishmael. You are part of the mission, my mission. You understand?'

Seneca fixed me with his burning eye, and drew his face close to mine, so close that I felt his warm breath on my skin.

'You are now my other leg, the one that beast devoured. You are that leg come back to me, and I will stand, and defeat that devil, through you. You are now part of this.'

For some unfathomable reason, I nodded as if I grasped what this meant. Fear gripped my soul, I could only concede. To resist the captain would be to tempt an outburst of his rage.

Then Seneca raised his right hand, and I was dismissed.

I was already outside the cabin, but I could faintly hear Chinese words being spoken. The monk had begun to read the Chinese text from the I Ching. Foreign sounds, one after another. It sounded like a string of monosyllables, but it was musical all the same.

彖曰：屯，刚柔始交而难生，动乎险中大亨贞。
雷雨之动满盈，天造草昧，宜建侯而不宁。

VIII

I T WAS A FULL MOON, the ocean was quiet and still.
Unable to sleep, I went up on deck. Sleep had always
been difficult for me. I wondered if my wakefulness
that night was to do with the full moon, or because it
was December. I had left England almost a year ago in
December. Leaving England and making my first voyage
across the Atlantic to America had been the most
memorable experience in my eighteen years of life. It was
also in that same month that I discovered the harbours of
New York, New Bedford and Nantucket, and began to
understand what it is to be a sailor in America. It was in
December I had found the *Nimrod*, or the *Nimrod* found
me and took me in like an orphan. Almost eleven months
had passed on the ship, and we were now in the South
China Sea, a warm ocean with frequent sightings of red
snappers and silver-pink tilapia. The coastline was dense
with vegetation. During the day we could see plumes of
smoke rising on the distant islands as we passed by. I
wondered whether it was smoke from a campfire, or a tribe
gathering for food, or was it a forest burning? But I would
never find out, as the captain had no intention of anchoring
the ship.

The deep calm of the moonlit night seemed to harbour

some mystery. There was no one on deck, except for a mastman up high in his crow's nest. I stood on the starboard side, gazing at the faraway waves. I saw glimmering lights on the remote shore. Was it Formosa? Or a Japanese island? As I was watching the distant lights and wondering what life was there, I heard footsteps. A familiar step, light, slow and steady, not hurried. I turned round. It was Muzi. Under the bright moonlight he wore the same white silk shirt and black silk trousers. He carried the same small hand drum. When he saw me, he gave a gentle nod of acknowledgement. I nodded back, but did not want to disturb him, as I knew this was his time for prayer. But on this occasion he walked up to me and stood by my side. He watched the lights as I did.

'That's Penghu Island,' Muzi said serenely. 'We are close to where I come from, China.'

I turned to gaze at the Chinese man. For so many months, he had barely talked to anyone. It was not so strange, in a way, since he was very much like Kauri, who did not like to speak much either. Muzi stating that we were very close to his home was something unexpected.

'What's your home like?' I asked. 'Is it a village or an island?'

'It's a village, a fishing village, in Fujian province. Across from the great island of Taiwan. I grew up with fishermen. We built boats, made sails and went deep into the sea to catch fish.'

I looked at him, surprised by his sudden talkativeness. It must have been because we were so close to his home.

'That must be why you are a good sailmaker, Muzi,' I said. 'But how did you become a monk?'

'Maybe not a monk. In my language we say Tao-shi.'

'What is a Tao-shi?'

'A man of Taoism. A man who knows how to follow the deep way of the universe,' he said. 'I learned this from my grandfather. So I became a Tao-shi too. My grandfather was a Taoist minister in our village temple. When I was a child, we lived at the back of the temple. In our temple, we had many gods. Gods for the sea and gods for the land, and gods for the sky. Before I went to the sea with my father, I helped my grandfather burn incense and helped the villagers make their offerings and their prayers. I watched Grandfather chanting, practising qigong and making herb powder every day. When I was about twelve or thirteen, my father died in the sea. So my mother brought me back from the fishing boat to the temple, and did not want me to sail again. From my grandfather, I learned how to make rituals with musicians who played gongs and cymbals. I recited the poems from *Tao Te Ching*, and I practised t'ai chi. I became a young priest when my grandfather was too old to receive the villagers. But one could only become truly wise if one travelled far and saw the colours of the world. So when I was eighteen, I left the temple. I became a nomad, a you-xia, as we say in Chinese.'

'A nomad? A you-xia?'

'Yes, a you-xia is a wandering man. I am a sea nomad. I travelled from boat to boat helping people who believed in Taoism, and I worked from island to island as a sailmaker. I let the ships take me to wherever they would sail. There were ships carrying tea, silk and spice travelling between Cap de Verd and South Asia, so I ended up in the Cape where I met Captain Seneca years ago. We were both young men then. There were many yellow men like me in Cap de Verd where we worked for the ships. But I did not forget Tao. So I built a temple in the Cape, and started again my role from where I left it. Tao shows me the way to live my life. It guides me. It enlightens me. I live a quiet and peaceful life even on the sea that always moves where we kill whales.'

What a journey, I thought. He had come as far as I had, and from the other side of the world. The fishing village, the grandfather, the herb medicine, the death of family members, and the desire to travel. Perhaps we were not so different after all, regardless of the different scriptures we followed and our different languages.

'Do you miss your home?' I asked.

He shook his head, then pointed up to the heavens: 'The sky is my home.'

I smiled. We both looked up at the night sky. The moon was sliding towards the south-west, the ocean was illuminated by the silver light. Yes, this sky sheltered us. The sky was our home.

'The sky is not a great void,' Muzi went on, 'stretching forever, crushing us into nothing, but is a giant pair of hands that reaches down to hold us up.'

I loved what he had said. Suddenly I felt less alone, and wiser. But then I thought of the strange men of this ship and their stranger chief.

I asked: 'Do you think Captain Seneca will find his white whale?'

Muzi sighed. Then he said with great simplicity: 'According to Taoism, a wise man needs to possess three treasures.'

'What are the three treasures?'

'Compassion, frugality and humility.'

I repeated these words in my head: compassion, frugality and humility. What should I make of these supposed 'treasures' of a wise man? From what I had observed of our captain, I did not see much evidence of them. To me, these three qualities seemed to be possessed by Mr Hawthorne, and perhaps by our first mate Drake. But definitely not by our captain.

Before I could ask more, Muzi had turned and was walking towards the bow of the ship, where he always sat for his prayers. I watched him sit down and soon he began to chant. I pondered again on those words Muzi had just spoken: compassion, frugality and humility. I might be neither wise nor a man, but did I possess these three treasures? I searched inside myself, but received no answer. As I looked out at the distant lights glimmering on the horizon, I thought, we can only know ourselves by acting in the world. It is in our conduct, the way we treat others, be they men, whales or fish, that our character will show itself. And I had not yet been fully tested.

CHAPTER THIRTEEN

Polynesia

I

WE LEFT THE CHINA SEA, and sailed out into the Sea of Japan. The water was blue-green, the currents flowed intricately, often in a tangled way, carried by the changing winds. Drake said that he had never understood the tides in the Japanese Sea and along these coasts. The Sea of Japan was an enclosed water, and so the channel created different layers of streams. 'If you dip your hand in the water, one moment it is very warm, next minute it is icy cold,' the first mate remarked. 'Why so?' I asked. 'Perhaps because the exchange between the northern part of the sea and the southern part is rapid. So on one island you see many sea lions and on the next there are only bamboo and reeds. But I have to confess that I do not know much about the Asian seas, not as much as I know about the Atlantic.'

We were short of crew members for whaling and for the work on deck. Drake believed that we should rely on the locals as the Asian seas were foreign to us, and we did not want to run into trouble with local fisheries. Captain Seneca did not object to the idea. In Yokohama, we tried to hire some Japanese whalers, but due to difficulties with language, we could not convince them to come with us. We

even asked Muzi if he could communicate with the islanders, thinking their languages might be similar, but the
islanders did not understand a word. Eventually we gave
up, and sailed on. Muzi suggested that we pick up locals
from a more remote island, as the harsh life there might
incite them to leave.

So we sailed towards the east, and stopped at Kagoshima.
We anchored at the south-western tip of the island of
Kyushu, which was covered with large and old camphor
trees. There, we managed to hire four Japanese seamen.
They seemed to be whalers, but they may have hunted
other fish too. Judging from the way they wielded their
harpoons, how nimbly they climbed the mast and handled
the riggings, they seemed very skilled. Two of the four
were older, their long white hair tied into buns, while the
other two were in their teens. None of them could
communicate with us, though, so we had to find a translator.

Moored outside Kagoshima for the time being, the
captain ordered Muzi to accompany Drake in the search
for a translator – an unusual but interesting task. Not only
did we need to hunt whales, but also we had to hunt a
translator! Eventually, Muzi and Drake brought back a
man called Taiji, who spoke both Japanese and English. I
was not sure what wages Drake promised Taiji, but he
would only stay on the ship for a month, then he would
have to go home.

'To see my family, sirs,' Taiji explained. 'I have three
small children.'

We asked if his family knew he would be working for an
American whaling ship.

'No, but it's no difference to them who I work for,
because we live on the island of Taiwan, or Formosa as you
call it!' Taiji explained. 'I am Chinese!'

This fact surprised us. We had passed the island of Formosa a few weeks prior, but we did not stop. From a distance, the island looked lushly green in the mist. I thought it seemed an idyllic place. I was intrigued that Taiji was from Formosa but could speak several languages.

'I speak Chinese too, of course,' he said. 'That's how your sailmaker Muzi found me. We are sea people, so we know the languages along these islands!'

We are sea people. Was that true of me? I could not say for certain if I was a sea person, though I felt comfortable on the sea. But more and more, I grew to miss the land after being away from it for so long.

'Do you know what Kagoshima means, Ishmaelle?' Taiji asked.

I shook my head. How could I?

'It means Island of Fawn.' He squatted on the ground, using his finger to draw three characters on the sand: 鹿儿岛.

The three characters looked curious and complicated to me. 'Is that Japanese writing?'

'No, these are Kanji – Chinese characters. In Japan they use some Chinese characters too.'

How big the world is, I thought, and how much of it I don't understand! This reminded me of how I first met my Polynesian friend Kauri in New Bedford, and how I tried to teach him to use the English words 'you' and 'me'. I wondered if I would ever need to learn a new language. I only realised that I spoke English when I met people who spoke other languages. I liked talking to Taiji, and told him I wished to see his island Formosa, and even China, one day.

Drake too took some interest in talking to Taiji, as he believed we would have to rely on locals for a while since

339

the captain intended to cruise around in this part of the world.

'We wanted to be in Asia because there are plenty of whales, not because we have to find the white devil,' Freedman murmured in a gloomy voice.

Since the disappearance of Jacques, Freedman was not the same jolly, simple man of before. He had been affected by the whole situation under Seneca's command.

'That's true. But we will remain around the waters here, unless –' Drake eyed the quarterdeck – 'unless Seneca is told by that Book that we have to turn the ship in a different direction.'

Taiji listened to this conversation, and remarked:

'Well, as soon as you know when you will leave the Asian seas, I will find a boat to return home. My wife will be waiting.'

Drake nodded. He looked melancholic. So did Freedman. It had been warm, so Drake no longer wore his Quaker's frock, nor his breeches. His sailor's shirt was stained, so were his trousers. All of us looked filthy and aged, after all these months at sea.

11

WHEN WE SAILED DOWN to the Philippine Sea
we saw many whales. One morning we sighted
a school of whales and lowered our boats. I
was instantly ordered by the captain to lead the third boat.
'You, Ishmaelle, you will lure the white devil with your
men!' I was with the harpooner Tyrone, three Japanese
whalers, as well as Taiji who would serve as an oarsman
while doing the translation. It was an odd assignment for
me. My role involved everything the third mate would
ordinarily do, and on top of that I had to work with the
Japanese whalers. Even though I had been on the whaling
boat to hunt many times already, I had never been asked to
give orders or make decisions for the crew. As the boat
bobbed violently on the waves, the sight of a tail caused my
Japanese whalers to cry out in their tongue. But they each
pointed in a different direction to signal to the oarsmen
where to head, and in no time the whale had disappeared.
We rowed on, watching for any movement in the water.
Then I spotted a patch of paler water swirling about. I
stood behind Tyrone and shouted instructions to the
steersman and the oarsmen each time the whale resurfaced.
But my words had to be translated by Taiji and his
translations seemed to be much longer than my own speech.

I was never fast enough and again and again we lost sight of the whale. I heard my Japanese crew shouting: 'Eesheemal, anattaa wwa oso sugimasu! Anattaa wwa oso sugimasu!' Perhaps they were cursing me, as Taiji did not offer a translation.

Fortunately, these men were excellent whalers. In the late afternoon, we hunted one down. But when we pulled the whale closer, we realised it was a calf, even though it was still as big as our boat. An argument broke out, infused by the language problems between the Japanese whalers and us westerners. It took me a while to understand the issue. Apparently, the Japanese whalers wanted to let the calf go, according to Taiji, but Tyrone the harpooner refused that idea straight away. He argued that even a small whale could yield at least five barrels of oil. Why would we want to waste it? Besides, we had been chasing the whales for hours.

Taiji translated Tyrone's opinion back to the Japanese crew. But they seemed not to budge. Normally in such a situation the mate on the boat would decide the matter, but I felt uncomfortable with this newly imposed role. In fact I agreed we should give up the young whale – a whale could live a very long time, so why kill such a creature before it even managed to find its life in the world? But I could not say my opinion out loud – Tyrone would be enraged. It was already strange for everyone to have a woman on a whaling boat, and I feared the consequences of either decision once we returned to the *Nimrod*. So I listened to their arguments, without knowing how to solve the conflict.

Then Taiji turned to me, and said with some frustration:

'Listen, I understand we are hired for your American ship, and we must do what we are told to do. But the

Japanese whalers have their ways. They never hunt juveniles or cow and calf pairs. It is respect for whales.'

I told him that I agreed with him, but I did not think the captain or the mates wanted to let any whale go once they had been hunted down. My speech was interrupted by the Japanese whalers. They were saying something fervently, addressing me and Tyrone:

'Kiru, rōpu o kiru!'

We turned to the translator.

'They say that if they had known the whale was a young calf, they would not have thrown their harpoons in the first place,' Taiji said. 'And now it is dying. Look at the blood! They want you to cut the rope and let it go.'

As we spoke, the ensnared whale attached to our boat struggled and made a huge splash. It was making a last effort to escape despite the harpoons and spears on its back. The boat swung furiously in the waves. The blood streamed like a red river as we steered. I had to steady myself to avoid being thrown overboard. Tyrone jumped into the water and tried to stab the whale to finish it off. More blood spurted. The Japanese whalers all shouted and gesticulated at Tyrone in anger. A terrible scene. I looked at the young whale; it seemed to have stopped struggling. It was dead.

I thought this might be the moment for everyone to stop the argument, but there seemed to be only more trouble and more animated Japanese speeches, which Taiji translated:

'They say they have to hold a funeral service on the ship for the young whale as it was not meant to be hunted and killed. They will do it in the Buddhist way, and if you don't do it, we will all have bad luck. The aggressive male whale will chase the ship and destroy it as revenge. And the dead whales will curse us and eventually we will die in a typhoon.'

I was speechless. What would Jacques have done if he was leading this boat? And what should I say to the officers when we returned to the *Nimrod*? I felt I understood the Japanese crew perfectly, but I did not believe that our captain and our mates would be so understanding.

'Tell them we will do what they ask once we get back,' I said.

Through the pool of blood the whale had shed, we steered our boat back to the ship.

III

BACK ABOARD THE *NIMROD*, I reported to Drake that the Japanese team wanted to hold a funeral ceremony for the calf we had hunted and killed. His expression upon hearing this clearly indicated he thought this was a peculiar act.

'But you did say we should adopt the customs of the local whalers since we must rely on them in this region,' I suggested.

Drake did not object to what I had said. But he enquired:

'What will they do after the funeral? If they had a whaler's mind, they would agree we cut it and take the oil.'

I said I was not sure, but I would go to Taiji to attempt some negotiation, and hopefully the group would agree.

I told Taiji the funeral could go ahead, but we had to proceed with the cutting right afterwards to take the blubber oil.

Taiji went to talk to the Japanese men. After lengthy discussions, everyone seemed to be nodding. The four Japanese went down in the forecastle to change their clothes for the ceremonial event, while the rest of us set about preparing for the cutting of the whale.

We brought up the empty barrels and firewood, but with the whale laid out on the deck, there was no space to move about. The body was bloated and the smell was strong, which attracted not only hundreds of gulls whirling above us but many sharks. By this time, Captain Seneca had come out to the deck. He limped to the uncut whale, slightly puzzled. With exasperation on his face, he asked:

'What is this folly?'

'The Japanese whalers want to do a funeral service on board because we hunted a calf and they believe it will bring bad luck for us if we don't. They must observe a burial rite in order to ask for forgiveness.'

As I spoke, the four whalers, dressed now all in white, reappeared. They brought with them a small wooden statue and some fist-sized drums. Taiji was holding incense and a burner. He had donned a white top but kept the same grey cotton trousers.

Some of us stopped our work and watched the scene curiously. The oldest of the group, Shinya, carried the wooden statue towards the dead whale. He seemed to be looking for the right place to set it down. At last he set it by the windlass, near to the whale's head, which happened to be right beside Captain Seneca's ivory leg. Seneca did not move an inch as the object was placed next to him. The others followed Shinya, and knelt around the whale and the statue.

The little statue was a godly-looking man with a laughing face, without arms or legs. The predominant feature on his body was his large manhood. This incredibly powerful-looking manhood seemed to hold the laughing man's whole body weight. But since the statue had no arms or legs, I found it disturbing. I glanced to my side to catch the captain's reaction. He seemed to be frowning, unsettled by such a strange or even grotesque-looking god.

'It is our sea god Ebisu. He will bless us and forgive us for any wrongdoing,' Taiji said.

'But why does your god have no arms or legs?' Seneca asked.

'Oh, he was born a very sick child, and his mother saw he was sick so she decided to abandon him. Ebisu grew up without any protection, and as a result the animals in the forest ate his arms and legs. But he survived on an island by eating fish, and he became the god of fishermen. He protects the men on the sea.'

Now the men in white began to burn the incense. They hit their small drums with their open palms and hummed a tune. The drum sound and the humming reminded me of how Muzi prayed at night. The scent of the incense diluted the terrible smell of the decomposing whale flesh. It was a curious scene.

Once they finished the ritual, they folded their palms together and bowed to the dead whale. Then they stood up, gathered their drums and incense burner, and went below deck to change their clothes. Shinya went last, carrying the little statue Ebisu. Once they disappeared from sight, we got ready to begin the cutting. But when they reappeared, Taiji said the Japanese whalers wanted to open the head first. Their way of working was methodical and effective. With two men standing on each side of the head, they peeled its skin upwards with their knives in a skilful way without breaking any parts. After the peeling, they cut into the blubber layer and carved out the oil mass in the most elegant way. They performed the entire task without a word and without a pause.

'If we American whalers could work like this,' Freedman remarked, 'we would not need three years on the sea! It

347

could be three months! Then we would head home to see our wives and to eat our roast pork!'

The captain did not comment. He seemed to be affected by the burial scene, or perhaps by the story of Ebisu, the sea god without arms or legs. Hobbling on his ivory leg, he retired to his cabin.

IV

FOR A FEW DAYS, we tried to outrun the storms, but with contrary winds whipping us from all directions, we could not turn the ship as we wished. From the Philippine Sea, we headed south, even though it would have been advisable to go north to avoid another typhoon. But Captain Seneca believed that the area around the equator in Polynesia was Moby Dick's home territory, so that was where we headed and where we had to linger. We could have stopped at an island in Indonesia and waited in a harbour until the weather changed. But the Japanese whalers vigorously protested the idea. Taiji explained that the Japanese men had had violent encounters with the natives of those Indonesian islands, so we should avoid unnecessary trouble. Captain Seneca ordered us to stay on the open sea, and we would sail on once the typhoon passed.

But try as we might to find a safe spot on the sea, it seemed we were constantly assaulted by rainstorms. The bow was damaged, to a degree that a group of us were assigned to bail water out non-stop. Even the cat was unhappy. She wandered about, and eventually found the driest place to hide – under Muzi's bunk.

Since my bunk was next to Muzi's, I got to know his

349

daily rituals. He slept very few hours. Most of the night he meditated and chanted. With the storm, he did not go up on deck, meditating and chanting on his bunk instead. He spent some time looking at his books. He possessed two books in Chinese script, as far as I could tell. He had explained to me that the book he used for readings with the captain was the I Ching, or the Book of Changes. The other one was the *Tao Te Ching*, an ancient book about his religion of Taoism.

Even though I had observed how Muzi threw his divination sticks I understood absolutely nothing. So one early evening when the rains had imprisoned us all inside, and after hearing the tinkering of Muzi's sticks from behind my curtain, I poked my head out and launched a conversation with him.

'Sir, if each throwing of the sticks brings a different pattern and changes the reading, then what's the point?'

'That's exactly the point. One has to read the changes. Only changes matter.'

Muzi answered in his firm and idiosyncratic tone. He did not seem to mind that I had interrupted his practice. Perhaps he also needed to speak with someone, especially in this dreadful weather.

'Is that what the I Ching book is about?'

'Yes, but the book is not important. Only the Tao is important. The Tao means the way.'

'What is this way?'

Muzi tidied up his sticks, and changed his sitting position, so he could face me properly. He thought for a moment, then slowly he explained:

'The way is the spirit of the universe, the flow. The universe always vibrates or dances. We want to be one with this movement. You only know yourself, and know your path, when you know the vibrations and the dance.'

'Know myself?'

'To know yourself is to know your movement through the universe.'

'How so?'

'For example, throwing this bunch of sticks brings you to Hexagram 17. That was what I did. That pattern of hexagram is named sui – 隨. It means pursuing or hunting. Then you have to look at the lower trigram, which is ☳, zhen – quake and thunder. You look at its upper trigram ☱, dui, meaning open and swamp. Then you need to be very careful in your pursuit and hunting. It is a dangerous action without a clear mind.'

I had not understood. Hexagrams? What were they exactly? Were they patterns of sticks, with Chinese names on them?

'But what do those squiggled characters mean?' I asked. 'Can the universe read them? And why should the universe read Chinese?'

'We humans name the universe. We bring things into being by doing that. There are thousands of names, and so thousands of things. Different names in different languages. It makes no difference which language. With the sticks we ask the universe a question.'

'But how can the universe answer?'

'We are the universe too. Our minds are also the universe,' Muzi said, and touched his beard.

'How is my mind the universe?' I asked, more puzzled than ever.

'Listen to me now. You are the universe appearing as Ishmaelle. Muzi is the universe appearing another way. But there is only one true universe. So, to know yourself is to know the universe. So, to ask a question to the universe is to ask a question to yourself.'

I nodded, even though I did not really understand. Still, I felt something. Every now and then, especially when I looked up at the clouds and down at the waves, or I watched a bird in the sky, or I wandered across a field in Denge Marsh, I felt I was somehow at one with the world, like God was tapping me on the shoulder, or breathing with me. And the love I felt in my breast was not just me but something beyond me. Perhaps that was what Muzi meant by me being the universe appearing one way. In those moments I felt at peace with myself. But most of the time, I felt alone and in danger, separated from the world. I did not feel I had the universe within me. I was trapped inside a body, surrounded by strangers and strange happenings. The world of the *Nimrod* did not make sense. It had become a dungeon. An island of craziness, floating by itself. Here on this wretched ship, with flensing and chopping and oil burning, how could men hear the universe speaking to them, when their craving minds had drowned out all feeling and sense?

I left Muzi so he could continue with his ritual. I pulled the curtain back around my bunk, and thought more about what Muzi had tried to explain to me. The rains and the wind were ceaseless all night, they gave no comfort to my troubled mind.

V

A T LAST, the ship escaped the bad weather. Two days later, the sky was incredibly blue, the sea peaceful and tamed. The universe changed as Muzi returned on deck to do his praying and chanting. We adjusted the riggings and sails, and drew towards the Palau Islands. The officers decided to stop briefly around Kayangel where there was a cluster of rocky islets. We would staunch the leaking bow, repair the rigging, and send out a small boat to get some fresh food from the island. As soon as the *Nimrod* was settled just off the isles, Drake ordered a boat to be lowered. With Taiji and two oarsmen, we set off in search of supplies.

Once in the boat, I saw colourful corals as we steered towards the shore. So near to me and so incredibly strange when their branches waved slightly in the water, I reached down and touched them. Then I saw seahorses! I had never seen real seahorses before. Taiji spotted a large orange one below the surface and pointed it out. I noticed its vertical body coming up with a pointed snout, then a smaller one following. Were they mother and child? What were they doing? Was this a good sign or a bad one? I wished my great-aunt Gladys could see this and tell me what the creatures were doing at that moment.

When we passed a small isle of debris and weeds, I saw a strange-looking octopus swimming towards us, like an enormous water spider with outstretched arms. For some moments I was mesmerised, and wanted to touch the mysterious creature. Suddenly, I heard Taiji's voice behind me.

'Be careful with the blue-ringed octopus – it is poisonous! Don't touch it or even get close!'

I brought my hand back quickly and we continued rowing towards the island.

Taiji warned Drake that we should be cautious around this area, as earthquakes and volcanic explosions were frequent.

'Once you have hunted some whales, you should return to the ship as soon as possible! You never know when the earthquake will happen, so do not linger long.'

Drake nodded. And I thought that perhaps Taiji was wanting to return to Taiwan to be with his family.

The water around this area was so clear and green that we could see very deep – almost all the way down to the seabed. Taiji pointed out large sea cows – dugong – their plump bodies like a lady resting on the meadow. Apart from Taiji, none of us was familiar with dugong. But we knew that the locals hunted them for their meat and oil.

'I can see that you westerners also like dugongs, though the Chinese never hunt them,' Taiji said.

'Why not?'

'It's bad luck to kill a sea cow – if they did, the men would become infertile and their wives would never get pregnant! But Filipinos hunt them aplenty for their meat and oil.'

He paused, then addressed himself to Drake:

'Sir, in my opinion, you don't have to chase whales.

These sea cows are as good as whales. They might be smaller in size, but their oil is the best!'

Drake did not comment on that. I thought, that's right, sea cows are as good as whales. But I could not imagine that Captain Seneca would lead us across all these seas just to hunt the dugongs. He would laugh himself to death if he was told he should hunt black sea cows rather than the white whale.

VI

NEXT MORNING, the sails were still being repaired, and the whale watching resumed. We had some new supplies – jackfruit, papaya, dragon fruit, durian and rice. But the sun was already strong in the early morning and the air humid. We would have to eat the fruits quickly before they rotted. I tried a papaya; its soft yellow flesh tasted sweet, a mixed flavour of banana and honey melon. I also tried a durian. But the durian was so large that I shared it with Hawthorne and Muzi. Apart from us three, no one else seemed to be very interested in this strange-odoured spiky fruit. As we tried to cut its tough skin, I could not quite describe this stink – it was almost unpleasant, as Hawthorne put it. The fruit tasted rubbery, like I was chewing a soft lump of caramel. I watched Muzi chop the flesh and add the pieces of durian to his porridge. He ate everything with his chopsticks and from his own special porcelain bowl which he had brought on board in Cap de Verd. We were always mesmerised by the way he ate.

The watch for the day was the young sailor Loick. Having barely recovered from the typhoon and a series of sleepless nights, he was still slumbering while we were eating breakfast. Since he was late, he went straight from his hammock to the masthead without eating. He was not long at his perch, when a cry was heard. We looked up to see a falling man in the air. The cry was followed by a violent bang as Loick's body caught the edge of the forecastle. But instead of coming to rest, the angle of the collision, together with the sheer force of the impact, caused his inert frame to be tossed over the starboard rail and into the sea. We rushed to starboard, and looked down into the water, just in time to see a few white bubbles in the blue.

Instantly, Freedman called for the lifebuoy to be dropped. So far we had not needed to use the lifebuoy – a long slender cask which hung from ropes attached to the stern. For months the sun and the rain had beaten down upon the cask, and over time it had shrunk in size. As Freedman lifted the cask and steadied himself to throw it into the water where Loick had fallen, we could hear water sloshing inside. We could see from Freedman's strained expression that it was much heavier than we knew such a cask should be when empty. The wood was not intact either, but bulged here and was splintered there. Yet there was no time to fetch anything else. As Loick sank deep down into the sea, we saw the cask tilt upright then it too sank down. Neither Loick nor the lifebuoy could be seen. We looked again and again, but there was no sign, not even a bubble where Loick had fallen. Drake called to lower a boat. The two oarsmen rowed round and round, but it was too late.

Drake reported to Seneca what had transpired. We all felt a great measure of despair, though none of us uttered a word. I felt sickened. Loick was the same age as me – eighteen. His death seemed to have neither meaning nor weight. He fell with a splash. The end. It was simply a

357

terrible accident. Would my death not be just as meaningless?

There was no time to grieve. We were soon called by the mates to resume our roles. Another sailor was ordered to climb the mast. Two more were assigned to the afternoon and the evening watch. And the lost buoy had to be replaced. Drake was directed to see to it with the carpenter. They went down to the hold, but they found no cask of sufficient lightness for the purpose. This was a moment of crisis in our voyage; we were losing men every month and we needed to have some security on board. Any of us could fall into the sea without hope of being rescued. Then Kauri came up. He said he would offer up his coffin as a replacement.

'A lifebuoy of a coffin!' cried Drake.

'Rather queer, that, I should say,' said Freedman.

Though both men looked amused by such a suggestion.

Kauri said: 'Me coffin make a good enough one.' He then waved in my direction. 'Ishmaelle help to carry my coffin. It save you, it save everyone.'

I came close to Kauri and nodded. I noticed that he had begun to use those special words I had taught him: 'me', 'I', 'you', even 'my'. In these months on this ship, this enclosed wooden jail on the sea, the sailors too had made him learn these English words. And now I heard them spring from his mouth. When he used them I felt something between us was different, like a barrier between us had melted. He was mine and I was his in our strange intimacy. We were from other sides of the globe, he from the south, me from the north, but our paths had now been tied together, and the ribbon of that bond was plaited now with those words, I, you, my, in his mouth, and the same in mine . . .

'The carpenter made the coffin airtight. Best lifesaver.'

'Well, Kauri, bring it up then,' said Drake, after a melancholy pause.

Woody was listening to all this, frowning. He did not like this new purpose for his specially made product.

'The lid will need to be nailed down, Woody.'

Woody stared at Drake, feeling almost insulted.

'What do you mean?'

'Don't look at me like that. It is not my idea. But we must have something ready if anyone falls into the sea!'

As they debated, Kauri went down to his quarters, and I followed him swiftly as I could see he was impatient to have his coffin converted to a lifebuoy. In no time, we cleared out the clothes and items in the canoe-coffin, then Kauri carried the coffin, and I carried the lid, which was much lighter, and we clambered back onto the deck.

There it was, a perfect and beautifully made coffin in the middle of the deck. The carpenter fetched his tools and began reluctantly to modify the coffin.

Everyone gathered around to watch. We all felt queer; a man we had lived with for a year had just drowned, and we were turning a coffin into a lifebuoy.

'Listen, sir, if you tell me to nail down the lid now, I will do it, but don't tell me I have to crack it open another time! That won't be a good thing to do!'

'Aye,' Drake promised. 'You won't need to open the lid again.'

Bang bang. Woody hammered down the first nail into the lid. Bang bang. He hammered the second. Bang bang, the third. Everyone watched as if they were seeing a great spectacle. Kauri's eyes were glistening, and he was almost smiling.

When the lid was securely in place, Woody turned to Kauri.

'Listen, you asked me to make the coffin perfect for your size. Now you don't want it, right? So you won't ever have it. I won't open it again.'

Kauri nodded. 'Kauri has no use of coffin,' he said.

Woody now turned to Drake.

'And I suppose I must caulk the seams, sir?'

He had brought a caulking-iron along with the other tools.

'Aye.'

Now Simon the cooper came up with some tools too, and asked:

'Shall I add some handles on the side, so the men can grab it easily and throw it to the sea?'

'That's very good,' said Drake.

'But, sir! The purpose of a coffin should remain its sole purpose,' the carpenter protested. 'I don't like this cobbling sort of business – I don't like it at all; it's undignified; and if the hull goes down, there'll be thirty fellows all fighting for one coffin, a sight not seen very often beneath the sun!'

Freedman ran out of patience.

'Away with it, I say, Woody! Make a lifebuoy of the coffin, and speak no more.'

Woody made no more complaints. He sealed the coffin thoroughly. At the same time Simon used some old metal pieces from the harpoons and made handles on the sides. Kauri watched the whole process while smoking his pipe. He was thinking of something, but I had no idea what.

VII

I N THE DAWN, a bird had been screeching 'eh-eh . . . eek eek' as it circled continuously around the *Nimrod*. From my bunk, I saw Gladys scampering up the stairs. The bird's squawk now mixed with the sound of the mewling cat, making an unpleasant din, so I got up, and went on deck. It was an albatross, a white bird-god with huge wings, whirling just above the deck and squealing down at us. How strange for the albatross to fly so low, I thought. The sun was beginning to rise over the blue waves. The din of the animals combined with the red seascape of sunrise to form a curious opera. A mastman was climbing up for the first watch of the day. Captain Seneca appeared, Dilly holding a tray with a teapot and cup following behind.

We all looked up at the whirling albatross. Its wings were so large they blocked the sunrise behind at times and the shifting shadows cast by the bird fell over us. Gladys was chasing the shadows, running hither and thither. I had not seen the cat so alive since her tail had been cut.

Then I heard Seneca say: 'Ishmael, have you the pistol?'

I was surprised – what did he want me to do? Shoot the albatross?

'Yes, sir, but not upon me,' I answered. 'I was woken by the bird.'

The albatross made an even louder cry above us.

'You bird!' Seneca shouted. 'What have you got to say, eh? Are ye dooming us or blessing us, eh?'

Strangely, the enormous white creature rose higher into the air, and then suddenly dived towards the billowing waves and skimmed across the foam, screeching as it did so, then it turned and abruptly flew away. There were no more shadows of its wings mottling the deck.

'What got into you, damn white devil of the skies?' Seneca exclaimed. 'I will shoot you the next time your wings shadow our fair ship!'

The cat was now quiet, crouching by the windlass, looking up at the empty sky.

At this moment, I noticed that the surgeon was by the windlass watching the scene too. Naturally, someone like Hawthorne, a man with keen knowledge of plants and birds, would be curious about the albatross's strange appearance.

'What do ye say about that white devil of the sky, Mr Hawthorne?' Seneca asked.

'Well, sir, a wandering albatross might be a sign of trouble,' the surgeon said, frowning. 'He might be looking for his mate. Because albatrosses are known for their monogamy. They mate for life, and the male usually flies with his partner between long flights at sea.'

'You mean he has lost his wife? What balderdash!'

Mr Hawthorne scanned the horizon as if to search for the lost partner of the albatross, but Seneca was losing interest in such a subject, and went back to Dilly for his morning tea.

This observation from the surgeon interested me greatly. I went over to him and asked:

'Mr Hawthorne, how can you see that the one that just flew away is a male?'

'Oh, I am not sure, Ishmael. With the albatross, it's very difficult to tell males from females. In general the males are slightly larger, and their bodies are flatter, with wider heads and wider bills. But that is not always the case.'

He paused, and gazed at me. His gaze made me queasy and a little uneasy.

'That albatross we saw could well be a female, Ishmaelle.'

I noticed he had changed the way he called my name.

Well, I thought, am I an albatross, not recognisably female or male? Do I have both sexes? Should I want to be one or the other, or somehow both, or neither? I recalled that when we were in Cap de Verd, Mr Hawthorne told me that the plants have female and male parts and how the insects would climb into the flower petals as a love bed. All this wonderful knowledge about female and male, about love and mating, did not seem to have much use here on this ship! Perhaps this sea life made us genderless, sexless, loveless. Or perhaps the sea was our partner, the ocean our mate for life.

While I was lost in my thoughts, Mr Hawthorne said despondently:

'I think his partner has died. Because the mated albatross pairs normally never split up until one dies.'

Gazing at the empty sky, we both fell into silence. Gladys now came to me, rubbing her warm furry back against my legs. Her stub waved slightly, back and forth, as though it was still attached to its phantom tail.

VIII

I T WAS NOON and I was mending harpoons with Kauri, when we heard someone crying on the deck. It was not just crying, it was screaming, followed by the sound of blows. We went up to find a brutal scene. Our mate Freedman was beating poor little Dilly with a broomstick. The boy twisted and squirmed in an effort to avoid the blows. His resistance seemed to make Freedman more furious. Blood oozed from the boy's nose, and we saw red marks across his arms.

As soon as Dilly saw me, he ran over and hid himself behind my back. With outstretched arms, I tried to parry the broom as it descended upon us.

'What is this all about, Freedman?' I cried.

'The little brat keeps stealing! First it was meat! Then coins! And now Mr Hawthorne's watch!' Freedman cursed furiously. Then he tried to push me aside and grab the bawling boy, but Dilly used this opportunity to scurry up the rigging of the mainsail, disappearing behind the billowing sails.

The surgeon and others had now gathered on board to witness the scene.

'No more beating the boy, Freedman,' Hawthorne said. 'I suspected he was the one, but he's a mere slip of a lad!'

Panting with anger, Freedman threw down the broom, took the watch from his pocket, and handed it to the surgeon.

Mr Hawthorne put it in his shirt pocket, pinning the chain on a button. We could hear distant sobbing from the mast above. Poor Dilly.

'He deserves it!' Freedman grabbed the broom and stormed back to the quarterdeck.

I looked up to where Dilly was. Instead of hiding behind the sails, he was now staring out to sea, and had ceased his crying.

'What's up with you, Dilly?' I shouted.

'A ship! There!'

His arm was extended towards the west. We went to the bulwark and, indeed, saw a large ship sailing directly towards us. We watched in silence as it got closer and closer. The flag was American, and soon Drake with his spyglass reported its name: the *Sirena*.

The captain of the ship was by now visible on the deck, surrounded by his men. A boat was lowered and rowed in our direction. The captain, holding a small trumpet to his mouth, stood up in the boat and called out a greeting.

'Good morning, the *Nimrod*!'

The mates acknowledged with a wave of the hand.

'Away from home long?' the captain of the *Sirena* called out.

Seneca, appearing from the quarterdeck, responded with his usual cold manner and his customary refrain:

'Not long. Have you seen the white whale?'

'The white whale? Aye, yesterday,' said the man. Then he added in a worried tone: 'Have you seen a whaleboat adrift?'

'Where was he? So he is still alive!' said Seneca, ignoring the man's question.

By now the captain of the *Sirena* had arrived at our ship. Grasping the chains by our boat davits, he sprang to the deck. Immediately Seneca recognised him for a Nantucketer he knew, a certain Fitzroy. Still, no formal salutation was exchanged. It was Drake who went to greet Mr Fitzroy, and who called out to Dilly to serve tea.

Before Mr Fitzroy could explain about his search for the lost whaleboat, our captain went on:

'Where did you see him yesterday?'

'The white whale?' Mr Fitzroy raised his eyebrows. 'It was yesterday morning, when we sent out three boats to chase a school of whales. The creatures led them four or five miles from the ship, and while they were still in swift chase, we saw the white hump and head of the white whale.'

'Did he have a crooked jaw and harpoons stuck in his back?!' cried Seneca.

'That's him. He had loomed out of the water, not very far to leeward. So I called for our fourth boat – a reserved one – to be lowered in pursuit. After a keen sail before the wind, this fourth boat – the swiftest of all – seemed to be gaining on the whale – at least, that was what our man at the masthead was telling us. The fourth boat went quite far with the white whale. Our mastman then saw only the tiny speck of the boat far in the distance, then only a gleam of bubbling white water, then nothing more. I sent up my spyglass, but there was no sign of that whaleboat. So we concluded that the white whale must have managed to run away with his pursuers, as often happens.'

'Which direction did he go?' Seneca chased with excitement.

'That way.' Mr Fitzroy pointed south-east. 'Last night, we placed lamps along the riggings. In the dark we picked up the three whaleboats, and they brought with them one whale. We cut the whale that night and made a fire in our brick furnace to do our try-work and so we could keep the fire all night as a beacon. Every other man on the lookout. Today it will be the same – we need to find the fourth boat and the lost men.'

Dilly served tea and rum; his nose had stopped bleeding. The captain of the *Sirena* took a draught. His eyes turned westward, his gaze mournful.

'Who are the men on the fourth boat, Captain?' Drake asked.

Mr Fitzroy sighed. 'My boy. Yes, my own boy is among them. He is but twelve years, for God's sake.'

Dilly stared at the man, forgetting to move away with the empty tray.

Mr Fitzroy now looked to Seneca in hope and in desperation. 'I beg you, Mr Seneca, you can help me. If you can spare your men to look for the boat and my boy for the next two days, I'll pay you! He is my only son, my only child!'

Seneca made no response.

'I am sorry to hear this,' said Drake. 'We will look for that boat!'

'We must save that boy . . .' Freedman muttered.

'I will pay if you can help! He might have drowned along with the rest on that boat, but I won't give up. I must carry on searching for him!'

Captain Seneca's eyes were turned towards the south-east. The sun was strong and he squinted. He did not say anything to Mr Fitzroy.

'You know my son, Captain. He is a little lad, twelve years old. William is his name.'

Captain Seneca was now looking up to our masthead man. He was perched up there, watching the distant waves.

It looked like Seneca was anxious that the mastman might have missed a sign of the white whale.

'I know you had a child too, Captain Seneca. A child is perhaps even more precious than a wife. So you will understand how important William is to me. Will you help look for him?'

'Avast,' cried Seneca. 'Captain Fitzroy, I will not do it. We must sail on. Even now speaking to you is losing time. I must go, I must hunt him! Drake, look at the binnacle watch. We sail to the south-east.'

Hurriedly and averting Fitzroy's gaze, Seneca retired to his cabin.

We were shocked at Seneca's reaction. Drake looked down, and Freedman's shame could be seen in his awkward bearing. Captain Fitzroy rose silently, followed by his men. They climbed the rope and lowered themselves down to their boat.

'Goodbye!' Fitzroy said softly, as Drake, then Freedman, shook his hand.

'May God go with you,' Freedman said.

We watched them return to the *Sirena*.

Soon the two ships passed each other. But the *Sirena* seemed to be heading in no specific direction. It glided along in the water very slowly. We could see that there were many men clinging to the mast, watching. And we knew that those masthead men were there not to sight a whale, but to find the lost fourth boat, with its child of twelve years old.

I turned and found Freedman standing behind me, his gaze focused on something far away.

'Are you all right, sir?' I enquired, puzzled by his troubled look.

He shook his head, and I saw his eyes were moist.

'Ishmaelle, you may think I am a hard man beating up a little boy. But sometimes we hurt those who are closest to us. Dilly . . . he is . . . my son.'

'Dilly is your son?!'

He turned to look at the sea, and spoke in a low and mournful tone:

'I met the woman who was to become his mother after I had already married my wife. I did not tell my wife about it. We already had children. But after Dilly was born, I promised his mother I would help him as much as I could. Then she died. Poor woman! I decided to bring the boy on board.'

This ship was full of secrets and strange confessions. The longer I lived on the *Nimrod*, the more it seemed to want to tell its tales. And perhaps they would become my own tales.

CHAPTER
FOURTEEN

The Chase and the Book
of the Changes

I

The White Whale Surfacing

Hexagram 19

This hexagram is named 臨 (lín): nearing or approaching.

Lower trigram: ☱ (兑 duì) open = (澤 zé) swamp; upper trigram: ☷ (坤 kūn) field = (地 dì) earth.

The lines: the yang line below is the solid field, the yin line above is the abysmal water.

The judgement: go to the goal

The image: a vast swamp

The action: to approach

Midnight, Seneca alone, pacing up and down on the deck.

I know you are the devil swimming slipping through the depths below these very decks yes you might be a mile from me I would smell you and if you venture near this boat I'll feel your leather skin of serpent I'll smell you out and smite you I'll cut out your tongue soon enough and eat it I'll pluck out that great dish of a devil's eye and feast on you

You fish do not know the boyhood in my sleeplessness I remember the me that was long ago I was a twelve-year-old boy I was on my first sea voyage I was a child serving the captain and the mates I was frightened by the waves and by the storm until the first thunder struck in the dark sky I cried out that I wanted to go home but I reminded myself that Papa Po had died and Mother had left for good I had no more home I was no longer a child of the Quakers I let the thunder and lightning strike me and suddenly there was no fear no tears no boy's heart or sentiment and I had no pity for that boy next morning

When I was seventeen I struck my first whale with a harpoon yes I was a boy-harpooner and I felt with that strike the shudder of the whale and then the rushing of the rope and the chase of death skimming over the surface and then the blood and the kill I pulled that first great carcass with my chapped hands weeping red upon the rope but I felt a joy I had never felt before then month after month year after year I plunged the steel and sharp barbed blade into the dumb flesh and rode the waves and pulled on the ropes as the blind creatures drew us men through the brine like harried corks oh how many harpoons have I cast sprung from my arm like holy arrows and messages of hate and how many whales have I hunted until that day the day the white monster cursed me from nowhere like an avenging angel of brute barnacled beastliness

When I think of this life I have led the desolation the solitude weaving through days from sunrise to sunset through storm and rain through chase and escape what a folly is man what folly to have made that woman my wife tied to this single obsessional man over there on the American land a wife and a dead child born from her sin that spawn the sign of uncontained lust

Mother after abandoning me I had missed those long winter nights when I was hurt like a dog but I no longer miss her and she is long dead now my hair is all white and I will join her I do not belong to the land I have to escape those streets and houses and the small talk of the good men and women and honest citizens when I enter those houses I feel a weariness come upon me I would rather eat mouldy crusts with the putrid salt beef and the worm-infused hard biscuit than stay confined in streets that are cages to the soul rather be away and be ready to disappear with the white devil as soon as I throw my last harpoon to join with it and find my hell or heaven

When I left my wife I left with a dent in our marriage pillow an imprint of my white-haired head oh wife ye are rather a widow with her husband alive oh child ye should be not dead your white father should have claimed you and I should have struck him with my harpoon with the same force that I will strike thee, whale, and I must chase ye because all the worth and meaning of a man lie in this strife of the chase till the arm falls weary the palsy-stricken arm at the oar shrivels and drops the iron and the lance fall by the wayside or to watery graves then all shall be over and the sea can consume all and peace will lie across the waters

I ought to brush this old hair from my blinded eyes for I find that I seem to be weeping in my greyness and in this quiet morning I weep like a tin can riven with holes and I catch the sight of this face in the mirror oh Lord age stares out at me a Methuselah I feel deadly faint and bowed and as though a crippling disease chose to make me its home and humped as though I were a lone Adam staggering beneath the piled centuries since Paradise was lost and Eve ate her apple and the serpent laughed at its work and God expelled the hapless pair and Eve was my mother surely but she has left the garden this world behind and she left old Adam alone in this world

Drake Freedman Ishmael stand close to me and let me look into a human eye which I dread to do so it is better that I gaze into the sea the sky the fish or even better gaze upon God but when I gaze into my mates' eyes I see the magic glass and I see my wife and her dead child in the garden oh I won't return to that garden that soil that land that once bore life

II

The White Whale and the Abyss

Hexagram 29

This hexagram is named 坎 (kǎn): the abysmal water and the gorge.

Lower trigram: ☵ (坎 kǎn) the gorge; upper trigram: ☵ (坎 kǎn) the gorge.

The lines: this hexagram consists of a doubling of the trigram 坎. A yang line has plunged in between two yin lines. Yang is closed in by yin like water in a ravine.

The judgement: falling into the abyss

The image: the abiding abyss

The action: to stand by and let the action be revered

We had been heading eastward towards the Ellice Islands, just below the equator. A few crew members had sailed these areas during past voyages. Drake and Freedman had anchored at one of the islands. They mentioned that the natives could be strange, even hostile, and thought that unless we had to stop for supplies we should just keep whaling. I knew my Polynesian friend was from this part of the world, so I asked him if he knew where he was.

'Kauri know this water, Kauri know this sun, but Kauri know nothing of where we go.'

I told him that the captain wanted to stay in this area, and would not go further south towards the sea off New Zealand, where we would be closer to his native island.

'Kauri know he will not go home.'

'You will not go home?'

'No more home.' Kauri seemed melancholy.

I wondered what he meant. Did he mean he would never return to his island of giant Kauri trees? Or did he mean that we would never return to Nantucket, the place where we began this journey? Home was a strange concept on board for everyone. We came from so many different parts of the world. Was England my home? I had no desire to return to Saxonham, even though I thought of that place often during my sleepless nights. Where was my home, really? Perhaps I had become like Captain Seneca, with a dread of going back. Home was a place to depart from, not somewhere to stay or return to.

'Will I return, Kauri?'

Kauri looked at me, his eyes like two pools in which I could drown. I felt he was conjuring up my future, his pipe's smoke wrapped around his bald dome, and his breath softly joined the sea air, with a stillness that seemed to be forming an answer.

'You say prayer for Kauri. Make prayer, for all men. Your shadow is the whale. He your god. He your spirit. You make prayer. You dance. Don't cry.'

He then began to sing softly in his native tongue with a slow, sombre repetition. He uttered his ticking and clucking words enigmatically. I did not understand them, but knew somehow that asking more would break his trance and not make me any wiser.

This morning I heard again the cry of an albatross squealing above the deck. The cry was piercing, as sharp and persistent as the first time I heard it. Seneca and Muzi were already on the deck when I went up at dawn. The same game resumed between the cat and the bird, the cat meowing at the sky while the bird whirled around above us. It was a queer scene to see. Seneca was much more irritated this time. He turned to me and ordered:

'Ishmael, get the pistol!'

I was again taken aback by such a request, though I had the pistol with me now, buried deep in the pocket of my trousers. Hesitantly, I reached down to it.

'Sir, I have it. What do you want me to do?'

'Will you shoot the damn bird?!'

I stood on the deck, frozen. The cat and bird game continued, though the cat seemed to be tiring.

'Do as I say, Ishmael!'

As if under a spell, I brought out the pistol. It felt heavy in my hand. I released the safety catch, and raised the revolver, grasping it with both hands. I pointed at the bird as best I could, for it was a moving target. I had no desire to kill the bird. Indeed, I felt it would be a sin. But I was sure I could not hit it anyway. So, I pulled the trigger. The albatross made a shriek and flew up. I fired again, into the air. The bird was indifferent to these vain gestures of violence. I was not surprised! The bird's cry was a mocking laugh, echoing in my ears even though it had already flown away. I cried out in my mind, 'Fare thee well, bird. Don't return to this ship of fools!'

379

Seneca was disappointed by my pathetic marksmanship. But his attention instantly moved away when the mastman shouted:

'Watch out! There is a white streamline that way! As straight as an arrow!'

We looked up. The mastman was pointing at the starboard. Rushing there, we could indeed see a long white trail, like a streaking cloud, in the ocean. The line ran parallel to the *Nimrod*.

'The devil's path!' the captain announced excitedly. 'That's where he went! The devil has appeared, or I am no mother's son!'

Alarmed, we observed that the long white line seemed to be stretching as we watched. We knew that such a long and uninterrupted stream could only mark the path of a large male whale.

'Man the mastheads! Call all hands!' Seneca cried out.

Tyrone jumped up and called upon everyone to gather around. Some men, still in slumber, appeared with their clothes in their hands.

'What did you see?' cried Seneca, flattening his face to the sky.

'Nothing yet, sir!' were the words that came down in reply from the mastman. 'Though the straight white line is stretching further that way!'

'Change the sails!'

Everyone ran to pull the rigging, and two more men were ordered to climb up the mast so they could look in different directions for the whale.

In no time, a man on the mast cried into the air:

'There she blows! There!'

'Is it him? The white devil?' Seneca cried, lifting his spyglass to observe the distant waves.

'He has got a hump like a snow hill! There!' the mastman shouted down.

Seneca narrowed his eyes, then his voice cracked through the air:

'It is him! Moby Dick!'

Fired by the cry which seemed simultaneously taken up by the three lookouts, the men on deck rushed to the rigging to behold the famous whale they had so long been pursuing. Drake and Freedman ordered us to get the supplies for the whaleboats, while the harpooners fetched their tools.

'There I saw him!' Seneca cried in his long-drawn, coarse tone. Then he put down his spyglass and shouted to the men:

'Stand by three boats. Mr Drake, stay on board, and keep the ship. Lower, lower, quicker!'

Clutching his stick, Seneca staggered towards the edge of the ship where the whaleboats were being lowered.

'Sir, are you sure that you want to go down with the boats?' Drake enquired amid the commotion.

Captain Seneca gave no answer. He was already moving towards the opening where the boats would exit, Kauri and four steersmen following behind with extra lamps and water supplies. As soon as the first boat was in the water, Seneca was on the roped chair and slid through the air to the whaleboat.

Freedman and Tashe's team too were getting ready. For the third boat, Drake ordered me to take the lead with Tyrone and the Japanese crew. This time, I had no hesitation. It felt almost natural that I had to be the third mate leading the Asian team, though I still understood nothing of their speech, apart from 'yes' in Japanese: hai! with a firm nod.

Soon all the boats were dropped. And with the sails set and the paddles plying, we were shooting ahead to leeward. As my boat left the *Nimrod*, I turned and saw Muzi on the deck. He was watching us with an expression I could not read. His palms were folded together at his chest and his lips moved very slightly as though he was sending a prayer to us. If he could predict the future, or if he could find the answer from his cosmic book, what would lie ahead of us?

III

First Battle

Hexagram 3

This hexagram is 屯 (zhūn): sprouting/trouble at the start.

Lower trigram: ☳ (震 zhèn) quaking and (雷 léi) thunder; upper trigram: ☵ (坎 kǎn) gorge.

The lines: the yang line below is the arousing thunder, the yin line above is the abysmal water, the yin line at the top means tears flow.

The judgement: continuing

The image: cloud and thunder

The action: let it come, bring it forth

As we followed the streamline in the ocean towards the white whale, the waters gradually grew calm, and we progressed as smoothly as though we were gliding on a carpet. Our three boats were steered parallel to each other, all aiming to the east where the whale seemed to be heading. Suddenly, about a league from us, the leviathan emerged from the water. What a sight! The white hump was huge and impressive, the fountain that shot up from the blowhole was so high it became a rainbow-coloured mist in the reflection of the sunlight.

My Japanese whalers made a curious singing sound, something I could only describe as a sort of crying and laughing at the same time – a very particular Asiatic way of expressing excitement. I saw Seneca and Freedman's boat was placed at an angle to the ungodly creature, so I told my men we should turn to the right to form a triangle with the other two boats. As we got close to him, we took down the small sail and brought out the oars so that we could better control our speed and direction. Now I could see the wrinkly skin of his enormous head. Oh, an old man of an old whale! As he moved, bright bubbles rose and danced by his side, and his sudden shifts produced such a wavy tumult that at times we could not see the other boats at all. We jerked and bounced in the waves, up and down, everyone drenched by the violent splashing of the water. It was almost impossible for us to maintain our balance.

We tried to turn the bow so that the harpooner could take aim. Then I heard Captain Seneca's voice from across the water.

'Aim for the head on, Kauri! Give it to him! Yes, throw it!!'

I could not see what was happening. Some harpoons were certainly thrown out to the whale, but what followed were even more violent waves surging towards us. Before we could understand what was wrong, the whale jolted – perhaps his back writhed in pain or his tail made a mighty splash – and our boat flew into the air. All of us were thrown into the sea.

I choked and struggled in the liquid hell as I thrashed

desperately, trying to grasp anything near me. But the waves were crashing onto me so savagely that I lost the direction I should swim towards. I was in a life-and-death battle. Somehow I managed to raise my head above the water before another frenzied wave crashed down, and saw that my Japanese crew were swimming for dear life. Nearby I saw our boat – well, not even half of the boat. The oars were floating aimlessly on the water.

Some moments later, we managed to get hold of some of the planks – all that remained of our broken vessel. Thank God there was no sign of the whale. We saw Freedman's boat coming towards us.

'How many are missing?' he shouted in the chaos, throwing us a rope.

No one could answer his question. He sent out the distress signal with his flare gun in the direction of the *Nimrod*, and after I climbed onto Freedman's boat, I realised that only Tyrone and two of the Japanese crew members were with me. Where had the other two gone?

Crowded in Freedman's whaleboat, we steered out from the whirlpool of the waves and tried to ascertain where the whale was, and where the captain's boat had gone. Meanwhile, we looked out for our missing men. After about twenty minutes, we rescued one of our Japanese crew. The older man – Shinya – was injured. His head was bleeding. He must have hit his skull on the bow when the boat capsized. He was semi-conscious when Freedman's team pulled him from the water. But by the time we lay him down in the boat, he was barely moving. He continued to bleed. And there was still one man missing.

Carrying on our search in distress and confusion, we saw the *Nimrod* sailing towards us. It was only then that we

385

spotted Captain Seneca's boat, rather far away. We could tell it was the first boat from its bright red sides. They were at least a mile from us, but the waves again rose and fell, such that we lost sight of the boat. Nor did we know the whereabouts of the whale.

IV

Second Battle

Hexagram 32

This hexagram is 恆 (héng): persevering/duration.

Lower trigram: ☴ (巽 xùn) ground = (风 fēng) wind; upper trigram: ☳ (震 zhèn) quake = (雷 léi) thunder.

The lines: the yin line at the bottom is the gentle wind, yang lines in the middle mean persistent humiliation and endurance.

The judgement: relentlessness and constancy

The image: thunder and wind

The action: to endure

In the chase, thoughts had no more substance than froth on waves, and the turbid agitation of the swells seemed to mirror my own desolation.

With the third whaleboat under my command destroyed, we had to return to the *Nimrod*. Still missing one Japanese man, I had to wait for Drake's instructions on what we should do. Upon my return, Freedman and his boat immediately set out again on the chase. Since Captain Seneca was leading the first boat and they were still pursuing the whale, Freedman wanted to make sure that he could assist, especially if the captain was in trouble.

We busied ourselves with the task of getting warm and dry. The surgeon, meanwhile, was trying to give succour to Shinya. His head was still bleeding heavily, and none of us held out much hope. Mr Hawthorne wrapped Shinya's head with a cloth but something in the gentleness of his manner told us that the man would not survive the next morning. Taiji, who had known Shinya for many years, was very upset. The two remaining Japanese sailors prayed at the side of the dying man.

Moses and Dilly brought us hot tea but we could barely drink it due to our distress. After changing into a dry shirt, I went to talk to the first mate. He was in the captain's cabin, having some exchange with Muzi. Never before had I seen Drake consult with the Chinese monk – usually our captain kept Muzi for himself, unless Muzi was guiding us in the making of sails. So it was surprising to see the two talking closely. Had Drake changed his mind about having the strange cosmic book guide us on the *Nimrod*? I waited by the door, and a few moments later Drake came out, his face looking gloomy. I made my report nonetheless.

'Sir, I am very sorry about the situation. We lost the boat, and possibly two men.'

Drake nodded, then sighed. 'I don't usually talk to Muzi, but since Seneca has been consulting him I have to know what is in his mind.'

'Perhaps it was not a good sign to go on the chase?'

'It is not for me to tell the old man what to do, but perhaps you have some sway over him, Ishmaelle. So, take our spare boat now and lead the men! If you manage to hunt the white whale with Seneca and return in one piece,

388

then we shall drink our rum and even head home soon! But . . .' He paused, and raised his head, as if searching the horizon for the whale and the crazed old man. 'But . . . if we were to lose another boat, then I would say we are definitely not heading in the right direction. In fact, the Chinese monk has already predicted it.'

'Has he?'

'Well, it is seldom that Muzi reveals his thoughts and mood. But I noticed, I thought, that his footsteps this morning were faster than usual when he paced the deck, his face somehow darker. He will have to tell Seneca – that is, if Seneca manages to find his way back to the *Nimrod* tonight.'

I found his last words frightening. But before I could ponder on the matter, I was ordered to lower the last boat – our spare one. All men were called on deck to help us gather the necessary equipment: oars, ropes, harpoons, lamps, sails, water, spears, shears. But with one whaler boat already chasing, plus the injured and missing, we did not have enough strong men to go out. So Drake ordered the carpenter to accompany us. At least Woody could row the boat as long as the chase would take. Poor Woody, he was not happy but he did not complain. All he said was: 'Ishmael, I told you, life is a task but death is not.' And he lowered himself down into the boat.

Strangely, even in the intensity of the moment I noticed that everyone called me by my male name, Ishmael, though most had become used to calling me Ishmaelle since discovering my identity. What made them switch back to my adopted name? Did my new task, assigned by the captain and the mates, make them believe that I was after all a male in a female body? My thoughts were quickly interrupted by the commotion of getting the boat ready to set out.

'The last time I was on a whaleboat chasing a fish was seven years ago! Poor me!' The carpenter squatted down and reached towards the oarlock. 'Oh! If I'd known this rowing seat was so uncomfortable, I would have made a special low chair with a cushion! Remind me when we get back, Ishmael!'

So we six left the ship and rowed our boat towards the battlefield again, except that we could not see where the whale went, only a small dot on the distant waves that was perhaps the boat led by Seneca.

As we got closer, we saw the white creature once more. There were several harpoons on his back. But this was not a good sign. Seneca and Kauri had thrown out so many harpoons that the ropes had become dangerously entangled. The waves were also against the small whaleboat – the steersmen could no longer control the tiller. We could see that both Seneca and Kauri were caught in a spider's web of ropes. Our Japanese men shouted urgently as Kauri struggled in the mess of pulled lines. Finally he managed to grab his knife and cut the rope around his shoulder, then the one around Captain Seneca's neck. As soon as the lines were cut, the boat and the whale were as though suddenly repelled by each other. And in no time, the whale dived into the water – and disappeared!

V

Third Battle

Hexagram 33

This hexagram is 遯 (dùn): retreat.

Lower trigram: ☶ (艮 gèn) bound = (山 shān) mountain;
upper trigram: ☰ (乾 qián) force = (天 tiān) heaven.

The lines: the yin line at the bottom means one must not
wish to undertake anything, the yang line at the top means
friendly retreat.

The judgement: withdrawal
The image: mountain under heaven
The action: to retreat

When the whaleboats got back to the *Nimrod*, it was near
midnight. There was no moon and it was almost pitch-
black even with the lit lamps. It had been a very long day,
and we were all exhausted. Captain Seneca was in a strange
mood. His face looked ghostly and his arm trembled as he
reached for his rum. He would not speak to anyone, and no
one dared to say anything to him. He soon returned to his
cabin, helped by Muzi and Dilly. Ragged and weary, we

were so fatigued that we could barely move. The chef had to get Dilly to carry the food up onto the open deck, so that the officers and the seamen could eat quickly together before falling asleep.

It was very unusual for all of us to eat together in the dark on the deck. Everyone was still in their drenched clothes from the chase, and no one had the energy to say anything. For a while, there was only the sound of chewing and swallowing from our dry mouths and throats. As I swallowed my last piece of salt beef, I thought of Shinya, probably dying in the surgeon's cabin. I did not see Mr Hawthorne anywhere. I also realised that we had not found the missing Japanese sailor. There would be little hope now.

Nevertheless, once we'd eaten, three steersmen were sent out again to search for him; everyone else went to get some rest. As I was making my way towards my bed, I overheard Freedman and Drake conversing by the stairs of the after house.

'Seneca would not even talk to the Chinese,' Freedman said. 'This is curious, is it not, Drake? But Muzi would not let the chase go on!'

Drake let out a deep sigh. 'For God's sake, and ours, I hope by the morning the captain will change his mind.'

As soon as my head touched the pillow I was asleep. But even in my sleep I was aware of how weary and exhausted I was. I had never been so tired in my entire life. I had lost all sense of time. At dawn, I had a brief moment of wakefulness. It was still quite dark, I realised. I felt the cat, my companion since the Cape. She must have come to my bunk in the night. But I could not move, as my arms were so sore and my legs as heavy as stone. My head was cleaved as though by a fiery knife. I felt like I needed to sleep for another day and night until I could gather my senses once again. I fell back to sleep in the dawn light. When I awoke again, the cat was gone.

In the morning, as we were having our breakfast, the surgeon came to tell us Shinya had died. Before anyone could say anything, the enraged captain appeared in front of us, his grey hair flying about wildly in the wind, his eyes like rheumy red sores. He ordered the three mastmen to go on watch, though none of them had finished their breakfast. He ordered everyone else to get the equipment ready as he believed the white devil was nearby. While we busied ourselves with preparations, we saw the Chinese man appear behind Seneca. I sensed that Muzi was attempting to communicate something urgent to the captain but in a discreet way. So with tools in my hand, I moved closer to them.

'The Book has said, Captain. You no go,' I heard Muzi utter with great solemnity.

'The Book, you pestilential monk?! Has the Book seen the white devil there under my eyelash?!' cried the old man.

Silence was the response from Muzi. I was stunned to witness this outbreak of conflict between the captain and his soothsayer. The Chinese man walked over to the piles of new sails we were preparing to take down to the whaleboats, and then he turned back to the captain.

'Be cautious with your bruteness. He sees. He hears,' he said.

The Chinese man looked to the bow and then the stern of the ship, his white silk shirt shimmering momentarily. He whispered something inaudible, and then shuffled away, leaving Seneca on the deck.

All of us carried on busying ourselves to prepare for the continued chase. When the white sun was burning our shadows into the deck, like a bolt of lightning a man on the mast cried into the air:

'There she blows! There!' A few moments later, the lookout confirmed it to us: 'It is him, the white whale!'

So the two boats were lowered. The order was different today. Seneca remained on board, ordering Drake to take the first whaleboat, I the second.

'Captain, I hope this pursuit will be the last!' Drake announced before he went down to the boat.

Seneca did not respond. None of us said anything either. Since we had lost some equipment in the chase the day before, we were not well prepared. And I knew certainly the Japanese were not happy even though they obeyed the order and went down with me. Taiji's face did not look calm.

As we settled in the boat, he spoke:

'Ishmaelle, I have told the mates that I must return to my family very soon, they are waiting for me.'

'Yes, I remember, Taiji.'

'But can I insist again? I want to return, as soon as the chase is over. I will seek passage on any ship that passes. Will you ask the mates for permission?'

I gazed at him. His black eyes were almost tearful. I nodded. He looked at me thankfully and off we rowed.

Within a mile or so, after observing the watery pattern where he had dived not long before, our boats arrived in the vicinity of the white whale. We waited and rowed slowly through the water. Then all of a sudden, the whale burst out of the sea, soaring high into the air, then came crashing back down with an almighty crack. This time, we were far enough from the violent surging of the waves, though still we clutched on to the sides of the boat to avoid being cast into the water. After some moments to reorient ourselves, Tyrone our harpooner stood with his arm raised, ready to throw out his weapon.

But then the whale dived again. It was playing with us. I felt panic. It was a dire situation as the whale was so close, and any movement he made could condemn us. He disappeared, but we knew he could only be below us, maybe below our very boat. I saw Drake's boat approaching and Kauri on the bow, his arm raised high above his shoulder and his harpoon straight.

In my heart of hearts, I wished the creature would dive as deep as he could, and that he would just swim away, away from us, further and further away from us, we the brutes, the heartless ones, the enraged and the greedy men! And what of the woman in their midst? There was no meaning in this. Only death, for the whale or for us. But for what purpose? 'Give me an answer, Lord, now, before it's too late,' I begged. I would need no persuasion if the Lord's answer was only half convincing!

There was a sea-quake, a whale-made hurricane, a man-made typhoon – the white whale rose in front of us and splashed his gigantic tail. He fell into the sea and in his wake he plunged us all into the water. Like a confused symphony of watery struggle, we all fell together, whale and all, into a whirlpool of mayhem, of bubbles, foam, froth and salty desperation:

guuuuurrrrrrrrunnnnnnnnnguuuuuuuuunnuruunnnnnnnnnngagagagggaggagaggg

guuuuurrrrrrrrunnnnnnnnnguuuuuuuuunnuruunnnnnnnnnngagagagggaggagaggg

guuuuurrrrrrrrunnnnnnnnnguuuuuuuuuuuuruunnnnnnnnnngagagagggaggagaggg

guuuuurrrrrrrrunnnnnnnnnguuuuuuuuunnuruunnnnnnnnnngagagagggaggagaggg

guuuuurrrrrrrrunnnnnnnnnguuuuuuunnnnnuruunnnnnnnnnngagagagggaggagaggg guuuuurrrrrrrrrunnnnnnnnnguuuuunnnnnuruunnnnnnnnnnngagagaggaggagagggg

guuuuurrrrrrrrrunnnnnnnnnguuuuuuuunnnnuruunnnnnnnnnnngagagaggaggagagggg

guuuuurrrrrrrrrunnnnnnnnnguuuuuuuunnnnuruunnnnnnnnnnngagagaggaggagagggg

Then silence and darkness. I seemed to wake after a time without reckoning. How long had we been in the water? How long had we swum our hearts out before the *Nimrod* found us? I was lying flat on the deck of the *Nimrod*, miraculously. I watched as others were dragged over the gangway to be landed like drenched lifeless slugs on the wood.

We had no idea what had happened to Drake's boat. But the men on the *Nimrod* saw all, and told us that it had been smashed. Mine had survived – it had sustained some damage but the carpenter was already repairing the leak. No one was missing from this attack, though.

So we had only one whaleboat left, the spare one, the one reserved for an emergency! What were we supposed to do? Anyone in possession of his senses would shout it out: stop this insane chase before it's too late! But anyone with a sober awareness would also see that it was already too late. Too late.

VI

Battle Intermission

Hexagram 37

This hexagram is 家人 (jiā rén): the clan/family.

Lower trigram: ☲ (離 lí) radiance = (火 huǒ) fire; upper trigram: ☴ (巽 xùn) ground = (風 fēng) wind.

The lines: the yang line at the bottom means seclusion within the family, the yang line at the top means nurturing and gathering good fortune.

The judgement: the perseverance of the woman furthers

The image: wind emerging from fire

The action: to return

The white whale's call of vengeance.

Whhhhhhhhhhhhhhhhhiiiiiiiiiiiiiiiiioooooooooo

Cooooooooooooommmmmmmmmeeeeee

Kkkkkkkkkkkkkkkkeeeeeeeeeeeeeeeeeeerrrr

WhhhhhhhhhhhhhhhhiiiiiiiiiiiiiiiioooOOOOOOO

Coooooooooooommmmmmmmmmmeeeeeee

Kkkkkkkkkkkkkkkkeeeeeeeeeeeeeeeerrrrrr

WhhhhhhhhhhhhhhhhiiiiiiiiiiiiiiiioOOOOOOOO

Coooooooooooommmmmmmmmmeeeeee

Kkkkkkkkkkkkkkkeeeeeeeeeeeeeeeeeerrrr

In the midst of the night, in my restlessness, I heard strange sounds. The gusts of wind seemed to funnel into our sleeping quarters a mix of whistles and clicks and squeaks. I was sure it was the whale. What was it crying out for? I also thought I heard a deep groaning from below the ship. I was too tired to open my eyes, nor did I dare.

Then, I felt someone shaking my shoulder. I opened my eyes and saw a face close by me, dim under the feeble lamp on the ceiling. It was little Dilly. He shushed with his finger and beckoned me to rise.

'The captain is wanting you. He is mad, he wants you to come. Now!'

My limbs still deadened with sleep, I managed to find my feet and follow the boy. I found the captain in his cabin, slouched in his armchair, dishevelled.

Beside a lone lamp, Seneca fixed me with his gimlet eye, his mouth slack and moist, his left hand seeming to tremble.

'Have you heard the whale? Of course you have! Tell the truth!'

'I . . . I have heard it, Captain,' I stammered.

'Aye, only a man like me or a witch like you would hear it. The whale is moaning! Moaning out its funeral dirge! It waits for us. We two! The whale waits for me, and waits for you! Hear me?'

'But, Captain, why would it wait for me? Why would it wait for anyone, let alone a poor soul like me? A woman. Surely, Captain –'

'Enough!' A surge of energy and power seemed to possess him. I was rooted to the spot, asking myself what madness possessed this man.

'You cannot lie to me and dissemble! You, witch, you have been brought to me, brought on this cursed bark. You are the path to the whale. You have beguiled that whale, you will ensure I prevail!'

He stood up now, tottering on his one leg and ivory peg.

'I have dismissed my Taoist, because he knows nothing. His magical sticks only rattle like bones foretelling disaster. He knows no future! But you . . .! Listen, do you hear it now? He is moaning and wailing out there, gnashing his teeth! Listen!'

Seneca grabbed my shoulders, and sealed my mouth with his rough swollen hand. His blazing black eyes were fixed on my brow, as if to see the sounds within my very head.

I could only murmur when he retracted his hand: 'I hear, sir.'

I took one step backwards; he one towards me.

'Ishmaelle, this is what it has all come to. I have lost trust in the men of this ship. I have lost trust in any man, in truth. All the men on this damned globe! All men have been a disappointment to me! You alone, the only woman I know who knows the whaling life, and who is more than a woman, you have not disappointed me. You hear me? You are going to lead us to the whale. If that damned Taoist was right, you are the only one destined to live. But that can only mean you will smite the whale! The magic of your witch's craft will do it. Show me how!'

He grasped my neck, as if he would strangle me, crying out that I must tell him the way, that I must pacify the whale and destroy its spirit. Then I must fly through the night, and enter the whale's brain, so as to relieve it of its power. His grasp was so strong I feared my life was in danger. All I could do was croak and, in desperation, lie:

'Yes, Captain. I will find the way. True, I am a witch. The whale speaks to me. I know how to end its spirit, to deliver it to you. Yes, Captain, but you must let me go. You must let me prepare myself . . . Captain, I will get you the whale! But you must let me live!'

Abruptly he released his grip, and stepped back. 'Tomorrow . . . I command you . . . deliver the whale unto us,' he whispered. 'Or you die . . .'

He then went back to his chair and sank into a near stupor.

'Your destiny lies with the whale. I know you feel the whale's mind. Draw it out of the deep so that he can be destroyed . . . Go now!'

I fled from the cabin, clasping my neck, and found a terrified Dilly, waiting by the door.

'Ishmaelle, I thought he was killing you!'

I could not speak, but staggered through the corridor, and up to breathe the air on the deck, under a starless sky. The Taoist was not there. Had he abandoned his beliefs or had he finished his prayer and returned to sleep? The night had closed in on us all. I felt myself swooning, and I collapsed on the deck in a ball.

Losing all sense of place and time, in utter exhaustion, I must have fallen asleep on the deck. I heard no more whale sounds. The sun rose. I could feel the rays and the warmth. But my body was cold. I opened my eyes and found Drake looking down on me.

'Are you all right, Ishmaelle?'

I nodded. I sat up, not sure what to tell the mate. I decided to say not a word about my conversation with Seneca. Had it perhaps been a nightmare? I shook my head. I needed to gather my senses. I stood up, feeling fatigued and listless. The pistol was heavy in my pocket. Almost stumbling, I moved towards the freshwater area by the bow, and washed my face.

VII

Final Battle

Hexagram 23

This hexagram is 剝 (bō): splitting apart.

Lower trigram: ☷ (坤 kūn) field = (地 di) earth; upper trigram: ☶ (艮 gèn) bound = (山 shan) mountain.

The lines: the yin line on the bottom is the receptive earth, the yang line above is the mountain keeping still.

The judgement: stripping away, no bounty

The image: the mountain rests on the earth

The action: to split things apart

The sea was eerily serene, the sky painfully blue. All the men looked like ghosts. Kauri, as if disenchanted, had stopped speaking altogether and avoided looking at me. He cast his eyes on the white foam of the grey waves. Even Mr Hawthorne, his face pale and anguished, stayed in his cabin, writing his diary as if he was sure only his diary would survive to tell the truth about the *Nimrod*. The carpenter had been up early working on our remaining whaleboat. With hammer and nail in hand, he was about to finish repairing the leak when the sun rose above the foresail. But the men on the deck murmured to one another, each chewing stale bread with an air of hopeless resignation. Obviously none of us felt that we could go on with one whaleboat. And there was no man on the mast yet to do the lookouts, perhaps because we wouldn't go on a chase.

Then Seneca appeared with Dilly following behind. Clutching on his whalebone leg, he had become unrecognisable – his beard was bushy and long, his eyebrows white, as if in one night he had grown a decade older. He had become the oldest man on this ocean. When he saw there was no one on the rigging, he fumed with rage.

'Where is the damn mastman?'

One of the men quickly swallowed his bread, jumped up and climbed on the mainmast.

'Watch with your eyeballs peeled!' the captain bellowed. 'The devil must be nearby – I heard him last night!'

'Nothing yet, sir!' the man shouted down.

All of us looked at the captain stiffly. In despair, Drake walked over to him and spoke:

'God is against this hunt, Captain, and it would be blasphemy to keep chasing the white whale!'

'What did you say? God? Which god? I am the god of the *Nimrod*! Keep silent, Mr Drake.' Seneca spat out his words.

Drake was shaking.

'Sir, allow me to plead,' Freedman challenged. 'We are not far from the islands of Bora Bora and Tahiti, and we could anchor there to get new boats and to prepare ourselves better, with all respect, sir!'

'You, coward rat! Away! It's our final chance! Final, you understand? And now we have our weapon, our tool!' Seneca then turned and pointed to me:

'We have the witch, standing there before us! Ishmaelle!'
I shuddered with horror.

'What?' Both Drake and Freedman turned to look at me, along with everyone else, with a mixed expression of incomprehension and bewilderment.

Suddenly, we heard the bird. It was not the albatross I feared, it was a black hawk pulling at the ship's flag. As we stared up at it, the hawk managed to pull the flag free from the mast! Off the bird went with the American flag in its beak. Someone was coming up on deck. It was Muzi the Taoist. He stopped at the sight of the bird. Then a look of recognition seemed to come over his face. His hands drew together, palm against palm, in a gesture of prayer.

Thud, thud, thud, Captain Seneca came towards me with a wild energy. Reaching out his hand, he grasped my arm and ordered:

'Listen, you, Ishmaelle, you take the lifebuoy-coffin, and go down to lure the devil. You know how to lure him, and you can hear him, so you do the witch's craft. Draw that whale towards us. Once he emerges, we will send our last boat to hunt him. You understand?'

His powerful grip on my arm pierced my flesh. I tried to pull back from him, shaking my head. With my other hand free, discreetly I reached down to the pocket in my trousers.

'Have you gone insane, sir?' Drake intervened with an anguished voice.

'Can't you see she is a witch, Drake?! How did she manage to be on this sea for so long, eh? A woman in man's clothes all the way from old England, with her herbs and hexes, and she can hear the whale and can sense the devil. Know you not this? Eh? Isn't it clear that she is practising witchcraft on all of us?'

Taking a chance while he continued with his mad

barking, my hand got hold of the pistol in my pocket and quickly I brought it out. My fingertips on the trigger, I pointed it at Seneca.

'Stop this, Captain!' I cried, with terror and desperation. Feeling outside of my body, I was surprised by my boldness.

But with lightning speed, Seneca grabbed hold of my pistol, with a furious swipe of his hand, and gained full possession of the weapon. Laughing like a crazed seal, he pointed it towards the mates and then towards me.

'Ishmaelle, you can do better than this! You don't need this toy! Go down to the water. Do as I say, and if anyone blocks you, he shall receive lead in his brain.'

As Seneca moved closer and closer to me, I stepped back. I was on the edge of the bulwark, his pistol pointed to my temple.

'You will seduce the devil, and with your spell upon the whale, we shall defeat him!'

All of a sudden, Kauri, my Polynesian, leapt out from the standing throng of men. Like a leopard, he jumped and ran towards the captain. He knocked Seneca down but then a bang erupted – the pistol fired into the air. I was pushed to the very edge of the deck while the two men were wrestling on the floor. Chaos descended on deck, and before I could understand what was happening, I found myself falling into the sea. There, suddenly I was sinking into the dark blue! In a daze of shock and terror, my heart beating, I regained the surface, and managed to get my head above the water. I heard a splash and saw the lifebuoy-coffin had been thrown down near me. I swam towards it and latched my body onto it. I lifted my head to find the ship, but it was already sailing on. Dilly called out from above: 'Hold fast, Ishmaelle!' But the stern had passed me.

And then, a white avalanche of waves gripped my coffin. I rose on a crest but I clutched on like a barnacle on a rock, my hands finding the handle on the side of the casket – that was my salvation. I was carried away by the wave. I could not see the ship for a while, but I heard the clicking sound, the very clicking and whistling sound I had heard last night. Then another wave came, this time a much larger one, an almighty power coming towards me. Was this it? My cursed life? Was this what I deserved, to be a witch cast adrift on the sea in a tempest? Then in a flash, an image of my great-aunt appeared. She once said witches were cast onto the water as a trial, and if they drowned they were proved not to be witches. Was this my trial?

I heard the clicking and whistling again. I knew the whale was coming and was very close to me. As soon as I surfaced and steadied myself on the coffin, I turned, and found the *Nimrod*, now quite far away from me. I could see the dots of men on the deck, moving about. Another ferocious wave arrived and I was smashed down into the liquid mass again.

TRIO

ISHMAELLE: Now I know my fate it all comes to this cast as a witch like my aunt of old into the cold absurdity of the ocean the waves about me a lone oyster with a mind screaming out to the abyss the end the end the end the end

SENECA: Calm your soul the witch is on the sea and she will go down and eat out the mind of the devil and deliver it to my mighty arms but I rage and feel the torrent and my heart beats stronger than a horse and the unknown is closing in the dark already and darker still the fate the dark the dark the dark and darker still beats the drum it comes it comes it comes

WHALE: Wwwoooooohhhhhh kkkkkkkkkkkkkkk www wwwooooooo ssssssssssssshhh

ALL TOGETHER: Lost in torment the sea devours all kkkkkkkkkkk wwwwwooooo ssssssssssssss

ISHMAELLE: Oh whale hear me as I ride this coffin don't crush it with your teeth but know I am with you I feel your strength your pain and I am not your avenger not the insanity of men but if the end comes take this body down with you . . .

SENECA: It comes it comes it comes I am ready for all my life achieves its meaning apotheosis I am becoming a god

WHALE: Wwwooooooohhhhhh kkkkkkkkkkkkkkk wwwwwwooooooo ssssssssssssshhh

ALL TOGETHER: Lost in torment the sea devours all kkkkkkkkkk wwwwooooo sssssssssssshhh

Then suddenly, in the space between me and the ship, out of the green and blue waters, a white mountain rose. There he was, the white whale. With his giant head he was charging the *Nimrod*, the great flukes of his tail rose up behind him, and propelled him forward into the stern of the ship. From a distance, I watched the *Nimrod* tremble, shake and shudder, as though a hurricane had descended upon it.

Baaaaaaaaannnnnnnng

Buuuuuuuuuunnnnng

Whooooossssshiiiiiiiiiii

Rooohhhhhhhhhoooooo

Baaaaannnnnnnnnnnng

Rooohhhhhhhhhoooooo

Baaaaannnnnnnnnnngg

Bannnnnnnnng buuuuuuuunnng whossssssssssss yeeeeeeeeeeooo whossssssssssss an almighty explosion a gargantuan rush and burst of sound like the crack of doom the masts the riggings snapped the sails broke and everyone flew into the air and the sky took them to its sphere all there was in this world were cracking timbers and wild scattering of ropes and sails and barrels and tackle and poles and the screams and the limbs the arms the foam and the swallowing of great volumes of rushing salt water hammering and driving onto everyone and everything where was the captain and where were the mates and where was my friend Kauri and the surgeon the carpenter the cook the cabin boy the cat where was any living one bannnnnnnnng buuuuuuuunnng whosssssssssssss yeeeeeeeeeeeoooo whosssssssssssss I saw the white whale with his jaw open like a horrifying tooth-lined chasm and his head making another assault on the fragments of the ship which seemed to have been sucked into a giant groaning vortex and a spinning whirlpool which finally gurgled and released a vast burst of air the last bubble of life and then silence save for the mist and the waves and the screams of birds and the foam and the deathbed of the waterquake oh Lord save me oh Lord no man was visible all was awash and only the sole sea and the scream of seagulls and wail of wind the world of the ship had now been expunged my cat Gladys and all and a void of ocean was all that remained.

Baaaaaaaaannnnnnng

Buuuuuuuuuunnnng

Whooooosssshiiiiiiiiiii

RooohhhhhhhhooooOO

Baaaaannnnnnn**nnnng**

RooohhhhhhhhoOOOOO

Whooooossssshiiiiiiiiiii

Baaaaannnnnnnn**nngg**

FINAL ARIA

Captain Seneca's last thoughts, while sinking down by the tail of the white whale.

WHITE WHALE WHEREVER you roam and whatever you devour you will not miss me I am your head your jaw your blubber your blowhole your tail your shadow and I am your fate your carcass your spirit

You waves ceaseless churn and rush forward and backwards swell subside and you inhabit me our swallowing mouth will take my ignorance my weakness my pride my passion and my sorrow

You clouds far above in the aeon float and unspoken you will witness my fate under this sun this moon this starry night this stormy air this world of elements and a man's cries

You Papa Po long gone from the dusty cornfields where I stole a cornstalk and roasting it burnt my finger Master Cutbush's dog chased and bit me oh Papa Po your scorched final day is my drenched final minutes and the sand has passed through the hourglass

The birth is a sleep and a forgetting and a laughter and a final disappearance and in that darkness I hear the echoes from the clouds the waves the talk of the seamen the ship the oars the thunder the lightning the rains the albatross and the white whale

The world I have seen and I will see no more

In that absolute darkness I will once again awake and see the tears of Mother and the view of windows with the lake and water lilies and slippery stones which I fell into once as a child one summer when the woman abandoned the house and I called Mother as I was drowning but all that was the past the dust of the memory of an old man

ALL PERISHED. Seneca, Drake, Freedman, Kauri, Tashe, Tyrone, Hawthorne, Washington, Moses, Woody, Simon, Dilly, Muzi, Taiji, my cat Gladys and the Japanese whalers along with the rest of the crew, all gone, swept into the deep of the ocean. Only the witch survived.

That lifebuoy-coffin, that small house of death, gave me life. It carried me along, floating through the Polynesian Sea, the warm ocean and the gentle sky above. It drifted for two days and one night. Days of parchedness, my tongue like a dry lizard in my mouth, and a cold night of endless stars and hopeless thoughts. Until a miracle. A ship caught sight of me. I knew that ship and I knew that captain. It was Captain Fitzroy of the *Sirena*, Captain Fitzroy who had been searching for his lost son. Instead, he found me, an orphan of the sea. I was taken on board the *Sirena*, along with my coffin. It is here that I must pause my story, though, and return to the shipwreck.

When I was floating on the coffin, passing the debris from the ship, I saw the white whale. He was swimming towards me. But this time, he was calm. When he approached, he slowed down, the giant head, scarred and barnacled, slipping through the crystal water. From my bobbing tiny craft, my coffin saviour, I looked down at the creature. He turned, and I saw his great eye looking up, wise and true. I felt the world come to a standstill, as the eye seemed to hold me in its vision. And then, with the merest stroke of his great fins, he swam on. The sea was entirely calm, as if under his command, as if the whale was preparing the way for me to float and then tell my story.

CHAPTER FIFTEEN

Saxonham

I

I HAD RETURNED TO THE WORLD.

A week after the *Sirena* brought me back to Nantucket, I found myself in New York. While waiting on the harbour to check for the next ship to England, I thought of revisiting Five Points in Manhattan. I thought of the pond where I sat and wept after hearing of the death of Captain Mackay. I sat by that pond till evening came and the night swallowed me. I recalled seeing Gemini and the black crows above me. Oh, that was more than a year ago, when I was a raw and inexperienced girl in man's clothing! When I sat and slept by that foreign pond, I could never have imagined what awaited me. I was just looking for a man I hardly knew. Perhaps Captain Mackay was the man who knew where the white whale was. Perhaps he wanted me to go on that voyage. Or perhaps he was like a mysterious whale himself, whom I had to eventually chase and encounter and then finally let go. Let him swim away. Let him pass by.

The whale decided that I should continue to have my life. And the soul of the Polynesian Sea – Kauri – decided that I should be blessed by him and by the spirit of the sea. How eventful and how tormented these months had been, my Lord! The memory-laden whaling voyage, like a finely wrought mesh rich in details, was still with me everywhere I went. It was part of my skin, deep in my bone marrow. I carried those faces and those speeches and those days and nights with me. Sometimes, a mere glimpse of the harbour and the sea made me tearful. I could not explain this pain. I could not speak of my sorrow. To say that I missed the men on the *Nimrod* was too light a thing to say. No, I did not miss them. I *was* them. Yes, *I was them*. I felt that part of me had died along with those men. And I knew it could never be reborn. What was that part of me that was wrecked and lost in the sea? The aggression? The violence? The vanity of conquest? I saw the part of me that was in the madness of Captain Seneca, the madness that had possessed me since I left England. The madness of Seneca that was his hunting the whale to the ends of the world. Such madness led me to the floating life of a half-man half-woman, a dangerous mix of possibilities. There I had been, a man then a woman. What had my womanliness done in that blood-drenched ship of men? Had I led all to doom or was there some salvation in their deaths?

I did not revisit Five Points. I waited by the harbour in New York for a ship that would take me home. Finally, I jumped on a merchant ship bound for the English port of Plymouth. I did not talk to anyone on board. I could not. There was a rock in my throat, my whole body seemed to be a piece of rock, I had turned to stone. Because if I had not turned to stone after coming back to Nantucket, I would have shattered, like foam on the sea. I would have died again and again.

II

IN A CARRIAGE on a winding road along the Kent coast, the familiar shingled beach and the white sea revealed itself before my eyes. The salty cold water was different from all the seas I had known. The sea here was grey-white in this season, the waves spoke a different language. As I caught a glimpse of the white petals of sea campions on the roadside, I realised that it was spring and that my nineteenth birthday was soon. Oh the white campions, the yellow cowslips, and the blue forget-me-nots! Here I returned, a nineteen-year-old woman-man. I wanted to shout out to this old wet landscape, to shout out to the swirling puffins and gulls, tell them what I had seen and heard. But where to begin? And where to end? Those stories could not end upon the shipwreck. Those stories could only end upon the final escape of the white whale. Yes, in my heart of hearts, I had always hoped the white whale would live. May he live forever. And may we never hunt him!

In the carriage, I learned from the coachman that Queen Victoria's nine children were all thriving, but that her husband Prince Albert had died. The queen was in deep mourning and would not come out from Windsor Castle. So our queen had become a widow while I was on the sea?

What was a queen after all? I asked myself, while the carriage rattled along the road towards Denge Marsh. I used to dream of becoming a queen when I was a child. Now I realised that a queen could just be a woman with children and a dead husband. For all my humbleness, I felt free and burdenless. I was my own queen. I pondered on this for a while and on my dead shipmates, and on the war that was going on in America, which no one here seemed to be aware of. Could there be a war here too? This was my country, but I had no idea if I would continue to live in this land. Had I turned into a kind of Captain Seneca, for whom a home was a place to leave, not to return? Or had I become my exiled friend Kauri, who was forever barred from returning home? Was I not a man-woman who was made for the ocean and for that permanent exile too? How could I stay in this land, when everyone I knew was either sailing on the ocean or at the bottom of it? My brother Joseph, I was sure, was somewhere out there, sailing across the sea. Perhaps when I got back to Saxonham I would find out more.

The carriage dropped me in front of the windmills behind our house. It was early morning. The windmills were covered in dense ivy. The ground was thick with overgrowth. The stinging nettles were everywhere and even with my linen trousers they managed to penetrate the fabric and sting my legs. But that particular windmill, the one my grandfather built and in which I had lived, seemed slightly different from what I remembered. As I stood among the nettles, with my canvas bag on my back, I realised that the mill's sails were missing. The wind and the rain must have completely destroyed them.

I stood looking at the windmill, without entering. For some reason, I feared going in. Would the barn owl still be living inside, in the crack under the ceiling? The owl I had cohabited with when I moved into the windmill after my baby sister died.

I turned away from the mill, and walked to our house. From the outside, it did not seem to have changed. Time had melted away and fused the past with the present. The same paint-faded sash windows, the same moss-covered stone walls, and the same thick door which my father made with a simple ornamented arch above the frame. The lock on the door was intact, though it was brown from rust. Our place to hide the key was always the same. So I walked back to the windmill. Behind it, against the wall, was a small pile of rocks. Under the largest rock, among earthworms, my fingers found a knotted piece of cloth. We wrapped the key in a piece of cloth so it would not go rusty – that had been my father's trick against time. Nothing had changed. Gripping the key in my hand, I opened the lock on the door.

When I had left the house, I had tidied up the kitchen and made the bed, and there was no chopped wood by the fireplace. But now I could see someone had used the fireplace. A few logs were still lying there, half burnt. The ash was cold. On the kitchen table was a porcelain bowl with a spoon in it. It was a large bowl we used for serving potatoes or soup. There was a tiny bit of yellow powdery dust on the bottom of the bowl. The air in the house smelled musty. A mournful feeling instantly enveloped me. Oh Lord. This had been my home, my world and my past. Could I bear to inhabit it again?

I put my heavy canvas bag on the dusty floor, and sat down on the bed. I felt something poke my right thigh. I knew it was one of the two parts of my seahorse lady. I reached into my pocket and brought them out. Laying them on the bed, I gazed at my broken seahorse idol. A spirit seemed to remain in this disembodied figurine. I was certain that this witness of my journey remembered everything.

It was utterly quiet except for some distant owls. The sheets felt damp, the pillow looked sulky and sullen. As I sat on the bed, I slipped my right hand into the pillow-case. This was where my brother and I would often hide our precious things in the past. In reality, there were not many precious things to hide. Occasionally Joseph would hide the money he got from working on the dock, and I would hide a bracelet or sometimes a coin. It was an old habit of my hand whenever I sat on the bed in that position. At this odd moment, when my hand reached for the pillow, I had not even realised what I was doing, but the hand went there, curiously and inexplicably. My fingers encountered paper. I took it out.

It was a letter.

A letter from my brother Joseph. Written the previous summer.

III

12 August 1861

Dearest Ishmaelle,

Where have you gone? I have returned to the house
twice in the last few months. This is the third time,
and I do not know when I shall return. I am going to
the sea for a while.

The last time I saw you was right after our baby sister
died. That was a very sad day and I am sorry that I
did not stay a few more days with you. But I was
desperate to leave and go seafaring. You did not know
yet what to do with your life, and what could I say to
you then? If I was wise I would tell you that you
should find a good man, well, a man beyond
Saxonham and perhaps beyond the Marsh, but I knew
your heart was set against that idea.

I heard that you knew a certain Captain Mackay from
the dock where I had worked. I have a vague memory
of him, as Father and I helped him to make containers
and fix his boxes, but I do not know anything more

about him. In February I came back to our house, and you were not here. Then I went to the rope factory in the village to look for you, and the women told me that you had decided to work no more there. I was very disheartened, and worried about you. The villagers told me they had seen you in a cabin boy's clothes. Then a few months later, my ship returned and I got back to the dock in Lydd. Someone who worked there told me that he knew a cabin boy who looked very much like me, who had been working there last December. I suspected that cabin boy was you. So I believe that you have gone to the sea at last. But so far I do not know where and how. Sister, you are mad!

As I am writing this letter on a summer's day, my heart is heavy. I do not know when I will see you again. I am leaving soon for Africa on a merchant ship. I hesitated before deciding to go on this trip, because it will be a long time at sea. I have something to tell you. I had an opportunity to meet a girl in Southampton a few months ago. She is the daughter of a seaman. She is a good person, and she made me want to stay on land. I could not make up my mind about what I should do. She hinted that I should marry her. But Lord, how can I marry her? Is my heart tied to her heart? I do not know, Ishmaelle. I wish you could tell me! I have missed you very much. I have thought a great deal of how we relied on each other, no one helping us, no one playing with us. Were we lonely as owls? Were we in terrible need of love like the two barren pear trees in our garden? Oh Lord, now you are a woman and I am a man and we have left each other for the great world out there! And I thought of all that when I met the girl in Southampton. I had to tell her that I cannot marry her. No. I cannot marry until I have sailed the seven seas and can know that my dear sister has found her rightful place. Am I making any sense, my sister? I miss you. I miss your wild spirit and waywardness. It is a blue summer's day out there in front of our window but I see no blue. I see our dead father and dead mother and how they would want us to be good and to be right. Are we being good and being right? I am sure you are, but I am not sure that I know what is good and right. All I know is that I will be heading off to sea, to Africa, very soon. And hope to see the world. May God bless me. And you.

I do not know when you will read this. But be sure that I want to see you when I return. I will come back to our house sometime in May. Yes, I think that will be the month I will return from Africa.

May you live and may I live to find each other again,

Your ever affectionate brother, Joseph

It was the 3rd of May. This letter had been written nine months ago, already old news but I had nothing else. Putting the letter in my pocket, I left the house. I made my way to the shingle beach and surveyed the bay. Towards the water's edge I found a barnacled rock to sit on.

I read the letter again. I knew that one day I would tell my brother how I had survived on the seas. Just *how* I would tell him I did not know. But now, the tide was rising, the waves dissolving into millions of bubbles as they washed over my feet. Fronds of green oarweed began to float around my legs, as though to entangle me in their web. Soon the rising waters lapped my knees and the salty spray misted my eyes. Oh Lord, the ocean here is cold! Colder, it seemed, than any I had ever sailed. The hem of my trousers pressed against my leg and then billowed out with the swell. My thoughts flooded like a tide: the sea has a great pull, we are of the land but still the sea is within us. I looked more deeply into the movement of the eddies; I saw the reflections of the sky and myself. The green light below and the golden light above seemed to merge. I felt both Ishmael and Ishmaelle being cast off like worn robes that have fallen away and are taken by wind and wave. I was alone, yet myself, and more than myself. I raised my eyes, somehow in expectation.

It was then, in the distance, that I saw it, although in some way I knew it was there already. A fine white streak gliding through the far blue. A burst of water, a shimmering spray. A flock of gulls gyring above. Will you wait for me? I had looked into your eye, after all that death and wreckage, and I knew we were entwined. Your eye, wise, old and true, beyond words, had remained within me.

Gazing into the blue expanse, all the way to the edge of the world, my body slipped from the rock. I swam out towards you. Letting the waters take me, I said 'yes' to your call, and 'yes' to life.

Appendix 1

Timeline

JUNE 1837	Queen Victoria begins her reign
MAY 1843	birth of Ishmaelle
NOVEMBER 1860	Lincoln elected 16th President of America
EARLY DECEMBER 1860	Ishmaelle leaves England
LATE DECEMBER 1860	Ishmaelle arrives in New York
END OF JANUARY 1861	the *Nimrod* departs on whaling voyage
FEBRUARY 1861	brief stop in the Azores
APRIL 1861	American Civil War breaks out
MAY 1861	the *Nimrod* arrives in Cap de Verd
JULY 1861	the *Nimrod* rounds the Cape of Good Hope
OCTOBER 1861	the *Nimrod* arrives in Batavia (modern Jakarta)
EARLY DECEMBER 1861	the *Nimrod* docks at Manila
MID-DECEMBER 1861	the *Nimrod* cruises through the Sea of Japan
JANUARY 1862	the *Nimrod* is whaling in the Philippine Sea then heads south
FEBRUARY–MARCH 1862	the *Nimrod* sails towards Polynesia
MID-MARCH 1862	the *Nimrod* sails below the equator, in the vicinity of the Marquesas Islands
MAY 1862	Ishmaelle returns home

Appendix 2

I Ching hexagrams in a nutshell

Yin (阴) and yang (阳) are represented respectively by broken
(- -) and unbroken (–) lines. The eight trigrams (八卦) are
formed from blocks of three lines comprising all broken lines or
all unbroken lines, or some combination of both. Each
symbolises a principle of reality, yet they are all interrelated.

Eight trigrams

Qian (乾, ☰): the creative force/heaven and sky

Dui (兌, ☱): the joyous reflection/lake and marsh

Li (離, ☲): the binding and bond/fire and glow

Zhen (震, ☳): the arousing thunder

Xun (巽, ☴): the gentle wind

Kǎn (坎, ☵): the abysmal water

Gen (艮, ☶): the refraining mountain

Kun (坤, ☷): the receptive earth

The three-line trigrams appear in six-line hexagrams, as in:

The hexagrams comprise 64 combinations. Divinations involve
interpreting the hexagrams which are produced by the person
doing the reading throwing sticks with patterns on them.

Acknowledgements

WHAT A TEMPESTUOUS transoceanic voyage
this has been. Obviously, Herman Melville's
Moby-Dick is the port from which I launched
my own journey, but I would never have arrived safely
without many wonderful people behind me. First, my editor
Kaiya Shang and my agent Rebecca Carter, two vitally
important people who contributed enormously to the
laborious work on this book. Thank you, Kaiya, for your
enthusiasm and faith all the way, and thank you, Rebecca,
for your knowing and wise counsel! My publisher Clara
Farmer laid her warm hand on my shoulder each time the
Nimrod needed to dock in order to take on new supplies.
Thank you, Clara, you are my captain! I am grateful also to
Graeme Hall who carried forth this book at different stages,
and brought it to a safe harbour where new crew members
could come on board to help me steer. My copy-editor
Katherine Fry has worked on several of my books over the
last decade. As always, she brought her razor-sharp editing
skills to bear upon my manuscript. A heartfelt thank you,
Katherine! And Jessie Spivey, what a dedicated, loving press
person you are! I am so lucky to have you. I am especially
grateful to Stephen Hickson for designing these pages and
to Rosie Palmer and Łukasz Łasisz for the beautiful cover,

to Bill Donohoe for drawing the map and Sarah-Jane Forder for proofreading. Thanks also to Victoria Murray-Browne, Beth Wood, Lucy Beresford-Knox, Asia Choudhry, Stephen Parker, Eoin Dunne, and the whole Chatto and Vintage team who worked on the book. A million thanks to my American editor Amy Hudley.

A very special person I want to thank is the brilliant historian and wonderful writer Edward Sugden of King's College London. Your thoughtful reading of my manuscript was so valuable for a non-western author like me. Given that I write in a second language, your suggestions have been crucial and I cannot thank you enough for your insight into the world of Melville.

For the research and writing part, apart from Melville's work, I benefited greatly from the research of the American historian Skip Finlay, specifically his *Whaling Captains of Color: America's First Meritocracy*. This remarkable book provided me with rich references that allowed me to create the character of Captain Seneca (who also owes much to Shakespeare's Othello)! The character of Ishmaelle is based on a number of nineteenth-century women sailors who travelled in disguise on the seas, in particular Ann Jane Thornton (born 1817 in Gloucestershire), and Mary Lacy (born 1740 in Kent). I was also deeply impressed by the adventures at sea of the American woman Annie Ricketson, as told so simply in her diary *Annie Ricketson's Journal*, published by Heritage Books in 2019.

I must thank the online resources provided by the Royal Museum Greenwich (www.rmg.co.uk) which greatly enriched my knowledge of nautical history and many other topics. The excellent website of the Nantucket Historical Association (nha.org) provided me with endless wonder and imagination and in particular the story of American whaler

Rebecca Ann Johnson (born 1830 in Rochester, New York). For whaling and further nautical knowledge, I cannot thank enough the New Bedford Whaling Museum (www.whalingmuseum.org), whose website is an infinitely rich resource for anyone who wants to understand life on board an American whaling ship. In a different but equally valuable way, Tom Mustill's *How to Speak Whale* and Philip Hoare's *Leviathan or, The Whale* were both for me immense reservoirs of inspiration.

I am extremely grateful to Esther Allen, who urged me to read the strangest essay by Melville, 'The Paradise of Bachelors and the Tartarus of Maids', which enabled me to gain an extra layer of understanding of Melville's oddity. And a big thank you to my German translator Anne Rademacher for her careful reading of my early drafts and valuable suggestions.

Now I would like to thank these fellow travellers, despite our vast difference in backgrounds. A life in writing is lonely, but it is enriched by your friendship and comradeship: Iain Sinclair, Gareth Evans, Andrea Zimmerman, Andrew Kötting, Anne Witchard, Paul French, Rana Mitter, Vanni Bianconi, Philippe Ciompi, Matthew Beaumont, Matthew Sperling, Alice Albinia, Nancy Seidler, Fiona Doloughan, Travis Elborough, Adam Biles, Mary Duncan and Sylvia Whitman.

And of course, my eternal gratitude to Steve and Moon. Together we have built our small but better version of the *Nimrod*, with a deck protected against the storms of everyday life.

ABOUT THE AUTHOR

Xiaolu Guo was born in China and now lives in Britain. Her books include *A Concise Chinese–English Dictionary for Lovers*, shortlisted for the Orange Prize, and *I Am China*. Her memoir *Once Upon a Time in the East* won the National Book Critics Circle Award. Her novel *A Lover's Discourse* was shortlisted for the Goldsmiths Prize 2020. She has also directed a dozen films, including *She, a Chinese*, which received the Golden Leopard Award at the 2009 Locarno Film Festival. She is a fellow of the Royal Society of Literature.